THE DEATH OF A DZUR

Miklós followed the dzur's gaze, and gasped. He had never before been so close to a dragon. It is one thing to know that a dragon's head is taller than you are, another to see one close up. The dragon wasn't looking at him, but at the dzur; and all of its tentacles were fully erect.

Miklós stared, mesmerized, until he heard a loud snarl and a thin black streak launched itself into the dragon's face. As the dragon gave a bellow, the prince turned and ran.

STEVEN BRUST

BROKEDOWN PALACE

ACE FANTASY BOOKS
NEW YORK

This book is an Ace Fantasy
original edition, and has never been
previously published.

BROKEDOWN PALACE

An Ace Fantasy Book/published by arrangement with
the author and the author's agent, Valerie Smith

PRINTING HISTORY
Ace Fantasy edition/January 1986
Second printing / November 1986

ISBN: 0-441-07182-1

Ace Fantasy Books are published by The Berkley Publishing Group,
200 Madison Avenue, New York, New York 10016.
PRINTED IN THE UNITED STATES OF AMERICA

For:

Jerry
Bob
Phil
Brent
Robert
John
and especially for Billy and Micky

Acknowledgments

In addition to my fellow Scribblies, and Terri, and Val, and everyone at Ace, there are a few others who ought to be thanked here: Fred Haskell, for many useful comments; Berry Goldstein, for help on geology questions; Chuck Holst, for river behavior; David S. Cargo, for his help on castle architecture and historical verisimilitude; my father, for answering many language questions (usually at about 3 A.M.); Kathy Marschall, for the maps; and Jon Singer, for additional last minute proophreading. My sincere thanks to you all. I'll probably bug you again. . . .

A Note on Fenarian Pronunciation

In Hungarian—whoops!—in *Fenarian* we have one of the world's most phonetically spelled languages. Having once learned their alphabet, school children from this land do not waste their precious youthful years, as do their less fortunate English-speaking counterparts, in endless hours of drudging homework to learn orthography. Even as adults, many—perhaps most—speakers of English persevere, resentfully, as slaves of old Dan Webster. Hence, a spelling bee is an unheard of institution in a country where the language is pronounced exactly as it is written and written exactly as it is pronounced.

Another delightful plus for the native Fenarian (and an enormous bonus for foreigners learning his language) is the uniformity of accent. Unlike English or Russian or even German, Fenarian stress is permanently fixed: on the first syllable of every word. Only those who toiled to acquire any of the above three languages can appreciate what a blessing it is to confront such regularity. Still, despite the uniformity of stress, Fenarian is an exceptionally musical language whose underlying principle is based on vowel harmony, a feature of the linguistic family to which it belongs.

The Fenarian alphabet proper consists of forty letters. Of these twenty-six are consonants, but an additional five consonants, so as to include foreign words, give the language a total of forty-five characters. By the use of the long and short diacritical marks (which have nothing to do with accent) over the customary vowels—*a, e, i, o,* and *u*—these five are expanded to fourteen vowels, enabling every Fenarian sound to have its own distinctive symbol. It is a phonetic *tour de force*.

An approximation of these vowel sounds in American pronunciation would be: *a* as in *law*; *á* as in *father*; *e* as in *met*; *é* as in the *ay* of *day*; *i* as in the *ie* of *field*; *í* as *ee* in *bee* (longer than *ie* in *field*); *o* as in *old*; *ó* as in *oh* (longer than *old*); *u* as in *rule*; *ú* as in *pool* (longer than *rule*); *ü* represents a sound similar to the *ü* of German *über* or the *u* in French *tu*. For readers unfamiliar with these languages, *ü* can be thought of as a sound similar to the *i* in English *fin* but pronounced through pursed lips. The *ű* is a longer and tenser version of this sound. The *ö* is very much like the *ö* of German *schön* or the *eu* of French *meurt*. Again, some readers not familiar with these languages may be guided by the hint that *ö* resembles the *e* of *her*, only tenser and the *ő* is a longer and even tenser version of this same sound.

With the exception of *c, j,* and *s* the consonants are by and large not too unlike those in English. The *c* (and in older proper names the *cz*) is pronounced as *ts* in the word *hits*. The *j* has the sound of *y* in *you*. The *s* is like *sh* in *she* or the *s* in *sure*. The consonant combinations are as follows: *cs* is like the *ch* in *church*; *sz* as the *s* in *sun*; and *zs* as the *z* in *azure*.

Finally, the letter *y*, except in old proper nouns—mainly family names—or in modern foreign loan words when it is equivalent to the English *ie* in *field*, appears only as part of consonant combinations and palatalizes or softens the preceding consonant. The *gy* in *nagy* (big) would be pronounced somewhat like the *d* and the *y* in the words *mind you*, when pronounced rapidly. The *l* in the combination *ly* as in the name of the composer *Kodály* is mute so that the second syllable rhymes with *high*. The consonants *ny* as in *hanyag* (negligent) and *ty* as in *tyúk* (hen) *are* sounded and the *y* in both cases approximates the *y* in *you*.

—W. Z. Brust
March, 1985
St. Paul, Minnesota

Author's Note: The names Devera, Alfredo, and, in fact, Fenario, are *not* Fenarian, and one oughtn't use the above rules in pronouncing them.

—S. K. Z. Brust
Minneapolis, Minnesota

prologue

The Legend of Fenarr

LONG AGO THERE LIVED a mighty lord named Fenarr. Some say he came from the lands around the North Sea, where the cold winds had frozen his sinews until they were like fine steel. Others say the Great Plains to the east had tempered his heart with the burning sun, so he feared nothing. There are those who tell how he came from the ocean far to the south, through underground streams that emerge high in the Grimtail, the southeastern part of the Grimwall, where he learned to live with great privation. Still others claim he grew to manhood in the Western Mountains on the very borders of Faerie, and thus knew the denizens of that land better than any other mortal man.

Wherever he came from, he arrived one day in the land bounded to the west by the Western Mountains, which are sometimes called the Mountains of Faerie, to the north and east by the Grim Circle, and to the south by the Wandering Forest and the Great Marsh. In this land he found a people who had lived for long years, even then, beneath the shadow of Faerie. They were a warlike people descended from horsemen who had lived by plundering until they had come through the Grimwall Pass into the area they now inhabited. It is told that a great chieftain of the tribe was shown a clod of earth from the River basin and was given a taste of water from the River, and said, "We have found our home." From that time on they had dwelt around the lakes and in the great sweeping plains and hills and valleys of the land.

They lived with the threat from the west, and often they would bring out their straight swords and long spears, giving battle to the lords of Faerie who challenged them for possession of the land. There was no peace then, and the people suffered, and many spoke of returning to the old ways of riding and plundering—of leaving the land in the mountains.

Then Fenarr came and soon grew to love the land. When he learned of the troubles that beset it, he resolved to go into Faerie and win peace from those who dwelt there. He built a mighty army from the people of the land, even of the women and children, yet he could find no way past the borders of Faerie.

At last, in desperation, he went alone into the mountains to find a passage. As the days went by he became hungry. Yet he remained, searching for a way to pass the border. One night, he felt he was close to starving to death. Yet he had promised the people that he would find a way or die, so that is what he resolved to do. When hunger and fatigue finally overcame him, he fell asleep. Then, as he lay sleeping on a rock, a mighty stallion, all of white, caused him to waken. It spoke to him, for it was a *táltos* horse and knew the tongue of men. The stallion said, "Master, look beneath this rock and thou shalt find thy salvation."

So Fenarr turned over the rock on which he had slept, and beneath it was a Sword, taller than he (yet he was of great height), and filled with the power of Faerie itself. Then the stallion said, "Turn over the next rock." Fenarr did this, and beneath it was food enough to last him for many days.

When he had eaten his fill, the stallion bade him turn over the third rock. Beneath it were garments of silver. Fenarr dressed himself and took the Sword into his hand.

Then the stallion said, "Mount upon my back, master, and I will bear thee to the lord of Faerie. But first you must groom and brush me until my coat shines like the stars. Then you must make a fire. When it has burned down to embers, you must let me eat the embers, and bring me a cask of water to wash them down."

Fenarr groomed the horse carefully, using his cast-off shirt, until the stallion's coat gleamed so that it hurt his eyes. Then, using the Sword of Faerie, Fenarr cut down wood from the spruce that grew in the mountains. He built a great fire. When the fire had burned down to embers, the *táltos* stallion ate them all, then drank a cask of water.

"Come, master," he said. "We are ready."

So Fenarr mounted upon the back of the stallion, and the stallion carried him through secret ways in the mountains until they came to a land on the other side, where the sun hid its face from the lords of Faerie.

Fenarr came to them, even to the seat of Kav, mightiest of the lords of Faerie, and said, "Stay you in your lands, and we will stay in ours. Make war upon us no more." But Kav laughed, for he was filled with the power of Faerie, and he called upon his power to destroy Fenarr. But the stallion leapt up before Fenarr and was slain in his stead. Then Fenarr was filled with a terrible anger. He brought forth the Sword of Faerie and held it at Kav's breast. Kav was astounded and cried, "How hast thou a Sword from the land of Faerie?"

But Fenarr only said, "With this Sword will I slay thee, and all of thine, unless thou vowest to leave my people alone."

"I will vow this, indeed," said Kav. "But thou must return the Sword unto us, for 'tis not a weapon for humankind."

Fenarr did not trust him, and said, "An thou would'st have this Sword, thou must take it from me, and I will slay all who try, and thee first."

"Yet," said Kav, "thou can'st not slay us all." The other lords of Faerie gathered around, preparing to slay Fenarr if he should strike Kav with the Sword. But then fires poured from the mouth of the *táltos* stallion, and black smoke came from his nostrils. Then a voice came from his body, and it spoke to Fenarr, saying, "Master, thou can'st trust him. An he vow, he shall keep his word."

The lords of Faerie were astounded and filled with fear, but Fenarr said, "I will give this Sword unto thee, an thou vow never to harass the people of my land." So Kav did vow never to cross the Mountains of Faerie save in peace, and never to make war upon the people of Fenarr.

Then did Fenarr give unto Kav the Sword of Faerie, and he returned over the mountains to the land he had left. There he built a home next to the River of Faerie, and soon a city was built around it, and the city and then the land came to be called Fenario, as they are still called today.

chapter one

The Horse

FIRST, CONSIDER THE RIVER.

It began in thunder; a cascade from Lake Fenarr, pouring over the lip of Mount Szaniszló. From there it cut a deep, straight path through the center of Fenario, eventually joined by other, lesser rivers. It cut a gap in the Eastern Grimwall, after which it turned south toward the sea, passing beyond the ken of Fenario's denizens.

Once, when Miklós was eleven, he had been in a mood of pleasant melancholy and had gone down to the near bank, to a secret place between the Palace loading docks and Midriver Rock. There, hidden by rushes and reeds, he had sat holding a single yellow flower that he had wanted to present to his middle-older brother. But his brother had been busy and had brushed him off, which was the reason for his melancholy. So he had taken the flower and thrown it into the river. The idea was to watch it as it floated out of sight, while thinking of how the world mistreated him. With luck, he could bring tears to his own eyes, which would cap the event nicely.

But the River, perverse thing that it was, had carried the offering back to him, spoiling the gesture completely. It always did things like that.

Now, remembering this, Miklós decided that the River ought to rise from its banks and sweep his wounded, broken body away, out of sight to the east. But it wouldn't.

Miklós was twenty-one years old, and dying.

* * *

Next, the Palace:

It loomed over the bend in the River, over the city of Fenario, over the River Valley, over the land, and over Miklós's left shoulder.

It had stood for nearly a thousand years if you count the hut. Nine hundred and fifty years if you count the fort. Seven hundred years if you count the Old Palace. Four hundred years by any way of counting, and that is a long time. And for all of that time, back to when it was merely the hut where Fenarr had dwelt, the idol of the Demon Goddess had watched over it.

Miklós craned his neck to look at the Palace and to try to forget the pain. It jutted up against wispy night clouds and a few halfhearted stars. The central tower resembled a stiletto; the River Wall resembled a blank, gray shield. Above it and above him, jhereg circled ominously, their cries harsh and distant, commenting on his state and, obliquely, on the Palace itself.

It looked its age. The nearest tower had a perceptible tilt, and he'd overheard his eldest brother, the King, speak of the way the wind played games with it. The River Wall was cracked and breaking. Its bones were showing.

Are my bones showing? he wondered. *Enough of them are certainly broken, and I'm bleeding in enough places. There are probably a few bones coming through the skin.*

The thought would have made him retch, but he hadn't the strength.

Now, observe the interior:

Start at the bottom. The Palace had been built without a basement of any sort, but tunnels had been dug during the long siege when the Northmen came down from the northern Grimwall Mountains and swept over the land more than three hundred years before.

The siege had lasted five years, and by the end of that time the whole area beneath the Palace, and beneath much of the surrounding city, was riddled with cunning tunnels that were used to sneak food in, or to harass the Northerners, or to spy out fortifications. When the enemy was finally driven out, the tunnels were promptly turned into wine cellars—which is one of the reasons that the wines of Fenario are known for thousands of miles around.

Let us move up from the cellars.

The walls throughout on the main floor were done in the palest of pale blues, and thought had been given to the areas of darkness and of light. Rippling patterns from a candelabrum, unlit, drew and erased wavering lines on the floor before the entrance. Now, was the candelabrum responsible for the patterns, or were the hanging, swaying oil lamps? Both, certainly. One determined essence, the other determined shape.

Here was the nursery, when Miklós was very young. All thoughts of taste had been left for other chambers. Here was a cacophony of colors and hanging beads and flowing streamers. It had been filled with things that rolled and things that tumbled and things that pushed or pulled other things that rolled or tumbled.

When Miklós was five, it was time for Prince László, then fifteen, to have his own chambers. Miklós had to move out. The nursery was emptied of things that rolled and tumbled, and filled with things that cut and stabbed. It was emptied of bright colors and filled with tasteful decorations of people cutting and stabbing.

But let us not be heavy-handed.

Every room was in use. Many were used for things for which they were not intended. This bedchamber was once a library. That servants' dining room was once a private study. Miklós's bedchamber, which had been one in the original design, was in the process of becoming a study. Now, was the bedchamber a misused library, or has the change in function changed the definition? Do definitions matter?

Well, define "dying." How about: "that state where the absence of life is imminent."

It would seem clear that Miklós cannot be blamed for having received the beating when, really, all he did to bring it on was to be there for twenty-one years. But consider the candelabrum and the lamp.

If you don't find this a fair analogy, rest assured that Miklós didn't either.

Miklós thought that it would be nice, in any number of ways, if the River would pick him up and drown him or carry him off to die far away. The longer he lay there dying, the nicer the idea seemed. In his chambers at night, alone, death was a mysterious, terrifying mystery—a wall whose contemplation sent shudders through him while he couldn't help trying to see over it. But here, death was merely a relief from pain—a relief that he began to fear would never come. Above him, the jhereg had given up, save one whose cries now seemed to say, The River! The River!

Finally, Miklós used what little strength he had in his right leg (which had only a hairline fracture) to push himself down the bank and into the icy water, which should have been the end of it.

But, as was pointed out earlier, the River is perverse.

And the city:

It was called Fenario, as was the land. It was the largest city in the country—the largest for thousands of miles in any direction beyond it. Well, any direction except west. West of the land of Fenario were the Mountains of Faerie, and who knows what lay beyond? But the city was a huge, sprawling thing on both sides of the River, with a population of well over five thousand. From the city, the towers of the Palace—all six—were infallible landmarks. Each was distinct: the tall and leaning King's Tower, the pockmarked Tower of the Goddess, the squat and rotund Tower of Past Glories, the worn and threadbare East Tower of the Watch, and crowned West Tower of the Watch, and the graceful, silvery Tower of the Marshal. Though the dwellers in the city were unaware of it, they oriented themselves by these towers. Should the towers vanish one day, the merchants and artisans of Fenario would have suddenly felt lost.

The walls surrounding the Palace courtyard ended some two hundred feet from where the city began, and, by the natural course of things, it was the most prosperous of inns and markets that were located nearest, along with homes of noble families who chose not to live among their estates.

Oddly, from the Palace the city was all but invisible. The wall hid the view from the lower two stories, and the third story, containing almost nothing but the Great Hall, had only windows high upon it. The towers had no windows at all (these having been filled in during one especially cold winter some years before), save for the East and West Towers of the Watch.

The city was built where the River of Faerie joined the North River, and grew slowly. Along the North River came grapes, as well as lamb and bacon, both liberally spiced to preserve them against the summer's heat. The spices traveled back north much more slowly. Wool also came along this river.

Down the River of Faerie came cotton from the marshes to the south, and timber and mushrooms from the Forest. There were docks along the south bank to receive these things, and two bridges over to the north bank—the Merchant's bridge and the King's bridge.

Miklós used to wander the city during the day with Prince Andor, who was the second oldest and his elder by six years.

"What is that, Andor?" he said once, pointing to the clouds moving in from the west.

"The Hand of Faerie, Miklós," his brother answered. "The people say it bodes great ill when it covers the whole land."

"Does it?" asked Miklós in wonder.

Andor shook his head. "I've seen it cover the whole sky two or three times, and nothing ever happened except that it has blown away in a few days."

And Miklós nodded, content, and took his brother's hand. That evening, he asked his brother Prince Vilmos, who was only three years his elder. Vilmos grinned wickedly and, for two hours, told him stories of what had happened during "Dark Times." The next day, Miklós asked László, but the latter only grunted and returned to his studies.

In any case, the sky was clear and the stars were bright and piercing when, during Miklós's sixth year, half of the west wing collapsed. It had been snowing hard for a week, although this only sped up what would have happened anyway, sooner or later. The collapse injured Miklós's father and, indirectly, led to Miklós's present situation.

At night there weren't many of the denizens of the city who visited the Riverbanks, so it wasn't surprising that no one saw the youngest brother of King László being carried away, his head somehow staying above the water, by the River that runs down out of the Mountains of Faerie.

Finally, the land:

One could describe the terrain by the food—apples, for instance. North was crisp and tart, from the hills at the feet of the Grimwall Mountains, East was sweet, from the valley carved by the River, South, near the Great Marsh, were crab apples.

Corn from the silt loams along the River in the east. The

western forests had as many varieties of mushroom as the central plains near the city had varieties of pepper. The colder and dryer north gave wheat. Rice grew in the south. Cattle and pigs were raised below the northern hills; sheep upon the hills themselves.

The land was enclosed by mountains on three sides: the Grimwall to the north and east, the Mountains of Faerie to the west. In the southwest the Wandering Forest, which for the most part rested like a skirt at the ankles of the Mountains of Faerie, gradually meshed with and turned into marshland. Then fens and bogs as one went further south until, along the southern borders, the way was impassible save in the very depths of the coldest of winters.

Now consider early autumn. Consider the first hints of color from the birch and the elm and the hickory. Notice the strings of red peppers hanging like scraggly beards from the eaves of the peasants' houses. Find the place where a gentle curve in the River causes a small eddy before the exposed roots of an oak that has watched the Riverbank forever. Notice Miklós clutching the roots and wonder, as he does, why the weight of torn shirt, leather boots, and heavy cotton doublet hasn't dragged him under.

And we're ready to begin.

Miklós awoke to hot breath in his face and the corresponding sound of breathing—no, *blowing*. These things were accompanied by a dull ache in his lower back. His eyes opened to stare up into what he finally recognized as the nostrils of a horse.

Then it came to him that his back hurt—that is, that *only* his back hurt. His last memories were of swirling water; his mind clouded by the misery of broken arms and legs, cracked ribs, and a collection of cuts and bruises that had made consciousness an agony.

The human mind being what it is, however, he looked for the source of his current pain before considering the absence of his past pain. He discovered that he was lying on exposed tree roots. As he moved away from them, the horse backed away several steps, and Miklós got his first good look at it.

There were three distinct breeds of horses in Fenario. This was like none of them. It had the gray coloring sometimes found among the small, fast *lovasság* breed from the central

plains; was as large as the *munkás* workhorses of the north;
and had the high head, broad chest, strong shoulders and thin
ankles of the *repülő*, owned only by the proudest among the
nobility. Its legs were thin but strong, its stance seemed narrow.
Its eyes were wide and blue above a swirl of hair perhaps half
a shade lighter than that around it.

Miklós, though he had no horse of his own, had been around
them all his life, and knowledge of horses was so automatic
to him that he took no pride in it. As he studied the horse, it
stared back as if studying him.

Let us, then, pause long enough to say that Miklós was a
tall, lanky young man with light brown hair, brown eyes, a
thin face, and something of a distant look about him. His face
was clean-shaven but gave the impression that he would have
had trouble growing a beard even had he wanted to. His hands
were long and thin, his cheekbones high, his eyes perhaps a
bit narrow and slanted. His complexion was dark, with the least
trace of yellow if one looked closely.

After a moment Miklós rose to his feet, shakily. He looked
around. From the position of the sun, he decided that it was
early afternoon. He studied the River and saw that it had carried
him a long way. His clothing was only slightly damp, so he
must have left the River several hours before. His eyes returned
to the horse, which was still staring at him.

Just to see what would happen, he held out his hand, made
clucking sounds, and said, "C'mon, boy. C'mon." He was
surprised at how strong his voice sounded.

The horse shook its head and walked up to him. Its step
was high. It stopped only a few feet away. It opened its mouth
then and said, "I'm glad you have recovered, master."

Miklós felt his eyes widening, and sudden understanding
came to him. "You . . . you're a *táltos* horse, aren't you?"

"Indeed I am, master," said the horse.

"Then it was you who healed my wounds!"

"Who can say?" The horse flung his head back and shook
it.

Miklós shook his head, unconsciously imitating the horse.
After a moment of desperately searching for something to say,
he came up with, "What's your name?"

"I am called Bölcseség," said the horse. The prince's mouth
worked a bit as he tried to pronounce this. After a moment,
the horse said, "Bölk will do, master."

"Bölk," repeated Miklós. "Good. I can say that."

"But can you understand it?"

"Understand it?"

"Pay no mind, master. But tell me, if you will, how you came to be injured."

Miklós bit his lip but made no reply. Bölk continued to study him, his large, bright blue eyes somber. At last, Miklós sat down with his back against the hard ridges of the tree. He said, "My brother László did it." When Bölk remained silent Miklós added, "I don't really know why."

The horse blinked. "Your brother László," repeated Bölk. "Do you mean King László?"

Miklós said, "Yes, that's right."

"But you still think of him as your brother," Bölk said.

Miklós nodded.

"And yet," continued the horse, "you don't know why you were beaten?"

Miklós turned his head to the side and squinted, pulling up his knees and hugging them. "I see what you mean," he admitted.

"Tell me what happened, master," said Bölk.

"Well, I was in my room reading and —my broth—that is, the King entered, without announcement." Miklós paused, waiting for Bölk to make an interjection. When the horse remained silent, he continued. "He told me he needed my bedchamber. That he needed a room of that size to pursue his studies. He said he was having one of the servants' quarters cleared for me. I didn't argue—"

"Why not, master?"

"Well . . . he's the King."

"And it does you no good to argue in any case?"

"Yes, that's right."

"So what did you say?"

"That he could have the blasted room. That the walls were cracking anyway, and the ceiling was sagging, and what did I care."

"And he attacked you?"

Miklós trembled with the memory. "I've never seen him so angry! We've never gotten along well, but this! He drew his sword—he always carries it—and struck me with the flat and then with the pommel. He kept—" Miklós stopped, his eyes growing wide again. "My clothes!" he cried. "They were torn to rags! He half ripped my doublet trying to hold on to me and now it's whole!"

Bölk chuckled. "So, the mending of your clothing seems more startling to you than the healing of your body?"

"No, no, it isn't that . . . well, I guess it is. I don't know. How did you do it?"

"I had no part in it, master. But how did you escape?"

Miklós closed his eyes, trying to remember. Already it seemed so long ago. "It's mostly a blur," he said finally. "I remember crawling out of the door, thinking that Lász—that the King would follow me, but he didn't. I remember wanting to reach the River and to throw myself into it. I thought I was dying. I *was* dying! What happened?"

"Who can say, master?" said Bölk. "Yet here you are. Do you think your brother will pursue you?"

Miklós considered. "I doubt it. But I can't go back home now. I'm afraid to."

"You needn't," said the horse. "I will bear you wherever you wish."

"You will?"

"I have said so, dear master."

"But . . . *why* will you?"

"Because you have found me at a time when I needed to be found."

"But it was *you* who found *me.*"

"Was it?"

Miklós fell silent. After a time, Bölk said, "Whither shall we go then, master?"

"I don't know, Bölk. I have nowhere to go."

"And nothing to do?"

"Nothing that I know how to do."

"Nothing you want to see?"

"I don't know what to look for." He looked up suddenly. "Except—I would like to look for whoever or whatever healed me, so I can give thanks and perhaps do a service for him or her or it."

Bölk's head drooped for a moment and shook in that manner peculiar to horses and shake-dancers. Then he looked back at Miklós once more and said, "Do you really not know?"

Miklós closed his eyes. He thought of the Demon Goddess, but he hadn't called out to her, so how could she have known to come to him, even if she chose to? Then, suddenly, he realized that he *did* know. "It was the River, wasn't it?" he said quietly.

"The River," said Bölk, "flows down out of the Mountains of Faerie."

"Then," said Miklós, standing, "I wish to go to Faerie."

Táltos horse and young Prince remained still, as if this announcement had created or removed a barrier between them and they weren't sure which.

"Few from this land," said Bölk, "ever travel that way. Fenarr himself; perhaps others. Are you certain you wish to go there?"

Miklós shook his head. "No," he said, "I'm not sure. You asked what I wished to see, and that is the answer. But I'm not sure. I'm not sure of anything. Do you think it's a foolish thing to do?"

"I am not certain myself, master," said Bölk. "You may find there what you need. You may not. I have some knowledge of Faerie, but what I know causes me to turn from it."

"What do you mean?"

The horse said, "I have been there once. To return, one must embrace it. I reject it; I cannot go there. I can bring you to the border, high in the mountains, but no farther."

"You reject it?" said Miklós.

"I do. I must. But that does not mean you should. I am old, master. I am from another age. Once I was stronger than the power of Faerie. Now, it is stronger than I. Perhaps someday I shall be the stronger again. I know that in Faerie, should you go and return, you will learn much. But I don't know if this knowledge is good or ill. If you go, you must decide this yourself."

"'Another age...' Was it you who carried Fenarr? You, yourself? But I thought you had died!"

Bölk made that sound which is called snorting in a horse or a man. "Myself? Another? Who can say? The land has changed; I have changed; the world has changed. All things become what they were not, and I am no different. I remember Fenarr, if that is what you mean; but my memory differs from the legends, and I am not certain that the legends are not more accurate. But master, the choice is still before you."

As the horse finished speaking, Miklós suddenly knew that

all thought of not going had left him. He straightened his back and said, "Come then, Bölk. Take me as far as you may, and I will learn what I learn."

"But what will you do with what you learn, master?"

"Do?"

"Pay no mind. Only climb onto my back. We have a hundred leagues of plains before we come to the foothills that bring us to the pass the River has carved, and from there we must find our way to the great waterfall that is its source. I think we should avoid the city, and doing so will add yet more time."

"We're in no hurry, Bölk."

"Are we not, then, master?"

"What do you mean?"

"Pay no mind."

They emerged from the Wandering Forest late at night, after riding to it for four days and through it for another three. They camped just beyond its border. The next morning, Miklós rose, stretched, turned, and gaped.

The Mountains of Faerie stood before him, awesome and magnificent.

Ten millions of years before, a battle had taken place. On one side had been billions of tons of rock, mostly granite, wishing to go east. On the other, billions more tons of rock, mostly limestone, sandstone, and shale, desiring to travel west. The battle lasted for hundreds of thousands of years of pushing, withdrawing, looking for avenues of escape, and head-to-head duels of pure strength. In the end, the limestone had succeeded in passing beneath the granite.

The victorious limestone, except for occasional patches, remained invisible. The granite could be seen for scores of miles. All conception of distance left Miklós as he viewed the closest peak. Its base was near enough that individual evergreens could be seen, yet trees at the top were merely a blur. The peaks further back, and higher, gleamed white with snow in the early morning sun. Those still further back showed faint white that the sun couldn't reach because the Hand of Faerie loomed over them like a blanket, shaken, about to settle.

"It's beautiful," he said at last.

Bölk stood next to him, watching Miklós's face instead of the mountains.

After what seemed like hours, Miklós noticed the morning chill and hastened to don a plain gray cloak that he had purchased in a village on the other side of the forest, trading his ring for it and for other things Bölk had said he would need.

"We must leave soon, master," said Bölk.

"I know," said Miklós, almost to himself. "We'll be traveling—how far can you bring me?"

"To the base of the flats that come from Lake Fenarr and signal the beginning of the River of Faerie."

"How far is that?"

"There is a path into the mountain before us that soon joins the Riverbed. We will reach the path a few hours after we start, and the base of the falls a few hours after that."

"So today is our last day together?"

"It is, master."

Miklós said nothing, but stared at the mountain before him while laying a hand on Bölk's neck.

"You should eat, master," said Bölk, gently.

Miklós sighed and put wood into the shallow pit where the fire had been placed the night before. He kindled flame using flint and thin pieces of bark he had picked up while traveling through the forest. When the fire began to burn, he took a loaf of bread and cut it into strips which he set on the rocks next to the fire.

From the pack which he had purchased at the same time as the cloak, he took a slab of bacon and pushed a stick through it. Holding the stick with his left hand, he used his knife to make a checkered pattern on both sides of the bacon. Then he held the slab over the flame exactly the way his brother Vilmos had taught him.

By the time the bread was toasted, grease began to drip from the bacon. He used his right hand to occasionally hold pieces of bread under it to catch the drippings as it cooked. Bölk watched him in silence.

A gentle wind came from the west, shifting slightly every minute or so. Miklós sat facing the wind, though the smoke stung his eyes, so he could more easily stare at the Mountains of Faerie as he ate his breakfast and cooked his lunch.

"Bölk," he said at one point.

"Yes, master?"

"I've never seen you eat. Don't you?"

"Not as you do, master. I am fed by the use folk such as you make of me."

Miklós turned from the mountains to stare at him. "Is that true?"

"I cannot lie, master."

"But . . . then are you always accompanied by someone or other?"

"No. Often I go for years, or hundreds of years, seeing no one who needs my help. Or no one who can use it."

"What do you do then?"

"I starve, master."

Miklós continued staring at him. "I can't leave you!" he burst out at last.

Bölk chuckled. "Yet you wish to go to Faerie. So, from that time on, you can't make use of me whether you want to or not."

Miklós, with no answer to this, continued looking at the horse for some time until, at last, his gaze was drawn back to the mountains.

Miklós wiped water droplets from his face and turned his back to the spray. Behind and above him, the waterfall towered white and blue and brown, and there was thundering in his ears.

"You can go no further?" he asked.

"No further," said Bölk. "But I assure you that getting to Faerie will be easy. Up this cliff to the lake, then west, and down the other side. You can see that the climb will not be difficult."

Miklós studied it, then nodded (wiping more water droplets from his face).

"It's funny," he said. "You don't realize how sharply you're climbing until you see how far you've come."

"Mountain trails are like that."

"Yes." Then, "Will I see you again?"

"I don't know, master. Returning to Fenario will be harder than leaving it. But if you wish to, and you manage, we may meet again. But then, I will no longer be the same."

Miklós snorted. "Nor will I."

Bölk nodded slowly. "Perhaps," he said, "you will come to understand."

* * *

"What are you doing up here, little girl?"

"That was a pretty horse, mister."

"My name is Miklós."

"I'm Devera. Where are you going?"

"I'm on a journey to Faerie. The horse couldn't take me any further."

"Where's Faerie?"

"Huh? Why, just down the mountain, over there."

"Oh. Is that what you call it?"

"What do you call it?"

"What's down that way?"

"That's Fenario. Why don't you . . . say! You're *from* Faerie, aren't you, Devera?"

"Well, sort of."

"What are you doing here?"

"I have a . . . friend, who said I should go to . . . what did you say it was called?"

"Faerie? Fenario?"

"Fenario. He said I should go to Fenario because I would be able to learn something about—well, I'm really not supposed to say. But I must have missed, since I'm way up here, and that means I'm probably early, too."

"Early?"

"Never mind, Mister Miklós. I like your name."

"Thank you. You sound like Bölk. That's the horse."

"He talks? Or do you mean mentally?"

"How can you talk mentally?"

"Never mind."

"You *do* sound like Bölk. No, he talks. He's a *táltos* horse."

"What's that?"

"Never mind."

"Okay. I sure do like this lake, Mister Miklós."

"Yes, it's pretty, isn't it? It's called Lake Fenarr. How did you . . ."

"What is it, Mister Miklós?"

"Your eyes. For just a second there, I thought I saw something in them. Like a palace, but not like any palace I've ever—"

"Well, it was nice to meet you, Mister Miklós. I have to go down that way now."

"No, don't—"

"Oh, I'll be fine. Maybe we'll see each other again, Mister Miklós. Good-bye now."

"But . . . now where did she go?"

INTERLUDE

THE KING STOOD in the chamber that had been his brother's.

He had ordered servants to clean it and to remove the bloodstains from the floor and the walls. A few hours before, he had followed the bloody trail down to the River and into it. This would have convinced him that his brother was dead had he not just returned from his tower where he had a vision of the Demon Goddess warning him about Prince Miklós.

He considered the plans to turn this bedchamber to his own uses, but for some reason couldn't concentrate on them just now. He shook his head and walked out the door.

He left a footprint behind. He had been standing on a bloodstain that wasn't quite dry. A few drops seeped into a crack in the tiled wood of the floor and into a crack in the hardwood beneath. This chamber, where Miklós had spent so much of his time, had a drop of blood to remember him by. The Palace, where Miklós had lived most of his life, had this to remember him by. The land of Fenario, where Miklós had lived all his life, had this to remember him by.

We will return to it presently.

chapter two

The King

THINK OF THE CELLARS as feet, and the sandstone pillars emerging from them as legs. The east and west wings (the latter of which collapsed many years ago) are arms. The hallways are veins and arteries; the Great Hall on the third story is the heart. The high, central tower, where only the King is permitted, is the head.

Can we stretch our analogy even further? The kitchen on the second story is the belly, and the dining room below it is the digestive system. Nestled in among these organs is the room that, only two years ago, was occupied by Miklós, the missing Prince of Fenario.

This room holds a position analogous to that of a womb.

And that is going quite far enough.

László III, King of Fenario, watched his brother Vilmos out of the corner of his eye. László was pretending to concentrate on a large slab of veal cooked with white wine, black currants, red peppers, onions, and slices of imported orange peel. Vilmos, on the other hand, really was concentrating on his food.

László smiled to himself sadly. *If it were a half pound of raw beef*, he thought, *Vilmos wouldn't care. As long as there was enough of it*.

Across from Vilmos was Andor, older than Vilmos but younger than László. The King spared him a quick glance, then returned to his clandestine observations of Vilmos.

To give you the proper framework for this, we should explain the following: The meal was taking place in the Informal Dining Room, a small area next to the kitchen and above the Formal Dining Room. The decor was simple, and mostly beige. The table was large enough to seat eight. The three brothers clustered toward the end away from the kitchen. Serving dishes filled the near end, creating a sort of balance.

At the head was King László: thin, with curly hair and a long drooping mustache. His complexion was pale for a Fenarian, so his dark eyes dominated his face when he opened them wide. Deep lines were chiseled around the corners of his eyes and mouth.

At his right was Prince Andor. His hair was close-cropped on top of a thin head, with a large, strong nose, and what would have been a finely carved face were it not for the fat around his cheeks—visible despite the full beard he had grown to hide his double chin. He was also paunchy around the middle, though not excessively so. Seeing him for the first time, one might get an impression of physical strength, then reconsider. Andor, as László would sometimes reflect, often proved to be less than first impression made of him.

Across from Andor was Vilmos, the object of László's study. Vilmos did not appear to come from the same family as the other two. His hair was black and curly and fell to his shoulders. His face and head were huge, on a massive pair of shoulders. At fourteen years old, he had once had both of his older brothers face each other and, with one hand, picked them up by their belts. His eyes were deep and wide and brown. His mouth was full of shiny white teeth, his face full of soft brown beard. There were, around the Palace, chairs that had been designed for him in particular, and he had to be careful to use only those, lest his weight break a normal piece of furniture. This weight, you may be sure, was solid muscle.

As László surreptitiously studied this giant, he sighed to himself. *He has done so much for me—and for the kingdom. I wonder if he knows it? Probably not. My brain and his muscle. It's a good arrangement, and we both prosper by it.*

He sighed again.

So why am I so afraid of him?

László left the Informal Dining Room, following a relatively wide corridor around a corner and through an arch. The audience chamber lay beyond, around another turn in the passage and down a small ramp that Vilmos had put in one day when that part of the Palace had settled unexpectedly. But László, as always, paused here a moment.

This archway was of knotty pine, with strips of varnished rosewood around the edges. But through it, on a small shelf built into the wall itself, was a stone carving placed there by László's distant forebear, King Gellért I. It showed a man on a wild bull, holding a sword at his side as the animal reared. László approached it slowly, as he always did, and slowly took in more detail. Yes, he thought, touching the hilt of his own blade, the sword could only be Állam. And the way the rider's cloak was rippled by the wind, only a bit, made him catch his breath anew. Who was it? Where? What battle? Why a bull? Certainly, a *táltos* bull, but there were no legends that quite fit what was depicted. Perhaps it was merely a symbolic comment, tucked away where only the King and a few others ever saw it.

As László came closer still, the expression on the rider's face fascinated him, as always. There was no glee as of battle, merely a stern expression of duty done. At what was he looking—and why was he looking out instead of toward the target his sword had found?

Yes, it was a message—by and for the Kings of Fenario. Sometimes László thought it contained the most important lesson he had learned and was learning. It spoke of duty and of dignity. It was well placed.

He mentally saluted it. then continued through the corridor.

The audience chamber showed fewer signs of age than any other room in the Palace. As much work had been put in on the Great Hall one story above, but there was only so much that could be done with a chamber that size.

But the place where the King met with his advisors or with powerful lords from the outlying districts was clean, shining, and always in good repair. The walls were of pine. There were hanging lamps and a single table with room for twelve. Two doors led into the room: one from a stairway up to the Great Hall, the other, which László had taken, led to a corridor, and down another set of stairs to the ground floor.

When the King entered Rezső was waiting for him. He rose and gave a small bow, which László perfunctorily acknowledged. Rezső waited for the King to seat himself, then did the same.

Rezső was a short, squat, older man, descended from horsemen of the northeast. Though he had seldom ridden, his legs were bowed, as the legs of that people are. As he walked, he would lean slightly to either side. His round face was clean-shaven, with wide-set eyes beneath a fringe of light brown hair. He had been an advisor to László's father for many years, and his attitude toward László alternated between respectful deference and affection, depending on whether he agreed with any particular decision of the King. His tunic was mostly a pale yellow, and the embroidery on it might have been attractive once. He wore sandals. He didn't wash his feet often enough.

"Well, my friend," said László. "What is first, today?"

"It's been cold in the north, Your Majesty."

"And?"

"The wheat crop has suffered."

"I see. Famine?"

"It doesn't seem to be that bad, but the Count—"

"Északimező?"

"Yes. He writes of murmurs of uprising among the peasants."

László sighed. "That's nothing new up there, is it? My father mentions the same thing when I speak to him and in his diaries."

Rezső nodded. "As did his father, and his father."

László thought for a moment. "As I recall, my father sent a hundred troops up there, then a good supply of grain, then took the troops out. It worked, I believe."

Rezső nodded. "Should we do the same thing?"

"We'll try it at least."

"Very well, László. I'll attend to it."

"What next?"

Rezső scribbled some notes, then set the paper aside and found another.

"The Northmen," he said finally.

"Ah, yes. Are there new developments?"

"More of the same. The reavers seem to be gathering. I think it likely they'll test us before the year fails, unless they dispense with testing and invade outright."

"You think they might, Rezső?"

"It is possible, Your Majesty."

"All of our problems seem to come from the north, don't they?"

Rezső didn't answer, apparently interpreting this as a remark to kill time while trying to think of a solution. *He knows me too well,* thought the King, then he smiled at himself. After a bit, he said, "I don't have any ideas. But since we're bringing troops up there anyway, we could certainly bring a few more and maybe frighten them off."

Rezső cleared his throat. László knew enough to interpret this as the I-have-another-suggestion throat clear, as opposed to the that-may-not-be-the-best-idea throat clear, or the remember-I'm-here-waiting-for-you-to-notice-me throat clear, or the I-have-something-in-my-throat throat clear.

"Well?" he said. "What is it?"

"The Northmen invaded last about a hundred and fifty years ago," he said. "They caused a great deal of damage."

"I know that," said the King. "What of it?"

"About seventy-five years before that, they threatened, during the reign of King János the Third."

"And?"

"They caused no harm, that time."

"I see," said László. "Well?"

"The King was a very wise man, Your Majesty. He brought his army to the pass by the North River where the Grimwall meets the Mountains of Faerie, which is the only path from the north into Fenario."

"Get on with it, Rezső."

The latter blinked at the young King's impatience, and continued in his own leisurely fashion.

"When they entered, he harassed them but never actually fought them. They tend not to know our land very well, so he was able to guide them along the western edge of the Wandering Forest by pretending that he was ready for full-scale battle at any time. The Northmen are fond of such things, being confident that they can win in any battle."

"Hmmmph! I'm not sure they're wrong, either. Go on."

Rezső paused to remove a silk handkerchief from his sleeve and wipe the corners of his mouth where saliva had been collecting. László controlled an urge to look away. The advisor continued, "He led them south until they were near the Southern Marshes, which took months of careful planning and maneuvering. When the Northmen were practically at our southern border, he sent a raiding party against the southern marauders. Of course, he disguised this raiding party as Northerners. And he left a clear trail back to the Northmen."

László's eyes widened, then he laughed. "Yes!" he said. "And the marauders, of course, charged in and did to the Northmen what we couldn't do ourselves! Wonderful! Can Marshal Henrik do the same trick, do you think?"

"I believe he can, László," said the advisor.

László shook his head, still laughing. "Excellent! Have the order written up, and I'll sign it."

Rezső nodded and made some notes. Then he found another scrap of parchment and said, "There is a dragon."

"Indeed?"

"Yes, Your Majesty."

"Well," he said. "Well, well, and well. We haven't had a dragon in Fenario in close to twenty years. I've been wondering when it would happen."

Rezső remained silent.

"I assume it's to the west, near the border." Rezső nodded. "Has it done any damage?" asked the King.

The minister consulted the parchment. "It's frightened a few peasants and a few merchants, but nothing more than that."

László nodded. "Do you think it has something to do with the Northmen, or is it just coincidence?"

Rezső considered this, then said. "I think it's coincidence, Your Majesty. If the Northmen could control a dragon, they would either use it to greater effect or leave it hidden."

"Hmmmm," said the King. "We can't really spare part of the army, can we?"

"Not very well. In any case, history has shown that armies are a poor means of fighting dragons."

"Yes . . . well, I think I have an idea."

"Your Majesty?"

"Never mind. I'll take care of it. Anything more?"

Rezső looked unhappy but didn't insist. He carefully set the papers down, folded his hands, cleared his throat, and looked at the King.

László groaned. "Not again."

"Your Majesty," said Rezső, "it is my duty. You are thirty-three years old. To be blunt, every day past forty should be counted as a blessing. I know, because I have given thanks to the Demon Goddess every day for the past twenty years."

"I know, I know." László swallowed with difficulty and looked away. *Rezső must have studied with the old King and Queen,* he thought. *And more than statesmanship. He is the only man I know who can almost bring tears of frustration to my eyes.*

"Your Majesty, if Andor succeeds you to the throne, I shudder to think what will happen to the kingdom. And he is unmarried as well, for that matter, and hardly younger than you. Nor has Vilmos found a wife. That leaves the throne of Fenario going to some Baron or other who is probably descended from your grandfather's eldest sister or something."

"I know, Rezső."

"Your Majesty, I have a proposal here from the Count of Mordfal—an important county with the galena mines near the Grimtail Fissure and part of the defense against—"

László fought to keep his voice calm. *How can I explain to this old man what he is asking for?* "Rezső," he said finally, "I'll be blunt with you. Dalliance, as you are sometimes pleased to call it, is the only pleasure I have. I know it is unbecoming to complain, but by the Demon Goddess! My whole day, every day, is given to this damned kingdom. Show me a woman I'll fall in love with or who won't cause a civil war every time she catches me with a kitchen maid. If you do that, if she has a position that makes it a good match, I'll marry her. I promise. But in the meantime—"

"Will you consent to see her at least?"

"How old is she?"

"Fifteen."

"At least you aren't trying to palm any more children off on me." László sighed. *What's the use?* "Oh, very well. Whenever you want."

Rezső bowed his head. "Thank you, László. I will send for her at once."

"Hmmph. Now, is that all?"

"Yes, Your Majesty. That is all."

"Good. If you need me, I'll be in the courtyard, working off some of my excess passion in preparation for this charmer of yours."

Rezső bowed his head again as the King stood and left.

"Good day, Your Majesty," said Viktor.

László snarled at him.

Viktor smiled. His teeth were even, and no trace of yellow marred them. His smile was more a baring of the teeth than anything else. "One of those moods, Your Majesty?" he said. "I suppose Rezső the Righteous still wants you to get married, eh?"

"Just shut up and fetch the practice swords, will you?"

"I have them here, Your Majesty."

"Then give me one and hit at me with the other before I lose my patience and use Állam." He touched the hilt of the straight sabre that hung in the ruby-encrusted sheath at his side.

Viktor did as he was told, still smiling. Viktor was twenty-three years old, but still youthful. He seemed to bounce rather than walk; his long, straight dark hair doing its own bouncing above his shoulders, yet remaining perfectly arranged. His eyes were brown and full of light, his face had a square jaw rare in Fenario. He wore the bright red of the Palace Guard that he commanded, and his buttons always, always glittered. He had once joked that he was so strong, it would only take ten of him to defeat Vilmos in a contest of strength.

Still, he was well matched with King László. After their first few bouts, the King had learned, for the most part, how to avoid matching strength with Viktor. From then on it had been a contest of the captain's speed against the King's remarkable sense of timing.

Nor did they stop short of striking with the wooden swords, when an opening presented itself. They made the one concession to safety of not striking to the head save when wearing practice helms which neither liked. Other than that, the blows were as powerful as could be given with the light sticks. And, while a good *thwack* with such a weapon is unlikely to do more than sting, a thrust, which was also legitimate, could cause injury. So far, in the two years they had been partners, they had avoided such an injury. But not through lack of trying on either side.

As they practiced, some of László's anger worked itself off. Viktor sensed this and began talking. It was a sign of the condition of both men that, after three minutes of hard work, they could converse without gasping.

"So, Your Majesty," said Viktor, "has he gotten you to agree to a wedding date yet?"

László snorted.

Viktor chuckled. "If that means no, I'll tell you I met someone new in town yesterday."

"What good does that do me?"

"She has a friend."

"Ah, now! Keep talking, my captain, and perhaps I'll make you a Count."

Viktor saw what he thought was an opening and struck for the King's side. László sidestepped neatly and brought his wooden sword up over Viktor's and down for a satisfying thump on the shoulder. Viktor grimaced, acknowledged the touch, and waded back in.

"Being a Count, Your Majesty, interests me almost as much as being a married man interests you. But, as to this young lady—"

"How old is she?"

"Seventeen."

"And not married? I hate to think what she looks like!"

"Trust me, Your Majesty."

"If you let me down, the dungeon always has room."

"Trust me."

Viktor feinted a cut for the head, although this was not a legal target. László took the fake and Viktor struck the King just above his right knee. By their agreement, the forward leg, from the knee up, was legal. László stepped back, saluted, and went in again.

"Since when," said Viktor, "has the Palace had a dungeon?"

"It can have one in a matter of hours, my friend. Set me up with an ugly wench and you'll see."

"Yes, Your Majesty," said Viktor. He wove an intricate attack around the King's weapon, but before he could culminate it, the other slipped past his guard and landed a solid blow on his wrist. Viktor sighed. "That's two out of three," he said.

"Yes," said László. "And I feel much better for it. Go ahead and send me this wench."

"It'll be tonight, Your Majesty. I'll have her bring in a message from me so the guards will let her pass."

"I'll tell you tomorrow if you're safe from the dungeons." He gave Viktor his practice sword. "Have you seen Prince Andor?"

Viktor's face was expressionless as he said, "He's down by the River, Your Majesty. Planting flowers."

László's brows came together. "Planting flowers?"

"Yes, Your Majesty."

"Why, in the name of the Demon Goddess, is he planting flowers?"

"He didn't say, Your Majesty."

László shook his head. "This is going to be interesting."

"Marigolds," explained Andor, "must be planted each year; they do not return unassisted. Roses, on the other—"

"Andor," interrupted the King.

"Yes?"

"When did this sudden interest in flowers come over you?"

Andor looked up from the neat rows he had dug in the dirt of the Riverbank.

"Not long ago," he said. "A few days."

"I see. And what happened to your interest in the magical effects of proper diet?"

Andor made a brushing-off gesture. "Unimportant," he said. "Only the surface manifestation of a deeper principle."

"The principle of gardening?"

With obvious effort, Prince Andor rose to his feet. He wiped his hands on his royal garments, leaving brownish smudges across the bright blue tunic on either side of his ribs. László controlled his reaction.

"It's an expression of the life force," said Andor. "Every time I put a seed into the ground and bring it to fruition, I am strengthening my own force of life, binding myself closer to every other living thing. I am strengthening my will to live, my ability to—"

"I undersand," said László. "Or, well, I don't really, but never mind. I hope it gives you what you want."

Andor smiled. "Thank you, brother. It will. Sándor himself gave me the idea."

"I see. Sándor. And where is Sándor, since we speak of him?"

"Oh, around." Andor gestured vaguely.

"Well, if you see him, tell him I'd like a word."

"I shall."

László nodded and turned to leave. Andor said, "Where are you going?"

"To visit our parents."

"Ah! Yes! I'll have to do that myself, soon. Give them my regards."

"I shall, Andor. A pleasant day to you."

"And to you, brother."

László walked away as Andor, whistling, returned to his gardening.

They lay in beds next to each other in a room done in red and purple. The old King, János VI, and his Queen, Teréz, now slept most of the time, but awoke when László came to visit them.

János's eyes opened. "Who is it?" he asked in a whisper.

"It is I, father. László."

"Welcome, my son," said the old man, managing a feeble smile. "How rests the kingdom?"

"Well enough, father," said László. "There is a dragon to the west and Northmen to the north, but all is under control."

János nodded, still almost smiling. He was small, shrunken, and had not moved since losing the use of his legs when the west wing had collapsed many years ago, forcing his abdication. He had taken it well, though, and maintained an interest in the running of a kingdom that he had no part in. His face was animated and alert when László came to see him, as he did every day. Teréz could walk if she wanted, but seldom did, being content to sleep most of the time.

King János stirred. "Have you given thought to the Palace itself?" he asked, as he always did. "I admit that, in my day, I did little to see to its repair."

"The Palace is as it has ever been," said László, as he always did.

The old King seemed about to say more, but then he shook his head.

László looked at his father's withered face, pleased that he could meet his eyes, and said, "Andor sends his regards." János and Teréz accepted this without comment or change in expression. László sat on his mother's bed and took her frail, shrunken hand in one of his, and his father's in the others.

"Is there anything I can get for either of you?" he said, as he always did.

Teréz shook her head as she always did. János said, "Only your company."

László smiled sadly. He looked at his mother and for just a moment imagined he saw, reflected in her eyes, a vision of the Palace as she'd known it: bright, strong, alive with color and visitors. This, too, had happened before.

"Father?" said László suddenly.

"Yes?"

"Did you find, as King, that the more power you had, the more you must placate?"

The old King almost smiled. "That is not your only choice," he said. "You can also be a bad King."

László matched his father's smile.

János stirred. "Tell me something," he said suddenly.

"Yes, father?"

"Your brother, Miklós . . ."

"Yes?"

"You've told me often enough how much you regret what you did, but—do you miss him?"

Now, what brought that on? he wondered. He pressed the old man's hand. "Yes, father. I miss him. More than I can say."

János nodded, the sudden tears in his eyes matching the sudden tears in his son's. "Maybe," said the old King, "maybe someday . . ."

"Your Majesty, Sándor is waiting to see you."

"Thank you, page," said László, entering the Great Hall. "Send him to me."

The page left to do so. As the King sat down, the wizard entered. He was older than Rezső and, reflected László, looked it. He moved his small, wiry frame with an easy gait; yet beneath the long white hair and beard, he somehow gave the impression of frailty—that he was ready to fall over dead with no warning. His odd green robes—too hot for early winter and always looking as if they would make the old man trip—added an element of the ridiculous to the brew that made up Sándor. Still, he had been a fixture around the Palace since before László's grandfather's time.

"I was told," said the wizard as he drew near, "that Your Majesty wished to see me."

László nodded brusquely. Sándor's voice, unlike his countenance, betrayed no sign of weakness. It was firm, strong, and confident, and could have come from a youth of sixteen.

"Yes," said László. "Please, sit down." The wizard nodded and did so. "I'm wondering," continued the King, "about Andor. Do you know what he's doing now?"

"Yes," said Sándor. "Planting flowers."

László nodded. "He claims to have gotten the idea from you."

"I don't doubt it," said Sándor. "He asked me how I lived so long. I told him that my strength was the strength of Faerie. Which," he added, looking sharply at the King, "is only the truth."

"I don't see how he got from there to raising flowers," said László.

"Does his raising flowers bother you, Your Majesty?"

László considered this. "No, not in itself. But he seems to flit from one thing to another, without any sense to it. I worry about him as a brother."

"Hmmph. Well, there's nothing wrong with that."

László felt a sudden flash of anger. *Do you think I need your approval, old man?* But kept his thoughts to himself.

The wizard continued, "I spoke to him about how anything that wasn't growing was dying, as a principle of life. I used flowers as an example, and I went on to describe how the power of Faerie allows my powers to continue to grow. But, as usual, your brother heard only what he wanted to hear. He took the metaphor as the law, and by the time I realized this, there was little I could do to shake him of it."

"I see," said László.

"Don't let it worry you, Your Majesty." Sándor chuckled. "He'll find something else soon enough."

"That," said László, "is what worries me. But very well. There is another thing. Do you know a spell that will help a man defeat a dragon?"

The walls shook, the floor trembled, and the ceiling quaked. The page flung the door open but, before he could speak, László said, "Send him in."

A moment later, Vilmos entered, his muscles bulging within his tunic. "Greetings, brother!" he boomed, finding a chair and sitting in it. For perhaps the thousandth time, László wondered why it never bothered him that Vilmos didn't treat him as King, yet it had bothered him so much that Miklós hadn't. But it was a fruitless question, and led László to dwell on things that only saddened him. If he only could apologize—

He shook the mood from himself. "Hello, Vilmos. We have a problem."

"What kind of problem, László?"

"There's been a dragon sighted, just west of the Wandering Forest."

"A dragon!"

"Yes. It hasn't done any damage yet—"

"It will, though!"

"Exactly. Could you—?"

"Let me at it, brother!"

László breathed a deep sigh of relief. "Thank you, Vilmos. I was hoping you would respond in that way."

"Well, how else?"

"Sándor is preparing something—"

Vilmos's snort, which had the power of a small wind storm, cut him off. "Sándor! I need nothing from wizards!"

László felt suddenly worried. "But Vilmos, a dragon—"

Vilmos flexed his biceps and showed his teeth. "I need no wizard's tricks, brother. I'll drop a rock on the dragon's head. If that doesn't work, I'll strangle it. Hmmmph. Wizards."

László shook his head, smiling in spite of himself. "Why do you dislike Sándor so much, brother?"

"Huh. Why shouldn't I? I don't trust him, that's all."

"He's done a lot for the kingdom, Vilmos."

"He's done a lot for you, you mean. And our father, and his father. What's he done for me?"

"What's good for the King, Vilmos—"

"Yes, yes, I know. I still don't trust him."

László sighed. "As you wish, then. But be careful."

"Ha!" said Vilmos. "I'll leave in the morning."

He lifted his fantastic girth from the chair and made his way out the door. László, watching him duck his head under the doorway as he left, drummed his fingertips against the edge of his throne. *It's a good thing he agrees to help so much,* he thought. *It's good that everyone is so willing to be helpful just to be helpful. But if Vilmos chose not to, I couldn't make him.*

He nodded to himself. *That's why he scares me so much.*

It was early evening when László met Brigitta, the friend of Viktor's current lover. He took her hand, and she stepped down from the carriage, performing a graceful curtsy with the same motion. She was a short woman with bright, clear brown eyes and a finely carved face. Her hair was light brown, straight, and cut short. She wore a bright green gown of cotton that concealed her figure, but László decided that there would be little cause for complaint. What pleased him at once, however, was that she didn't seem to be as, well, *worn* as he'd expected of a wench her age.

"You are Brigitta?" he asked.

"Yes, Your Majesty. I'm honored to be able to present myself to you."

"It is my pleasure," said László. "Come. I'll show you the Palace, and we can dine."

She dimpled, and curtsied again.

As he crossed the courtyard, enjoying the gentle pressure of her arm on his, he overheard Vilmos's booming voice crying out, "All right, you cursed wizard! I'll take it! But by the Demon Goddess herself, if it betrays me I'll come tie you into knots and bounce you off the walls!"

László felt as if a burden had been lifted from his shoulders. Thank the Goddess for Sándor! The responsibility for losing *two* brothers would have been almost unbearable. He exchanged a smile with Brigitta and realized with a start that an understanding, an intimacy, had already begun to develop between them.

The world was certainly looking up.

If only Miklós could have been there.

INTERLUDE

ONCE THERE WAS A poor man who lived in the Grimwall Mountains and worked in the mines. He had about three hundred children, so you can imagine that he was pretty poor. Well, the youngest was a lad named Mózes, who was the handsomest youth you have ever seen.

One day, the poor man hears that the King is looking for a handsome youth to be the husband for his daughter, who is just getting to marriageable age. So he says, "Mózes, you must go to the city and become the husband of the King's daughter, or else your old father and all of your brothers and sisters will starve to death." So, being a dutiful son, he went off.

He hadn't been traveling more than a week and a day when he saw a calf lying by the side of the road, and there were two dzur just about to pounce on it. Well, Mózes felt sorry for the calf, so he walked right up to it, past the dzur, and carried it away. (Well, he was strong, too.)

He was walking along with the calf, when suddenly the cow comes up to him. "Ho there," it says, "that is my calf you have there!"

"Well then, mother," he says, "you may have it back, for I have just saved it from two dzur."

And the cow says, "If that is true, I will help you as best I may, but if you have lied to me and were taking my calf to be slaughtered, I will gore you to death." (In those days cows had horns.) So she asks the calf, and the calf tells her that what

Mózes said was true. "Very well, young Mózes," she said. "How should I help you?"

"Oh, mother," says Mózes, "I am to try to marry the King's daughter so my father and my brothers and sisters won't starve to death. How can I do this?"

"Well," says the cow, "you are handsome enough. But the King will never see you dressed as you are." And, quick as thought, she made him beautiful garments of silver. He thanked her, and went on his way to the city.

He got there and was sent in to see the King, who said, "You are handsome enough," so he introduced him to his daughter, whose name was Rózsa. Well, Rózsa was the prettiest girl who ever lived on either side of any mountain. She looked at him, and he looked at her, and bells rang, and everything else you can imagine. You can bet they were as much in love as anyone ever was!

So it was all set, except the King said, "Who is your father, Mózes, so we can invite him to the wedding?" And when Mózes said, "He is a poor man who works in the mines and has three hundred children," the King was mad as a Fásbot bull and tore out his beard.

When he had calmed down just a little, he said, "All right, Mózes, if you want to marry my daughter, you must do three things for me. First, you must make the River flow backward. Come to me when you have done that."

Right away, Mózes went to see Rózsa and told her what her father had said. "Leave it to me, handsome Mózes," she said. And she went over to her window and hummed a song that sounded like a flock of bluejays. Pretty soon a tall lady comes into the room. "What do you want, pretty Rózsa?" she says. "Oh, Demon Goddess, I want to marry Mózes, but my father won't consent until he turns the River backward." So the lady says, "Well, Mózes, how tall am I?"

Mózes says, "Why, you are twice as tall as I am."

And the lady says, "You are a clever lad!" and has her demons jump into the River and kick up such waves that it seems to run backward.

Well, the next day, Mózes goes to the King, and he says, "I see you have done what I told you to. Now let us see if you can make the stars shine during the day."

Well, Mózes runs up to see Rózsa and tells her about it. She just says, "Leave it to me, handsome Mózes." Then she goes to the window and hums a song that sounds like a flock of sparrows. Pretty soon an old lady comes to the window and says, "What do you want, pretty Rózsa?" "Oh, Demon Goddess," she says, "I want to marry handsome Mózes, but my father won't let me unless he can make the stars shine during the day."

"Well, Mózes," says the lady, "how old am I?"

"Oh, that is easy," says Mózes. "You are twice as old as I am."

"You are a clever lad," says the lady, and has her demons fly up and put a blanket over the sun, so the stars shine during the day.

The next day, Mózes came to the King again. The King said, "You certainly are a clever fellow, Mózes. But now the third task: you must move my Palace to the other side of the River."

Well, just like before, he goes to pretty Rózsa, and she goes to the window and hums like a flock of geese. Pretty soon, a fat lady comes in. When she hears the story, she says, "Well, Mózes, how much do I weigh?"

"That's easy," said Mózes. "You weigh twice as much as I do."

"You are a clever fellow," said the lady, and she had her demons move the River so it flowed behind the King's Palace.

Well, the King was really a good fellow, and he knew when he was beaten at his own game, so he gave the two young people his blessing, and they got married, and Mózes's father and his brothers and sisters all moved into the Palace, and when the old King passed away Mózes became the King, and if they haven't since died, they are still alive to this day.

chapter three

The Dragon

CLEAR WATER NIBBLED the toes of brown leather boots and made small, slapping sounds against the low rocks at the lake's edge. The boots supported legs wrapped in brown wool, and a body wrapped in a dirty green tunic over a stained yellow jerkin. On the breast of the jerkin a small animal was sloppily embroidered in black and white.

Miklós stood on a shelf of flat, grayish rock. Mountains rose behind him and to either side, some of them showing faint white cappings. Before him, as far as he could see, was a lake, also gray but with a blue tint. The lake covered nearly all of the mesa on which he stood, save for an unscalable mountain wall to the near side. On the other side, the north, he could see nothing but water. The breeze came from off the lake, chilly yet bracing.

Miklós squatted on the rocks. He dropped the branches he had picked up along the way, brushed off his hands, and scooped up a handful of the water of Lake Fenarr and tasted it. It wasn't, perhaps, as sweet as he'd remembered it from the first time he'd passed this spot, or as deliciously icy as he'd imagined it would be during his long years of servitude. Yet, it would do.

He stood once more and studied the spot where his shadow would be if the sun weren't hidden by the Hand of Faerie. It was more than two years ago that he had passed this way, traveling west. Then, he had known it as the source of the River. Now he knew it for a basin that collected water from higher mountains, and sent it forth both east and west. In the west, the Lake's spawn was called the Eastern River.

The first time he had come this way it had been morning and the water had been blue and silver in the sunlight. Now it seemed brown and gray. Then, his shadow had preceded him on the final stage to Faerie. Now, at the end of the first stage home, his shadow was so faint it was hardly noticeable.

Home . . .

His reason told him his memory lied, yet, in his memory, home was clean and fresh and strong and secure and a place of rest. His reason told him that László would have turned his room to some other use, but his memory only told him how safe he had felt in his bed.

Reason had done him no good during the last two years, but memory of home had kept him alive. It was reason that had held him there for as long as he had stayed—reason had told him that he was learning, that the strange, extra sense he had been given, the Pathway in his mind, wouldn't help him unless he knew how to use it.

Enough of that.

He gathered twigs and dried leaves together on the rocks at the water's edge. He called upon the Power and he demanded fire. After a moment it came, and the twigs and leaves began to smoke, then to burn.

He dropped the pack he carried on his broad shoulders. He pulled off his boots and set them by the fire. Then jerkin and tunic and leggings. Then he dived into the clear waters of Lake Fenarr. He swam with the long, easy strokes of one who has been around water since boyhood, augmented by muscles built from two years of toil.

It was almost dark when he emerged, dripping and cold, and sat naked by the dying fire. He threw a few small branches on it. When it was going well again, he threw into the flames yellow jerkin, green tunic, and brown leggings.

From his pack he took the worn, ragged clothing that had been his as a Prince and slowly dressed himself. Only the boots remained of the outfit he had worn upon arriving at this spot. The fire burned high and bright.

Prince Miklós slept.

The next day Miklós spent skirting the north shore of Lake Fenarr. The mountain wall on that side sometimes met the water, forcing Miklós out into it, but usually he could walk between lake and mountain. Diminutive streams and waterfalls fed the lake, forcing Miklós over, through, or under them. But this, too, was all right. He ate a few of the biscuits he had taken with him, and slept without a fire. It was around noon of the next day that he began to hear the distant roaring of the waterfall. An hour later, after passing a ledge of rock that forced him into the lake up to his knees, he began to see the fine mist kicked up by the cascade.

Then he was on a ledge above the falls. He looked down, but the bottom was hidden in the mist and spray. He remembered the climb up, though. Nearly a thousand feet, the water fell. Yet the path had been easy. He looked for signs of it, but didn't see any.

Some of those he had lived with (the term "friends" never entered his mind) had been able to leap from great heights, landing as soft as a leaf. But they had been old and had practiced the use of the Power for many times the length of his life. He wouldn't be able to do that with the little he knew.

He walked along the ledge for nearly an hour until he had convinced himself that the path was no longer there. This being the case, there was nothing to do except go down without one.

There was no point in hesitating. He took a good look over the edge, found a footrest below, and made for it—going feet first over the edge, scrabbling and straining. He found a small ledge a little further down. His hands gripped rock, his feet settled onto the shelf.

He carefully turned himself around, scraping his right shoulder, and looked down between his feet. A momentary vertigo he banished with an act of will.

The next ledge was wider but farther away. He slowly bent his knees, letting his back scrape against the side of the mountain, until he could sit. From there he turned quickly while grasping with his fingers. He hung for a moment, then let go. The drop was only a few inches, yet for an instant he nearly went over backward. He recovered his balance, then his breath.

It occurred to him that descending a mountainside was its own art—one that could probably be studied and learned. There were many things to study and learn. He would have a chance to study none of them if he were unable to make his way safely down the mountain.

As he faced away from the cliff, the edge of the waterfall

was visible fifty feet to his right. He twisted and looked up. The top, from which he had started, was about fifteen feet above him. Only nine hundred and eighty-five feet left to go.

He began looking for another hand- or foothold below him.

He slept in a shallow cave halfway down the cliffside. He had made considerable lateral progress away from the falls, though at one point had had to go nearly under it. His descent had been painfully slow after the first two hours, as he was afraid that exhaustion would do the job of carelessness.

While he sleeps, let us explain why it is that the path he had taken on his journey to Faerie was no longer there for his journey back. For thousands of years, water had been seeping into the flaws in the cliff face, slowly dissolving granite and making large cracks of the small ones. Few ever came this way; Miklós had been the last to use the path before it finally collapsed of its own weight and went crashing onto the ground at the base of the falls.

The new cliff wall, while it had no path in it, was jagged and uneven. An experienced mountaineer would have had no trouble. Miklós, on awakening fresh the next morning, and with a day of climbing experience behind him, made his careful, painstaking way down the rest of the cliff to the pile of rubble and broken boulders at the bottom by afternoon.

He spent the rest of that day there, at the source of the River, never quite dry because of the spray from the falls, but not minding. In the evening he moved off a short distance to where it was dry and built a fire. He ate a few more biscuits, then lay down next to the embers of the fire and fell asleep.

He dreamt.

In his dream, he saw the Palace that was his home. He saw it as he remembered it, not as it was. He saw jhereg flying around it, and he became aware that each time one flew near, it would take a bite out of the Palace, and he realized that soon there would be nothing left of it.

When he awoke, he knew that he must set out for home at once. Yet he paused for a moment, delighting in the sun in his eyes, though it nearly blinded him.

In all his bitter days in the land of twilight that men called Faerie, he had not been aware of how badly he had missed the morning sun. Looking back to his time in Faerie, he realized that he had never really believed the sun would not appear. It had always seemed to him that the sky would clear on the morrow.

He turned away from the sun. When the spots cleared from his eyes, he stared up at the height from which he had descended the day before.

He was certainly safe from his master now. His master would not follow him—in fact, would probably not have considered following him in any case.

It wasn't, Miklós reflected, as if his escape had been difficult. The others he had lived with and worked beside had seemed to accept their lot, and he had been expected to do the same. There had never been anything to prevent an escape. Nothing except the difficulty of breaking patterns that, in only a few days, seemed to have become ingrained. And, as well, always the question of where to go, and what to do when he got there.

But he could only take so much. Finally, one morning he had put his old clothes and a small bit of food into his pack and had walked away from the master's fields and into the mountains he had come from. No one would miss him, that was certain.

Miklós was going home. As for what he would do there, he'd know that when he did it.

. . . And he was in the Forest.

It came up that suddenly. For a few hours after leaving the base of the waterfall, he was walking along a path through hard, rocky ground, with the River a distant, wavering line on his right. Then there was a blur ahead of him as he began to notice grass beneath his feet. Then the blur took shape, and then he was in the Wandering Forest—amid the hickory and the birch and the heaken and the oak—with the clean scent of growth all about him and cool wind in his face.

He wasn't sure why, but he moved away from the path. He walked through thickets and around trees, jumping over puddles and disturbing teckla that scurried and norska that hopped. As he walked, humming songs from childhood and listening to the chatter of the birds, he considered again what he would do upon returning.

He would see his parents, of course. He realized with a sudden pang of guilt that they might have died while he was gone. Then he laughed to himself. He had hardly left the Palace of his own volition. Yes, he would see his parents, if they yet lived. And dear Andor and big, laughing Vilmos. And László.

László. The King. *King,* he thought to himself. His master had owned ten times the land that László ruled, yet was called the name that means "Baron" in their tongue. Miklós shuddered as he thought of the power his master had wielded. An effort of will, and he could be miles away. A snap of his fingers and a hovel would burn and crumble and disappear as if it had never been.

And pitiful László called himself a King.

Miklós realized that he no longer feared László. What he had learned in Faerie was little enough next to those who had worked the fields beside him and insignificant next to his master, yet next to László he could be a god.

But as Miklós walked, and hummed, and listened to the sounds and smelt the smells of the Wandering Forest, this mood passed. László had always had a temper, and did things he later regretted. László had, in all probability, spent the last two years regretting that night. He probably believed Miklós dead and tormented himself with the thought.

No, punishing László was not what he had returned to do. Returned to do?

He considered this thought. Where had it come from? Why the feeling that there was something that he needed to do? He had a life to live. People to meet. Lovers to love. Maybe he could learn to climb mountains.

Then he remembered his dream of the night before and spent much of the rest of the day wondering.

Miklós awoke the next morning to a drizzle of rain that threatened to become a downpour. He quickly gathered his pack together and ran until he found a broad oak under which to take shelter. By mid-morning the rain ended, and the sun was glimmering through fat oak leaves.

Miklós began walking. He was well into the Forest by now. With each mile his mood seemed to shift; sometimes anticipatory, sometimes apprehensive, sometimes eager, sometimes ambivalent.

He had noticed this and was pondering it (he had always been introspective) when the woods around him became quiet. In the Wandering Forest it was no great feat of woodsmanship to notice the silence; it was a place filled with birds that piped, small animals that chittered, larger animals that growled. When they unceremoniously stopped the orchestration (leaving Miklós feeling vaguely stupid for having missed whatever message they had all received), Miklós stopped as well, listening intently and looking around.

On a branch of the oak nearest him sat an athyra with its thick brown plumage and hooked beak. A little way off, a teckla sat up on its back legs, motionless except for quick, furtive movements of its gray, whiskered head. Nothing else moved.

Miklós dropped to one knee so he wouldn't tire of standing. He realized that he knew, as well as any of the other animals, that something was coming. He had to keep reminding himself to breathe. Gradually, though, he adjusted to the rhythm of the Forest—the tensionless waiting, the alert calmness.

He had been kneeling, motionless, for several minutes when it appeared, as a flickering movement through a thicket, far off to the right of the direction he was facing. He watched it carefully, not wanting to move until he knew what direction it was safe to move in.

The teckla knew this before he did—it darted off to Miklós's left. Miklós considered briefly, then followed. He glanced back, but the athyra hadn't moved. He looked over to where the movement had appeared and had a sudden, clear vision of a monstrous head—narrow, triangular, and reptilian. He had never seen it before, but his stay in Faerie had taught him to recognize it. Three small tentacles, which Miklós knew to be sense organs, descended from its chin. There would be larger ones around its neck, but Miklós didn't remain to see them. He raced off through the woods, hoping the teckla knew enough to pick a direction opposite the one the dragon would choose.

The Wandering Forest wrapped itself like a sheet around the base of the Mountains of Faerie. Here and there, intermixed with trees, brooks, weeds, and shrubs, were outcroppings of granite—an advance guard, as it were, for the eastward march of the mountains. Some of these were almost high enough to be considered mountains themselves, or at least hills. They were new, as such things go, and hadn't been around long enough to develop a layer of topsoil for the use of grass and trees. Only occasional weeds sprang from flaws in the rock.

It was from a shelf on one of these that Miklós, perched like a hawk ready to dive (though feeling more like a teckla ready to scurry), watched the dragon, trying to guess its path. Even from this vantage, forty feet above the floor of the forest, he could only rarely glimpse the massive form of the beast, weaving in and out of trees that it doubtless found as strange as Miklós did. Odd how silently a dragon could move, even on unfamiliar terrain.

The dragon was a mountain animal, he reflected. Odd that it was only when he came down out of the mountains that he encountered one.

The dragon stopped suddenly, and the Prince could see its neck tentacles becoming hard and rigid. He chuckled to himself at the vaguely sexual impression it gave. Then he realized that the dragon was standing in almost the same place he had vacated a few minutes before, and he was very pleased he had moved. But what had it found? The athyra?

Then he saw the dragon's head snapping at the branch of a tree and knew that it was true. He shook his head in sudden sympathy with the foolish bird. Apparently dragons were so rare in the Forest that the athyra didn't know how to contend with one. The athyra was a hunting bird; it lured its prey to it with mind-tricks, sending out silent messages of safety and food. Its means of defense were similar—hiding itself and sending messages of fear to keep predators away. It was a shame, Miklós reflected, that it didn't know better than to play mental games with a dragon. Or maybe it did know, but the dragon had snared it in the same sort of web it wove, so it was powerless to escape.

The dragon struck again, and the prince's straining eyes could almost make out a few feathers, drifting softly to the ground.

An hour before, Miklós had had some idea that he was traveling in the right direction. Now, he had none. He had blundered by many streams and pools, but not the River. Was he anywhere near it? He had had no time to search. Whichever way he went, it seemed, the dragon was behind him.

Yet the oddest thing was his feeling, almost a conviction, that the dragon *wasn't* following him. Certainly, there was no reason why it should, unless it had gotten a good, strong scent where it had killed the athyra, but there was no indication that it was following or looking for anything. It was more as if, no matter which way Miklós turned, the dragon happened to turn that way, too. And every time Miklós turned, he became that much more lost.

Yet the fires of Faerie had tempered him, and even pursuit by a dragon didn't shake the stubborn confidence he had learned among that people—fighting for everything he needed during days of labor and nights of hopelessness. He was lost and he was pursued; he was not frightened.

He heard a snarl off to his left and stepped back, alert. He found himself staring into the yellow eyes of a dzur, about thirty feet away from him. Five hundred pounds of black death.

He let out his breath. "Nice kitty," he remarked.

Thoughts of the Power came flickering through his mind, but he brushed them off; even his master would have feared to use it against such an animal. The dzur snarled again.

Miklós had encountered dzur before and knew that they didn't usually attack men. He watched its rear legs and took a slow step back. The cat continued watching him. Miklós sensed, rather than saw or heard, that the dragon was approaching. Another step back and he bumped into a tree. His start almost made the dzur leap, but not quite. He stepped around the tree, and the dzur's head suddenly swung.

Miklós followed the dzur's gaze, and gasped. He had never before been so close to a dragon. It is one thing to know that a dragon's head is taller than you are, another to see one close up. The dragon wasn't looking at him but at the dzur; and all of its tentacles were fully erect. This time Miklós found nothing amusing about it. He stared, mesmerized, until he heard a louder snarl than he'd heard yet, and a thin black streak launched itself across his line of sight and into the dragon's face.

As the dragon gave a bellow, Miklós came to himself enough to turn and run. The bellow echoed through the forest and left the prince with a ringing in his ears that went on and on and on. He wasn't really aware that it had stopped until, some time later, as he lay face down at the edge of the River, another sound came to him from behind.

This far-off sound he recognized as the death wail of a dzur.

Two hours later Miklós lay on his back, chuckling to himself. Instinct, of course; his own and the dragon's. The dragon had never been following him, and he had never really been lost. Both of them had been making for the River.

And why not? It was cool and pleasant to his legs. Lifting his head to look downstream through a tunnel of elms dotted with occasional willows, he was certain it was cool and pleasant to the dragon's feet as well. He chuckled again.

There was, however, a more serious side to it. Now that he was at the River, it would be dangerous to leave it; he might become lost indeed. But the dragon was *down*river from him, and he did not relish the idea of walking past it. Dragons, unlike dzur, had no objection to manflesh; or so the stories said.

He lifted his head and considered crossing over. That would be a solution, except that here, fresh from the waterfall and the trip down the mountain, the water was cold, fast, and deep. A raft? That would do, if he could make sure the raft would bring him to the other side before it brought him to the dragon. The idea of floating into the dragon's maw was not appealing. A pole? Would that be enough?

As much to test his skill as for any other reason, he found a large tree and brought forth the Power, forcing his mind through the rigid paths and strict logic required to bend it to his will. The tree fell. The dragon looked up, startled, then went back to drinking from the River.

Using the same Power, Miklós cut the tree into eight even sections. He laid them next to each other and concentrated still harder. Using the power of Faerie to destroy was hard; using it to build was even harder. Or, at least, using it to build something that would last.

The Power was there, and the Pathway in his mind, and the Source whence came the Power. All that was needed was understanding—strict, inflexible rules guided the use. They must be remembered without error and applied without hesitation.

Three hard, sweating hours later he lay back, exhausted. The sun had set long ago, but he had scarcely noticed. He wasn't even sure if he had succeeded, but that was for tomorrow. Now he needed sleep.

The next morning he studied his raft. It was bound together by the Power of Faerie, and only by his desire could those logs be broken from each other. He dragged the raft over to the River (yes, the dragon was still there) and made sure it floated. Good. Now, for a pole.

He pulled the raft ashore, found a sapling, and cut it easily. He used his shaving knife to trim off the small twigs and branches. Good.

Now, of course, the question was did he trust his ability as a waterman to carry him past the dragon, or, alternately, did he trust the dragon to leave him alone?

He was considering this when he heard the sound of splashing from downstream, surprisingly loud over the rushing of the River itself. He couldn't see the cause of the splashing, but apparently the dragon could, for its tentacles were growing stiff and its head was turned to look further down the River.

Miklós stood up and took a hesitant step forward, then changed his mind. The dragon turned ponderously to face the shore; evidently whatever it was was coming on land. Then he heard another sound—so strange he couldn't believe he had heard it—a human voice shouting.

He heard it again but still couldn't make out the words. But—didn't that voice sound familiar?

He began walking toward the dragon, almost against his will. It couldn't be. . . .

He was a hundred feet away when he saw that it was. He stopped. He would have yelled, but his tongue felt frozen against the roof of his mouth. Some analytical part of the back of his mind said, *So this is what being paralyzed with shock is like. I hadn't thought it would ever really happen.*

And his brother Vilmos, now close enough to hear, had eyes only for the dragon. He cried out, "All right, monster. My turn first." He held up one of his massive fists, and there was a sudden flash of light. Miklós, now beyond surprise, felt the emanations of the Power.

The dragon felt them, too. It flinched back and roared, sending waves rippling down the River that knocked Miklós onto his back, though only his feet had been in the water.

He got to his knees and heard Vilmos cursing wizards in general and Sándor in particular, and saw him heaving something up over the dragon's head and away, apparently in disgust.

The dragon seemed surprised, but not harmed. It was on Vilmos faster than Miklós would have believed possible. For a moment Miklós feared the worst, but then his brother emerged from the River, his back to Miklós, having dived under the dragon. He was waist deep in water, but his strength allowed him to stand against the current, at least for a while.

Miklós thought of calling out to him, but feared it would only distract him. Miklós began running.

He was fifty feet away when Vilmos leapt onto the dragon's back, crying, "I said I'd strangle you, and by the Demon Goddess I will!"

Even his massive hands couldn't come close to actually fitting around the dragon's throat, but he took one of its great tentacles and twisted and pulled it.

The dragon lurched and fell into the water. Miklós stopped, then shook his head and continued at a walk. He didn't know whether the moisture on his face was from the River, from sweat, or from tears.

Vilmos stood up in the water at the same moment that the dragon did, towering above him. It spotted him at once, and its head came crashing down. Vilmos threw himself out of the way, then rolled quickly up onto shore. The dragon followed, leaping.

Vilmos spun around, as if looking for something, then threw himself once more out of the way of the dragon's jaws. Teeth, however, are not the dragon's only weapon. A claw that was as big as Vilmos himself swung out too quickly to be seen, but somehow Vilmos wasn't there. He retreated, still searching the ground. Then the dragon was between Miklós and his brother.

Miklós broke into a run again. He was only twenty feet away when the dragon struck again, first with one claw, then the other. Vilmos screamed, and Miklós heard himself scream as well.

The dragon's head came down hard, and the ground shook with the force as it missed its target. Miklós saw his brother, his chest soaked with blood. Over his head, Vilmos held a rock half as big as he was. For an instant their eyes locked, and Miklós saw his brother's widen. Then Vilmos brought the rock crashing down on the dragon's head.

Its body gave a great spasm. The neck struck Vilmos across his chest, throwing him out into the middle of the River, where he began splashing against the current. Miklós started to run toward him. Then, out of the corner of his eyes, Miklós saw the dragon's tail whipping around. It hit him, and he felt himself flying through the air. He had time to be amazed that he seemed unhurt before he noticed a tree rushing toward him, as if desperate to catch him before he hit the ground.

Miklós had never seen a wall like that before. It seemed to be made of millions of small, fuzzy things, that . . . oh. So was the sky. He blinked a couple of times and realized that he wanted very much to throw up. He knew that if he could just throw up he would feel so much better. He rolled over onto his stomach and pushed up with his arms. If he could only . . . the ground rushed up at him, much as the tree had. He had time to be glad that he hadn't tried to stand up.

The next time he woke, his vision was clear, but he still felt sick. He rolled over onto his back to see if he could, and nothing hurt more than it had before. He saw that it was either early morning or late evening, depending on which way he was facing. He decided to look for the River. Deciding was as far as he got.

It was night. Time to sleep, he decided.
   So he did.

Miklós didn't know how many days had passed, but he was finally able to stir himself. He pulled himself up by holding onto a nearby tree. It occurred to him that this was the one he had hit. He resisted looking for marks of where he had struck the tree for fear that he might find them. He stumbled away to practice walking and to clean himself and his garments, which he apparently soiled sometime in the last day or two or three. . . .
   He bathed in the River, upstream from the body of the dragon which lay in the water, covered with jhereg. Of Vilmos there was no sign. It occurred to him that, if it weren't for the meal the dragon offered to the local scavengers, he wouldn't have survived, helpless as he had been. He shuddered.
   While his clothing dried, hanging over the bough of a tree, he kindled a fire. He took out his shaving knife and held it. He drew once more upon the Power, and soon a norska came to him. He killed it quickly, skinned it, and roasted it over the fire. He ate every bit of meat and much of the fat.
   Then he washed himself again, allowed wind and fire to dry him, and put on once more the ragged and tattered clothing

which identified him as Prince Miklós of Fenario.

He took his whetstone from his pack, sharpened his shaving knife, and put knife and stone away. He smothered the fire and returned to his raft. He picked up the pole he had crafted, pushed off, and carefully negotiated around the body of the dragon. Several jhereg hissed at him. He hissed back.

Soon dragon and jhereg were lost behind a bend in the River. The Palace was ahead.

INTERLUDE

A SINGLE DROP OF BLOOD, deep in the floor boards . . .

Yet, let us be careful not to put too much emphasis upon its effect. There is a strict limit to how much blame may properly be assigned to any catalyst. There are always the questions: would there have been another catalyst? Would any catalyst have been necessary?

There was a thing in the Palace, built into its very structure from the beginning. Why? Perhaps it was carried on a log sent downriver from the Wandering Forest when the Palace was built. Perhaps only because the Palace was built next to the River that flowed down from the Mountains of Faerie. Perhaps it was in the very nature of the Palace itself. Perhaps these things cannot be separated.

Nevertheless, there was a thing in the Palace. It waited, very much like a seed, for the proper time to sprout. Call it a seed. Two years ago, a single drop of blood had touched the seed, and things began to happen. Not fast, nor in any way apparent. Yet, it began to grow.

At first it was weak, as such things will be. But gradually it acquired a shape, still hidden. Had its shape not been hidden, at this point, it could have been easily destroyed. Yet, if it had been, another would have begun to grow.

Whatever it was that caused this growth to sprout had, at the time, seemingly unlimited strength. This would not always be the case.

Rest assured, we will return to this again.

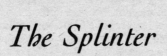

chapter four

The Splinter

ANDOR STIFLED A CURSE and looked at the forefinger of his right hand. He squeezed it, and a tiny drop of blood appeared near the tip just to the left of the nail. He looked closer but didn't see the sliver.

He ran his thumb back and forth along the finger, trying all directions until he found the way of rubbing it that felt as if he were being poked with a needle. He rubbed it a few more times, wincing, then raised it to his mouth and tried to pull the sliver with his teeth. After several tries he thought he had it, but discovered when rubbing still hurt that he had only removed a small piece of skin.

He took time out to scowl at the windowsill, then closed the shutters with his left hand, holding the forefinger of his right awkwardly to the side.

He had gotten the sliver while absent-mindedly running his hand along the sill, staring out at the Riverbank where he had planted his flowers. The sill had had little use before Andor had begun the planting; there had been nothing to see from the window except the River. But these last several mornings he had risen, thrown open the shutters, and strained to see if any growth had broken through, before running outside to take a close look.

The sliver, however, had driven all thoughts of flowers from Andor's mind. He brushed aside the curtain that separated his room from the corridor outside (carefully, so as not to knock

53

the rod out from where the braces were coming loose), and
went looking for—

Let us pause here. In this world, or any world, there are
people who never need help in removing splinters, people who
need help in removing splinters, and people who need help in
removing splinters but can find no such help.

Of those who made their home in the Palace, only László
had never felt the need to have help with a splinter. Andor had
gone to his mother for many years, until the accident, after
which she had moved to the tower with her husband and so
was unavailable. Miklós had gone to Nurse.

Nurse was gone now, as was Miklós. László still needed
no one. Andor needed someone, and so had settled naturally
on Sándor. Vilmos, from time to time, came to Andor, but—

Did we have three categories, there? Pardon, there is a
fourth: Those who need no help with splinters, but aren't aware
of it.

Andor trudged up the stairs, still holding his finger off to
the side. The steps shifted and grumbled beneath his weight,
but they had been doing that for as long as he could remember.
At the top, he turned left (avoiding a small puddle—there had
been a light rain the night before) and went back down. As he
followed the next turning of the corridor, he spared a glance
for the carving of the bullrider. It seemed such a silly place to
put a carving. He came to the audience chamber.

László, alone in the room, looked up.

"Where is Sándor?" asked Andor.

"The Old Library," said László tersely.

Andor muttered his thanks and followed the corridor to the
indicated room. He paused in the doorway for a moment, looking at the edges. *It is odd,* he thought, *how much more aware
of cracked wood one is when one has just received a splinter.*

After he entered, it took him a moment to find the old
wizard, hidden as he was behind stacks of books. The room
itself was large, and seemed curiously empty despite the piles
of books that nearly filled it. The books in the Old Library
were mostly stacked on the floor, for much of the shelving had
fallen down over the years. The books in the New Library were
all copied and bound in Fenario by clerks and monks in the
service of the Demon Goddess. The Old Library held books
brought over the border from far lands, or traded for the wines
and spices of Fenario before being given to one or another King

on one or another occasion. Many of these books, if truth be told, were in better shape than the room that contained them.

Andor approached Sándor and sat down next to him. The wizard held up a forefinger (in unconscious parody of Andor) while he ran his other finger along lines of ancient script. Andor winced in false sympathy to see him rubbing his finger, and looked away. Then he looked back, once more admiring the wizard's calm demeanor. Dignity, that was it. Even the unpretentious pale green robes added to the effect of calm self-assurance.

After a moment, Sándor looked up. "Yes?"

Andor was flustered for a moment to be caught staring, but he held out the injury. "Do you think you could help me with a sliver? I've tried digging it out, but I can't seem to—"

"Certainly," said Sándor. He grasped the end of the finger tightly, turning the tip purple, and reached down deftly with the fingernails of his other hand. Between the pressure from the squeezing and the light pain from the digging of the nails, Andor didn't actually feel the sliver come free, but Sándor was holding it, and rubbing now produced no pain.

"Thank you," he said.

Sándor nodded brusquely. Andor settled back and sighed. Sándor seemed to resign himself to a long conversation. "What is it?" he said.

"The flowers," said Andor. "They don't seem to be coming up. It's been more than a week now, and—"

Sándor snorted.

"What is it?" asked Andor.

Sándor snorted again. "Late autumn is not the time to plant flowers, my foolish friend."

Andor, who had been prepared for either a shocking revelation about the Nature of Truth or a severe tongue-lashing for lack of trust in the Power of Life, felt his jaw drop with amazement.

After a moment, he managed to stammer out, "But you said—"

"I said nothing. I was speaking in generalities. You chose to take my examples literally and wouldn't listen when I tried to correct your error. Flowers, indeed!"

Andor stared at him, trying desperately to understand. At last he said, "Please, Sándor."

"Please what?"

"Help me. There is something...."

"Yes?"

"Something missing. Something that I'm not seeing or doing."

"And it's making you unhappy, is that it?"

Andor nodded miserably.

"You feel an emptiness in your life, and you come to me because I seem to be fulfilled."

"Yes."

"You think there must be some secret that I have, knowledge of how to be happy."

"No, but—"

"No *buts*. I can hear it in everything you say."

Sándor's expression was midway between exasperation and disdain. Andor looked down, like a child confronted with the evidence of a dish found under his bed with remnants of months-old pudding still on it.

Sándor said in a suddenly gentler tone, "It isn't that easy, Andor. I have paid for my peace of mind with the burden of power, and paid for the power with years of study. The ways of the Goddess—"

"The Goddess?"

"Certainly, the Goddess. She is the living embodiment of the power of Faerie. That is why we worship her."

"Then the power comes from her?"

Sándor frowned, considering. "In a manner of speaking, I suppose it does, but—"

"I understand!" cried Andor. It felt as if, after hours of chasing lanterns, he had emerged for the first time into the full light of day. His pulse raced as exhilaration swept through him.

For years, he realized, he had been going through the duties of worship and obligation to the Goddess as if such things were separate from his personal life. The more he thought about it, the more he realized that again and again the Goddess had spoken to him, but he had chosen not to listen.

Little things, such as the flowers refusing to grow, or the fountain breaking down when he had been looking forward all day to cooling off in it, or his consistent failures at tests of arms, or even today, the splinter received while watching for flowers that would never break the soil. Hundreds of things should have pointed him in the right direction, but he had been blind.

Well, that was over, now. His search had been long, but at last he was on the right path. He could feel it.

Andor realized that Sándor was still talking.

"I'm sorry," he said. "I missed that. What were you saying?"

Sándor stopped, then looked exasperated. He threw up his hands and sighed. "Never mind. You'll do what you'll do, as always. I don't know why I bother. Now go away and—"

The door burst open. Andor turned to it, so he didn't see the peculiar color that came over Sándor's face. Instead he saw Vilmos, and a scream froze on his lips.

His brother's tunic was torn, and there were deep red stains over the tatters of it, running down to his blue leggings. His bare chest was a mass of scabs. His lips were drawn up in the snarl of a wild animal, his eyes were wide and blazing, even his beard seemed to stand on end.

Vilmos took a step into the room. He didn't bother to duck under the doorway; his head cracked against the wood at the top, breaking off a piece of the intrados. He didn't seem to notice. He took another step. Sándor rose to his feet. Andor backed up.

Vilmos took another step, then another. Sándor spoke in a low, even tone. "Tell me what happened, Vilmos." The giant growled and took another step.

Sándor stepped behind a table and backed up again. "Didn't the spell work, Vilmos? I can't think why it didn't." Vilmos lifted the table with his right hand and flung it casually behind him. Andor heard the sound of wood cracking and splintering when it landed, but he didn't look around. Sweat poured from Andor's brow as he tried to think of something to do. He took a hesitant step forward, but froze when Vilmos half turned to him.

Sándor scurried back. "Please, Vilmos!" he cried. "At least tell me what happened!"

Vilmos stopped, a look of scorn replacing the rage. "Can't you see my chest, wizard?"

"But the spell—"

"Yes! The spell! It made the dragon angry, wizard. I killed it anyway, but do you see what the thing did to me? And all because I was fool enough to listen to you!"

He lifted his hands and walked toward Sándor again. His massive back blocked Andor's view of the wizard. In desperation, Andor screamed. "No, Vili! Don't—"

"Quiet, brother," said Vilmos without turning.

"Vilmos," said Sándor, fighting to remain calm. "You need rest and healing. Look how injured you are."

The giant was upon him now, and his hands began to descend. A blue light suddenly flickered around Vilmos. He jumped back, startled, then advanced again.

"Your tricks are useless against—"

"No trick, Vilmos. I'm healing you. See? Already your chest is better, isn't it."

Vilmos looked down, then growled. For a moment, he seemed unsure of himself. The blue light flickered again.

"Do you see, Vilmos?" came Sándor's quivering voice. "Don't you feel better?"

The giant stirred. "Nice try, wizard," he said, stepping forward again. "But—"

"Vilmos!"

Andor turned, and László stood in the doorway. The King entered quickly, his eyes flicking from his brother's chest to the crumpled, frightened form of his wizard.

"Did his spell fail you, Vili?"

"It did, brother. But we need never worry about that again." He turned back. But with speed that amazed even Andor, who thought he knew him, László ran up and leapt between giant and wizard.

Vilmos stopped. "What are you doing, Laci?"

"I need him, Vili. The kingdom needs him. If you want to harm him, you'll have to harm me, too."

"I could destroy you, Laci," said Vilmos.

"I know," said László.

For a moment, Andor studied the tableau as an outsider. The giant's hands were still raised, but László stared up calmly. The loudest sound in the room was Vilmos's breathing. Andor became aware of a pungent odor, and realized that he was smelling his own perspiration.

Then, with a curse that Andor shuddered to overhear, Vilmos turned and stormed from the room, his head making yet a new dent in the structure of the doorway where he refused to bow upon passing through.

László reached out a hand and helped the old man to his feet. Sándor made his halting way to a chair that László had knocked over. Andor hastened to set it upright.

"What happened?" asked László.

"I don't know," said the wizard. "He would only tell me that the spell hadn't killed the dragon." He was silent for a moment, then: "He must have been near water. That's the only thing that will weaken that spell."

"Didn't you warn him about that?"

Sándor sighed. "To what purpose? You fight a dragon where it is, not where you want to." He shrugged. "It doesn't matter, in any case. The dragon is dead, Vilmos is alive. All is well."

"Sándor, you are a fool."

Sándor glanced up at the King; the expression on his face was unreadable. "That has been said by many kings before you, Your Majesty."

Sándor stood up and left, bowing to László. Andor started to follow him out.

"Andor," said László.

"Yes?"

"Will you do something for me? I'm expecting visitors the day after tomorrow. Will you make sure there are suitable arrangements?"

"What visitors?"

"A certain Count of Mordfal and his daughter, Mariska."

Andor smiled. "Daughter? Is Rezső trying to get you married again, brother?"

László shrugged. "Will you see to the arrangements and make sure there is an honor guard for them? I expect them in the forenoon."

"Certainly," said Andor. "But what about Brigitta?"

To Andor's amazement, László actually flushed.

"Shut up," he said. He stood and walked out of the room.

Andor shook his head in puzzlement and went up to his own chambers to meditate on how best to please his Goddess, before making the arrangements his brother had requested. He found himself trembling with delighted anticipation.

In his dreams that night, Andor stood on a cliff, clothed in garments of white, his hands uplifted. Wind from the sea (which he had never seen, but which he envisioned as like a lake only bigger) ruffled his hair.

He stood at the very edge of the cliff and felt a sudden fear, not of falling, but of jumping. His actions seemed to be pre-destined, and he could only wait to find out what he would do.

He became aware that a cloud had descended, so that it was directly before him. He had no memory of its arrival, yet there it was. In the dream, this didn't seem odd. He thought he must be high up indeed for there to be clouds, and for the first time he wondered where he was.

Then the cloud changed (again, he wasn't aware of the process, merely that a transformation had occurred) and it assumed the features of a face—a face he knew to be that of the Demon Goddess. In his dream, it didn't seem strange to him that she looked exactly as he'd pictured her (the artists of the land never really agreed on her features, and to Andor none of them were close). In his dream or out of it, he never noticed how much her face resembled that of his mother—thin, with high arching brows and deep, round eyes beneath a tall fore-head.

She spoke to him (though her mouth never moved), saying in a voice that pierced his heart, "Andor, will you serve me?"

He watched himself tremble, seeing himself seeing her, yet seeing through his image's eyes at the same time. He felt his own awe almost vicariously. "I will serve you," he heard himself say as he said it.

"Then I will guide and protect you," she said, "and make your life full and meaningful."

He bowed his head. "What must I do, Goddess?"

"You must aid and protect László."

He felt himself feeling puzzled. "Protect him from what, Goddess?"

"From those who would thwart his aims, which are my aims, and from those who would tear down your home, which I have sanctified. And, above all, from himself, when he doesn't understand that it is sometimes best to throw a lamb to the wolves."

"I don't understand, Goddess."

"Trust your heart, Andor, my child," she said, and there was only a cloud before him. Then that, too, was gone.

Andor awoke, then, and rolled out of bed. He cast himself full-length onto the rough wooden floor and prayed.

The next morning he became aware that he had picked up

another splinter, this one on top of his right foot. Before doing anything else he set off in search of Sándor, limping slightly.

It was still early in the morning when Andor decided what he must do to fulfill his promise. Firm with new resolve, he set off in search of Vilmos.

Calling at his brother's door brought no answer, so he tried the next obvious place and found him at once. Vilmos knelt on the floor in the alcove beneath the stairway to the wine cellars, looking incongruously huge in the tiny space. He was feeding scraps of vegetables to several norska in a small enclosure built there.

Andor watched for a moment, trying to keep the disgust off his face. Even Vilmos's clothing—dirty wool leggings, boots that bunched around his ankles, a tunic of some indefinable color that was ripped along the side—bespoke one who had no understanding of his role, who took no pride in his station. Finally Andor said, "Don't you get tired of the smell?"

Vilmos looked up, seeing him for the first time. He grunted "No," and went back to the feeding.

Andor braced himself and said, "We need to talk."

Vilmos grunted again, this time not even looking up.

"We need to talk *now,* Vilmos."

The giant administered another scrap of something green and leafy, then sat back on his heels.

"Well? What is it then?"

"It's about your attitude toward our brother and our Goddess."

Vilmos cocked his head to the side. "You say them as if they were the same."

Andor paused, startled, then began again. "No, but it's all part of the same problem. I am older than you, Vilmos. My memory stretches back farther than yours. I remember when László first took the throne from our father."

Vilmos nodded solemnly and waited for the other to continue. Andor blinked. "I think you should consider your duties. Yesterday you were near to killing—" he choked, then continued, "—actually *killing* Sándor, who is vital to the kingdom."

Vilmos snorted. Andor raised his voice and said, "Yes, vital. How could you do that? As I think about it, Vilmos, I see that your attitude toward the Goddess is perfunctory. Yes, you perform the rituals every seven days, but is your heart in them? If you could but see what I see, you would understand that the Goddess is the one who protects the kingdom, and our prayers and sacrifices to her are part of how we all contribute to the well-being of each other. Yet you seem interested only in ... those animals of yours, as if they were more important to you than your duty to the kingdom. Do you understand what I'm saying, Vilmos?"

Vilmos looked at him and blinked twice. Then he went back to feeding the norska. Andor felt himself suddenly filled with anger.

"Must you learn it only to your sorrow?" he cried. "To all our sorrow? You have benefited by living here, by your position as Prince of Fenario. Can you only take without giving?"

Vilmos stood up and faced his smaller brother. For a moment, Andor had the sudden fear that he'd pushed his brother to violence, but Vilmos didn't approach him. Instead, he ripped open his shirt, showing Andor three pink (already nearly healed) scars that went from high on the right side of his chest across his belly almost to his left hip. He gave Andor a look of contempt and returned to feeding the norska, making small clucking sounds.

Andor gritted his teeth, trembling with rage. He said, "Bah!" and half walked, half ran ~~ck up to the main floor of the Palace.

Dinner that evening was much as usual, except for the underlying tension between Andor and Vilmos. It occurred to Andor that László probably wouldn't notice it, absorbed as he was with the problems of the kingdom, especially since, he suddenly realized, there was a great deal less conversation among the three of them than there had been a year or two ago. During the silence of much of the meal Andor pondered this, and decided that it was probably due to their falling away from the Goddess. If so, he realized, it was up to him to remedy the situation.

He cleared his throat and said, "I understand, László, that there have been problems with the Northmen."

László appeared startled at the sudden break in the silence, but collected himself and said, "There have been, yes, but we seem to be dealing with them adequately." He turned his attention back to—what was it? Some kind of bird covered with a reddish sauce. Cherry.

"How is that, László?"

"Hm?" The King appeared faintly annoyed, as if he had been thinking about something. But after swallowing he said, "Marshal Henrik is attending to it." He took another sip of wine and attacked his food again.

"What is he doing, then?"

László put his knife down, wiped his lips with the white linen napkin, and replaced it on his lap. He leaned forward and said, "He is defeating the enemy."

Andor realized that this was not accomplishing what he wished to accomplish, so he smiled and nodded, somewhat embarrassed, and turned his attention back to his own food. Vilmos, across from him, had never stopped eating.

The rest of the meal proceeded in strained silence, broken only by eating sounds and the unobtrusive coming and going of servants. Andor occasionally followed one of them with his eyes. What was her name? Juliska. There was something pleasing about her: quiet, small, slim, and with a perpetually frightened and vulnerable look about her. But, he reminded himself, she was below his station, and it would be unfair. László, whatever his own faults, never used his position to force his attentions on an unwilling wench. Andor resolved to be guided by this.

That he had made similar resolves in the past and failed to keep them troubled him not at all. He was renewed now, he had found his life's path, and everything was going to be different. It made life easier to remain firm in his resolve that Juliska seemed, without giving any overt sign, to be aware of his attention, and that it made her nervous. Her hand almost trembled as she set down the glasses for the after-dinner wine. Andor found this embarrassing rather than stimulating.

As we have said, nothing of significance happened for the remainder of the meal.

Before we leave it, however, let us take a moment to shift our perspective. It was mentioned earlier that László, as King, sat in a position between his two brothers. But after his encounter earlier that day, Andor had unconsciously edged his place closer to László's right hand, so he was no longer directly across from Vilmos.

Looked at from above, this would actually make it seem that Andor, not László, took the middle position of the three. It may be true that this had been the case all along, but only the now-apparent tension made it obvious.

It was not really obvious, however, for the simple reason that there was no one hanging from the ceiling to view things from the one perspective that would make it so.

Perhaps, if Miklós had been there, that is where he would have been.

It was almost noon of the next day that the carriage, drawn by the obligatory four white horses, pulled into the courtyard. They were accompanied by six retainers, all riding *repülő* horses, though the ones drawing the carriage were of the sturdier *munkás* breed.

Andor stood at the spot where the carriage stopped (the coachman knew his business), dressed in his royal best: tight hose, black boots, dark blue tunic, and silver cloak (the combination did much to disguise the slight bulging of his middle). His hair had been carefully done, as had his nails, and he had bathed in lightly scented water (heated indoors, now that the fountain didn't work anymore). Even his teeth shone. Behind him stood an honor guard of twenty soldiers in two ranks.

The Count of Mordfal stepped down first, graciously declining Andor's offer of assistance. He was a solid man of about five-and-forty, with short legs, a muscular build, and a neat fringe of graying beard. He bowed to Andor, then allowed the Prince to assist his daughter from the carriage.

Mariska of Mordfal ("Countess" by courtesy) was, at fifteen, the personification of grace. She had dark, slanted eyes and very dark hair piled high and held in place by small, tasteful gems. Her skin was pale, her face thin, her legs a bit long for her height (which was average, if not a bit short), and she had generally a look of frailness and delicacy about her. In her left hand she clutched a small white fan.

Andor handed her down, noticing that she put no weight on his arm. She stood facing him, fully erect, for just a moment. Then she gave him a graceful curtsy. Andor mentally compared her (on his brother's behalf) with Brigitta. The wench was more curvaceous, perhaps, but couldn't compete with the Countess of Mordfal for natural grace and poise. It occurred to him suddenly that she resembled Viktor, the Captain of the

Palace Guard. He almost turned to him to look, but realized in time that the captain might interpret this as an order to do something.

As she rose from her curtsy, he stepped back a pace so he could address both guests at once. He said, "On behalf of the King, I welcome you to the Palace and offer you all the hospitality we have. The King wishes you to look upon his Palace as yours."

The Count bowed again and said, "Thank you, Prince Andor. We are honored far above our station."

Andor returned the bow, saying, "If it would please you to see the King at once, he is awaiting you. If you would rather refresh yourselves after your journey, your rooms are prepared with, I trust, all that is necessary."

"The journey was easy," returned the Count. "We should be happy to see the King as soon as it is convenient for him."

Andor bowed once more, then offered Mariska his arm and led them both to the Palace proper. Behind them, the coachman shuffled off to see to his horses, asking someone about the quality of oats in these parts. As Andor led his guests through the doors, he was suddenly uncomfortably aware of the cracks in the stonework of the floor and the warping of the walls inside the entry. Neither of the guests gave any appearance of noticing, however.

Andor conducted them to the Great Hall and had a page run off to tell the King they had arrived. He offered them brandy, which the Count accepted but the Countess declined. Andor looked around the room. It was nearly empty, save for a far corner where Vilmos and three guards were playing some sort of card game. Andor smiled to himself. Good. At least he would be spared the necessity of introducing Vilmos to the Count and Countess. How could he have explained that the monster wearing the rags of a peasant was a Prince of the Blood? He hoped the card game would keep them occupied for a long time. He turned back to studying the Countess, wondering how she could be so calm and self-assured. She caught his eye and sent him a small smile, then her eyes strayed to the fan she was holding, and she clutched it tighter.

Andor felt himself becoming envious of her poise, and despised himself for it. He must ask the Goddess to banish this from him; it was unworthy.

At that moment the King was announced, and the three of

them rose. "Thank you, Prince Andor," said the King.

"Your Majesty," said Andor, bowing. Then he bowed to the guests and departed the room, his task completed. As he turned back toward his own rooms, he expelled air from his lungs with a great sense of relief.

Suddenly, without knowing why, he made his way toward Miklós's room, which he had not looked at since the young Prince had vanished.

He pushed the curtains aside hesitantly, as a child going where he knows he doesn't belong. Direct sunlight came in from a window and struck his eyes. He saw where the shutter had broken off and fallen. He thought of fixing it, but some feeling of disquiet about being here prevented him from entering the room. There was something about the room that frightened him, but he couldn't identify it.

He was unable to understand that this room, with its dust covering, broken shutter, and shattered furnishings, epitomized the decay of the Palace around him. He was even less able to understand that it was this sense of decay and corruption that had caused his unhappiness over the last few months and years.

Also, the sun was in his eyes. This, as much as anything, must be blamed for the fact that he didn't see, though it was directly before him, what was growing from between cracks in the flooring at his feet.

He backed out carefully, as if threatened by the ghost of Miklós. He let the curtain swing shut and watched the patterns its shadows made on the floor as it swayed to and fro before settling.

INTERLUDE

ONCE THERE LIVED a poor farmer with three sons. One day, the farmer needed wood for the fireplace, because it was growing cold outside. "Go into the forest," he told his oldest son, "and bring back wood so we don't freeze to death."

So the oldest son took the axe and went into the forest. He came to a place where paths went off in two directions. He took the path to the right. Soon he saw a wolf sleeping by a stream. It was the biggest wolf he had ever seen. He was filled with fear and turned to go the other way.

But when he got back to the place where the paths met, there was an old hag standing there. "Good morning, mother," he said.

She said, "Good morning, eldest son of the farmer with three sons. Why have you turned away from the other path?"

"Oh, mother," he said. "There is a great wolf that way."

"That is a good reason," she said. And she turned him into a teckla. He had not run three paces when the wolf came up behind him and gobbled him up.

Soon the farmer grew impatient. He said to his middle son, "Go and find your brother and bring back wood so we don't freeze to death." So the middle brother went out. When he came to the place where the paths diverged, he took the path to the left and soon met the old hag.

"Good afternoon, mother," he said.

"Good afternoon, middle son of the poor farmer with three

sons. Why have you not gone the other way, where a great wolf guards the path?"

"I did not know it was there," answered the youth. "But I have no fear of wolves." And he promptly turned and walked back to the place where the paths met. There he saw a great wolf waiting. He took up the axe he found at his feet (which his brother had been carrying) and was about to set to the wolf when the hag came up behind him and turned him into a cock. Then the wolf gobbled him up.

Soon the farmer said, "Well, I don't know of your two brothers, but we still need wood so now you must go and get it so we don't freeze to death."

So the youngest son went out, and when he reached the place where the paths divided, he saw there was an axe on the road. He picked it up and looked around very carefully. Soon he saw the old hag standing on the left-hand path.

"Good evening, mother," he said.

"Good evening, youngest son of the poor farmer with three sons. Why are you waiting here?"

"How do you know who I am, mother? And what has become of my brothers?"

"I know what I know," said the hag. "And as for your brothers, one was gobbled up by the wolf because he was too cowardly, and the other was gobbled up because he was too rash."

"Well," said the youngest son, "I am neither too cowardly nor too rash, but I wish to have my brothers back." Then he struck the old hag a great blow with his axe so she fell dead at his feet. He went down the right-hand path until he saw a great wolf sleeping next to the stream.

He removed his boots so that his feet would make no sound and crept up on the wolf, and he struck such a blow that it died at once. Then he cut open its belly and out popped a teckla and a cock.

As he was wondering what to do next, the hag came up to him, only she was no longer a hag but a beautiful lady, and he saw that she was the Demon Goddess.

She said, "You have shown yourself to be a youth of courage and sense. So now dip your hand into the stream and see what happens."

So he dipped his hand into the stream and poured the water over the teckla, and there was his brother, whole and sound.

Then he dipped his hand again and poured the water over the cock, and there was his other brother. Then he dipped his hand a third time, and found that his hand was filled with silver coins.

He dipped his hand five more times, until each of the brothers had a pocketful of silver. Then he said, "That is enough. We need no more."

And the three brothers collected wood and returned to their home with enough silver to live in comfort for the rest of their lives. And if they have not died, they are still alive to this day.

chapter five

The Coachman

UNDER COVER OF DARKNESS, Miklós pulled the raft into a
hidden spot beneath lilacs that had already lost their leaves. It
was, in fact, from this very spot that he had departed two years
before. He stared at the Palace, looming dark and huge against
the stars, and shuddered as he thought of that night. His hands
opened and closed.

The need for a decision on what action to take became
suddenly real and immediate. He tried to envision his next step.
Should he walk up to the Great Gate nearly half a mile away
and demand entrance and an escort, then allow himself to be
conducted—where? To see his brother? He would look like a
prisoner. No, that wouldn't do, at least not at night. Sleep,
then, until morning? Like a beggar waiting outside the door?
Or sneak in like a thief? And what if he was caught?

He studied the outlines of the Palace towers as best he could.
Odd, he thought, how he had never noticed before that the
River served as a defense against attack. He knew the Palace
had been built as a seat of the Crown, not as a defensible
fortress; yet, by design or chance, elements of defense had
been included. He saw many things that went toward defending
the Palace, things he had never noticed before. The height and
thickness of the walls, the positioning of the towers, the way
the wings faced the main doors. Why were these things so clear
now, when the Palace itself was barely visible?

He began walking along the bank until he came under the

portion of the Palace that hung over the River (housing the latrines and the garbage gate). He watched his own actions with a peculiar sort of detachment, as if he were dreaming. He found the loose board among the planks that had been used to replace the crumbling sandstone near the water line.

He pulled himself inside, past cobwebs and small, scurrying animals, and closed the makeshift latch he had installed as a child. He smiled to think that there had been this breach in the Palace defenses for two years, and that his first act on returning was to close it up.

He found himself walking through puddles in the narrow corridor. It was lit only by the very faintest penetrations of starlight and by reflections of the Palace lights from the River that found their way through the broken slats of the River Wall. He ran his right hand gingerly along a rotted wall that sagged when he pushed against it, almost as living flesh. He shuddered to touch it, but had no other method of finding his way. The corridor ended where the wine cellars began.

The darkness here was absolute; the musky smell only relative. Miklós felt a brief moment of panic when he realized that his bare feet no longer remembered the path to the stairs. He held himself still, his eyes straining to catch the least bit of the light he knew he wouldn't find. When it became intolerable to remain motionless, he edged his right foot out, sliding it, with his hand extended at eye level, then slowly shifted his weight onto that foot. He repeated this action a few more times until his hand touched a wooden shelf and the bottles on it. This started to bring back memories. It was with a little more confidence that he sought the sandstone pillar that ran from the cellar up through the Palace, helping to support floors, ceilings, and, ultimately, the roof.

When he found it, closer than he had thought, he used it to guide himself toward the stairway. As he left it he was no longer holding a hand in front of himself. Instead, he brushed his hands together to remove the particles that had clung to them from the crumbling sandstone.

By the time he had crossed the fifty paces to the base of the stairs he was moving with confidence. Without the need to think of where he was going, he was able to concentrate more on what he would do. Up into the Palace proper, certainly; then where? Should he see László first? Or last?

He heard the chittering under the stairs, and smelt the clean/

dirty/clean smell of a nest of norska, and was pleased that Vilmos still raised them.

He was only a few feet from the stairs when he realized that there was another sound. He stopped and listened. Yes. There was someone before him: the sound of breathing was unmistakable. Moreover, he began to smell strong liquor, over and above the scent from the wine casks.

"Who is there?" he said.

A voice he didn't recognize came back. "That was to be my question, young sir. But, as you have managed to ask it first, I suppose I should answer. I am called Miska."

"And what are you doing here?"

"Now, now," said Miska. "I've answered one question of yours, good fellow. It's only fair that you answer one of mine."

Miklós stared into the darkness. Who could this be? A man, sitting in the dark in the cellars of the Palace? Should he reveal his name? Would the man recognize it.

"Have you light?" he asked.

"More questions! I seek answers and receive only questions. Are you a *garabonciás?*"

Miklós laughed suddenly. "Do you know, I think I am! Yes, by the Goddess, I have never thought of it before, but I have traveled far away to a place you have never heard of and returned . . . and returned. Yes, I think I am a *garabonciás.*"

He stopped, feeling rather breathless. But Miska's voice remained even. "You are a strange *garabonciás* then, if you can speak of the Demon Goddess."

Miklós shrugged, then realized the other couldn't see him. After a moment, there was a scratching sound, a flare, and the room was lit. It took a moment for Miklós's eyes to adjust to the light. The norska had stopped chittering.

The one who had called himself Miska was holding a torch in his right hand. Next to this hand was a long-necked ceramic bottle of some pale color. He was dressed all in black, with bright silver buttons. His boots gleamed in the torchlight. On his head was a cap, set at a rakish angle, with a bright feather in it. He had long, drooping mustaches and thick black hair. He studied Miklós for a moment, then transferred the torch to his left hand. He picked up the bottle with his right and passed it to Miklós.

The prince hesitated, not wanting a drink just then, but hoping to draw this strange creature out. He accepted the bottle and drank from it. It was *pálinka;* strong but good.

"You are dressed as a coachman," said Miklós, handing the bottle back.

"That's well," said Miska. "I am a coachman. You are dressed as a Prince."

Miklós smiled. "Am I then? Good. Yes, I am Prince Miklós."

"As I'd thought. I am the coachman for His Excellency the Count of Mordfal." There was, perhaps, a hint of irony in the way Miska said "His Excellency," but Miklós didn't press it.

"What are you doing down here, Miska-coachman-to-Mordfal?"

"What am I doing, Miklós-Prince-of-Fenario? I am getting drunk, that is what I am doing. I suggest you do the same."

"No," said Miklós, "I think not."

"As you wish."

On impulse, Miklós sat down on the floor of the cellar. Miska looked at him questioningly. "Tell me a story, friend Miska, and I won't tell your master what you are doing."

Miska laughed loudly. "Fair enough, my Prince." We should explain, I think, that coachmen in Fenario spent their time in the stables with the grooms and stable hands, yet it was considered beneath their dignity to help with the work. So it was that they would help their comrades by telling them stories as they worked, thus relieving the tedium of the day. To this day saying of a story, "It is a coachman's tale," is the highest of praise.

"Well, then," said Miska, "a brief tale only, I think, for the hour is late and I must be getting on with my journey to oblivion. Hmmm. Yes. Would you hear a tale of your own family, my Prince? I will tell you a tale of the occupation. You know of it, I hope: how the Northerners came into our land, and only those of us in the mountains to the east escaped their yoke.

"Well, in that time, the King was trapped in his Palace, like a norska in a chreotha's net. They were then only beginning to build the tunnels in which we are now pleased to sit, my Prince. But life went on as it would, for many. Yet among the Northerners was a young man who had a barbaric sounding name that I will not try to pronounce, who fell in love with a young woman of Fenario. She loved him too, I should add, but she loved jewels even more. So she begged this Northerner to give her the biggest diamond he could find."

The coachman took another drink of *pálinka* and offered

the bottle to Miklós. The prince shook his head but didn't speak. Miska continued.

"The Northerner went to all of the jewelers in the city— for as you know, the finest of the diamonds found in the Western Mountains are sent here—and he found one that he thought was good enough for her. He asked the jeweler for it. The jeweler handed it to him but, foolish man, asked him to pay for it. 'Here is your payment,' the Northerner said, up goes his sword, and off comes the jeweler's head.

"Well, it so happened that one of the Goddess's demons was walking around trying to make mischief for the barbarians. He sees this and tells the Goddess. She sends a dream to the King's youngest son, since I'm told that is how she speaks to your family, and lets him know about it.

"Well, to leave off half the story, this young Prince goes into his father's bedchamber and takes hold of Állam, the sword of the kingdom. Then he goes into the courtyard, finds a *táltos* bull, and they leap right over the Palace walls. So he goes riding right through the Northern army (who, after all, is going to get in the way of a *táltos* bull?) and comes into town. He finds this Northerner, all cozy in bed with the girl, who is all cozy in bed with her diamond. He barges in, and before you can say *garabonciás,* he runs him right through, while she cries about how she'll never love another and all like that.

"There is much more, my Prince. I could tell you of how he had to win back to the Palace through the entire Northern army, after she betrayed him to them. I could tell you how Állam swept back and forth in all its battle-madness, killing scores of barbarians at a blow, but that isn't the end of the story. The end of the story, Prince Miklós, is that when this young man returned to the Palace his father had found out that he had taken Állam, which only the King may wield, and so he had the sad duty of cutting off the young man's head.

"And that is the end of my story. Come to me when I'm sober, and I'll tell you a longer one."

Miklós studied the coachman, who sat back with an ironic expression on his face, drinking *pálinka* from the bottle. "What happened to the girl?" he asked, as he knew he was supposed to.

The coachman smirked. "She married the demon," he said.

Miklós nodded his appreciation and watched Miska for another moment. Then he asked, "What, exactly, is the point, good coachman?"

Miska snorted. "Point? I don't know, my Prince. Maybe, within this story, there is a prophecy of the tale of your own life. Maybe more. Maybe the point is the futility of all human endeavor. Maybe it is the triumph of justice, whatever the cost. The point? I don't know. You wanted to hear a story so I told you a story. Ask yourself the point. If you were entertained, that is enough for me."

Miklós looked at him some more. At length he stood. "Yes, Miska," he said. "I was entertained. Thank you. Drink well. Perhaps I'll see you later."

Miklós climbed the stairs past the sodden coachman. The story the coachman had told him came and went in his mind as he considered what he should do next. He made no effort to be silent, as he knew the sounds his weight made on the wooden slats of the stairway would blend with the Palace night sounds. He reached the top and slipped past the draperies. The warmth inside made him realize that the cellar had been chilly.

All was still in the Palace itself. He walked past the buttery, the corridor toward the servants' quarters, the hall that led to his old chambers, and so came to the grand winding stairway that led to the Great Hall (called so mostly by tradition—in the Old Palace the Great Hall had started on the ground level and gone up three stories).

He reached it and found a guard sleeping outside of the door. He walked past and the other never stirred, leaving Miklós to wonder if losing his boots hadn't been a stroke of good fortune—or else the guard had become so accustomed to the creakings of the Palace that little could have disturbed him.

Miklós stepped into the hall, where fires were still burning in two of the five hearths. He stepped beneath the doorway at the far end. This put him on a very small winding stairway (he had to turn sideways to ascend). He followed it easily. There was now a certain amount of light, both from torches in the Great Hall below and from narrow window slits high above him, letting in starlight. It occurred to him that he had never really noticed the transition, as he walked, from darkness to faint light. These stairs were less familiar to Miklós than most of the rest of the Palace, so he went slowly, using both hands to guide himself.

There was a small lamp glowing in the chill room at the top, smoking and giving off the pungent odor of burning oil. It was set on a table between two beds.

Miklós's breathing echoed loudly here, as if the rest of the Palace sounds didn't penetrate. He had the sudden feeling that he was entering a different world—one bare of the luxuries of the Palace, yet also without its decrepitudes.

Decrepitudes? he thought. *Now, where did that notion come from?* His mind traced back the path he had just walked, through a dank, smelly cellar, past cracked wooden panels and crumbling sandstone that he somehow had not seen as he actually passed them. Sudden tears sprang to his eyes.

In the test of memory against reason, reason had achieved the final victory.

The air was chill against the back of his neck. He looked at the pair of beds from the which soft, disjointed sounds of his parents' breathing could be heard. He realized that he had nothing to say to them.

As softly as he could, he made his way back down the stairs.

The Great Hall was as quiet as ever. Miklós stood in the middle of it, feeling its vastness and trying to decide where to go from there. Several doors led down: one to the hallway that led to the sleeping rooms, another to the King's audience chamber, still another to the kitchen and servants' quarters, yet another led up to László's private chambers. Miklós considered long and quietly.

At last, though he couldn't have explained why, he took the one that led to the chambers of his brother Vilmos. This was a small stairway that curved but didn't wind. The corridor it led to was wide but empty. One oil lamp was lit at the far end, revealing several others that were not. Miklós walked softly, and was near the curtains of Vilmos's room when a shape appeared in front of him.

He jumped back, stifling a cry, and heard the sound of another cry being stifled. He stood motionless, as did the other, and he could dimly make out a pair of eyes looking into his. He stood thus for perhaps half a dozen heartbeats, then Miklós said, "Who are you?"

"That was going to be my question," said a soft, feminine voice. "But I am Brigitta."

Miklós walked past her to the lamp at the far end, stood

under it, and turned to her. "I am Prince Miklós," he said.

Her gasp indicated that the name was not unknown to her. She approached him, as if to see better, and in doing so he saw her as well. He studied her face, and said, "You must be here at László's request."

She nodded, still wide-eyed. "He is entertaining a prospective bride, but he asked me to remain here, so he gave me a room to sleep in." She continued to stare at him, and her voice changed. "He *said* you were still alive. No one else believed him, but he said he knew it." Miklós nodded. She seemed fascinated by him, as if he were a vision or a specter. He carefully kept any expression from his face. "You know," she continued, "he told me what he did to you. He regrets it terribly. I think . . . thought that was why he refused to admit you were dead."

Miklós nodded once more, then stifled a gasp. Whether it was a trick of the flickering lamps, he couldn't say, but for just an instant her staring eyes seemed to contain a reflection of the Palace itself, seen from the outside, with all of its crumbling walls, broken towers, and sagging arches highlighted. The vision was so strong that Miklós looked away.

"What is it?" she said.

"Nothing." He swallowed. "Are you from town? I don't think I've seen you before."

"No. I used to live by the marshes, in the county of Nagyláb."

"How long have you been in Fenario?"

"Since spring. My mother died last winter."

"I'm sorry."

"Don't be," she said with only the tiniest trace of bitterness. "It wasn't much of a life."

Miklós was about to ask more when he caught a flicker of motion from over her shoulder. She followed his glance as Vilmos, dressed in a pale nightgown, emerged from a room down the hall.

"Who by the demons is out there?" he thundered.

Miklós said, "Hello, Vili."

Vilmos stared, then a grin erupted all over his face. "Miki!" he cried. He rushed forward, almost running over Brigitta, and embraced Miklós.

"Careful," said the smaller brother.

"Then it *was* you! I thought I saw you—"

"With the dragon. Yes. I would have said something, but the dragon threw me one way, and the River carried you another."

Vilmos nodded and released him. He held him at arm's length to take a good look at him. "You've been hurt," he said.

"The dragon threw me into a tree. I'm all right now. How are you?"

"Never better. I almost murdered old Sándor, but—why are we standing here? Let's go to the kitchens or somewhere and talk! By the Goddess, it's good to see you alive! Where have you been?"

Miklós nodded to Brigitta, suggesting that she accompany them, and began walking toward the stairs up to the kitchen.

"Not that way," said Vilmos.

"Eh?"

"We have to go around and up. Those stairs collapsed a year ago."

Miklós sighed and followed his brother further down the hall toward another archway. "This whole Palace is going to collapse one of these days," he said.

"Is it indeed?" said a new voice.

They turned. The King was clad in a purple dressing gown with fine embroidery, and showed no signs of sleepiness. Oddly, the sword at László's side did not seem incongruous. Viktor stood next to him, holding a lamp.

"Good evening, László," said Miklós.

"The whole Palace is going to collapse, I think you said?"

"Aren't you going to welcome me home, brother?"

"I was prepared to do so, Miklós. Indeed I was, when the Goddess woke me up in a dream to tell me that you had arrived. Until I came down here, Miklós, and heard you, once again, holding forth on—"

"Did the Goddess tell you to greet me armed, László?"

"No, brother. Viktor did. He came as I was dressing to say that he had heard whispers down here and that one of the voices was Brigitta's."

Miklós looked over at her. She was staring at László, her face unreadable.

"And you wanted to protect your property, is that it?"

"Don't bait me, Miklós. I don't know why you have returned, but if you wish for peace between us, this is your chance to beg for my pardon."

Miklós felt suddenly stung. He knew that, almost against his will, he and László were falling into the old patterns. Yet his answer came before he could stop it. "Beg? For pardon? Yours?"

"Hauteur doesn't become you, Miklós."

"Then tell me what I am to ask to be pardoned for?"

"Trying to convince our brother of . . . whatever it was that you were trying to convince him of."

"I wasn't trying to convince him of anything, László. He told me that the stairway to the kitchens had collapsed. I said—"

"Don't repeat it!"

"As you wish."

"Well?"

Miklós felt himself beginning to tremble. This was going so wrong! He hadn't wanted it to start all over again. He closed his eyes for a moment to collect his thoughts. "László," he said slowly. "It is not my wish to offend you. I am sorry you heard what you did. I—"

The King's eyes had narrowed to slits. "You are sorry I heard it; are you sorry you said it?"

Miklós looked at his brother. As he did so, the last two years came rushing back to him in a flash—the endless hours of toil, the pain of learning to use the Power, the true grandeur of which László and kingdom were such a pathetic parody. *To the devils with him, then!* he thought. "Are you sorry it is true, elder sibling?"

László's answer was to draw his sword. Even in the dimness of the flickering light, the plain, functional blade stood in glaring contrast to the ornate sheath from which it was drawn.

"I can see," said the King in a soft voice, "that you are going to need a better lesson than you received last time, if I am ever to have peace from that flapping tongue of yours."

He advanced on Miklós as he spoke, slowly, much as Vilmos had avanced on Sándor before. Brigitta slunk to the side. Miklós, without turning from László, said, "Well, Vili? Will you let him kill me before your very eyes?"

Vilmos said, "I . . . stop it, Laci."

"Hold him, Vilmos."

"Protect me, Vili."

The giant stood as if paralyzed. László lunged suddenly, like a yendi striking. Just as quickly, Miklós stepped behind Vilmos.

"Hold him for me, Vilmos."

"Help me escape, Vili."

"I . . ."

For a moment it was comic; Vilmos standing as if he were a pillar, while the other two played a deadly game of roundies. But then Laśzló snapped, "Viktor." The latter moved to one side as the King moved to the other. Miklós stepped directly back from Vilmos, grabbed Brigitta, and pushed her into Viktor. She gasped and stumbled. Laśzló instinctively paused to see that she was all right. When he turned back, Miklós had vanished down the corridor.

Miklós ran to the end of the hallway, ducked under a low arch to his right, and made his way to the east wing, up through the servants' hall, around, back into the central area, and down. As he ran, the gongs and bells of the Palace rang out. When they stopped, Miklós paused to listen, but heard no sounds of pursuit. He pushed aside a curtain and entered a room.

His brother's eyes were open and he was looking around blearily. "Wha—Miklós! You're alive!"

"Shhhh!"

"But—"

"I need help, Andor."

"What kind? Where have you been? How—?"

"Hide me."

"Hide you? From what?"

"There isn't time."

"But—"

"Please."

Andor blinked twice. "All right," he said. "Where?"

"Here. If anyone asks, you haven't seen me, all right?"

"Yes, certainly, brother. But—"

"Later."

Miklós stepped into Andor's wardrobe and hid himself behind a silver-blue tunic and a thick gray-dyed woolen cloak. He had barely settled in place when he heard Laśzló's voice.

"Andor!"

"What is it?"

"Miklós has returned. He's in the Palace somewhere, and we must find him."

"Why?"

"He's up to old tricks again."

"Why are you holding your sword?"

"Don't question me, Andor."

Miklós tried to breathe as quietly as he could. He wondered how it could be that he felt no fear of his brother, yet was aware of the danger he was in.

"Well?" demanded László. "Will you rise and help us search? You know the Palace as well as any of us."

"But can't you give me some idea of what happened?"

"I have explained all you need to know. Miklós has returned. He—has offended me. I was awakened by a dream sent by the Goddess, and found him—"

"The Goddess!"

"Yes, that's right. I dreamt of her, warning me. But there is no time—what is it?"

"I have to think. Are you sure it was the Goddess?"

"How can I doubt it? What's wrong?"

"It . . . Miklós. He is hiding in my wardrobe."

"Here?"

Miklós sighed and stepped out from between the garments. "Thank you, Andor," he said coolly.

László stared at him, then his lips curled into a smile. "You don't understand," said Andor plaintively. "The Goddess—"

"Be silent, Andor," said László.

Viktor stood behind the King. Another member of the Palace Guard, one whom Miklós didn't recognize, stood next to Viktor. All three held naked swords. The King raised his until it was pointed at Miklós's breast.

Miklós studied the tableau, thinking furiously, yet still feeling no trace of fear. Állam, the Sword of the Kingdom, was pointing at him; the other two swords were held uncertainly, as if their wielders didn't quite dare raise them to a Prince. Andor stared at the scene with an expression of amazement and horror, as if he couldn't believe he was about to see one of his brothers attack another.

Miklós reached a decision. He opened his mind to the Pathway. The Power came quickly. *Union of fabric and flesh. Feel the tang beneath and within. Motion within that, now speed. Expand. Spread out. Draw, pull from the fabric, from the flesh, from the air. Faster. Yet faster. Power is speed and speed is heat. More—*

His concentration was broken by screams. Viktor and the other guard dropped their blades and clutched at their hands. László still held his, but his face had become pale, his eyes narrow, and his jaws were clamped tightly together. Miklós could actually see smoke rising from where hilt and flesh met.

Well, thought Miklós, *this will have to do.* He found a water pitcher on the table next to Andor's bed, and flung it at the King. As László's hand and sword went up, Miklós ducked past him, pushing him to the side, ran past the other two (who were still clutching their hands), and out into the corridor.

He fled back down the hallway, his bare feet slapping against planks of the floor—long stripped of lacquer—around a sharp corner and up a flight of stairs, with boards half-broken and feeling none too sure. He heard footsteps behind him. He slipped under the pale archway, through the Informal Dining Room, and down another flight of stairs. At last he came, through no conscious plan, back almost to Andor's room—into his own chambers.

Here he stopped, amazed.

Before him, growing out of the very timbers of the floor, was what appeared to be a plant, higher than his ankle. Somehow the idea of this shocked him more than the other signs of decay and disrepair he had seen in the Palace. Yet there was something else about it. Something strange. He wished he had the time to decide what it was.

The footsteps were coming closer. He stepped up to the window from whose broken shutter he could see the River below.

He turned back and found László standing in the doorway. Next to him were Andor and Sándor.

To Miklós, the run had been small exertion compared to his labors in Faerie, but he saw that Andor was breathing hard. Sándor, too, seemed a bit breathless. László, like Miklós, didn't seem to have noticed the run.

Moreover, László was still holding his blade. "The power of Faerie doesn't seem to affect you, brother," said Miklós.

László shrugged. "I felt it. I just didn't let it bother me."

"I see. Good morning, Sándor. You are awake early, are you not?"

"I greet you, Prince Miklós," said the old wizard.

Without turning to him, László said, "Whatever he tries to do. Sándor, stop him."

"Yes, Your Majesty."

Miklós nodded to himself, realizing that Sándor could do as he'd been told. The young prince had had enough experience with the Power of Faerie to know that he had only touched on what could be done with it, and it was clear to him now that Sándor had had his own Pathway to the Source for many years.

László advanced on him. Miklós retreated to the very edge of the window. Then, with thought for nothing but escape, turned to jump—

—and found that he couldn't move. Iron bands seemed to hold his limbs and body motionless. He struggled with all the strength in his body, with no thought for matching his control of the power against Sándor's. For a moment it seemed to be working, but then the grip tightened.

"I can't hold him this way long, Your Majesty," said Sándor.

"You needn't," said the King.

Then the floor trembled, and the walls shook. Miklós knew exactly what this meant: Vilmos was coming. Too late? Probably.

More shaking, and he was suddenly free. He heard Sándor curse, as he stepped to the side and ducked. He felt a blow to his side; more as if he'd been hit with a stick than a sword, and was surprised to hear his own voice crying out. He turned around and saw László drawing back for another strike, as Vilmos stepped into the room.

For a moment it seemed that Vilmos would wrestle László's sword away from him. But the King said, "Don't move, Vilmos," and the giant didn't.

Once again, Miklós said, "Help me, Vili." And he added, "Save my life."

And, once again, Vilmos seemed gripped by indecision. Andor hadn't moved the entire time. Sándor watched the King, waiting for new orders. Miklós felt himself growing weak and knew what the sticky wet feeling in his side meant.

In the moment he had to do so, he turned and launched himself out the window. He felt a burning pain in his calf as László's sword made one last try for him, then, almost at once, he struck the water as if it were solid ground. He wasn't aware of the waves closing over his head.

INTERLUDE

CONSIDER A TINY CRACK in wood that had once been bright and polished, but was now dull and neglected. Something appeared through the crack. What was it? Maybe a leaf. Maybe the first shootings of a new seed, straining for the light in a lightless room, from the dark of a soil that wasn't fertile before it became dull and neglected. Perhaps a weed that will exist for a time, then sink to death and decay, as the Palace itself does.

A lightless room?

The foundations of the Palace shifted. Just the least bit, by such a small amount that no one felt it. But it was enough to make the slats in this room tremble. The trembling put the final touch on the job of loosening a wooden pin that had been working its way out of the wall for years.

The pin went, with a clunk that no one heard. The shutter went, with a dull crash that blended into the sounds of the Palace that everyone had grown accustomed to.

For the first time, daylight struck the small growing thing in the floor. The thing drank it, ate it, and almost waved to it.

The Palace?

The Palace strained in the wind, as if it would pull itself apart. Rotted beams and cracked timbers creaked and grumbled beneath the weight of stone that defined it and furnishings that made it seem more than it was: a shelter from the rain and the snow and the storm.

The Palace was more than four hundred years old and had served its purpose; it would be unbecoming to despise it for showing its age. But there was now one spot within it of something new. Turn your thought to it for a moment. One incongruous new idea amid a marsh of stagnant facts.

chapter six

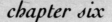

The Giant

VILMOŚ, CROUCHING IN THE alcove beneath the cellar stairs, sighed. It was certainly Bátya again. Csecsemő was too little to upset an earthenware bowl, and Húga was too passive to want to. Vilmos replaced the water in it and reached into the hutch. He grasped both of the norska's ears with his left hand and slipped his right under its hindquarters. It struggled a little, then settled into his hands. He held it up so its nose was directly in front of his, while he stayed ca. fully out of range of its incisors.

"What's wrong with you, Bátya? Why do you always go throwing the water around, eh?" He looked between its legs, spreading the fur apart. "Are you getting too old to live with your sisters anymore? Is that it? You want a room of your own, eh? My brother wanted one too. It got him into trouble."

He held its nose to his once more. "You behave yourself. Any more trouble from you and I'll give you to Cook. So."

Bátya quivered his nostrils at Vilmos and didn't seem to take the threat too seriously. The norska was put into a temporary hutch along with his two sisters while Vilmos cleaned their home, very slowly and carefully, running an abrasive cloth dipped in lye over every inch of wire, then rinsing it off several times. He replaced them, then swept the manure out from under the cage and collected it into a bag to give to Viktor, who raised his own worms for fishing.

He repeated the process for the other hutch, which at this time held only Atya and Anya—the buck and doe who had produced the other three. Only when both hutches were cleaned, as well as the third, temporary hutch, did Vilmos pour feed into two bowls and place them in the hutches.

The feed was his own mixture: some grain, a few roots and leaves, a little grass, and a small measure of meat, carefully ground. Norska required small amounts of meat for good health, but would refuse to eat any they had not killed. Vilmos had found, through years of experimenting, that if the meat were hidden well the norska would not notice it. Or, as he often speculated, they would pretend not to notice it. The superstitious part of him was afraid to discuss the meat aloud, for fear they would understand, become indignant, and refuse the feed altogether. The nonsuperstitious part of his mind, rebelling at the other, insisted on discussing it all times.

"I know what's bothering you," he told Bátya, who was slowly becoming his favorite in spite of his belief in neutrality. "You're upset that I didn't bring some any dragon meat for you. That's what you want, isn't it? But if I gave it to you, Bátyini my friend, you'd turn up your little black nose at it. You'd say, 'It's been dead too long,' and refuse to touch it. So. Well, the River carried me away too fast to take any home with me, and by now I fear the jhereg have it all."

Bátya stared back at him between mouthfuls. (Norska ate by filling their cheeks almost to bursting, then slowly chewing each morsel, sometimes for minutes, while periodically swallowing minute fractions.) His eyes were blue-gray, his face rather long, and he had the pure white coloring of his mother, without his father's black ears. Shortly after being weaned, he had somehow picked up the habit (who knew where norska got their habits?) of alternating small sips of water with his food, giving Vilmos the impression that he was carefully keeping himself clean. The trait was endearing as well as amusing, and reminded Vilmos of László. Sometimes when the brothers were sharing their evening meal, László would notice Vilmos watching him with a grin, but László would never condescend to ask what Vilmos was smiling about, and the giant would certainly never tell him.

He moved over to the other hutch, so the older norska wouldn't feel neglected. It was part of the cleaning day ritual that he watch them eat part of their meal, and Anya, at least, would sulk if he ignored her.

"Well, dear heart, how are you? Enjoying your food, are you? So."

Atya chittered at him as he swallowed.

"Fine, fine," said Vilmos. "Thank you so much for asking."

Atya chittered again, then took another mouthful.

"My brothers? Well, not so good, Atya. Not so good. Sometimes they seem to want to kill each other. Sometimes they cry because they aren't together. Who knows? Sometimes they want me to help them kill each other or cry with them. Silly, aren't they?"

Atya didn't answer, but stared somberly back. Anya didn't seem interested at all, but Vilmos was convinced she enjoyed the conversation anyway.

The discussion, one-sided as it was, was interrupted by the sound of footsteps coming down from the main floor above. Vilmos crept out of the alcove beneath the stairway and carefully straightened his back, which had become stiff from being bent over for so long. By the time he had done so, László was before him, dressed in robes of dark blue, with his sabre at his side.

"Good afternoon, Laci," said the giant, smiling.

"Good afternoon, Vili. How are your friends?"

"Fine, thank you." Vilmos reflected that, of his brothers, László was the only who asked about the norska, and Miklós the only one who cared about them.

"Good," said László. "And yourself?"

"I'm feeling well," said Vilmos.

"Do your wounds still bother you?"

"No, thank you."

"Not at all?

"No."

The King's face changed. "Then why," he said, "were you unable to help me with Miklós this morning?"

"Help you?" repeated Vilmos.

"Yes, help me. Is the idea so foreign to you?"

"But, Laci, you were trying to kill him."

"Oh, come, Vili. You know I wouldn't have actually killed him. What do you think I am?"

Vilmos shook his head, feeling suddenly very puzzled. "But, well, you seemed so angry."

"If you thought I was going to kill him, why didn't you help him, instead?"

"Because I—" Vilmos stopped. He thought back to the morning, trying to puzzle it out. Had he really believed László would kill their brother? "I don't know," he said at last. "I just didn't do anything."

"I know you didn't do anything, Vili. That's why I'm upset with you, because you didn't do anything. If you'd—"

"I'm sorry you're upset with me, Laci."

László sighed. "I just want you to understand, Vili. I love Miklós, too, just as you do. But I'm suspicious of him. He was away for two years, and now—I've been warned about him by the Goddess, and I hear him up to his old tricks again, and—do you know where he was when he was gone?"

"No. We didn't talk about it."

"I'm not surprised. But Sándor—"

"Sándor!"

"Please, Vili. Sándor says that he must have gone to Faerie."

"Pah! How can he know that?"

"Because of this," he said, holding out his right hand, palm forward. The fingers were red and swollen, and the palm itself was thick with blisters.

Vilmos gasped. "Laci! What happened?"

"Miklós did it. He made Viktor and Károly drop their swords, because they became so hot."

"How could Miklós do that?"

"The power of Faerie. The same power Sándor has."

"But how could Miklós have such power?"

"That's what I was saying. It comes from Faerie, and Sándor says that he had to go to Faerie to find it and to learn how to use it. But think, Vili: why would Miklós want such power? What will he do with it?"

Vilmos considered as carefully as he could. "I don't know," he said at last.

"Neither do I," said László. "But it worries me, so it should worry you. And the next time I ask you to help me with him, you should. For your good as well as my own, and maybe even for Miklós's. Do you understand?"

"I think so, Laci. I'm sorry about your hand."

"Never mind my hand. Do you promise to help me, next time this happens?"

Vilmos considered carefully. "Laci," he said slowly, *"were* you trying to kill him?"

László met his eyes, but he seemed to be looking some

distance away. "I don't know," he said softly. "I hope not."

Vilmos nodded. "I'll think about what you have told me, brother."

"All right," said László. He went back up the stairs. Vilmos crept back under the stairway and found that Anya and Atya had finished their meals.

"Pay no attention," he told them. "It's just silly things we talk about, and not worth worrying yourselves for. Have you finished your meal? Well, that is good. I'll be back in a while. I have to give Viktor your droppings so he can grow worms in them. Funny, isn't it? What Cook won't use, I give to you; what you won't use, we give to the worms. What the worms don't use, grows vegetables so we can give them to Cook along with the fish that Viktor catches with the worms. Funny, isn't it? Ha! Ha! Ha!"

Laughing the while, Vilmos climbed back up the stairs, which bent and complained, but still bore his weight.

It was somewhat later in the day that a messenger from László found Vilmos, who was resting near the Riverbank. Vilmos followed the messenger down the stairs into the cellar. Vilmos wondered if there were some problem with the norska, but the messenger continued to lead him straight into the wine cellars, until coming to the area that was nearly under the main doors themselves. There he found the King waiting, along with Sándor. He scowled. Then he noticed several tendrils like thin tree roots that seemed to come from the ceiling and embed themselves in the floor.

He came closer and studied them curiously. There were four or five of them, all coming from almost the same spot above. This spot seemed to be a crack in the wooden planks, but whether the roots had made the crack or had used the crack, he couldn't tell. They were well buried in the dirt floor of the cellar.

László and Sándor nodded to him.

"What do you think?" asked the King.

Vilmos blinked. "Why ask me? Ask him."

"I have. He doesn't know whether it is the Power of Faerie or not. But as for why I am asking you—do you know what is above us?"

Vilmos considered. He looked back toward the stairway, now hidden by wine racks, and tried to estimate distances.

"I am not sure," he said.

"We stand below Miklós's room."

"Oh."

"And this has appeared the day after he returned. Doesn't that suggest something to you?"

"You think Miklós did it? I don't know, Laci. It seems to be something that has been growing for a while now. No one visits this place often. How did you find it?"

"One of the cooks found it, bringing up wine for my dinner with the Countess this evening."

"Oh. How are things with her?"

"Never mind that. I wanted to show this to you. Whatever it is, Sándor will destroy it; but remember that we were lucky to find it, and it comes from Miklós's room. Who knows what it would have done in a month? Or a year?"

"Yes," said Vilmos. "Who knows?"

That afternoon, Vilmos made a discovery. He had never re- alized before that he could identify his brothers, and many of the others around the Palace, by their footfalls on the stairs down to the cellar. He discovered this when he heard someone descending and became aware that he didn't know who it was.

He clucked to Bátya and returned him to his cage, then backed out of the nook under the stairway and looked up. A gown of some light color, perhaps a pale blue, was descending into the gloom of the cellar, accompanied by careful, hesitant steps.

Eventually gown and footfalls were revealed as belonging to the Countess of Mordfal. At the bottom, she turned and looked around, until she spotted Vilmos. He bowed to her. She curtsied.

"I would like to see your norska," she said.

"Oh," he said after a brief pause. He felt strangely reluctant, but motioned her over. He held a lantern under the nook. She came over and knelt down. He stepped in next to her.

"This," he said, "is Atya. This is Anya. These are their children; Bátya is the oldest, then Húga and Csecsemő." He stopped, feeling as if he should say more but not knowing what else to say. How could he speak of them to someone who didn't understand norska, and didn't know him?

"May I hold one?" she said.

"All right." He opened the cage, hesitated, then took hold

of Húga by the base of the ears, quickly putting his other hand under her hindquarters, shifting the first hand to support her head.

"This is how you hold her," he said. "Go on. She's the gentlest of them. She won't try to nip you." This wasn't quite true. Csecsemő was gentler, but more delicate.

He waited until she, apparently with some hesitation, set her fan on the floor next to her. Then he transferred the norska to her arms, carefully positioning her. He felt Húga tense to jump, but the Countess evidently didn't. He kept one hand on top of Húga's hindquarters and stroked her with the other. His fingers brushed the top of the Countess's breast over her low-cut gown and she looked up sharply, but he noticed neither the contact nor the look. After a moment, Húga relaxed into her arms and Vilmos removed his hands.

"She's so soft," said the Countess, almost whispering.

Vilmos nodded, not knowing what to say. Soft? Well, certainly she was. All norska were soft. What could this Countess from the East Grimwall Mountains know of the special way Húga would lick Csecsemő's fur, or bound toward her protectively when a stranger (that is, anyone but Vilmos) came near? She couldn't. All she could know was that she was soft.

Suddenly desperate to change the conversation, Vilmos said, "Countess, are you going to marry my brother?"

She looked at him with an expression of curiosity. "Call me Mariska," she said.

He grunted. "You don't want to answer?"

"I just did."

He grunted again and thought about it. "That means you are, then?"

"Yes."

"When?"

"We haven't decided yet. A year perhaps."

"Well. Good. Rezső will be pleased."

"The old advisor? Yes, I imagine so." Then, "Your brother is a strange man, Vilmos."

"How, strange?"

"I don't know. Strange."

László? Strange? Well, maybe. He had never thought of it before. Marriage was strange. He somehow couldn't conceive of it, despite all of the time he had spent with Anya and Atya. "Do you love him?" he asked.

She inhaled sharply and glanced quickly, almost involuntarily, at the fan at her feet. Then she said, "No. But I can happily be his Queen."

"Why is that?"

"I'm not sure. We have similar interests. He's very dedicated."

"Yes. He is."

"There is something . . . we should be together, somehow. I can't explain it. Perhaps Brigitta would understand."

Once again Vilmos was startled. "You know about Brigitta?"

"Oh, yes. We've met. The King explained why she is here."

"Oh."

She sighed. "I don't know why I'm telling you of this." She went back to stroking the black and white fur of the norska. "The norska is very proud," she said after a moment.

Vilmos felt his eyes widen. "What do you mean?"

"I don't know. But . . . what was her name? Húga? Húga has a great deal of pride. She's haughty. That's why she's so gentle; she isn't afraid of anyone." Mariska handed her back.

Vilmos nodded, too surprised to speak. How could she have known that?

As he did, Mariska said, "Thank you, Vilmos. I've wanted to see them for some time."

"You are welcome, Mariska," he replied, surprised to find that he meant it.

She nodded. She picked up her fan again, looked at it and clutched it tightly. Then she put her other hand into the pail of feed, sniffed it, and nodded.

"That is all they will eat, when they are kept this way," said Vilmos, who somehow felt the need to justify the feed, as if she would think it too poor for such fine beasts.

She nodded. "What do they eat in the wild?"

"Mostly dragons," said Vilmos.

That evening in the Great Hall, Vilmos listened to a minstrel from somewhere near the southern marshes. He was a rather chubby man, with long, stringy dark hair shot through with gray and a beard that matched. He sang songs from his home in a soft quiet voice that Vilmos had to strain to hear, while accompanying himself on a long-necked *lant*. Halfway through the third song, Andor approached Vilmos.

"We need to talk," he said.

"Shhh," said Vilmos. "I am listening."

"That can wait."

"Why?"

"I've been thinking about your failure yesterday."

"Failure?"

"With Miklós."

"Oh."

"We should talk about it."

Vilmos turned in his chair and looked fully at Andor. Then he turned back. "Shhh," he said again. "I am listening."

Andor stood next to him for a moment, then left the Hall.

Vilmos listened to the minstrel for a while longer, until the King and the Count and Countess of Mordfal bid the room good night, threw the minstrel a purse, and departed for the evening. In a little while Vilmos found himself alone in the Hall, sitting on a great chair that had been constructed for his frame and piled high with cushions. Eventually, he drifted off into a pleasant doze.

Some time later he heard soft footfalls behind him but didn't turn to see who it was. When they stopped in front of his chair, he opened his eyes.

"Hello, Brigitta."

"Good evening, Vilmos. May I sit with you?"

"Yes."

She pulled a chair over next to his. He studied her, comparing her to the Countess. Brigitta was solid where Mariska was almost frail. But after speaking with Mariska he realized—in a way that he couldn't express even to himself—that there was a core of strength inside of the Countess. Now, looking at Brigitta, he wondered if, within her, there was a corresponding weakness.

"You like this room, don't you?" she said, suddenly, interrupting his thoughts.

"Hm? Oh. Yes, I do."

"It's peaceful, after everyone has left."

Vilmos nodded.

"When I was very little, and my father was too drunk to make liquor, I used to collect mushrooms. I'd go out walking until I was in what you call the Wandering Forest. To us, it was 'the woods'—as if it were our own, private part of the Forest. We'd go out and collect the mushrooms there, and sometimes sit until sunset. It was like this room: big, peaceful, and empty. You would have liked it."

Vilmos nodded again.

"Most of the trees were old in that part. There were a lot of elms, especially, that were actually rotting and falling apart. Some of the biggest and best mushrooms grew around trees like that, as if somehow the rot of the tree was helping them grow.

"But from time to time, a big, old tree would just collapse. We'd see it coming, over the years, because branches would fall off first, and of course there'd be no leaves on them. I noticed that sometimes the tree would fall over on top of the mushrooms and crush them. Then, again, sometimes the tree would rot almost completely away without ever really falling, and the mushrooms would be as big as my father's hand. That's where I got the idea that they were feeding off the tree. Of course, I was little then."

Vilmos studied her, not understanding but not saying anything. After a moment she sighed.

"I like this room," she said. Then she nodded, "I wonder where Miklós is?"

Vilmos didn't answer, and Brigitta didn't speak again. She left a little later to be replaced in short order by László. Vilmos had the sudden feeling that he was at the center of the world; that everyone, even the King, came for his own reason, to convince him of something or to ask for something. He knew, at the same time, that it wasn't so. The Great Hall was the center of the Palace; if one waited long enough, everyone would arrive.

Yet the illusion persisted.

László made a brief greeting, seated himself next to Vilmos, and said, "You have heard that I am to be married?"

"Yes. Congratulations."

"Thank you."

The King stretched his feet out in front of him and stared at his toes. "There will be some changes in how the Palace is run, of course."

Vilmos stirred. "What sort of changes?"

"I don't know. But having a Queen in residence again will certainly have some effect."

"Will we be getting things in shape for her?"

László glanced up sharply. "What do you mean?"

Vilmos indicated the room around them. "You know. The

woodwork, the flooring, the plastering—"

"What's wrong with them?"

"Huh? They're crumbling, falling apart—"

László stood up. "Silence!"

Vilmos stared at him, puzzled. "What's wrong, Laci? I was only saying—"

"You were parroting your brother Miklós. That is exactly what I was afraid of."

"How am I—?"

"It seems I can't exchange three words with you or Andor without Miklós, and his absurd claims about the Palace, coming up one way or another." He glared down at Vilmos, his brows drawn together.

The giant tried to understand the reason for his brother's anger but could find no explanation for it. "I'm sorry I've upset you, Laci," he said. "I didn't mean to."

The King sighed and sat down again. "I know, Vili. It's just that I see the Palace as a member of the family—as if it were a person. Do you understand that?"

Vilmos tried to, but at last he shook his head.

László said, "This Palace has kept the rain off our heads. It has provided a place for our meals and allowed us to sit together as a family. It has been the center of our realm for hundreds of years. It has stood up to war, to wind, and to floods. Doesn't that mean anything to you?"

The giant's mouth worked as he tried to reason this out. At last he said, "I don't want you to become angry again, Laci, but I don't understand."

Vilmos saw his brother fighting to remain calm. "What don't you understand?" László said at last.

Vilmos spoke slowly. "The Palace has only kept the rain off our heads because I have repaired the roof. Isn't that true?"

László made a brushing-off gesture but didn't speak.

Vilmos continued, "It's given us a place for our meals, but it wouldn't if I hadn't put the beam against the kitchen wall where it was falling in last spring. Yes?"

"But—"

"And," said Vilmos, beginning to gain momentum, "It was the men in it who stood up to war, not the Palace. Wasn't it? And we could have been together as a family anywhere. And sometimes the wind comes through the cracks in the door and travels all the way down to the cellar, when I'm with my norska.

Yes, it has been the center of the realm, but, truly, Laci, what is that to me? Do you think I would be a member of the family any less if I were not a Prince? Or would you, if you were not King?"

As Vilmos spoke, László's expression went from anger to puzzlement to sorrow. When the giant had finished, László said suddenly, "What about your norska, then? You can't deny that the Palace has provided a shelter for your—your norska."

Vilmos wondered briefly what his brother had almost said, but didn't comment on it. Instead he said, "No, Laci. I had to build a place for the norska. If I hadn't, they'd have become lost in the Palace, and Cook would have used them—"

"But you built those places *within* the Palace, Vilmos."

"They could have been anywhere. László, I'm sorry to differ with you, but I must say what I feel. To me, the Palace is where I am, and I do what I must here, but I feel no loyalty to it. It is a place. When it begins to crumble, I try to repair it. When—"

"It isn't crumbling!"

Vilmos studied him curiously. "I think," he said, "that we should not talk about this anymore. What was it you wished to see me about?"

László, bristling with anger, stood up. "To warn you, Vilmos. It may be, when the Queen comes into her own, that she will feel there is no room in the Palace for small, furry animals who contribute nothing and are owned by someone who fails to appreciate the sanctuary they have been given for all these years!"

He turned and strode out of the room, leaving behind a puzzled and hurt brother who stared after him with open mouth.

As he broke his fast alone the next morning, Vilmos considered seeking out Mariska and asking her if László had any basis for his parting words of the night before. He was on the point of deciding that he didn't know how to broach such a subject when she wandered into the kitchen's breakfast nook. She was holding two steaming cups, over the lips of which he saw slices of orange. Her fan was cradled under her arm.

She put one of the cups in front of him and sat down in the other chair. Vilmos blew on it, then sipped, not noticing the absurd appearance his massive hand gave holding the delicate teacup.

"Thank you," he said. "I like it."

"It's a red tea with cinnamon. This is how we drink it at home. The oranges come from only a few hundred miles down-river."

"Yes. You trade them for pepper, don't you?"

"And other things. How are you?"

"Well enough. And you? How are preparations for the wedding?"

"They are—good day, Sándor."

Vilmos turned and saw the wizard at the same moment the wizard saw him. Sándor stopped for just a moment, as if he were afraid to come too near Vilmos. But he came up anyway.

"I won't hurt you," said Vilmos.

Sándor's face darkened.

"I didn't mean it that way," said Vilmos quickly. "I wasn't trying to mock you, I—never mind."

"I actually meant to speak to you later, Vilmos. But if now is a good time . . ."

"As good as any."

"Should I leave?" asked Mariska.

Vilmos gestured noncommittally; Sándor gave no sign.

"What did you want to speak to me about?" asked Vilmos.

"It has to do with the upcoming wedding. There are things that ought to be done that you can do."

"Such as?"

"The ceiling of the Queen's chamber is sagging. The work-men need help holding it up while they put a support beam in place. Also—"

He was interrupted by the giant's laugh. "Did László ask you to speak to me about these things?"

Sándor seemed puzzled. "No, although I'm certain he would appreciate your help. Why?"

"It is nothing. He and I had words yester eve. No, Sándor, I am afraid I will be unable to help László make repairs that aren't needed."

"Aren't needed?"

"So says my brother."

Mariska put a hand on his arm. "Vilmos."

"Yes?"

"Be patient with him. He's still upset about Miklós."

Vilmos snorted.

"Please?" said Mariska. "As a favor to me?"

Vilmos looked at her, then sighed. "Very well. The ceiling. What else?"

"There is also that strange growth in the cellar."

"What growth?" asked Mariska.

"Why not use your powers?"

Sándor studied the floor for a moment, then said, "I tried. For some reason it is impervious to the Power of Faerie."

"Ha! When you sent me—"

"Please."

Vilmos sighed once more. "Very well," he said. "Let me finish my tea, and I'll go into the cellar and pull the roots."

"Thank you, Vilmos," said Mariska, smiling gently.

Vilmos nodded, and turned back to Sándor. "Will you be there to help?"

"No, I'll be gone for most of the day, I think."

"Oh?"

"Yes, I have an errand, with Andor."

"What errand is that, wizard? Will you take him to meet the Demon Goddess?"

Sándor shook his head. "No. We're going to find Miklós. We are going to bring him back."

INTERLUDE

IT HAPPENED WHEN I was a lad of nine or ten. There was a fellow who worked in the mines in Bajföld. His name was Péter, and he came to visit us from time to time. One day we learned that he was dying, so my father took me to see him. We sat down and took out the *pálinka*, honey muffins, and stuffed apples that my mother had prepared. He couldn't eat anything because he was so weak, but he drank some of the *pálinka*. He was so happy that we had come to visit him that he said, "Now I will tell you what I have never told another soul, so that when I am gone you will remember and pass it on to your children." Then he began his story.

"I had only been working the mine for a year or so when I saw a small vein of black stephenite along one of the walls. Well, said I to myself, somehow no one has found this yet, so I'll just go see where it leads and maybe find a big fresh deposit. Then we'll see what the Count has to say to me (for we worked for the Count of Bajföld then as now, but it was the old Count then).

"So I went following it with my little oil lamp and, sure enough, it ran to a part that we weren't working anymore. I moved the boards that were set up over the tunnel and went through, still following the vein. Well, I just kept following the tunnel and following it for what must have been three days, when I fell through a hole, right in the floor of the tunnel.

"I don't know how long I fell, but I must have been knocked

right out of my senses when I landed because the next thing I remember I was sitting on the floor of a wide hallway made of the purest crystal you have ever seen, with lamps of glass all around me.

"I went looking around a bit, and the first thing I saw was a tree growing right up through the floor, and instead of leaves it had pots of pure silver. I was looking at it, just staring, when up comes a demon, as calm as you please. I knew right away it was a demon because it was only as tall as my waist and had bright red skin, a pointy little head, and a tail it could wrap around itself six or seven times without stretching.

"Well, quick as you please, I hid myself behind the tree to see what it was going to do. It went right up to that tree and pulled a bucket from it, then went back down the hall. I followed after it, a good distance behind, and pretty soon, it came to a big room where there were thirteen old women sitting in a circle around a fire. I sat and watched them, and there was a whole string of demons coming to them with buckets full of silver. The demons were throwing the silver onto the fire, and pretty soon this black stuff would come pouring out, and I could see it was pure stephenite. More demons were collecting it in more buckets and running off with it.

"Well, by now I was mighty curious. As soon as I could, I grabbed one of the demons around his neck, and I held up my pick. I said, 'Look, you, you'd better tell me what's going on around here pretty quick.'

"Well the demon started gibbering, but then it said, 'This is where we make all the silver for you to find up there.'

"'Why do you do that?' I asked.

"Well, it didn't want to tell me, but it could see that I meant business with the pick, so it finally said, 'The witches want to bring you down here so they can suck all your souls, to make themselves young again.'

"When I heard that, I can tell you I was scared enough! I tied that demon up with his own tail and took off down the hall. When I came to the tree, I picked a bucket of silver, then I started climbing. Pretty soon I looked down, and there must have been five hundred demons climbing after me.

"Well, I don't have to tell you that I climbed as fast as I could, but there were still a few who caught up with me, and I had to stop and use my pick to send them back down where they belonged. When I was finally shut of them, I was back in that same tunnel I'd been in before. That's when I saw that I'd dropped all of that silver from right out of the bucket. But I wasn't about to go down there for it! Not for anything!

"But if you want to yourself, you can try to find it because we're still finding silver in that mine, so I guess the tree is still there."

So that was old Péter's story. I know it is true because before he died, he showed my father and me the bucket he had carried up. I've never tried to find the tree myself, but now that you know, you can go looking if you want to.

chapter seven

The Meeting

THE RIVER HAD MANY songs, Miklós realized. Further upstream it sang in rippling joy, almost a tinkling laughter. Near the Palace it hummed in sweet harmonies. Here, it sang a tranquil song of healing.

He sat with his back against the same oak, and saw again that the River had healed him. He shook his head. How long could this go on? Once before, he had left the Palace injured and in fear of his life, and the River had brought him, alive and well, to this spot.

And yet it was different, too. This time he had received a lesser injury than before, and he was less puzzled—or at least puzzled in different ways. He had seen and learned much since then. The River itself? The water wasn't the same. Even the River's shape had changed, subtly. Perhaps more of the roots of the oak were exposed now, though it was hard to tell for certain. As before, he had fled his brother. But that time, his brother's anger had been a senseless thing. This time—? Overhead, there were no jhereg circling either; merely a few songbirds.

"Things repeat," he muttered aloud, "but they are never the same."

He studied the landscape more closely than he had before. The River was wide here, gently curving away from him; the opposite bank perhaps a quarter of a mile distant. The grasses were long and were nearly the only flora of the region, save the oak. He looked upon a green-swept plain. Someday it would be settled, cleared, and peppers would grow here. He stood up and looked across the River. No, nothing. Only the unending sameness of grasses as tall as he was and sand along the Riverbank. In the distance, to his right, he could almost see a few more scattered trees. All around was the clean smell of growth, yet not so overpowering as it had been in the Forest.

Well. What to do now? Perhaps he could—

He heard a thud from behind him and caught a simultaneous flash of movement. Perhaps it was fear from having just escaped with his life, but reflexes he didn't know he had came into play. He spun away from the oak, crying aloud. The Pathway to the Source was there well before he could have thought to ask for it, and lightnings danced from his fingertips, hissing and crackling in the air and playing about the sudden form that loomed before him in the mid-afternoon sun.

Then he stopped as suddenly as he had attacked.

"Bölk!"

"Yes, master," said the horse. "I see you have learned from your stay in Faerie."

"I'm sorry, Bölk. Have I hurt you?"

"No, master. That is not how you could hurt me."

He stood and approached the horse, surprised to find a lump in his throat and his eyes moist. "Bölk," he whispered again.

"Yes, master. I have awaited you."

"You knew that I would be here?"

"Someday."

Miklós considered. "You were right," he said. "I am."

Bölk nodded his great head. Miklós sat down with his back against the oak once more. The horse moved around so they could study each other.

"You've changed," said Miklós. And he added, "Of course."

"Yes. But little. My coat is darker, I think. And I've grown thinner. But I always change. There was a time, not too long ago, when I was a bull. This is nothing." He laughed.

"It is good to hear you laugh," said Miklós.

"It is good to feel myself laugh," said Bölk. "We have a long road ahead of us, master, and I may not have the chance again. Yet I am pleased to see you, and to see you so well. Physically, at least."

Miklós, for the third time since Bölk had appeared, bit back the urge to say, "What do you mean?" In some things, at least, he was sure the horse wouldn't have changed.

"I was just reflecting," said Miklós, "that things repeat themselves, but are never the same. It seems that this is true of you, too."

"Yes, master. I am glad not all things repeat, however. It is better that you don't run off to Faerie a second time."

Miklós chuckled.

Bölk continued, "But when things repeat, they don't have to repeat fully. We are able to control them."

"Yes. It is surprising what we can control. And what we can't."

Bölk's nostrils flared. "There is *nothing* we can't control."

"Indeed?" said Miklós. "What about others, who, in turn, wish to control us?"

"You quibble," said Bölk.

"I don't think so."

Bölk was silent for a moment, then he stated, "You have fought with your brother again."

"Yes."

"Over what?"

"It seems that, for some reason, any small thing I say criticizing the Palace is taken for a deadly insult."

"For him, it *is* a deadly insult. The most deadly insult."

Miklós stared at him. "Why?"

"You have been to Faerie, have you not?" Miklós nodded. "Then you know that, by comparison, Fenario is not much of a kingdom, nor is the Palace much of a palace."

Miklós nodded. "I remember reading, years ago, descriptions of the 'fortress' that was here before ours. The historian became excited recording that it had a stairway and a window with glass." He chuckled. "By the standards of Faerie, we have hardly improved over that. Our little Palace is to them a fortified house—and poorly fortified at that."

Bölk nodded. "But consider that, to your brother, it is the center of a kingdom—the mightiest kingdom he has ever known. To him it isn't a mere building, it is the heart and mind of this kingdom, and he takes his responsibilities for it seriously. Perhaps there is no rational reason for him to feel as he does, but then, there is no reason for him to be rational. When you make light of the condition of the Palace, you, a Prince, who should be one of the kingdom's staunchest guardians, are striking at its heart and, to his eyes, weakening it."

"Then why doesn't he simply repair the damage? Then the subject wouldn't come up."

"Suppose it cannot be repaired? It is old, master. There may be nothing he can do that would help beyond delaying the inevitable for a few years. Perhaps he is aware of this. If so, then isn't he better off pretending not to see it?"

When Bölk fell silent, Miklós considered for a long time. At last he said, "What you say echoes much of what he has said. Perhaps I should speak to him of this. Perhaps if we understood one another better—"

"It wouldn't help, master. This may be difficult for you, but understanding isn't the same to everyone."

Miklós blinked. "I don't see what you mean."

"You are a scholar by nature. You see a thing, and you think of the general thing; the group of things to which it belongs. You see a swallow, and think bird, flying animal, then animal. You try to understand it and the rules by which it functions. Others don't. Others see a thing and act upon it instinctively. In you this is a weakness and a strength. In others, the same. But you must try to understand that merely pointing something out to someone such as your brother will not move him. He will not take it as you intend—he is too firmly committed."

"What you say about me may be right, but how is it a weakness?"

"You are too little committed."

"I don't understand."

"I know that too."

"I—"

"Wait, master. Someone approaches."

Miklós stood and looked upstream, surprised to find that the Pathway to the Source was sharp and ready. Bölk's ears had picked up the sound of footsteps before the person was in sight, but Miklós recognized her as soon as she appeared.

"Brigitta!" he called.

She looked up and ran to him. "Miklós! I've found you! Ah! It is good that you have a horse."

Miklós almost began laughing but contained himself. "Hardly," he said. "Brigitta, meet Bölk. Bölk, this is Brigitta, a friend of László's."

"Good afternoon, Brigitta," said Bölk.

She stared, looked back and forth between Miklós and Bölk, then silently mouthed the word, *"táltos."*

"Yes," said Miklós.

She started to curtsy, then stopped, looking puzzled. "I don't know what to say," she said finally.

Miklós laughed. "Yes, I usually have that problem with him."

"Speak of your problems," said Bölk.

Brigitta looked startled and almost insulted. "I would have no reason to lie," she said.

"What?" said Miklós.

"But you dwell, for now, within the Palace," said Bölk. "And, within the Palace, everyone's life is interconnected. We cannot address one problem without addressing all, for good or ill."

Brigitta considered this, then nodded. "I see what you mean, then," she said. "But I can't always tell what I'm feeling. Sometimes I do things, then decide why afterward."

Bölk nodded, and Miklós wanted to ask what was going on but was somehow afraid to. Instead he said, "Why are you here, Brigitta?"

She turned to him as if she'd forgotten he was there. "Oh, yes," she said, blinking. "I want to warn you. Sándor and Andor are coming for you. They're only moments behind me. I slipped out of the Palace when I heard them preparing to leave."

"I see," said Miklós. Then, "Why?"

Bölk turned to him. "To warn you," he said.

Miklós was about to answer that he knew that but wanted to know why she wished to warn him. He was distracted by Brigitta, who, at Bölk's words, blushed and muttered, "There was no need to say that."

Bölk said, "It is the truth."

Brigitta said, "You didn't?"

Miklós said, "What, in the name of the Demon Goddess, is going on around here?"

Bölk turned back to him. "What is going on is that two persons from the Palace are coming, presumably to take you back. What do you wish to do?"

Miklós glanced at Brigitta, who was nodding. Then he said, "I can run, or I can wait for them."

"Yes," said Brigitta. Bölk nodded.

"I'll wait, then."

"Very well," said Bölk.

"I'll wait with you," said Brigitta.

Bölk trotted over to the Riverbank, looked up it, and came back. "I can hear them," he said. "They'll be here soon."

"All right," said Miklós.

Brigitta shot Miklós a quick, puzzled glance; then said, "I don't know. Perhaps the same way I did."

"A reasonable plan," said Bölk.

"I just followed the River and hoped," said Brigitta.

As she finished speaking, Andor and Sándor appeared from behind the bend. Miklós, Bölk, and Brigitta turned to wait for them, the afternoon sun forcing them to squint to see the new arrivals.

"Good day, wizard," said Miklós. "Brother."

Andor tried to meet his brother's eyes, but couldn't. "Miklós," he began, "I—"

"Keep silent," said Sándor. "I'll speak to him."

Without being aware of making a decision, Miklós found that he had stepped forward and slapped Sándor across the face. The old man stepped back, his eyes wide.

"Have a care how you speak to my brother," said Miklós softly.

Andor winced and took half a step back, as if he were the one who had been struck. Sándor glared at Miklós. "You are not making this any easier on yourself," he said.

"I'll learn to live with that," said Miklós.

"Will you, indeed?" said Sándor. He didn't quite sneer.

Andor seemed to notice Brigitta for the first time. "You!" he said. "Why are you here?"

Brigitta smiled cynically. "I felt such distinguished visitors required someone to announce them."

Sándor snorted. "Yet it seems he didn't take advantage of the announcement to flee."

"I have fled twice already," said Miklós. "I think that is enough. Besides, I have fled from the King. I don't see that I am required to flee from his lackey as well."

To his surprise, Sándor didn't take offense at this. "If that was supposed to be an insult, I see no shame in being lackey to the King of Fenario. It says a great deal to me that you do."

Miklós was silent. Bölk said, "He is right, master; it does."

Andor gave a cry and stepped back. Sándor's eyes grew wide. Brigitta laughed. "I'm sorry," she said. "I should have introduced you. This is Bölk. Bölk, this is Prince Andor, and this is Sándor, the King's wizard."

Andor recovered from his surprise enough to manage a sneer. "Introduced to a talking horse by a serving wench and whore! I never thought a Prince of the realm would come to this!"

For a moment, Brigitta's gaze darkened, then she laughed. "I take no shame in being the King's whore," she said. "It says a great deal about you that you think I should."

Andor flushed. Sándor, who was still staring at Bölk, said softly, "A *táltos* horse!"

"Indeed," said Miklós.

"A pleasure to meet you," said Bölk.

Andor looked puzzled. "What did he say?"

But Sándor's face grew flushed. "How dare you!" he cried.

"What?" said Miklós.

Brigitta said, "He was only stating his position, Sándor. He didn't threaten you."

The wizard didn't seem to hear her. He stared at the horse long and hard. "What gives you the right to say such things to a representative of the King of Fenario?"

"I exist outside of Kings," said Bölk.

"I will too," said Brigitta.

"What?" said Miklós.

"What did he say?" said Andor.

"By the Goddess!" cried Sándor. "I have come by my powers by toil and risk! I will not have them sneered at by anyone—*táltos* horse or not!"

Brigitta looked at Miklós. "There is something going on here that I don't understand."

"Huh," said Miklós. "I'll say."

Andor said, "Miklós, what has the horse been saying? I can't understand his speech."

Miklós put a hand up to shade his eyes for a moment, and shook his head. "I'd rather know what Sándor has been hearing."

Bölk said, "He hears what he must hear, being what he is."

"Gah!" cried Sándor. "I will listen to no more of this. Prince Miklós, I am here to return you to the Palace. Will you come?"

"Yes," said Miklós.

"Good. Then let us—"

"In my own time."

Sándor's face was flushed; his breathing heavy. "How am I to interpret that?" he said.

"However you wish," said Miklós.

"If your own time is not now—"

"It isn't."

Sándor paused, and seemed to get his anger under control. "I must insist," he said.

Miklós laughed. "Insist away."

Sándor looked at him. For perhaps half a dozen heartbeats, there was silence except for the sound of the River against the roots of the oak. When the wizard spoke again, his voice was softer, and more threatening.

"I don't know what this *táltos* horse can do, Prince Miklós. But I have been sent to bring you back. Unless it has more power than I, and you know something of mine, you should return voluntarily. You know that my abilities are greater than yours. If I must force you, we will both be the worse off."

"I understand," said Miklós.

"Well?"

Miklós glanced at Bölk, but the horse remained motionless, staring at Sándor. "I will return to the Palace," said the Prince.

"Now? With me?"

"No. Later. At a time, and with company of my own choosing."

"To me, that is the same as a refusal."

"You may take it as you like."

"Well, then, if it is your desire—" Sándor raised his hands, and Miklós felt, as if from a distance, the faint tremblings of Power from a Pathway that wasn't his own. Bölk moved slightly, and Miklós noticed that the sun was no longer in his eyes. Bölk had not interposed himself between him and the wizard, but Miklós was in his shadow.

Sándor relaxed. "You seem able to protect him, horse," he said. "But can you protect yourself?"

"Sometimes," said Bölk.

The wizard raised his hands again. This time, to the surprise of the rest of them, Bölk spun and kicked with his hind legs, the left one catching Sándor squarely in the forehead. The latter gave a short cry and dropped senseless to the ground.

No one moved or spoke for a moment, then Andor knelt at the wizard's side. "Is he . . . dead?" he asked, as if they could tell better than he.

Bölk snorted. "Such as he are not so easily destroyed," he

said. "Although they can sometimes be made harmless for a while."

"What did he say?" said Andor.

Brigitta answered before Miklós could. "He said he should be returned to the Palace," she said.

Miklós stared at her, but said nothing.

Andor blinked. "But . . . how am I to take him back? I can't carry him."

Bölk chuckled and said, "Throw him in the River, and let him make it flow backward."

Miklós laughed. Brigitta gave him a puzzled look.

"What did he say?" asked Andor, hysteria beginning to creep into his voice.

Brigitta answered him. "He said if you bathe his face he may recover enough to walk with assistance."

Andor nodded and did as she had suggested. Sándor seemed to rouse somewhat, and Andor helped him to his feet. The wizard seemed content to be led back toward the Palace.

As Andor led him away, he said, "What about you, Brigitta?"

She stared at the ground for a moment, looked at Bölk and Miklós, then said, "I'll return soon."

Andor nodded. "And you, Miki?"

"I will be coming, brother. I don't know when yet, but I will be coming. You may tell that to the King our brother."

Andor nodded and led Sándor away.

After watching them leave, Miklós resumed sitting with his back against the oak. He sighed, then smiled at the horse. "Thank you once again, my friend," he said.

"It is only my duty, master."

"Is that what it is? Why?"

"I serve those who can use me," he said. "As I told you two years ago."

"I see. Then tell me this: why is it that everyone who hears you, hears something different?"

"Because no two people who listen to me are the same. And because not everyone listens to me."

Miklós looked at Brigitta, who seemed puzzled but was remaining silent. He spoke again to Bölk.

"I suppose," he said, "that if I asked who heard you correctly, you'd only say, 'all of you,' or 'none of you,' or something obscure like that."

Bölk chuckled. "Not quite, master. It is a question of understanding. Sándor is a part of the kingdom and the Palace, and hears all with the King's ears. Andor is torn between King and family, so, hearing both, he understands neither."

"I see. And Brigitta."

"For that, you must ask her."

Miklós looked to where she sat with her back to to the River. Her knees were pressed against her chest, her arms wrapped around them, and her face buried in her arms.

The Prince turned back to Bölk. "It seems that you can't be hurt by the Power. You protected me from it, and earlier, when I attacked you, you didn't seem to notice. Why is that?"

Bölk considered. "It isn't completely true, master," he said at last. "It isn't easy for the Power of Faerie to hurt me, but it can. The Power of Faerie is a manifestation of something that I have little to do with, and has little to do with me. It is rare that we can hurt each other."

Miklós nodded. "Then that is why you couldn't cross over to Faerie itself."

"Yes," said Bölk.

"The power is manifestation, you said. Of what?"

"Of the use men make of it."

"I don't understand."

"I know that, master."

Miklós considered for a while longer. "Is it the Demon Goddess?"

Bölk's head snapped up. "No, master. But the question is astute. The Demon Goddess is a manifestation of the power of Faerie. That is why I am powerless against her."

"Against her? Why should you be against her?"

"Because I am what I am."

"The thought makes me uncomfortable."

"I hope it will become less uncomfortable. You must defeat her."

Miklós gasped. "Defeat her!"

"Certainly," said Bölk. "The Goddess is a tool in the hands of your enemies. You must defeat her to gain what you want."

"How—? I don't even know what it is I want! How can you say—?"

Bölk chuckled softly. "You wish to assume your rightful place as Prince of Fenario. The Goddess aids those who would stop you."

Miklós started to argue, then remembered László's dream and how the mention of the Goddess had caused Andor to betray him.

"I can't fight a Goddess, Bölk," said Miklós. "I can't fight anyone. I'm not a fighter."

"That is the problem, master. As for the Goddess, I cannot fight for myself, but I may be an effective weapon against her. Not alone, but I may be useful in the right hands."

Miklós shook his head again. "I still don't understand."

"No," said Bölk. "You cannot. Your weapon is the Power of Faerie, but you cannot best Sándor with wizard's tricks; he is better at them than you are."

"I already know that."

"Then you must find other weapons and learn to use them."

"What? Swords? László is better than I ever will be. Longbow? There are guards who—"

"None of these, master."

"Then what?"

"That I cannot tell you. All I can say is before you can pick up another weapon, you must drop the one you carry."

Miklós felt himself flushing. "How can you tell me—?"

"Another thing, too, master," said the horse.

Miklós stopped. "Yes?"

"You must decide to fight. That is the first thing. I am a warrior's mount, master. Remember that."

So saying, Bölk turned away and trotted up to the River and stared upstream toward the Palace. Miklós watched him and then saw that Brigitta was no longer looking down. He caught her eye.

"Were you listening?" he asked.

She shook her head. "I tried to at first, but what you said and what he said didn't make any sense. I gather that that is what you were talking about at first. After that, I don't know."

"He explained it—a little. But tell me something. When I asked you why you'd warned me—"

"No," she said.

"All right."

They sat facing each other, both of them glancing at Bölk periodically. Suddenly Miklós said, "Do you really consider yourself to be the King's whore?"

She caught his eye, her face somber, and he felt as if there were an explosion in the pit of his stomach. But she said, "You must understand, Prince Miklós, how great an improvement that is over my previous state."

She stood up. "I think I'll return to the Palace now. Perhaps I'll see you there."

Miklós stood up also. "I didn't mean to offend you."

She met his eyes and gave him a small smile. "You didn't, Miklós. Don't worry."

He bowed his head. "Very well, then. And Brigitta—thank you."

She nodded and turned away. "Farewell, Bölk."

"Farewell, Brigitta," called the horse.

Whatever she heard made her gasp. She turned and hurried away back up the River. As Miklós watched her leave, Bölk returned and stood next to him. After a moment, Miklós sighed and seated himself once more.

"What now, Bölk?"

"What do you wish to do, master?"

"I don't know. I want to return to the Palace, but—"

"Why?"

"Eh?"

"Why return to the Palace?"

Miklós chewed his lip, then said, "Because it is my home."

"No," said Bölk. "It is László's home."

"Oh? At least one room of it is mine."

"I had thought László took that room two years ago."

"He was going to, but it seems he didn't."

Bölk cocked his head to the side. "That is interesting," he said.

"Why?"

"Is it like your brother to change his mind about something like that?"

"No, I suppose it isn't."

"Well then."

"What do you make of it?"

"I'm not certain, master."

A memory came to Miklós then. "Perhaps—"

"Yes?"

"Perhaps he is using the room after all. I noticed something strange in it."

"What sort of thing, master?"

"I'm not sure. A growth, a plant of some kind, that seemed to be growing from the floor."

Bölk's nostrils twitched, and his ears came forward. "Could you tell nothing at all about it?"

"Only what I said. It was green, perhaps as tall as my calf. I saw no flowers or buds on it."

"This is very peculiar, master."

"Yes."

"Were others in the room with you?"

"Yes, for a while. They attacked me there."

"What did they seem to think of it?"

"None of them noticed it, as far as I could tell. They were too busy trying to kill me."

"It is in a corner, then? Hidden?"

"No; as a matter of fact it is in the middle of the floor."

"In the middle, master? Calf high? And none of them noticed? They must have had to step around it to attack you."

Miklós closed his eyes, remembering. "Yes," he said at last, "they did."

"And yet they seemed not to notice this plant?"

"As I have said, Bölk."

"That is very peculiar, master."

"Well, now that you mention it . . ."

"I cannot conceive of what it might be, but I am certain it is important."

"In that case," said Miklós, "that is another reason for me to return to the Palace."

Bölk pawed the ground. "You are right, master," he said after a moment. "I can think of no other way. You must return."

Miklós smiled. "Good. Will you bear me? It is a long walk."

"Let us rest for today and tonight. Tomorrow I will bear you to the gate."

"And then?"

"I do not know, master. Perhaps I should return here, and await the next time the River sends you to this spot."

"I doubt that will be necessary, Bölk."

"Do you?"

"Yes. I think that the next time the River sends me this way, I will be dead."

INTERLUDE

IT HAD SENT ROOTS searching down through flaws in the floor, and they had had a long struggle indeed to find a path to good, solid earth, but they managed. And all of this time, the small seedling was soaking up the sunlight, sending its shoot higher and higher into the room.

The roots were firmly entrenched now, and had worked their way deeply into the earth below the cellars. Back in the room with the broken shutter, what had seemed before to be a small plant began to grow up and out.

The branches were still thin, but there were many of them. Oddly, they sprang in all directions, not just toward the light. The leaves, though each was thin, were now so thickly clustered that they formed a shell around the trunk. The total height was about that of a man's waist, and thin branches and stringy green leaves, the latter of which reached down to the floor, acted to hide its center.

Some water it brought up from the roots. Some it took from the very air around it, moist as it was from the River below the window.

Sometimes at night it seemed to shimmer in the starlight.

Sometimes it swayed in the wind.

Sometimes it swayed in the stillness.

chapter eight

The Captain

VIKTOR TOOK THE WOODEN sword from László's hand. "Another round, Your Majesty?"

"Not now," said the King. "That helped, however. Thank you."

Viktor nodded brusquely and watched his master buckle on Állam, in its bejeweled sheath. He had only seen it drawn three times in his life, and on only one such occasion had been able to get a good look. What a weapon! Its edge fairly gleamed, its delicate lines shouted its perfect balance, its hilt asked to be taken into the hand and used. Oh, for such a weapon as that!

He sighed under his breath as he wiped sweat from his forehead onto his tunic and adjusted the bandage on his hand. László walked away, then stopped and turned back.

"Yes, Your Majesty?"

"You know that Sándor was unable to remove those roots in the cellar?"

"No, I hadn't heard. Are you going to ask Prince Vilmos to help?"

László looked away. "I'd rather not. See if you can do it."

Viktor wondered at this. Was there some new trouble between the King and Vilmos? But he said, "Very well."

The King walked away again, and Viktor had the pleasure of seeing him rub his upper arm where the captain had landed a clean strike. Smiling to himself, Viktor replaced the wooden swords and strapped his own belt around his waist.

He walked the same path the King had, past the stables, through the central courtyard, and so into the main door of the Palace. Károly stood just inside. Viktor nodded approvingly to himself. Károly was young, undisciplined, loud, brash, and as fearless as a dzur. Viktor allowed the young guardsman to see a small smile.

"How is your hand?" he asked.

Károly held up his own bandage. "Fine, Captain. Thank you. And yours?"

"Well. Thank you. All quiet?"

"All quiet, Captain. The King has just been by."

"Yes."

He continued past. As he walked, he idly ran a finger along the plaster covering the wall, amusing himself by watching the fine dust fall in a stream from where his finger passed. His high, black boots clicked against the floor, sending echoes against the walls, the metal plates on the soles sounding crisp and sharp. He went through the doorway that had once led to the west wing and now only led to a stairway going up to the second floor and a smaller stairway leading to the cellars.

He took the latter, grabbing a lamp and striking a light to it on the way down. The instant his head crossed the level of the floor, his nostrils were assailed by the musky odor of norska, mixed with the ageless smell of dust. He grimaced. As he walked away from the alcove where Vilmos kept the animals, he heard them chittering.

He walked around the back of the first tier of wine racks. To his left, to his right, and ahead were the mouths of other tunnels, now locked and barred, that led under the city; all of them filled with aging bottles, barrels, and casks of wine. It was as if the Palace had grown tendrils which were supporting the city, with wine as the blood flowing through them all. The thought pleased him.

He held up his lamp, looked around, strode forward, and stopped short. The roots, which only two days ago had been thin tendrils, had thickened until they were as big around as his fist. He came closer, started to grasp one, and drew back. It was unnatural. Weird. The thought of touching it made the hair on his arms bristle and his heart palpitate. Then he cursed at his own cowardice and touched it anyway.

It was hard and tough, with the feel of tree roots that had

been years growing. His jaw worked as he walked around the edge of the jungle of roots that had seemed to sprout from nowhere. He knelt and studied one where it entered the ground. There was a small crack in the earth leading from it and extending perhaps a foot in either direction. He tried tugging on the root, but felt no give. He put both hands to it, straightened his back, and lifted with his legs. Nothing. It was as if he were trying to lift the Palace itself.

He took the lamp again and stood up. He was somehow afraid to walk among the roots, as if being surrounded by them were tantamount to being encircled by an army. That, he decided, was ridiculous, so he quickly stepped past the outermost circle. Though nothing happened, the feeling intensified there rather than disappeared.

As he stood considering, a sudden feeling of dread came over him, and he almost cried aloud as he tried to back out of the center. Each time he bumped a root, like bumping the bars of a cage, his panic increased and he wanted to whimper like a frightened puppy. After what seemed like minutes, he stood gasping outside of the circle once more. The light jumped and flickered from the trembling of his hand, and he found himself wishing for more lanterns to dispell the darkness that seemed to be nourishing whatever it was that was invading the Palace.

It was only then that the full import of the king's statement reached him: "*Sándor failed to remove those roots. . . .*" Sándor had failed. The wizard had not managed to hurt them. All at once this strange plant became a threat to the realm itself. Worse than a threat, in fact: an enigma. The King had been right after all; Miklós was up to something.

And yet, with that thought, his attitude changed. Finding a cause for it, a human cause, made it somehow less of a mystery. And that was enough to alleviate his fear and confusion as quickly as they had come, to replace them with anger.

The King didn't tell you to analyze it, he berated himself. *He told you to destroy it. So destroy it!*

He set the lamp back down in the pitted and pockmarked dirt of the cellar floor and drew his sabre. He took one deep breath, made sure he had room to swing, and struck the root nearest him with all of his strength. A dull thud issued forth, accompanied by a faint overtone, almost metallic in quality. At the same time, a shock traveled up his arm and into his shoulder, jarring his teeth in his skull. This only made him more angry. He struck again, and yet a third time, and a fourth. He put his left hand over his right and, using both of his arms, struck again and again and again, until, at last, the sabre dropped from his exhausted fingers.

Brought to his knees by his own struggles, he finally stood up, lamp in hand, and inspected the root he had been attacking.

Not the least scratch marred its surface.

He picked up his sword and inspected it. The edge was notched in several places. Perhaps, in some sense, he should have felt despair, but the number of emotional turnabouts that he had experienced in the last few moments were too much for his normally cool makeup. He stood for the space of several heartbeats considering, then, lamp in one hand and sabre in the other, he turned and walked back around the wine racks, up the stairs, and into the Palace proper.

Guards snapped to attention as he walked by, ignoring them. None commented on seeing, through the high Palace windows, their captain stride purposefully past, in full daylight with a lamp in one hand and a naked sabre in the other. None among those who saw him closely commented on the sweat that covered his forehead and neck, nor on the light brown smudges of dust upon the knees of his bright red uniform. The guardsmen who saw this were startled, certainly. The captain was normally cool and clean, and garbed in a uniform crisp and pressed. Yet, startled though they were, it occurred to none of them that this must mean that someone, or something, had brought the captain to his knees. They were, to a man, incapable of thinking this. The King was the King, and they would gladly have died for him; but the captain was their own personal god—he to whom they looked for help, punishment, and justice in all its fine nuances. They knew that nothing could humble the captain.

He took the spiral stairway from the dining room up to the kitchen, unconsciously shifting his sabre to allow for the narrow walls and tight curve. From there he made his way to the audience chamber, stopping for a moment in front of the fine stone carving. His eyes took in the chipped ear of the bull and smudging of the rider's eye, and he *tsked* to himself. "Stay with it, old fellow," he told the statuette, "it will all come home for you someday." He continued to the audience chamber.

Tóbiás, on duty outside of it, at first made a motion to bar his way. Seeing who it was, the guard stepped back, then seemed to hesitate, as if he weren't sure whether his captain should be admitted or not. He held out a tentative hand as if to stop him. Viktor, without appearing to see him, handed him the lamp, muttered "thank you," and entered the room.

The King seemed to be in a deep discussion with Rezső. László was seated, staring down at a piece of parchment, while the advisor stood looking over his shoulder and pointing at something on it. Rezső's clothing, if it could be dignified with such a term, tried to be yellow. The rags of stitching upon them had once, perhaps, been embroidery. He seemed to have made no effort to comb his hair. Viktor felt his lips tighten. *If I were King, my advisors would dress as if they served a King.*

When King and advisor noticed Viktor's presence, Rezső straightened up and seemed annoyed. The first expression to cross the King's countenance was anger; then he seemed to take a closer look at Viktor's face. His eyes came to rest on the sabre, and, for the briefest of instants, something like fear came over his features, to be replaced by wary curiosity.

"What is it, Viktor?" he asked evenly.

Viktor stepped forward around the long table. When he was halfway there, he set his blade on it, hilt first, and slid it toward the King.

László stopped it, then turned back to his Captain of Guards.

"Yes, Viktor?"

"Look at it, Your Majesty."

The King did so. He ran his thumb carefully over the notches, then looked at Viktor again.

"Yes?"

"I attacked the roots."

László blinked twice, then looked back at the notches marring the sabre's edge.

"I see."

Resző looked from one to the other. "What is it, Your Majesty?"

"Never mind, Rezső. We will continue this later. Leave me now."

The old man bowed and picked up the parchment along with several others that lay on the table. He gathered them to his bosom as a mother will her baby, and, bowing again, left the room with one brief glance at Viktor, containing equal parts of confusion and resentment.

When his shuffling footstep had faded from hearing, László said, "I take it you did them no damage?"

"None," said Viktor. "They've grown. They are thick and well buried. I see no way to hurt them."

The King nodded and stood up. "Very well, then."

"Are you going to ask Vilmos to help?"

"Not just yet. I will if I have to. First, though, I want to see something. Come with me."

He led the captain out of the room and down, until they came, with much winding and little ceremony, to Miklós's room. They stood for a moment in front of a curtain of drab gray cloth—moth-eaten and ragged as it was, it seemed to be a wall separating the corridor from another universe altogether. King and captain looked at each other. Then, as one, they stepped through.

At first glance, Viktor saw no difference from the night before. His eyes lit on the broken shutter, the still-made bed, the layer of dust covering the hardwood dressing table. He started to take another step forward and realized that his path was being blocked by the very object of his search.

It came almost to his chest—green, full, and bushy. It looked like a small tree, perhaps, such as grew on the banks of the River. He studied it closely while next to him the King did the same. The leaves were long and narrow, and there were tiny buds buried within. He brought his head closer and looked carefully inside one of the buds. It consisted of several tiny stalks, each of which had a pair of connected, fingerlike appendages around it.

Viktor blinked and pulled back, surveying the entire growth. The leaves were so thick, it was impossible to see to the trunk. He pulled a handful aside, and was unsurprised to discover that the center was even thicker and stronger looking than the roots had been.

"It is odd," said the King, "how long it took us to notice it."

"Yes. And that we didn't when we were here last night."

They knelt next to it, pushing more leaves aside, and studied the floor beneath it.

"Does it seem to you," said László, "that the stem is tearing the floor apart?"

"Yes," said Viktor. "The longer this continues, the worse it will get."

The King nodded. "Well, then," he said, "let us see what Állam can do."

Viktor stepped back. The King drew his blade with a flourish, and held it back, palm down, to cut crosswise. Viktor drew his breath in, staring at the sabre. The air before his eyes seemed to crackle and spark, and he could almost imagine he saw a kind of aura, a reddish haze, outlining Állam. László cut, then, and Viktor heard the same dull sound as before, with the same faint, metallic overtone. Two of the thousands of leaves fell from the tree.

The King inspected his blade, then resheathed it. Viktor sent him a puzzled look.

"It isn't notched," said László. "Or bent or broken. I want to keep it that way."

"But we can't—"

The King cut him off. "Now," he said, "we speak to Vilmos."

"Yes," said Viktor.

They turned their back on the growth, and Viktor followed the King out of the room.

They found Vilmos just coming up from the cellars.

"How are the norska?" asked László.

"Fine," said Vilmos. Viktor kept his reaction to himself. "Were you looking for me?" asked the giant.

The King nodded. "I have a request."

"Yes?"

László's jaws worked, then he said, "It concerns those roots in the cellar. We want—"

"Ah! You want me to tear them out."

"Yes. If you . . . that is, I know I—"

Viktor held a grimace behind his face. To be King, yet to be made uncomfortable in asking a service from a subject, was absurd. But Vilmos smiled and gently put a hand on the King's shoulder. "It's all right, Laci. Sándor asked me to do this already."

Viktor could see that there had been something between them, but made no effort to guess what it was; it was sufficient to him that the King seemed relieved.

"Thank you, Vili," he said.

"It is nothing."

László nodded. "We'll be in the audience chamber."

"I'll do it now."

Vilmos walked back down to the cellar. As Viktor and László started back up, one of the Palace Guard caught up to them.

"Your Majesty, Prince Andor and Lord Sándor are return-ing."

The King looked at him. "Alone?"

"Yes, Your Majesty."

He turned to Viktor. "Should we await them here?"

"I can hardly meet them like this, Your Majesty."

The King looked him over, trying to deduce what he meant, until his eyes came to rest on Viktor's empty scabbard.

"Very well," he said, almost smiling. "Stop by the armory, then meet me in the audience chamber."

"Yes, Your Majesty," said Viktor, bowing slightly. He fol-lowed the maze of hallways to the guard hall in the east wing, and received a new sabre of the armorer. He noticed the way the loud, bantering voices of guards dropped into respectful whispers as he approached, and smiled to himself. *About time I changed boots,* he decided. *They know the sound of my walk too well.*

He retraced his steps to arrive at the stair leading up. When he reached the entrance he found Vilmos emerging from the stairway. At once, he noticed a strange, faraway look in the giant's eyes. *Odd,* he thought ironically. *One might almost believe he's been thinking.*

Vilmos almost walked into him before noticing the captain.

"I'm sorry," he mumbled.

Viktor grunted. "Well?"

Vilmos opened and closed his mouth, then shook his head.

"You couldn't do it?" Viktor prompted.

"No . . . yes. I'm not sure."

"What do you mean?"

Vilmos shook his head once more. "I don't know," he said at last. "There was something—there is something about those roots."

"What?"

"I just . . . I couldn't bring myself to touch them."

Viktor stared at him. "What do you mean?"

"I don't know. But I stood there, and they seemed so frail—"

"Frail!"

"Yes. I touched one and pulled a little, and it would have been so easy to just pull a little harder. . . ."

"I don't believe it."

"But I couldn't bring myself to do it. I don't know. I've never felt anything like it."

Viktor snorted, feeling disgust well up in the back of his throat. "Couldn't bring yourself to do it," he said. "Something that put notches on my blade and remained untouched against Sándor's wizardry, and you have the power to destroy it, yet you won't. I don't believe you, Vilmos."

The giant looked at him, quizzically. "You saw them?"

"Of course I saw them. You were there."

"Yes. That is right. Didn't you . . . feel anything?"

"Yes. I felt—" He stopped, then went on. "I felt fear, at first. Then anger."

Vilmos shook his head. "But didn't you feel anything *for* them?"

"I don't know what you mean."

Vilmos sighed. "Never mind."

"I think," said Viktor, "that you should inform the King of this, before you go back to playing with norska."

Vilmos nodded sadly. "Yes. Of course. I'll do that."

He turned away. Viktor leaned against the wall and watched his retreating back. He had the sudden feeling that the ground was no longer stable—that things upon which he had depended were falling away. The King unable to give orders, the wizard unable to kill a tree. And the tree itself, by the Goddess! Growing right in the middle of the Palace! He sighed and started to follow the giant up to the audience chamber. As he walked past the double doors to the courtyard, he saw that the main gate was opening again. A lone figure came through it and began walking directly toward the entrance of the Palace, past the idol of the Demon Goddess. Viktor waited.

"Good afternoon, Brigitta."

She nodded brusquely and continued past him.

"Brigitta . . ."

She stopped and turned. "Yes?"

"Where have you been?"

She looked him up and down. "I do not believe I must give you an account of my actions."

He frowned. "I didn't mean to ask for an account."

"Then what did you mean?"

"I was only . . . never mind."

She nodded and turned away again.

"Brigitta, wait."

This time when she turned around he could detect a trace of exasperation in her face.

"I would like to show you something," he said.

She blinked. "What?"

"Are you aware of what has happened in Miklós's old chambers?"

She peered at him. "Happened?"

"There is something growing there."

"What do you mean, growing?"

"Come with me."

She hesitated. "Why?"

"You have just been with Prince Miklós, haven't you?"

"And if I have?"

"Perhaps you wonder why the King has been wroth with him."

"Perhaps."

"Then, the next time you see Prince Miklós, you may ask him to explain what this is and how it came to be in his chambers."

She studied him for a moment, then nodded. "Very well. Let us go, then."

He led the way toward Miklós's chambers. They passed Vilmos on the way, who grunted at them. His brows were drawn together, as if they'd been knitted there. His massive face was drawn into itself, prunelike. A few paces behind him was Mariska.

"Were you coming to see me?" she asked.

Brigitta shook her head.

"No, Countess," said Viktor. "We are going to look in on Miklós's room. It is just down the hall—"

"I know," she said. "I've been looking at it myself."

"Indeed?" said Viktor. "What do you think of it?"

"It serves no purpose," she said. "Excuse me, Viktor, Brigitta."

She continued past them, following the still audible footsteps of Vilmos. *Serves no purpose?* thought Viktor. *How odd.* He noticed Brigitta following the Countess with her eyes, and decided that she was probably wondering the same thing he was.

When they pushed aside the curtain into Miklós's old chambers, Viktor found that László and Sándor were there before him. At the same moment, he heard Brigitta gasp. He turned to her, and saw that she was staring at the tree, which now was fully as tall as he was.

The expression on her face, however, was less one of surprise than of delighted wonder. Of all the reactions she could have had, this he hadn't expected. He looked up to see László and Sándor were also staring at her.

After a silence that seemed to stretch the length of the River, László said, "What is it, Brigitta?"

She shook her head, as if words failed, but finally managed to whisper, "It's beautiful."

Viktor felt himself gripped by an icy rage. Beautiful! Beautiful? A tree, growing in the middle of the Palace, impervious to all efforts to remove it? Tearing apart the very floor? Looking as if it would explode the very room that contained it? Beautiful?

Yet, before he could speak, László cut in.

"Just what do you find beautiful about it?" Viktor took satisfaction in hearing that the King's tone of voice matched his own feelings.

Brigitta just shook her head. "I don't know," she said. "But seeing it growing there, amid these stone walls—seeing something fresh from all of this ... decay ... Seeing—"

"That will be quite enough," said the King in a tone cold enough to freeze the fires that burned behind his eyes.

Brigitta seemed to catch herself, and Viktor could see her suddenly realizing what she had said and to whom she had said it. There was a moment when no one spoke, and Brigitta seemed about to form an apology, but then her lips tightened and her face set. She said nothing.

The King nodded almost imperceptibly, then said, "Leave my presence at once. If I need you for anything, I will call on you. Until then, stay out of my sight."

She curtsied, seeming to find dignity in the air around her. "With your permission, Your Majesty, I will return to town."

"You do not have my permission, until I decide what will become of you."

She bowed her head, straightened it, and looked directly at him. "As you wish, Your Majesty." She turned and left the room, somehow making it look as if she had chosen to leave rather than been dismissed.

When she was gone, László turned to Viktor. "Did you have some reason for bringing her here?"

Viktor bit his lip. It did not seem the time to speak to him of his guesses about her involvement with Miklós. Perhaps Sándor knew and had spoken of it. If not, he, Viktor, wouldn't either. He contented himself with casting his eyes down and saying nothing.

After a moment, the King grunted. "In any case," he said, glancing at Sándor and Viktor, "the question is: how are we to deal with this . . . thing?" He gestured toward the tree.

Sándor crossed over to the window and looked out. "It is the River that nourishes it," he muttered.

"Fine," said Viktor. "All you need to do is stop The River, then."

Sándor scowled but didn't answer.

"Be serious," said László.

"The danger, Your Majesty," said Viktor, "comes from the way the stem is pulling apart the floor tiles, and from the danger that it will continue to grow until it puts pressure on the walls."

"Yes," said László. "And?"

"Is there some way to secure the walls and the floor so they will not be broken apart?"

"This has been suggested by the Countess." He asked the wizard, "What do you think?"

"I'm not certain," said the wizard. "It is worth thinking about."

"The only other thing we can do is destroy it," said Viktor. "And I see no way to do that."

"Except for Vilmos," said the King. "And he won't."

"Perhaps you should speak to him again, Your Majesty."

"Perhaps."

"I see no other way. Neither Sándor nor I can hurt it."

"We could burn it," said the wizard.

László snorted. "Certainly. And the Palace with it."

"There is also Állam, Your Majesty," said Viktor carefully.

The King nodded. "Yes. I have not fully tested Állam against it." He stroked the hilt of his sabre. "Somehow I don't want to."

"Why not?" asked Viktor.

"I'm not sure," said the King. He chuckled. "Perhaps because if Állam doesn't hurt it, we'll *really* be powerless."

Viktor forced himself to smile, despite the sudden rage this invoked in him. But he said only, "If we have a weapon that might solve the problem, though, we should consider using it."

The King studied him. "What do you know of the sword?" he asked.

"Nothing, Your Majesty," said Viktor. "Why?"

"Never mind. I'll think about it."

"And I," said Sándor, "will consider the matter of strengthening the Palace."

"Should I speak to Vilmos?" asked Viktor.

"No," said László. "Don't bother. There is something I must do before any action is taken."

He stopped. Viktor and Sándor glanced quickly at each other to see who would ask the question the King obviously wanted asked. Finally, Sándor said, "What is that, Your Majesty?"

"I am going to spend the evening in the Tower. I wish to consult with the Demon Goddess."

The next afternoon, as Viktor entered the Great Hall, he noticed someone who seemed to be asleep in a corner. Looking closer, he recognized the coachman of the Count of Mordfal. At that moment, the other opened his eyes, as if he'd felt the captain's stare. The coachman nodded. Viktor approached and sat down next to him.

"Good afternoon, Captain," he said in a sonorous voice. Viktor looked for, and found, several empty wine bottles at the foot of his chair.

"You're drunk," said Viktor.

"My name is Miska," said the coachman, as if that were an answer. But he went on, "My master says we are to be leaving soon. I am preparing for the journey."

"If any of my men 'prepared' themselves the way you do—"

"Oh, come, good Captain. There is no need to be so serious."

Viktor didn't answer. He wondered, though, why a gentleman such as the Count would keep on a sodden fool like this. Viktor noticed the coachman's bloodshot eyes were fixed on him. He suddenly felt uncomfortable and, consequently, irritated.

"Don't be angry with me, good Captain," said Miska. "Shall I tell you a story?"

Viktor hesitated, then, "Very well."

Miska nodded and closed his eyes. "Many, many, years ago—hundreds of years ago—there was a babe born in this very castle, to the King and Queen. He was normal enough at birth, but by the time he was six months old he weighed thirty pounds. By the time he was a year old, he could lift twice his own weight.

"As he grew older, he became larger and larger, until he was so strong—"

"Vilmos," said the Captain.

"Please," said Miska. "There are giants born to this family every four or five generations. Now, then, where was I? Well, never mind. Now, he had a brother, did this giant. I don't know which brother was the older. Perhaps they were twins. But this brother was so smart that he learned the languages of the birds and the beasts, and he knew how to make the River run backward, and how to make the stars shine during the day.

"Well, one day the strong brother said to the smart brother, 'I am so strong, I could break our father's sword in two.' And the smart brother said, 'I am so smart, I know enough not to try.' And the two brothers had a good laugh about this, then went off to do other things."

Miska closed his eyes again. After a moment, Viktor said, "Well?"

The coachman opened one eye. "Well, what?"

"Is that the end?"

"What more is needed, Captain?"

"Which one became King?"

"Neither. There was war with the Northmen and the strong brother was slain in battle, while the smart brother ran away and was never heard from again."

Viktor stared at him for a moment, then turned his back on the coachman. He filled a bowl with potato soup from the large pot near the kitchen and sat down to eat it.

After a moment, Sándor came in and sat down next him.

"How is it today?" asked the wizard.

"The soup? Too hot for Rezső, I think," said Viktor. They exchanged a smile.

Sándor filled a bowl and returned. "Not bad," he said, tasting it. "I wonder if any of the potatoes will be left tonight?"

"Maybe," said Viktor. "It tastes like they used lamb *and* beef this time. Probably still trying to impress the Countess."

They ate in silence for a while, Viktor holding his bowl in one hand, Sándor having set his on a low table next to the chair, and leaning over it to eat. The pose looked uncomfortable to Viktor, but he said nothing. He thought about the coachman's story, but, if there was a point to it, he couldn't see what it was.

"Have you seen the King?" asked Sándor eventually.

Viktor shook his head. "I wonder if he learned anything."

"Yes."

"I wonder why he needs to?"

Sándor looked at him sharply. "What do you mean?"

"There are at least two things he could try that don't require asking questions."

"I assume one them is Vilmos."

"Yes. When he spoke to me, it was clear that he had the strength to pull up the roots. Why doesn't the King order him to?"

"I don't think it is that easy a thing, Viktor. He has influence on Vilmos, but he doesn't command him. If he were to put Vilmos's loyalty to a strong test it might break, and that could have dire results for all of us."

Viktor snorted. "He is one man, Sándor!"

"His strength makes him more than that. I think the King is right not to push him unless he has to."

Viktor bit back a reply of, Then he isn't a King. Instead he said, "Then I don't understand why he doesn't use Állam."

The wizard's eyes burned brightly for a moment. "To be blunt, my friend, neither do I. And I know as much about it as he does."

"What is it about that blade, Sándor? Both you and he have alluded to it, but—"

"Have the King tell you. He will, if he's in a talkative mood. But something about using it against the tree frightens him. I think—no, never mind."

"Don't start on that, Wizard. What is your theory?"

Sándor sighed. "My theory, Captain, is that he fears his own blood lust. That once he begins wielding Állam against that tree, he won't stop until he actually *has* killed his brother. It is that kind of weapon, and the King is that kind of warrior."

"Well then, so be it," said Viktor.

"It isn't your brother we are discussing."

"Perhaps. But then he could let me wield it. I am not likely to lose control in battle."

Sándor set his spoon down in the bowl and searched Viktor's eyes with his own. "Have a care," he said. "Who holds Állam holds the kingdom."

"Well then," said Viktor softly, "so be it."

Sándor studied him for a long moment. "Why are you saying these things to me?"

Viktor answered his question with another. "Did you know that I am the eldest son of King Vendel's daughter? And that she was older than Gellért, János's father, by—"

Sándor smiled. "Monika. You are Monika's son. How is she?"

Viktor stared at him a moment. Then he swallowed. "Well. But without ambition."

Sándor nodded. "Does the King know who you are?"

Viktor shook his head.

"I see," said Sándor. Then, "Why are you choosing to trust me? And why now?"

"I trust you because I've known you for five years. You serve the kingdom more than the King. And you can see as well as I what is happening around us. As for why now? I think you know that, too."

Sándor studied him for five blinks. At last he grunted and resumed eating. "Have a care," he said again.

Before Viktor could respond, he was interrupted by the arrival of László and Mariska, who approached and greeted them. Servants brought chairs, and soon they had made a small circle. Viktor noticed that the King seemed tired, as if he had spent a sleepless night.

"My friends," he said, "I have spoken to the Goddess."

Viktor leaned forward intently.

"What did she say?" asked Sándor.

"She said that, unless we do something, there is no doubt that the tree will destroy the Palace. She also said that it wasn't a tree, but wouldn't say what it was. It isn't good, whatever it is. We must destroy it at all costs."

Inaudible sighs seemed to pass around the rest of them, as if a fear they had felt all along were confirmed. For Viktor, the words that remained ringing in his ears were, "at all costs." *I wonder, does László understand what that means?*

Mariska said, "Did you ask her about strengthening the supports of the Palace?"

"No," said the King. "It didn't come up."

"You should have."

He looked at her. "My bride," he said, "have you ever communed with the Demon Goddess?"

"She has never chosen to come to me, and I am not permitted to visit your tower."

"Then do not speak of things you know nothing about."

Mariska's face turned red and Viktor thought she was going to leave, but she only clutched her fan tighter and settled back into her chair.

Viktor said, "What about Állam, Your Majesty?"

The King looked away. "Állam," he repeated softly. "Yes, there is Állam. When Fenarr, my ancestor, returned from the land of Faerie, he ruled from a keep that was built on the same spot this Palace stands upon. He ruled for forty years. They say that when the Goddess came for him at last, he begged that his son be given something to help him hold the kingdom against the Northern barbarians."

He looked directly into Viktor's eyes. "They never found Fenarr's body, but on his bed was the sword, Állam." He stood up and drew it, holding it in front of Viktor's eyes. It was a light-looking blade, the metal of silvery-gray and shockingly plain against the ornate hilt and jeweled scabbard. Viktor thought that he had never seen anything more beautiful.

The King held it in front of him for the space of several breaths, then fluidly resheathed it and sat down.

"Fenarr's son became King József the First. He led the kingdom to war against the Northmen, and there Állam was tested. They say that when József drew it, he became a demon and slew many of his own men as he ran in and out of the ranks of Northmen, like a living spear.

"And there is one more thing: all Kings of Fenario are granted a death-boon by the Goddess. Fenarr's gift was the sword. József asked if the sword could be made so enduring that it would last as long as she, the Goddess, should live. We are told that the Goddess replied, 'It cannot be done. The sword is destined to live longer than I.'

"This, Viktor, is the sword whose power you wish me to unleash within my own Palace. Are you certain you are wise in what you are asking?"

Viktor knew that he ought to consider carefully before risking an answer, yet the words came out of him before he could check them. "Yes, Your Majesty, I am certain."

The King studied him, then turned to Sándor. "And you, wizard? Are you, also, certain that this should be done?"

"No, Your Majesty, I am not. Yet what else can we do? Can you convince Vilmos?"

László sighed. "Perhaps."

Sándor nodded. "Because, if not, I see no other—"

"If I may be permitted," said Mariska suddenly.

László nodded to her. "You may."

"Are you quite certain, Your Majesty?"

He flushed, then suddenly smiled. "Yes. I am sorry, Countess. I should not have spoken to you so. I have had no sleep, and am worried. What have you to say?"

"Are you still convinced that the growth is Miklós's fault?"

"It is likely," he said dryly. Sándor nodded.

"Then perhaps, before doing anything else, we should ask Miklós to remove it."

"Ask Miklós! If he put it there—"

"Are you certain he knew what he was doing? That it could destroy the Palace? And are you certain he would still want to? It would do no harm to ask."

"A reasonable thought, Countess," said Viktor, "but Miklós isn't here."

"This is his home, Captain, whether he likes it or not. He will be back."

The King stared at her. "I will consider the matter," he said. "But I cannot afford to wait. Each hour, it seems, that thing in his room grows and becomes stronger. Whatever we do must be done soon."

Mariska bowed.

At that moment a servant appeared at the King's elbow.

"Yes?" he said.

"Your Majesty, a horseman has appeared at the gate, asking for admittance."

"Well? What of it?"

"Your Majesty, he says he is Prince Miklós."

INTERLUDE

LONG AGO, IN THE days of your grandfather's grandfather's grandfather, it was the time of Tividar the Renewer. Now, as is well known, the King had many sons and daughters. One of his sons, who was called Jani, courted a lady named Margit who dwelt in the city.

It was their custom to spend time in the city in the public houses, for Jani was well-beloved by all the people, as were all the sons and daughters of the King then. On a time, they came to one such house they often chose and found that all of the people were gathered on the street outside.

"Is it a fire, then?" asked Jani.

"No," they told him. "There is a man inside who is bigger than a house, and he is fiercer than a dzur, and he is carrying a great sword, so we are afraid to enter."

"Well," said Jani, "what have you done?"

"We have sent to the Palace for aid."

"Then that is right," said Jani.

But then Margit spoke of how Jani needed no one else, as he was so brave. Some of the people laughed at this, so Margit took one of her gloves and threw it as far as she could inside of the doors. Then she asked Jani if he would return it to her.

"Certainly," he said, smiling. And, though he carried no weapon, he walked into the house. Well! You can imagine how this made the people gasp. A moment later he came out again, and you may cut my tongue from my mouth if he wasn't carrying her glove. My father was there, right in the front of it, so you may be sure I am speaking the truth.

Well, he hands her back the glove just as calm as you please. And the people said, "Didn't he hit you with that great sword?"

Jani smiled at this, and said, "No ordinary weapon may harm a Prince of Fenarr's blood. I was in no danger."

Well, then Margit says, "But Jani, you would have done it anyway, wouldn't you?"

So Jani shakes his head and says, "You will never know that." And he walks away, and from that day forward, he would never have anything to do with her.

As for where it happened, why, by the Goddess herself, we're sitting in the same place now! If you don't believe me, ask old Pista over there; he'll tell you the same as me. But I'll have more wine, first; talking is thirsty business.

chapter nine

The Homecoming

LET US, FOR A MOMENT, move backward along the flow of time and look up Miklós and Bölk, the one upon the other, as they progress toward the Palace and, temporally, to the point at which we have, with the assistance of Viktor, already arrived.

After crossing to the north bank of the River they made slow, steady progress westward, passing before diminutive villages stuck onto the Riverfront like an afterthought of whoever had crafted the landscape. Between the villages, the strings of peppers were gone from the peasants' houses, replaced by new caulking to prepare the stone and wood frames for the winter.

The sky was a deep, powerful blue, enhanced by occasional clouds dotting it in the same way the villages dotted the Riverfront. The air had turned chilly, and Miklós folded his cloak tightly around him. No one took notice of them, though Miklós, for his part, was fascinated by the brief glimpses he received of people. Hundreds of people going about their business with no thought for the Palace or those who lived in it.

"I don't wish to sneak in this time," he said suddenly.

"There is no need to, master."

"But the guards—will they let us in?"

"Indeed, master. Are you not a Prince of the realm? They will let you in. The question is, what will happen to you after that?"

"Yes. But do you think I should just go up to the gate?"

"You didn't fare well the last time when you tried stealth."

"True, but—"

"There may come a need to hide what you are doing, but as long as it isn't necessary, you shouldn't."

They saw, on the opposite side of the River a tall, narrow house of some Baron or perhaps a minor Count. It was built all of wood and had been painted yellow. The paint was fresh. The houses of peasants became more frequent, as did the villages. Soon, almost unnoticeably, they were in what seemed to be one village, on both sides of the River. It was not so much large as *long*. That is, the houses and markets and an occasional inn (distinguishable from the houses only by a badly painted sign hung to one side or the other) were built only on the Riverfront itself, never back from it; yet they stretched unbroken.

The wall that marked the city of Fenario was broken in more places than not. Looking closely, Miklós was able to see where sections had been shattered by rams during the siege of King István II or had been pulled down by ropes and oxen after the invasion during the reign of King János IV. There were neither gate nor guard, but the places for both were still discernible.

Riding through the streets of Fenario almost brought tears to Miklós's eyes. He hadn't seen these streets for more than two years, and they gave him a sense of peace and serenity that he hadn't known was in him. He attracted no attention, except from those who stopped to admire Bölk, so Miklós could ride and gawk as if he were a visiting peasant.

The streets were, for the most part, narrow and winding. They were both long and short at the same time; that is, a street would run for the entire length of the city, sometimes even to a bridge over to the other side of the River or out of town, yet during that span it would change its name ten or twenty times. And any stranger looking for a house on Fenarr Street would have a hard time of it indeed, for nearly every street became a Fenarr Street at some point on its journey.

In Fenario, unlike the villages along the way, the inns were easily identified: they were big, sometimes two or even three stories tall, and the signs were large and often accompanied by a statue or device. Miklós passed one which boasted a pair of life-sized black dzur, crouching, guarding the door. He remembered his experience in the forest and shuddered. He continued on his way, stopping now and then to take his bearings by the Tower of the Goddess and the King's Tower. Soon the

Tower of Past Glories came into sight, and Miklós thought once more of his parents. He had seen little of his father when he was young, but much of his mother. She had spoken of little except to be sure he understood what a fine King her husband was.

But thinking about it now, with the decaying Tower before him, he realized that there was much truth in what she'd been saying, as hard to accept as it had been at the time. King János had held his kingdom together with little change, and what more could a King do? The Kings that history spoke of as great had been those who had rebuilt the land after a disaster or defeated an invasion. And more, Miklós realized, it took a special kind of man to step down from such a position when he felt he could no longer fulfill his role.

And as for his mother . . .

He smiled. No one could remove a splinter as painlessly as she.

Perhaps he would have something to say to them after all.

They came at length to the gates into the courtyard of the Palace.

"Halt!" the guard-chief cried. "State your business!"

Taking a deep breath, he answered: "I am Miklós, Prince of Fenario, and I seek entrance to my home."

The guard stared down at him, wide-eyed, fidgeting with the spear in his right hand. "A moment, Prince Miklós. We will, that is . . ."

There was a hasty conference of three guards in the tower atop the wall. Miklós smiled gently in sympathy and said nothing. Then the gate swung open.

"It is time, Bölk," said Miklós. "Let us see what he has in mind." He entered the courtyard. He saw someone running off, doubtless with a message to László saying he was here. How would László react?

He sat a little straighter. A servant whose name Miklós could almost remember approached respectfully.

"May I see to your horse, my Prince?"

Miklós considered briefly, then nodded. "Take special care of him," he said, dismounting. "See that he is well fed and well groomed."

"Yes, my Prince."

Bölk was led away, giving Miklós a glance that the Prince couldn't read. He began to walk toward the doors into the

Palace. As he passed the icon, another guard, coming to him and bowing, said, "My Prince, the King has been informed of your arrival."

"Very good," said Miklós.

"If you would care to wait here, I'm sure we will be told—"

"Nonsense. I am entering the Palace. Do you know any reason why I should not?"

"I—that is, no, my Prince."

"Good. Neither do I."

He resumed walking forward. Yet he was still twenty paces from the doors when one was flung open from the inside by the servant who had carried the message. The servant stepped to the side, and, framed in the doorway, was his brother László, King of Fenario.

They looked at each other, each refusing to be the first to show his feelings, whatever they were. Miklós felt a brief flash of regret that Bölk wasn't there to advise him on this, but what could he have said, anyway? Memories came and went through Miklós's head with the speed of arrows. His earliest memories, seeing László as a stranger. The years of desperate efforts to please him. The shock of the discovery that László would be King some day, and how Miklós had not dared to speak to him for a week. The brief times when László would sit down and tell him stories of the great battles to maintain Fenario's independence, or legends of Fenarr, or the history of their fathers' sword, which László now wore strapped to his waist. And the way László's eyes would get when he told such tales—dreamy, distant—and Miklós would understand that they were a part of a thousand years of history, and shudder with pleasure.

A woman that Miklós recognized as Mariska, daughter of the Count of Mordfal, appeared behind László and gently squeezed his arm. Had they spoken of him? Doubtless. What had she said?

At that moment, László gravely inclined his head. "Brother Miklós," he said. "Welcome back to your home. The lamp is lit, the table is set. We greet you." Then László, with his own hands, opened the second of the double doors into the Palace.

Once again Miklós felt tears welling up in his eyes. In the flash of a timeless instant, all of his intentions, plans, and stratagems for dealing with his brother were washed away in a flood of the purest, cleanest joy he had felt in years. "Brother," he said softly, and then he and László were in each other's arms.

László whispered in his ear, "Welcome home, Miki."

"Thank you, Laci," said Miklós. "Thank you."

A few minutes later they were in the Great Hall. It was filled, as usual, but the two of them were given a respectful distance by everyone else.

They tried to make small talk, but Miklós refused to discuss what he had experienced in Faerie, and László seemed reluctant to discuss his marriage or the problems of ruling the land. Soon an uncomfortable silence settled. Then Miklós cleared his throat.

"Laci, I feel that I should apologize to you. I know how strongly you feel—"

"You don't need to speak of it, Miki."

"Perhaps. But I feel I should. May I?"

The King huddled with himself for a moment, then nodded brusquely. His hands settled on the arms of his chair, as if he were prepared to grip them if he needed to.

"I know how strongly you feel about the Palace," Miklós continued. "I have said many things I shouldn't have said, for many reasons. None of them good. In the future, I will try to curb my tongue." He looked at the room around them, seeing the cracked plaster, crumbling sandstone, and rotting beams; but also seeing the shadows the lamps made against the walls, the arch of the timbers that held up the ceiling, the graceful carvings over the doorways. "I love this place, Laci. Perhaps not as much as you or in the same way, but I love it. You should know that."

The King closed his eyes and seemed to be trying to master his emotions. "Thank you, Miki. That is good to know. For my part," he paused and looked around much as Miklós had, "I admit that all is not perfect here. Perhaps now that the four of us are together, we can repair it—put it into the kind of shape it was meant to be in. The kind of shape it can be in. I've spoken to Mariska of it; she has many ideas. With your new skills and your travels, you should have ideas that will be helpful."

"Yes," said Miklós. "We will work together." His smile matched the King's.

Then László's face darkened.

"What is it, Laci? If there is a problem, now is the time to speak of it."

"Yes, Miklós, I am prepared, now, today, to forgive you anything, if forgiveness is required."

"I am prepared to ask for it, Laci, if I have committed a wrong."

"That is the question. Have you?"

Miklós felt his brows contract. "If you speak of something in particular, I don't know what."

"Your room. The thing that is growing there."

"Ah! The little plant. Yes, I—"

"Little plant!"

Miklós frowned. "What is it?"

The King stood up. "Come with me," he said. "Let us look at this little plant of yours!"

Miklós followed him down and to his room. László threw aside the curtain and Miklós gasped.

"By the Goddess!"

"Yes," said László. He gripped Miklós's arm—hard but not painfully. "Miklós, I am asking you. Is this your doing?"

With an effort, Miklós tore his eyes away from the tree. He searched the King's face. Then, looking directly at him, he said, "László, I have no idea what this is or how it came to be here. If it was any of my doing, I don't know how."

László nodded. "Very well. I believe you." He chuckled. "But I am forced to surrender a theory that I liked."

"That I was behind it? Why did you like that theory?"

"Because I hoped to persuade you to take it down."

"Take it down? Can't it be cut down? Or pulled out?"

"Viktor notched his sword on it. No one but Vilmos has the strength to pull it out. You can see that we could not bring enough men or machines in here to do it. And Vilmos, for some reason, won't."

"What about Sándor?"

"His wizard's tricks don't seem to affect it, either."

"Hmmmm. If you like, László, I will speak to Vilmos. He and I have always been close. Perhaps I can convince him—"

László clapped him on the shoulder. "Yes! Thank you, brother. That would be a help, indeed."

"I'll do it then," said Miklós.

They left the room and walked back up toward the main hall. "Until this plant is destroyed," said László, "I don't see how you can stay there. When the Count of Mordfal leaves, we will have a room free. I will see that it is prepared for you."

"Thank you, Laci. Where is Vilmos, now?"

"I imagine he is with his norska. You will see him at dinner. I was going to dine alone with Mariska, but now we will all be together, and I don't want to delay our first dinner as a family in two years."

"Yes. I look forward to it."

"Oh, and Miki, speaking of two years . . ."

"Yes."

"I, too, am sorry. That night when I drove you away. I—"

"There is no need to speak of it, Laci. Please don't. I understand." The King put his arm around his brother's shoulders, and so they returned to the Great Hall; taking the long way up because the circular stairway would not accommodate two abreast.

They found Andor in the Great Hall.

"I was told you had returned," he said.

Miklós nodded.

Andor said, "We will look for better things from you in the future."

Miklós heard the sharp intake of breath from László, but neither of them answered. Miklós made himself smile, then walked away. He heard sharp whispers from behind him, but couldn't catch the words that were spoken.

He was the first into the small dining room, followed by László escorting Mariska, then Andor. László took his place at the head of the table; Mariska took hers at the foot, László indicated a place for Miklós. He was moving toward it when he heard the familiar rumble from the floor and walls. An instant later Vilmos stepped into the room, freshly washed and changed from working with the norska. His eyes fell on Miklós, and his face lit up like the Great Hall on Ascension Day.

"Miki!" he cried. "You are back! Are you back?" He lumbered forward and they embraced.

"Yes, Vili," he said when he could breathe again. "I am back."

Vilmos looked at him, grinning from ear to ear. "It is good," he said, as if it were a proclamation.

"Yes," said Miklós.

"Let us eat," said László, but he, too, was smiling.

Miklós fairly bounded into his chair, set between Vilmos and Mariska. He chuckled. "I've been smiling so much today that my face is starting to hurt."

László matched his chuckle. Vilmos let go a booming laugh. Andor half smiled, half scowled, then looked down. Mariska watched László.

Juliska came in from the kitchen, looking fresh and bright in a lavender dress with embroidered white apron, her hair drawn up into a tight bun. She set before each of them a small plate which held a steaming towel, boiled in lemon water. Miklós pressed the towel against his face. It was just short of scalding, and the scent reminded him of things he hadn't known he had missed for two years.

He quickly ran the towel over his hands and set it down for Juliska to pick up. She vanished into the kitchen and emerged almost at once with five large bowls of the same soup that Viktor had remarked on the day before. Miklós, in his turn, smiled after his first taste. The soup was thick with potatoes and onions, and strongly flavored with garlic and red pepper.

"I know what the main course is going to be," he said.

"Yes," said László.

"I don't think I have yet congratulated you and the Countess. Good luck. I'm certain everything will be—"

"Why did you return?" said Andor suddenly.

László slapped down his spoon. "Stop it," he said.

Andor said, "I want to—"

This time he was cut off by a low rumbling sound from Vilmos. He grimaced and went back to eating his soup. There was a brief silence, broken by Mariska saying, "Thank you, Prince Miklós."

Next Juliska appeared with cabbages stuffed with rice, pork, onions, tomatoes, and mushrooms, covered with a red pepper and garlic sauce and sour cream, and each wrapped in a thin slice of bacon. With this, Máté, Juliska's assistant, brought out the first wine. It was the famous "Sandwine" from the east fermented near Mariska's homeland of Mordfal. She smiled to acknowledge the compliment. Máté presented the wine to László, but he indicated that Miklós should approve it.

As was customary among the family, there was no talk during the second course or the third, which was a suckling pig roasted whole and stuffed with peppers, mushrooms, onions, and lamb—to make a transition to the fourth course. It was just before this course that the men adjusted to their second trouser buttons.

Juliska brought out another wine, this one a light wine from the north, as the chef himself, Ambrus the Fat, presented and served the potatoes. Two halves for each of them, stuffed with lamb and beef. The potatoes themselves consisted only of skins, as the rest had gone into the soup, along with the meat juices that weren't used in the sauce. Only the tiniest hint of wine could be identified in the meat.

Vilmos grunted to the chef and said, "Good."

Miklós said, "There is plenty of garlic. Thank you."

Mariska said, "It is beyond praise. This is happiness."

Andor said, "Very nice. Yes. Very nice."

László stood and bowed to the chef. Smiling, the latter retired to the kitchen. Máté served bean sprouts and green peppers with ginger and lemon peel while Juliska poured the wine, then the two servants also returned to the kitchen.

"I had forgotten what eating was like," said Miklós.

László smiled. "I told Ambrus that you had returned."

"Ah. I'm flattered."

Andor scowled into his plate. László ate in small bites, alternating with sips of wine. Miklós noticed Vilmos watching the King eat and smiling, but avoided asking what he was smiling about. Instead he said, "When is the wedding?"

"A few months," said the King.

"My father," said Mariska, "will see to the arrangements at home. He is preparing his departure now."

Miklós nodded, then said, "Laci? Would you rather not discuss the problem in my chambers while we eat?"

László tapped his knife against the table, then said, "Yes. I would rather wait. Thank you for asking."

Andor seemed about to say something, but was stopped by a look from Vilmos.

Before the salad course, everyone went to his third trouser button—except, naturally, for poor Mariska. The salad combined fruits, vegetables, and cheeses in a way that no one but Ambrus could do, and was covered with a mild vinegar made from the Rozsanemes apple that grew in the eastern River Valley. Miklós turned his attention to surviving until the honey-cakes.

*   *   *

Miklós made his way to his old chambers for the customary
after-dinner nap, remembering halfway there that these rooms
were no longer usable. He paused, then continued anyway,
feeling a desire for another look at the strange tree that grew
from the floor of his room.

He pushed aside the curtain and saw that the room was
already occupied. Brigitta, standing off to one side, was staring
intently at one of the long, narrow leaves. As Miklós entered
she turned to him, nodded, and stepped back to survey the
whole once more.

Miklós stepped closer to the tree, through the thickness of
branch and leaf, and studied the web of cracks where the trunk
emerged from the floor. He stepped out again and studied its
height—perhaps a handbreadth from the ceiling. It wasn't close
to the walls around it yet, but then, it wasn't too far from them
either. Behind him, Brigitta said, *"tsk."*

"What is it?"

"You're looking at it wrong."

"Wrong?"

"You aren't seeing what's important."

He studied her, standing half in the shadow of the tree, half
lit by the evening sun peeking through the window. "Very well.
What is important, then?"

"Look at a leaf. Do you see the way each one curves in on
itself, like a hand? Study the veins. Or, if you want to look at
the whole, look at the fresh green or the perfect symmetry of
its shape."

Miklós did these things, then said, "I still don't understand."

"It is beautiful. Can't you see that?"

Miklós felt his eyes growing wide, but he turned back and
studied it more. Beauty? It was a tree, and trees were beautiful
in their own way—certainly he had enjoyed walking through
the Wandering Forest for that reason. Yet here it was only
incongruous. He said as much.

She nodded sadly. "I thought you'd feel that way."

He leaned against a wall, then sat on his haunches. He
spoke, as much because he wanted to continue speaking with
Brigitta as for any other reason. "Can you teach me to see it
another way?"

"I don't think so. I feel it, I don't think it."

"What if I think I *should* feel differently than I *do?*"

"I don't know. Ask Bölk."

"Perhaps I will."

He watched her watching the tree.

In the winter when he had turned seventeen, his portrait had been painted, as was done for all Princes at that age. He had compared his to the one of László. What had caught his eye had been the squareness of his older brother's shoulders, as compared to the roundness of his own. His brother had seemed strong and complete, himself weak and vacuous. Yet Brigitta's shoulders were rounder even than Andor's, and they seemed right for her. The line made by her shoulders, neck, and cheekbones seemed more graceful to him than the idol in the courtyard.

He said, "I think *you* are beautiful."

She looked at him, then back at the tree. After a moment she said, "Thank you."

The silence became uncomfortable. Miklós stood up and dusted himself off.

"I think I will see Bölk then, as you suggested. Would you care to accompany me?"

"No, thank you."

He watched her a moment longer. "The tree—it fascinates you."

"Yes."

"Why?"

"As I've told you, it's beautiful."

"Yet no one else seems to think so."

"No one else has looked at it."

"Oh. Well, perhaps later then."

"Yes."

He stood up, stepped back into the corridor, and started toward the doorway. As he passed Vilmos's room, his brother called out, "Miki!"

Miklós poked his head in. Vilmos lay on his massive bed, fully clothed, with three pillows holding his head up. "Yes?" said Miklós.

"Are you up from your nap so soon?"

"I haven't taken a nap."

"Ah! Busy."

"Yes. I'm going to see my horse."

"Your horse? That you rode here? I have been hearing that it is an amazing animal."

"Yes."

Vilmos pushed himself to a sitting position on the bed. "May I see him?"

"Certainly, Vili. If you wish."

The giant got himself up, and the two of them walked out to the stables.

"You have changed," said Vilmos as they walked.

"Have I?"

"I'm not certain how. Tell me, Miki, did you really travel to Faerie?"

"Yes."

"Why?"

"I had nowhere else to go."

"Oh." And, "What happened there?"

"I found out who I am."

"Oh."

They walked a little further.

"Who are you?"

"Your brother."

"Oh. Yes."

As they walked through the courtyard, Miklós glanced briefly at the idol of the Demon Goddess. He thought about what Bölk had said about her, then shook his head. Vilmos stood beside him, saying nothing.

Just outside of the stable door they found the coachman, Miska. He lay on his back holding a bottle and snoring. As they walked past him, he said, "Prince Miklós."

The Prince stopped and looked back. It was hard to see in the dimness of the courtyard, but it seemed that Miska's eyes were open. "Yes?" said Miklós.

"That is a fine horse."

"Yes," said Miklós.

They entered the stable and quickly found Bölk in a large stall. Miklós felt a curious sense of unreality as he watched the horse. It was as if the entire stable area was part of one picture, and Bölk part of another, and the scales differed. Bölk seemed larger than his surroundings in a different way than Vilmos did; it was somehow nonphysical.

"Good evening, master," said the horse.

"Hello, Bölk. Are they treating you well?" He glanced quickly at Vilmos, who was staring at the horse with his brows knit.

"Well enough. I would prefer to be unconfined, but I can understand the need for it while you make up with your brother."

Miklós frowned. Was there the slightest hint of reproach in Bölk's voice? "If you like, I will take you outside of the gate so you can go where you wish."

"Thank you, master, but it is best if I remain with you for now."

"Very well. Tell me something: what should I do if I feel one thing, but think I ought to feel another? Which do I trust?"

"Trust your thoughts, if you are thinking correctly; trust your feelings, if your instincts are right."

"Great," said Miklós. "How do I tell which is right, if either?"

Bölk turned his head away.

"Miki?" Vilmos's voice was soft and hesitant.

"Yes?"

"Miki, is the horse . . . talking?"

"Yes, Vili."

"This is a *táltos* horse?"

"Yes."

"I had never thought they were real."

"Nor had I, Vili."

"And he is yours?"

"He chooses to stay with me for now."

"Why?"

Miklós sighed. "If I knew that, Vili, I would understand many things that I would feel much better for knowing."

Vilmos nodded, though he still looked puzzled. Bölk made no response.

"The food is adequate, Bölk?" said Miklós.

The horse laughed. "You remember how I am nourished, master. The food is minimal, but the best I can get for now."

"Oh," said Miklós.

"It's almost as if I can understand him," said Vilmos.

"Yes," said Miklós. "Me, too."

As they walked back to the Palace, Miklós said, "Laci told me that you had some problems when you went to pull up the roots from the tree that seems to be growing in my old chamber."

"Yes."

"What sort of problems?"

Vilmos sighed. "I don't know, Miki. There was something about them that—I don't know."

"Did you think they were—" Miklós hesitated. "Beautiful?"

"Beautiful? No. It wasn't that. They seemed so determined, somehow. I can't explain."

"All right. Would you be willing to try again?"

They reached the doors of the Palace and entered.

"Let me think about it."

"All right, Vili. We'll speak of this again."

Vilmos continued toward his room. Miklós hesitated, then made his way down into the cellar to see how Anya was getting along. She had always been his favorite.

It was late at night when Miklós, unable to sleep, returned to his old chamber. He set his lamp down on the floor and slowly walked around the tree.

"Tell me, tree," he said in a whisper, "why are you beautiful? How should I look at you so I can see beauty in you? Can you tell me that?"

The tree remained silent.

The Prince approached it and took a leaf into his hand. It felt like velvet, but cool, and seemed stronger than its looks indicated. He held the lamp close to the leaf and traced its veins with his eyes.

"Why did you grow in *my* room, tree? Are you tied to me, somehow? Am I to climb you, out of the Palace, until I can walk from star to star? Is that what you are, tree? A ladder to the land of the gods?"

He stepped away from it and held the lamp high, studying the top where it brushed against the ceiling. It waved to and fro, like a dancer, it suddenly seemed. Miklós had a sudden image of Brigitta, dancing. Dancing for him alone, slowly, her long face somber, her eyes holding his, fascinated. He felt himself becoming aroused and smiled self-consciously at his fantasies.

Yet, still, the swaying top of the tree held his attention with its flowing, its dancing, its beauty.

INTERLUDE

THE LEAVES BEGAN to fill out a bit, and the trunk, still hidden behind the greenery, began to thicken. The attacks made on the roots had not been as unnoticed as the attackers would have thought. Though mindless, the growing thing seemed to know that it had been threatened. Just to be safe, it responded by sending a few tentative roots out to the sides, hoping to find more soil in case the roots below should be damaged.

The body still grew, but more slowly. Now it was brushing the ceiling. Now it seemed too large for the chamber it was in.

But this would not keep it from growing.

chapter ten

The Wizard

SÁNDOR SAT IN THE great hall, stroking his beard and considering the passing of years. Sometimes he could almost imagine that he heard them, rushing by like the River as he stood motionless on an island in their midst. At other times, like now, the passing of time stopped, holding its breath, waiting to see what direction it would take.

From time to time, the forces that drove events to become history would enter the sphere of his influence. Then he could put aside the toys and games and know that, with a push here, and a tug there, *he* was guiding the fate of the kingdom.

The beginning had faded almost beyond recall. He knew that he had made the pilgrimage across the mountains, but little of that time remained to him—and even less to those who knew him. No one except Rezső now remembered that he was not native to Fenario, and it mattered not at all to the King's advisor. Sándor had been one of the chosen few to make the journey to Faerie from his village in the land to the south of Fenario. They had sent him and a few other boys and girls as they did every year, hoping that one might return in a few years and be their high priest. And so it always worked. But of the many who never made it back home, some of them didn't choose to; so it was with Sándor. He no longer remembered what he had seen when he came back over the mountain to Fenario, but he remembered how he had felt. He still felt that way. This was his home.

"You're getting old, Alfredo," he chided himself in his birth tongue. "You have things to do or at least think about."

The tree.

What was there about it? It fascinated and intrigued him, and was the first thing to do so in—no point in that! But how could it be that the power didn't hurt it? How had it come to be? He had been around too long to feel the panic that the young King felt—nothing was as urgent as youth made it seem. Still, it was a mystery; one that he, Sándor, ought to be able to solve.

The youngest Prince, Miklós, had to be behind it. Sándor was not yet so old that he was dotard, and the tree growing in the Prince's room was a Sign if there ever was one. That Miklós was a close one, too. He always seemed so honest and young, like a puppy. What was he up to, and why? He had the power of Faerie at his command; was he scheming against Sándor for his position? If so, what form would the threat take?

In Viktor there was no hope. All of Sándor's life he had seen Viktors in one form or another. If you don't like someone, kill him. If you want something, take it. If you have power, use it. So crude, so vulgar. And, ultimately, so futile. Yet his plans could not be ignored. That these schemes at usurpation came up often was no reason to be certain one would not succeed. And the schemers always thought Sándor would help them. Why was that? But he wouldn't, of course; any more than he would warn the King. These matters were in the hands of the Goddess, and he would not interfere. Still, forget Viktor in the solution of this problem.

Rezső? Nonsense! In a crisis, he'd be better off depending on Andor, and this was becoming a crisis.

No, if there was anyone to whom he'd be able to turn for aid, it was the foreign Countess, Mariska. She had at least the seeds of understanding. Contain the problem, keep it from becoming worse. Of course, that was only the beginning. And where to go from there? How to turn it to the advantage of King and kingdom?

And, above all, why did his powers not affect it?

A nearby sound startled him and he opened his eyes—surprised that he had closed them—to find that young Miklós was pulling up a chair.

"Good morning," said the wizard.

"Thank you."

"Was there something you wished to speak of with me?"

"Yes. The tree in my old room."

"Well?"

"I was told that you attacked it with the Power." Sándor heard him pronouncing the capital letter and almost smiled.

"Yes, I did," he said.

"And it had no effect?"

"None."

"Do you have any idea why?"

"Not yet. Why do you ask?"

"Huh? Because I want that thing out of my room, that's why. I'd like to move back in there. I have spoken to Vilmos, asking him to try once more. I am not certain that I was able to convince him."

Sándor studied him, but found no flaws in his playing of the role, if that was, indeed, what he was doing. Sándor said, "There will need to be many improvements to the Palace, now that the King is to be married. Certainly, we will address that one, too."

"Do you think it will wait that long, Sándor? It is growing—"

"It cannot grow larger than the room it is in."

"Can't it?"

Sándor's eyes narrowed. "You think it could actually break apart the room?"

"It might."

"Hmmm. Our future Queen suggests that we strengthen the walls around it."

Miklós considered. "That might work. But I can't believe we are helpless against it. It seems absurd."

Sándor nodded and decided to risk honesty. "I would give a great deal to be able to understand it—where it came from, why, what it really is, and why my powers are useless against it."

"Yes. As would I."

The wizard considered him. He was quick, and his mind worked well. He was willing to listen to alternatives to his own ideas and appeared to actually consider plans. He didn't go rushing into things headlong, but was willing to take his time— or was as willing as anyone his age ever could be. Of course, Sándor still didn't trust him, but that argument ran in both directions. Yes. In fact, the more he considered it, the better the idea seemed.

"There is a thing, Miklós."

"Yes?"

"I am old."

"I know."

"Do you know how old?"

"Not exactly."

"That is well. I am old. The power of which we are both initiates has allowed me to extend my lifetime. But this will not last forever."

"What are you saying, Sándor?"

"That the realm of Fenario should not be left without a wizard."

Miklós squinted at him. "Do you feel you will be . . . leaving us soon?"

"Not soon as you count it. But someday. Perhaps during László's reign, perhaps not."

"I don't know what to say."

"That is because I haven't asked you anything yet. I do so now. Will you consent to become my apprentice? To allow me to guide you further into the mysteries, so that you can take up the task after me?"

Miklós's eyes grew wide. He stared at Sándor, as if he were seeing an apparition.

"Sándor, I—"

"Well?"

"I don't know."

"That is right. You do not know. There is much you do not know. Have you ever spoken to anyone, mind to mind?"

"Eh?" Something like a memory flickered behind the young Prince's eyes, but he said, "No."

"This can be taught. The power lies within you. And more— much more than you would have learned in Faerie."

Miklós swallowed. "What is involved in this?"

"Study. Practice. Hard work. As in any apprenticeship."

"And after? What duties are there? Forgive me if asking is tactless, but—what do you do for the realm?"

"Sometimes I am called upon to study the signs and make predictions to help guide the King. Sometimes I must counter the actions of other wizards who seek to disrupt our realm.

Always, I attempt to learn more of the way the world works and to make our land safer and more prosperous. It is not a bad life."

"No," said Miklós slowly, "it isn't. I can see that."

"Well? What say you?"

"I am honored that you ask me, Sándor."

The wizard grunted.

"I'm not certain," said the Prince at last. "I need time to think about it."

"That is well." Sándor nodded. "Take as much time as you need." He closed his eyes and leaned back. Presently he heard Miklós walking away.

Later in the day Sándor found the King in the audience chamber and spoke to him of what Miklós had reported about Vilmos.

László nodded. "Perhaps I should see him again. It can do no harm."

László stood and left the room. Sándor, on impulse, followed.

The Great Hall, thought Sándor, was like a mirror that reflected the state of the Palace, and therefore the kingdom. It was empty in the morning, full in the evening, and in between ebbed and flowed unpredictably. The conversation was subdued when the King was tense, loud when the King was happy. Now it was empty save for Vilmos, who sat in his special chair before an unlit fire.

"Excuse me, Vili," said the King.

Vilmos opened one eye. "Yes?"

László sat down. Sándor sat next to him. Vilmos ignored the wizard.

"I am told that Miklós spoke to you yesterday about the roots in the cellar."

"Yes."

"Have you thought about—"

"I went to look at them again, Laci."

"And?"

Vilmos looked down. "I couldn't do it. I am sorry."

"Why? What happened?"

For a moment, Vilmos didn't speak. Then he said, "I went there and I stood in the middle, with the roots all around me. I pulled on one, and it seemed to cling to the ground."

László stared, wide-eyed. "You couldn't pull it up?"

"No, no. It wasn't that. When I was there, in the middle of it all, I felt something. I—"

"Yes?"

"Forgive me, Laci. I have trouble with the words. But there was a feeling in there, that I belonged. That I was safe. But that isn't right either. It isn't that I feel unsafe, but it was . . ." His voice trailed off. He looked at his brother as if desperate for understanding.

"But you know that it may threaten the whole Palace, don't you? The Goddess herself has said—"

"I know, Laci. I know. But I couldn't make my fingers hold them or my shoulders pull them. I tried. I tried as hard as I could, Laci. I did. I'm sorry."

László stood up, reached over, and clapped Vilmos on the shoulder. "It is all right, Vili. You tried. That is all that matters."

He left the Hall, Sándor following.

The wizard tried to fit this into his scheme of things, knowing it to be important. But it was like nothing he had experienced before.

Where Miklós was a novice in the use of the power of Faerie, Sándor had taken it fully into his life. It colored all of his thoughts, all of his deeds and actions—even those that made no direct use of it.

To use the power of Faerie, one must know and understand a harsh, unforgiving logic. The mind must be disciplined and firm, and go where the will wishes it to. This discipline is all that limits the wielder of this power, for the Source will send as much as is asked for.

But there is a cost, as in all things.

He could still recall, though less vividly than once, the first time he had taken the power, as one will take a drink; not to use, simply to hold. The memory, the experience, might fade— but it would never leave him. Its effects lingered, and the effects of holding the essence of Faerie within himself as he had done again and again had left their mark upon him, upon how he used the power, and perforce upon the kingdom.

For Sándor, the shapes and patterns of the world around him became first symbols—means of expressing his desires so they could be turned into a form he could use. A lesser man would have lost his understanding of the difference between symbol and reality then, but Sándor refused this, and forced his understanding deeper.

Then he began to see all things as expressions of his power, and that each expression must fit into the patterns his mind cast. The world became patterns of the power, and events were beads the colors of emotions that made up these patterns. A break, an error, a failing in this pattern was almost painful to him.

Yet, the world being what it is, and not what we imagine it to be, these breaks in the patterns came often.

And so, the last stage: Sándor's life was one of finding a way to look at things—a way that allowed him to fit them into a pattern he could create, control, and manipulate. No longer painful, these discontinuities were challenges to his mind.

For one who would master the power of Faerie and not be mastered by it, there is no better way to look at the world. But, as with all things, there is a cost.

Sándor paid this cost gladly.

They passed the paintings on the walls of the upper corridor, and, as always, Sándor's eye was drawn to The Hand—reaching out for him, now as if to hold him, now as if to crush him, now as if to beckon. So simple, yet so perfect. And the stagnant pond, where there should have been no life, yet the potential, as it were, was captured beneath in the gentle disturbance on the surface where a stone had been thrown an instant before the moment the artist had chosen to portray. Ahead of him, he noticed László staring at the little statue, nearly crumbling to dust before their eyes, and almost sighed to himself. Always, with the Lászlós and the Viktors, it was the violence, the action, that appealed. But there was more power in the dark, stagnant pool than László could ever imagine. They began walking again at the same moment.

As they reached the audience chamber, Sándor forced his mind back to the problem at hand. "There is more at work here than I had thought," he said.

"What do you mean?"

"I had thought that Prince Vilmos was being contrary or stubborn, and—"

"He isn't like that."

"Perhaps. But there is more to it than that. Whatever it is that prevents my powers from affecting this tree is also stopping Vilmos the only way he can be stopped—by sapping his will."

László considered this, then nodded. "I think you are right." Then, "The Northmen?"

Sándor shrugged. "How is their invasion attempt progressing?"

"It is all but over. Henrik led them over the southern border, where they met with an enemy they deserve. They are now fleeing from our land as fast as they can. Henrik is hounding them to be certain they do no damage on the way."

"In that case," said Sándor, "I don't think it is they. If a man is doing this, he must be at it almost constantly, and why continue to harass us after they have been defeated? Besides, how can they do with the power of Faerie what I cannot undo?"

"I don't know," said the King. "I know nothing of these matters. If not the Northmen, however, then who?"

"Or what," said Sándor.

"What do you mean?"

"I am not certain. But I find it hard to believe that there is anyone who can do this. To use the power in such a way as to influence a man as strongly as Vilmos has been influenced is no easy task. And to create a thing that cannot even be affected by the power is beyond my comprehension—if it is the power of Faerie that is being used."

"Go on," said the King.

"Your Majesty, there are other powers than mine in the world."

"For instance."

Sándor shrugged. "You know, do you not, that there are still witches, hiding in covens in the Wandering Forest or in the marshes to the south."

"You think a witch—"

Sándor waved it aside. "No, no. It was only an example. I can smell their puny efforts when I meet them. It is nothing like that."

"Then what?"

"I am not yet certain. I must find out. I am only saying that it would be an error to assume—"

"By the Goddess, Sándor!" exploded the King. "I am assuming nothing! I want to know what is causing this, and how we can remove it."

Sándor sighed. "Do you know of nothing that has power other than Faerie, near us, of which the legends tell strange stories?"

László said softly, "The River."

"Yes," said Sándor. "Think, Your Majesty: We have a tree

sinking its roots into soil that is saturated with water from the
River. You and I, who have studied these things, know that
many strange tales have been told of the River. I, who have
studied the power of Faerie, know that these tales do not speak
of things such as that power would do."

László shook his head. "But how——?"

"I don't know. That is why I have been reluctant to speak
of it. But I am suspicious. I don't like that River——"

The King laughed softly. Sándor glared at him. "I know, I
know," said the King, still laughing. "You don't like the River.
You have spent more than a hundred years dwelling next to it,
and you have hated it every moment. And such impotent hate,
too, Sándor. The River provides the livelihood for half of the
people of the realm, it——"

"Not that many."

"Allows us to move our goods back and forth, it feeds us,
and more. And who could stop it anyway? You?"

Sándor shook his head.

"So," the King continued, "when you see something you
don't understand, you rush to blame——"

"No, Your Majesty," said Sándor firmly. "As I have said,
I am not yet sure, but I am not rushing to blame the River for
no reason. Think about what I have said. What else could it
be? We know that there is a mysterious power associated with
the River, and we know that anything planted near the River
grows faster than anything planted elsewhere. It affects people
strangely. It——"

"Why this hatred, Sándor? I have never understood it."

The wizard stopped and considered. Oddly, he had never
even asked himself this question. It had been an instinctive
thing, as far back as he could remember. What was it?

"Have you ever spoken to a Riverman?" he said at last.

"I have spoken to my brother Miklós," said László, laughing
lightly. "He spent nearly his whole childhood there."

"Miklós knows something of it," Sándor admitted. "But a
real Riverman, such as a few of the fishermen in town, can
tell you every tiny whirlpool along it, and where you can find
how many fish of what kind. Some of them know only a small
part of it, but they know it so well they could name every
pebble in it. It seems they know each time someone throws a
stick into the water."

"Well?" said László. "What of it?"

Sándor shook his head. "I don't know. But there is a mystery there that defeats me. Some are so fascinated by the River they make it their lives. Others take it for granted. Others fall in between. A few hate it. I am one of those. I don't know why."

The King nodded.

"But," said Sándor, "this in no way affects what I am saying. It would be just as true if I loved the River as Miklós does. There is something about it that is feeding and protecting that tree. I am convinced of it."

"It is true," said László, "that the River is known for making things grow faster. Yes, what you say may be. But if so, what do we do about it? We can't stop the River."

"I know. But I also know that for every problem there is a solution. I have not yet found the solution for this problem. Rest assured, Your Majesty, I will."

The King nodded. "Very well, Sándor. But whatever the solution, it should be soon. The tree is growing at a truly alarming rate. I begin to fear for the Palace."

"I am considering it." Then, "Your Majesty?"

"Yes?"

"Have you seen Miklós's horse?"

"The *táltos* horse? No. I've been almost afraid to. I never thought there would be a *táltos* in the Palace during my lifetime. Why do you ask?"

"I think it is involved in this."

"Do you? Why?"

"Because it is there."

"Eh?"

"Consider: the tree is growing in Miklós's room. Miklós turns up with this horse. The horse is arrogant and hostile to you and all you stand for. We know little of *táltos* animals, but they could have the power to—"

"What about the River?"

Sándor shrugged. "There is no reason why both could not be involved."

László shook his head. "What you are doing, without saying it in so many words, is accusing Miklós of causing this."

Sándor said, "I am not certain that he is. But consider the possibility."

"I have considered it," said the King. "And I still am. I don't think so."

"Why not?"

"Because I saw the look on his face when he saw the tree in his room, and I heard his voice while we talked about it."

"Could you not have been fooled?"

"I could have been. I don't think I was."

Sándor nodded. "Very well, Your Majesty. Perhaps—" He paused.

"Yes?"

"Perhaps you should see this horse, after all."

László looked at him. "Very well, then. Let us go."

They stood up, and Sándor slowly led the way down to the main floor, then out toward the stables. It was late afternoon, and the sun was nearly behind the outer walls. Sándor made a sign to the idol of the Demon Goddess as he passed.

They found the horse at once. It turned to look at them and Sándor caught a malicious gleam in its eye.

"Greetings, horse," said the King. "I am László, King of Fenario."

"Greetings, doomed King," said the horse. "I am Death."

Sándor heard the sharp intake of breath from the King, but controlled his own rage.

"Why am I doomed?" asked László carefully.

The horse seemed to consider before answering. "Because you have failed."

"Failed? How?"

"Look! Your house is falling down around you! What else could that mean?"

Sándor caught a flicker of motion as the King's hand went to Állam at his side. He didn't draw it, however. He said only, "Have a care, horse, if you can be hurt."

"I can be hurt, unhappy King," said the horse. "But not by the likes of you."

Sándor could see that László's lip was now trembling with controlled rage. The King said softly, "Miklós should have not brought such an animal to our home."

The horse's ears pricked forward. "He has done nothing," said the horse. "Nor have I. I can do nothing, while I remain out here. But the instant I am in your home, beware! I will be the end of you, King. And, more particularly, of you!" This last was said to Sándor, who suddenly felt the first fear he had experienced in more than a hundred years. In an odd way, it was almost pleasing to discover an emotion he had thought lost years ago. He smiled as he touched the scar on his forehead where the horse had kicked him before.

The King said, "Sándor, can we do nothing about this animal? I will at least ask Miklós to remove it from the stables, and judge him by his answer!"

"Poor judgment," said the horse, "is the mark of a poor ruler."

László's grip on the sword tightened, but he made no answer.

"We cannot easily kill him, I think," said Sándor. "He is *táltos,* and he is tricky. I tried once before." He again touched the scar on his forehead. "But perhaps we can make it easier if we—"

He turned away and rummaged around the stable until he found a good, strong rope. Then he came back. "Here now, horse. It seems that I cannot use my powers against you directly. But try this!"

He tossed a rope end into the air, and immediately drew upon his power. Like a snake, the rope wrapped itself around the horse's right foreleg just above the knee, then its left foreleg, then attached itself to the side of the stall. Sándor tied the other end to a hitching post. He found more rope, this time tying the horse's head so it couldn't move. The horse made no effort to resist.

"There!" said Sándor. "Perhaps that will keep you out of mischief for a while."

The horse still said nothing, but Sándor had the uncomfortable feeling that it was laughing at him.

"Perhaps, Your Majesty," said Sándor, "you should now use Állam."

The King, his temper under control, said, "No. Not without first speaking to Miklós."

Sándor nodded. "As you wish."

"Let us go," said the King. "I have seen enough."

They left the stables without looking back. As they passed through the courtyard, Sándor said, "Do you agree with me, now, Your Majesty?"

"That the horse may be responsible? Yes. It is very possible. With or without Miklós's knowledge."

Once more, as they walked by the idol of the Goddess, Sándor made a sign with his right hand.

They stopped and looked at it—tall and graceful, it was white in the pure daylight, but was now turning gray in the sunset.

The King said, "Does she have something special to do with your powers?"

Sándor nodded. "She has everything to do with them."

"They come from her?"

"Not exactly. It is more that she is the personification of those powers. I ask for her guidance in their use, and her help when I need it."

"I see. Has she ever failed you?"

Sándor chuckled. "With her, it is hard to know when she has helped, and when it would have worked out anyway. I believe that is how she wants it. I can say that I have never failed when it most mattered. I am still here, after all."

The King nodded. They stood silent for a moment longer. Sándor seemed to see a glittering light in her eyes.

"I imagine you will need her help soon," said the King.

"Yes," said Sándor. "I imagine I will."

The King grunted. "Than I hope you have it—for all our sakes."

A moment later he said, "You know, do you not, that Mariska thinks we can build up the strength of the walls and contain the tree that way?"

"Yes," said Sándor. "I heard her."

"Can you use the power of Faerie for that?"

"I think so," said Sándor.

They continued on into the Palace. Sándor stopped and addressed the guard at the door. "Tell Viktor that he is to have Prince Miklós's horse watched at all times. If it does anything, we are to be notified. Furthermore, no one is to untie it. No one. Do you understand?"

The guard nodded. László and Sándor continued into the Palace proper.

"Well done," said the King.

Sándor grunted. "What will you do about the horse, Your Majesty?"

"I will speak to Miklós about it. I want it dead, or out of here." Sándor heard that his voice trembled with rage and he regretted bringing it up. Or did he?

"Let me know what he says," said Sándor.

INTERLUDE

So, YOU WISH TO KNOW of the old King, eh? János, his name was. János the Sixth. Did you know how he met Teréz, his Queen? Well, he was a lad of sixteen then, and used to take himself around the countryside visiting places, and playing his fiddle everywhere he went. One day he came across a man who was looking for a cow that had wandered off. Now, János was dressed no different than you or me, for he wasn't a King yet, you see. So the man didn't know him at all, and just complained about how his cow was missing.

"Well," says János, "we'll find your cow for you, I think," and starts playing on his fiddle. Well, he had hardly started when up comes the cow, with a calf at her side. The man thanked him, of course, and said he could have the calf, in payment, but János just laughed and walked along.

As you may guess, this story spread pretty fast. Soon, everyone was talking about it from one end of the River to the other. János found that he couldn't go anywhere without being asked to bring back a cow, or a goat, or a horse, or a pig, or even a rooster. But he didn't mind, he just walked around playing his fiddle, and every time he found a stray, the man who owned it would offer him one of its young, but he always turned it down.

Well, you probably know what happens next, but I'll tell you anyway. One day a man comes up to János and says, "Are you the János with the fiddle who has been finding strays everywhere?" And János says he is, and the man says, "Well, we haven't been able to find our daughter for a week now, and that isn't like her at all."

So János says not to worry, and he sets out looking for the daughter. Well, he travels for a while, and pretty soon he crosses over into Faerie. Right there, on the other side of the mountain, she was lying asleep, and elfs were all around her. So János looked closer, and oh! but she was a pretty. Only fourteen years old she was, lying on a bed of roses, her hair all done up in ribbons, and János fell in love on the spot.

So he went there, and asked the elfs how she came to be sleeping. The elfs said they'd done it, because she was so beautiful and they wanted to look at her. János said he wanted to take her home, but they'd have none of it, and they had swords and like that, and looked mighty angry. Well, János plays on his fiddle, and pretty soon along comes a calf, only by now it's grown into a bull. And a horse. Then a billy goat and a big hog and a rooster. Then more and more of them. All of the animals János had been offered came running when he called them, because after they'd been offered, they were really his, you see.

So they charged down out of the mountains like nothing you ever saw before, and the elfs gave out a shriek and ran off. Then János tried to wake up the girl, but he couldn't. He was trying to think of what to do when the first bull comes up to him and says, "Master, if you can play your fiddle for as long she's been asleep, she'll wake up again."

Now by this time she'd been sleeping for a hundred days, but János didn't let that stop him. He took out his fiddle and played, and played, and played. He didn't stop to eat, either, so pretty soon there was nothing left of him but bones, but he still didn't stop. And sure enough, on the hundreth day, she starts to wake up.

The János says to the bull, "You were right, but I can't let her see me like this, I'm nothing but a pile of bones because I haven't eaten in a hundred days."

The bull says, "Don't worry, master," and it gives out a bellow, and all the other animals come running up. The goats brought him cheese, the roosters brought eggs, the bulls brought wine, and they had everything you can imagine. So János gobbles it all down until he had flesh on his bones again, and just about then the girl wakes up, sees him, and falls in love right there.

So all the animals bring them home again, and János goes up to the man and says, "Here's your daughter back, but now I want to marry her."

And the man says, "Well, you've done me a good turn and I'll be in your debt as long I live, but I can't let anyone marry my daughter who can't give her a good life."

So János says, "That's pretty fair, so I should tell you I'm the eldest son of the King, and I'll be King when he dies."

"What?" says the man. "You're János the Prince? Why, your father died a hundred days ago, and the whole country has been looking for you to make you King!"

"Well, they need look no more," says János. "I will be King, and your daughter Teréz will be my Queen."

And that is just how it was. If you don't believe me, ask my father. He was right there with me, and we saw the whole thing.

chapter eleven

The Stable

MIKLÓS STOPPED IN THE small dining room and helped himself to one of the loaves of fresh bread that had been put out for the family. Not stopping even to butter it, he went out to the stables to speak to Bölk.

There was much on his mind. Not only was the tree growing in his room still a mystery, but what about Vilmos and his strange reaction to it? And, more immediate, there was Sándor's offer to him. He had been awake half the night thinking about it. Why such an offer? Should he accept? What would it mean? Certainly, it would give some direction to his life.

His feet kicked up dust in the courtyard. He saw a guard all in shining red standing straight and tall next to the entrance to the stables. Miklós motioned him away. The guard moved; Miklós stepped inside.

His gaze fell on Bölk, tied by the neck and legs. A gasp escaped his lips, and red fury filled his heart. He rushed up to the horse, crying "Bölk!"

"I am well, master. This is nothing."

"Nothing?" cried Miklós. "It will soon be nothing!"

He was looking around for a cutting implement when the guard stepped through the doorway.

"You!" called Miklós. "Lend me your sword."

The guard looked uncomfortable. "I cannot, my Prince."

"What? You cannot? Then use it yourself to cut these ropes. I will not have this horse tied up!"

"I am sorry, my Prince, but I am commanded not to let anyone undo them."

"By whom?" snapped Miklós.

"The captain gave the order, my Prince."

"Viktor? I will deal with Viktor. Now lend me your sword, quickly."

"I cannot, my Prince. The captain says the order has come from the King himself."

"Oh, has it?" said Miklós. He glanced around the stable, but was unable to find a knife. He turned back to the guard. "For the last time, I command you—give me your sword."

In answer, the guard turned away, leaned out the window, and shouted something that Miklós couldn't quite hear. Then he turned back.

"Very well," said Miklós. He allowed the Power to flow through him. He had called for the Power when startled, and he had called for it when calm. Never before had he used this extra sense, this appendage, in the fullness of rage. It came to him and filled him, until he thought he would burst with exhilaration, and he realized how much easier it would be to attack the guard directly, rather than to use subtlety and skill. He resisted the temptation; he had made his decision rationally and he knew that to change it now would indicate that his emotions had power over his intellect.

Raising his hand, he stared at the hilt of the sabre at the guard's belt. At first, it seemed that his right forefinger was joined to the hilt by a single strand, thin as a spider's web. But then the strand became a string, then a cord, then a rope. Miklós began to pull, and the sabre slid freely out of the guard's sheath.

At that instant, however, the door burst open and two more guards stood in the doorway. Miklós's concentration was broken and the sabre fell to the floor. No one moved for a moment, then the guard picked up his sword, staring wide-eyed at Miklós as he did so.

The Prince composed himself to begin again, this time to take it forcibly from the guard's hand. But Bölk spoke then, saying, "It is not necessary, master."

Miklós turned to him. "What?"

"You need not."

"Why?"

"Because," said Bölk, and he reared back. The rope holding

his head broke as if it were the thinnest twine. He reared again, the ropes holding his legs stretched, frayed, and snapped. Bölk shook his head, and rope fragments fell from him, lying on the ground like dead snakes.

"The more tightly I am bound," said Bölk, "the harder I am to contain."

The guards backed out of the stable, turning to run the last few steps. Miklós nodded.

"I think I will speak to my brother now. There is no call for him to have done this."

"Perhaps not, master. But neither is there reason for you to speak to him about it."

"Why not?"

"If for no other reason, because it was not his doing. It was the wizard."

"Sándor!"

"Yes. He took ill many of the things I said to the King, and—"

"Said to the King? What did you say to the King?"

"Things not to his liking, I think. I asked him to justify his reliance upon the Demon Goddess."

"But—very well, then. I will have a word with Sándor."

"Will you, master? What sort of word?"

"One he will not soon forget!"

"I think you plan to attack him."

Miklós hesitated. "And if I do?"

"Then I am curious, master. With what weapon?"

"I—" Miklós frowned. Then he said, "You are the one who spoke of attacking. I only said I would speak to him."

"It is foolish to speak to an enemy without a weapon to hand, master."

"Then you think I should do nothing?"

"Master, never in the long, long years of my existence have I counseled anyone to do nothing. I merely question what it is that you plan to do, and why."

"Why? Because he had no right to bind you!"

"Because I am your horse?" There was, perhaps, the least trace of irony in Bölk's voice as he said this.

Miklós snorted. "From which I am to conclude that no, you are no one's, right? In that case, why do you keep calling me master? And even if you are not mine, he doesn't know that. And don't claim that you can take care of yourself. You didn't.

If there was a reason why you didn't, you'll have to explain it to me."

Bölk was silent for a while, then he nodded. "You grow, young master. I am pleased. For now, I only say that no good will be done by a confrontation with the wizard on my behalf, and I ask you not to start one."

Miklós chewed his lower lip. "Very well."

"Good. Now, did you have a question to ask me when you came in here?"

"Heh. Many."

"Start with the first then."

"What is it that is growing in my room?"

"What does it look like?"

"A tree. What do you think it is?"

"To be honest, master, I can't manage even to guess. Tell me about it."

"It is strong, so that Viktor could not scratch it with his sword. Vilmos could not gather the will to pull its roots out. Sándor could not harm it with the power of Faerie. Brigitta thinks it is beautiful."

Bölk considered this. "Brigitta thinks it is beautiful, you say?"

"So she has told me."

"Then it is. Brigitta is not likely to be wrong about something like that. But you don't find it beautiful?"

"Two days ago I spoke to you about not feeling something, when I think I ought to."

"Ah! You think you should see beauty in it, but you don't. Is that it, master?"

"Well—"

"Yes?"

"The last time I looked at it, for a moment . . . I don't know, Bölk."

"I don't understand this thing, master. It is important, somehow, but it escapes me. I mislike this."

"It is evil, though. Isn't it? I know Brigitta thinks it beautiful, but a thing may be both evil and beautiful, may it not?"

"Yes, indeed. I wish I could see this tree for myself."

"I also wish you could. But I can see no way to arrange it."

Bölk chuckled. "I wouldn't fit through the door." And he added, "Yet."

"What do you mean?"

"Pay no mind."

"Heh. All right, then. Since I cannot think of a way to make you smaller, I will return and study it some more."

"Tell me what you learn, master."

"Heh again. More likely *you* will tell *me* what I learn."

He walked back into the courtyard, blinked in the sunlight, and looked around. Several of the guards sent unreadable glances at him, but no one seemed to be looking for him. Strange. There had been plenty of time to have alerted László or Sándor. Was there some deception here? Had it not really been they who had given the orders? Or were they unconcerned with what he did? Or were they waiting?

They were probably waiting.

He walked past the idol and looked up at it. For a moment, it almost seemed as if the Demon Goddess was glaring at him. He shook his head.

Near the gate, a coach with four white horses stood ready. He saw a figure leaning against it, and the feather in the cap indicated Miska, the coachman. Miklós approached him.

"The Countess isn't leaving, is she?" he asked.

Miska smiled ironically and shook his head. "No. The Count is returning to his home to make preparations there."

"I see. Well, does this mean I am to get no more stories?"

The coachman looked at him carefully, his weathered face serious for a moment. "I don't think you want to hear any more stories, my Prince. If your horses will bear you to the end of yours, that will be enough. But I have something for you," he added, reaching under the seat of his coach. He pulled forth a bottle of *pálinka,* and handed it down to Miklós.

"Thank you, Miska."

The other nodded. "Think of me when you drink it."

Miklós stared at him. "Fare you well then, good coachman."

Miska smiled. "Fare you well, my *garabonciás.*"

Miklós turned his back on the coach and entered the Palace. He stood for a moment just inside the door and ran his finger along a crack in the sandstone wall. The wall had been painted white, and the paint was new, but the jagged crack could not be painted over. In other spots, the sandstone had crumbled, rather than cracking, and Miklós could see depressions in the wall.

"Is there something wrong, my Prince?"

He turned, taking a moment to focus in on the guard—what was his name?—who stood at the door.

"No, nothing, Károly," he said at last. Then he added, "If Sándor or the King should be looking for me, tell them I am in my old chamber."

He watched Károly's reaction closely, but the guard only nodded. "Károly," he said then, "I am sorry about your hand." The other flushed, the color of his face nearly matching his uniform.

Just as Miklós had said, he went to his old chamber and stepped past the curtained entrance. The tree had grown again. Now it was touching three walls; only on the wall with the bed was there a little space left. And now, everywhere that it touched a wall, the leaves seemed to curl backward, as if the tree were bracing itself to push. The ceiling had certainly stopped the upward growth, yet as Miklós looked closely, he saw nothing that made him think the tree was exerting pressure.

He sat down on the floor of the chamber and stared up at the tree. He thought once again to try to see beauty in it, if for no other reason than to have more to say to Brigitta, whom he seemed unable to get out of his mind.

Yet other thoughts intruded. The change in László—could he really trust it? The wizard—what of his offer? And more than these, the strange feeling that had come to him in the stable, flooded with the power, alive in a way he had never been alive before. It had felt so strange. . . .

On impulse, he tried something he had never done before. He relaxed in his seated position against the wall, took a deep breath, and opened the Pathway just a little. The Power came to him, as slowly as he wished, but he did nothing with it. He held it inside himself, and let it build.

He felt as if he were glowing. Tiny lines seemed to run across his eyes, and he seemed to be floating. He stopped the flow from the Source and concentrated on holding the energy within himself. He discovered that his eyes were closed and he opened them.

The air around him shimmered. Were there more lines, running through the room, around the tree, through the window, to the doorway? Were they real or imaginary? He discovered that he could allow himself to see them or not, and a kind of euphoria came over him. Yes, everything was connected—he could see that now. He saw the joining of tree to floor, and

realized that it was not a *wrongness*, but a necessity. Yes.
Everything was as it was because it must be that way. The
levels of connection between himself and his world were breath-
taking. And all of it so easily controlled. Just a tap here, or a
nudge there, and—was this what Sándor was offering him?
His heart beat faster. That felt wrong so he ordered it to slow
down, and giggled when it did.

"Hello? Who is there?"

He looked up and saw Brigitta. She was wrapped in light
of the purest green, and shimmered with it. He saw that he
loved her, and the revelation was almost painful in its intensity.

She was looking at him oddly. "Are you all right?"

"Yes," he said, finding he could answer. But why did she
need to ask? Couldn't she see him as clearly as he could see
her? No, of course not. But she stood out so sharply. And he
saw that yes, she could come to love him, too. She looked
down on him with an expression of puzzlement, but why did
she try to conceal her feelings, when with each little motion
of her limbs, each crease in her forehead, each minute adjust-
ment of her position, she shouted them to him. *I trust you,
Miklós,* she was saying, *and it scares me. I don't want to love
you. It scares me more.*

Even this wasn't as surprising as the realization that she had
been saying these things to him—shouting them—ever since
she had met him by the oak. He had been blind. Why? What
did it mean? They were part of the same world, the same
universe, the same life. That was important. He had never
before realized how important it was. It was—

"Miklós, you should sleep now."

He stared into her deep, deep, brown eyes. Even as he
looked he saw her melt, and wanted to laugh with the pure joy
of it. She cared for him so much. So very, very much. But
how could he let her know?

"Sleep, Miklós."

That was the answer. She wanted him to sleep. He would
show how much he cared for her by sleeping. He closed his
eyes, and willed himself to sleep. He felt, with a bit of sadness,
the Power drain out of him, then oblivion.

"Good afternoon, Prince Miklós."

He looked around, finding himself stretched out on the floor
of his old chamber. "Good afternoon, Brigitta."

She looked at him without expression—without acknowledging the experience they had shared. "What are you doing here?"

But had they shared it? Had it been a dream? It was gone now, save for the memories. But he did have the memories, and they were real. Real. What was real? He cleared his throat and answered her question. "Looking for beauty, Brigitta. I have found it."

She smiled a little sadly and shook her head. "But you still see none in the tree, my Prince."

The tree? How could she bring up the tree at a time like—but of course, she couldn't know. He glanced at it, noticing for the first time how much it resembled the fountain outside, when that had worked. The frondlike boughs and leaves erupted from the center and almost sprayed down around it on all sides in a splash of green, brushing the floor like spray at the fountain's base. He turned back and answered her question. "Only where it reminds me of you, Princess."

She laughed a little. "Where did you learn such sweet talk, Prince Miklós? You didn't seem to know it even yesterday."

"I don't know," said Miklós. "Perhaps Bölk taught me without my knowing it. Most of what he teaches me I don't know I've learned until I use it."

She nodded. "In any case, I am not a Princess."

"You are *my* Princess."

She looked back at the tree, as if to say that it, not her, should be the object of his attention and affection.

"Brigitta," he said at length. "Don't you understand that this tree may pull the whole Palace apart if it keeps growing?"

"It hasn't done any damage yet, has it? Save a few cracks in the flooring."

"That is only a start. László—I mean, the King—tells me that the Goddess has said it would happen."

Brigitta still stared at the tree's crown where it rubbed the ceiling. "I have only been here a short time, Prince Miklós. The Palace means little to me."

"It means a great deal to me."

She looked at him suddenly. "Why?"

"Eh? I've lived here all my life."

"Yes? And? Go on."

He considered carefully. "There have been many happy times here."

"I believe that, Prince Miklós. But happy times may occur anywhere. Why is the Palace important?"

"It has sheltered us."

"Any house would have done as much."

"And therefore, any house would mean something to me. This happens to be the one I've known. And you cannot deny that there is beauty here."

Brigitta made a show of looking around the dim, plain room, with dust covering faded pictures.

Miklós flushed. "I didn't mean this room in particular."

"Then what?"

"Well, the gardens, the—"

"Those are outside."

"All right, the furnishings in the—"

"Furnishings. You could have them anywhere."

Miklós glared at her. Then he said, biting out the words, "The other day, I was noticing the shape of the archways in the Great Hall. I think they are very attractive."

Brigitta nodded. "So. The Palace means so much to you because of the archways in the Great Hall."

"There are things other than beauty, you know!" Miklós found that he was almost shouting.

"I know that very well," she said. "You are the one who said the beauty of the Palace appealed to you. But tell me, if not appearance, what makes it so important to you?"

"It has kept my family safe for a thousand years."

Brigitta remained unruffled. "Not this Palace. Other buildings on this spot, perhaps. But we are not discussing other buildings."

"All right. Four hundred years then."

She nodded. "A long time. One should respect any structure that has stood for four hundred years. Where I come from, near the Wandering Forest, there are few trees that are four hundred years old. Most of them rot before then. We are sorry when such an old tree falls, but we make no effort to prop it up. That would be foolish."

Miklós continued glaring at her. "So. We should let the Palace fall like an old tree, just so a real tree, which you happen to find appealing, can be allowed to grow. Is that it?"

"I didn't say so. I merely pointed out—"

"I know you didn't say. You've been picking holes in what I say without giving anything in answer."

Brigitta frowned. "Yes, I suppose I have. I'm sorry."

"Heh," said Miklós.

Her lips were suddenly pressed tightly together. Miklós involuntarily took a step backward. "Very well, then," she snapped. "What if I say that this tree isn't a threat to the Palace, it is salvation to those who live here? What then?"

Miklós stared. "You can't be serious."

"I am quite serious, my Prince."

"Stop calling me that!"

This time it was Brigitta who took a step backward. "I'm sorry. I . . . what should I call you?"

"How about Miklós? That is my name. If you feel about me as I feel about you, you might even call me Miki."

"How is it you—? No, don't answer. Very well—Miklós."

He cursed under his breath. *You've ruined it now, idiot!* Then he said, in a calmer voice. "All right, Brigitta. Can you tell me how, in the name of the Demon Goddess, the tree is our salvation?"

In an instant, the expression on her face changed. For the first time since Miklós had known her, Brigitta looked miserable. She seemed close to tears. He had a great urge to take her in his arms, but he somehow knew that she wouldn't want him to. Very softly, she said, "No, Miki. I don't know how I know. I'm just sure of it. I wish by all the ancient gods of our ancestors that I *did* know. I've been certain of it since I saw it. I think Vilmos feels the same way. But he doesn't know why either."

Miklós slumped against the back wall. "By the River from Faerie," he said softly.

"Perhaps," she said hesitantly, "we should speak to Bölk."

Miklós nodded. "Yes. But not now. I want to think about this."

He went over and sat on his bed, fighting his way past part of the tree's leaf wall. It was the first time he had touched the bed in more than two years, and it felt surprisingly soft, almost too soft. He leaned against the wall and crossed his legs. Brigitta, in her turn, leaned against the wall where she stood, shutting her eyes.

Miklós cleared his throat. She opened her eyes, looking at him bleakly.

"What else do you know?" he asked. She shook her head. "Do you have any idea of what this tree—" he gestured at it with his head "—is going to save us from?"

"Not—not really," she said softly.

"What does that mean?"

"Since I saw that tree, I've been having nightmares."

"Nightmares? And you still think the tree is somehow good?"

"Please, Miki. In the dreams, I see a face. Always the same face. It isn't anyone I know. Sometimes she is angry, and I'm frightened of her. Sometimes she is laughing at me. Sometimes she just watches me."

Miklós nodded. "Go on."

"I—I think she is the Demon Goddess."

He nodded again. Somehow, he had almost known what she would say. He remembered Bölk, on the Riverbank near the old oak; "You must defeat her," he had said.

"Bölk agrees with you," Miklós told Brigitta.

"What?" She was suddenly alert.

"Bölk has said that I must defeat the Demon Goddess. I don't know what he means. I guess I thought—no, hoped— that he was speaking metaphorically. It seems he wasn't."

She shook her head. "I have never thought of her as anyone to be defeated, or, well, as anything. I've never heard of her actually manifesting herself, except in tales as old as the mountains."

"There are László's dreams."

"Anyone can have dreams."

"Sent by the Goddess?"

"How do you know?"

"I guess—you're right, I don't. But it's been accepted in our family for so long that the Goddess speaks to us in dreams, that—I don't know."

"I've seen that," said Brigitta. "You—that is, your family— prays to the Goddess, asks her for things as if she might give them. Outside of the Palace, it isn't that way at all. Most people seem not to really believe in her—or, at least, she has no part in their lives."

"I know."

"Why is it different here?"

"Because of our traditions that she is the guardian of the family and of the kingdom."

"But why do you believe that?"

Miklós shook his head. "There is so much. Growing up with the belief, I suppose. And the dreams. I—I don't know.

I can't accept the possibility that she isn't real."

"And yet, you are to defeat her?"

Miklós said, "I wouldn't know how to even begin. The idea isn't frightening, Brigitta, it's absurd."

"Yes. But Bölk——"

"I know, I know." He looked at the tree once more. It was daylight outside and a clear day. The tree shimmered with green.

Miklós said, "I found Bölk tied up when I went out to see him this morning. And guarded."

Brigitta gasped. "Tied up? Who did it?"

"László and Sándor."

"Why?"

"It seems Bölk said something about the Demon Goddess. Neither of them would like that. The guards tried to stop me from helping him. When they failed, I am certain they must have alerted László and Sándor, but neither have spoken to me about it."

"Did you free him?"

"I tried. But before I could, he freed himself. Isn't that odd? If he could have freed himself any time, why did he wait?"

"To show you something?"

"Undoubtedly. But what?"

"I don't know. Did you talk about the tree?"

"Yes. Bölk doesn't know what it is, either. He certainly seems intrigued by it, though."

"Humph. Intrigued. That is a great help." She smiled. He grinned with her. She continued, "Bölk always knows more than he tells, doesn't he?"

"You speak as if I know him. I don't really. But no, I don't think what you say is right. I think he tells us everything he knows as clearly as he can, and sometimes we just can't understand him. Whether that is our fault or his doesn't much matter."

"All right," said Brigitta. "But what do we *do?*"

"I don't know. I'll ask you another one, though."

"Yes?"

Miklós told her of Sándor's offer to him. Her eyes grew wide. "Miklós," she said when he had finished, "you must refuse."

"Why?"

"I don't know. But you must."

He studied her, standing near the window, hidden from the

neck down by foliage. Her eyes were almost burning, and for a moment he had the sick fear that she was developing brain fever. He turned his head and said in a whisper, "What is happening to us?"

She came over and sat next to him, putting a hand on his. "I don't know, Miklós."

He looked into her eyes, and his earlier experiences came rushing back to him. Before he could stop himself, he brought her hand up to his lips and kissed it. "Come with me," said someone speaking with his voice, his lips, his heart. He stood up. She followed him out of the room and down into the cellars. He led her past the dangling roots, now as thick as his wrist, and to the door he had made years and years ago, that led out to the Riverbank.

Trembling, and with his heart throbbing, Miklós led her to a place hidden by reeds and rushes. He said, in a voice barely above a whisper, "You are the only one I've ever shown this place to."

She nodded and looked around, and seemed to understand. They moved in among the rushes and out of the sun. Brigitta removed her cloak and spread it on the ground, then stood motionless as Miklós undid the clasps of her garments, letting them fall as they would. Naked, she stood before him. Miklós thought his heart would break, and he nearly wept as he gazed upon her. He moaned softly and came to her.

She made gentle sounds into his ear as she helped him to remove his garments, then they lay together on her cloak. Slowly, she taught him the games of love, and he taught her of an innocence she had never known.

The reeds swayed above them, but there was no wind to stir them.

INTERLUDE

ENCLOSED NOW ON ALL SIDES, it found that it had grown up in a cage. It gently tested the boundaries, and considered.

The roots dug deeper, finding wet, fertile soil in abundance. The leaves soaked up sunlight from the window and moisture from the River. The base of the stem grew thick, as a jumper preparing to leap.

Yet, *still* nothing had happened.

There was, around it, a growing sense of expectation, of readiness, that was becoming almost frustration. It could not tell that powers had been used, spells cast, and the walls built up against it. It would not have cared if it knew. It awaited a signal, a sign, the waving of a flag, before it would pit its still untried strength against a structure built by man.

And this, in itself, was yet another danger—for strength that is left unused can turn upon itself, and the urge for growth that is confined can become cancerous, and stagnant air breeds rot and decay.

Helpless in its majestic strength, it waited, as it must, unable to break out of its shell. Waiting, with the patience of history, for the single, not-quite-inevitable crack.

chapter twelve

The Cellar

I WILL BE QUEEN!

She sat in her chamber and demanded of herself an end to
the melancholy that gripped her. She clutched her fan tighter
and stared down at it, hating the urge to weep that came upon
her, even now, years later. It couldn't last. It couldn't.

I will be Queen!

But even this couldn't end the spell. She would just have
to wait for it to run its course. They were becoming less frequent
now, at least. . . .

She looked at the fan: petal-shaped, of white lace with tiny
wires running through it to hold it firm, made for the blistering,
breezeless midsummer of the Grimtail Fissure. *He is gone,* she
told herself. *Forget him. You saw him die, at your very feet.*
She shuddered and clutched herself, trying in vain to exorcise
the image. She had received the last smile from his lips and
the fan from his hand.

I was a child! she cried out silently. *I didn't know what I
was doing!* Nothing answered her. She stared at the fan once
more, closed her eyes, and waited for it to pass.

After a time she repaired to the dressing table and did what
was needful to her face. She stood, wrapped her arms about
her waist, and breathed deeply. Then she passed through the
curtain of her chamber and into the hallway to face the world
again. It was nearly time to dine.

She entered the Great Hall on her way to the informal dining room. She was struck at once by the silence there; the Hall filled with people not speaking. Her eyes were drawn to one corner where László, Sándor, and Miklós stood. Even from as far away as she was, she could see that wizard and King were glaring at the Prince, and the Prince was glaring back.

As she walked toward them, Andor approached and said, "Perhaps you shouldn't disturb—"

She brushed him off. Vilmos and Viktor stood side by side, a little way off. In a whisper, she said, "What is it, Vilmos?" He shook his head, which could mean anything. She went over to the trio, then, and László turned to her.

"Perhaps later," he said. "This isn't—"

"What is the problem?"

"Perhaps later," he repeated.

Miklós turned his bright, warm eyes to her speculatively. "Have you met my horse?" he asked.

"Miklós," said László in a warning tone.

Something deeply buried in Mariska wanted her to encourage these two in their conflict, but she was aware of that side of herself and stepped on it firmly. *I will be Queen!*

She nodded. "Very well." She made motions to Andor and Vilmos, then led them into the dining room. She glanced back at László. The look he gave her combined gratitude with pride. She could ask for no better.

She instructed the manservant—what was his name? Máté— to bring them a light wine. As it was being poured, she looked around for something to talk about, but Andor started in.

"You know," he said, "what they are speaking about?"

"No. But I am certain I will be told later. Do you like the wine?"

"Huh? Oh, it's fine."

She glanced at Vilmos, who was grinning. He drained his glass and poured himself another before Máté could do it for him.

"Are the repairs to the Palace going well, Vilmos?" She asked. "I am told that you are undertaking many of them yourself."

He grunted. "All right."

"I think it very important," she continued. "It isn't just its appearance, you know. I think there are parts of the Palace that aren't sound. We must strengthen and repair them. Don't you think?"

Vilmos grunted again. "I've been doing that all my life," he said.

"Yes, I know. László has spoken highly of your skill."

"That isn't what he should be doing," said Andor, glaring at the giant.

Mariska kept her voice pleasant and conversational. "Oh? Why is that, Andor?"

"The Goddess has spoken to László of the danger to the Palace, and she meant that tree that is growing in Miklós's room. Vilmos could tear its roots out, but he won't."

Mariska smiled. "Well, I am certain that he has good reason not to. Now—"

"Nonsense!" said Andor. "He just won't do it. He says he can't do it."

"Well, Andor, if he can't, then—"

"It isn't lack of strength, it is lack of dedication. He has fought the Goddess all his life. Because he is strong, he feels he needs nothing but strength. He—"

"I am quite certain that, whatever his reasons, they are good ones. Máté, may I have—thank you."

"But the tree is—"

"Have you considered, Andor, that if the walls and ceilings of that room were made strong enough, the tree would not be able to go through them. Then it would die on its own. Sándor has been putting forth his power to strengthen the walls—"

There was a snort from Vilmos. Mariska considered, then chose to ignore it. "—and if Vilmos will lend his help to the workmen we are hiring, I am certain this will solve the problem."

Andor stared into his wine. "What does László say to this?"

Mariska shifted uncomfortably but decided on the truth. "He isn't certain about it. He has, however, had Sándor put forth his powers. That means he thinks it at least worth the attempt."

Andor fell silent. Vilmos poured the rest of the bottle into his glass. Máté left to bring another.

"Well, Vilmos?" said Mariska.

"Well what?"

"Will you help?"

"Of course," he said moodily. "I've already agreed to. I've begun. Today I put support beams in the corners of Miklós's room. Tomorrow I will help the workmen who are connecting beams along them, to prop up the ceiling. Then I'll—"

"I'm sorry," said Mariska. "I hadn't known that you had begun."

He grunted. Then he said, "What about my norska?"

Puzzled, Mariska said, "What about them?"

"László said that after you are married, you may not want norska in the Palace."

Still more puzzled, she said, "When did he say that?"

"I don't know. A while ago."

"But Vilmos, you know I love your norska."

Andor sniffed."Norska! Is that all you can think about?"

Vilmos looked at him and blinked twice. "What else is there?"

"What else? The Palace! The kingdom! The Goddess! All of us are—"

"Brother," said Vilmos softly, "I begin to tire of this."

Andor quickly looked to Mariska for support, though he must have known he would get none. Mariska met his eyes but said nothing. He slapped his hands on the table and stood up.

"Máté," he called. "I will eat in the Great Hall this evening."

"Yes, my Prince," said the servant.

Andor left without another word.

"I am sorry," said Vilmos after a moment."I became angry. I should apologize to him."

"As you think best," said Mariska. "but *I* wouldn't."

"No," said Vilmos thoughtfully. "You wouldn't, would you?"

Before Mariska could ask him what he meant by that, or even decide if she wanted to, László and Miklós entered the room. They took their normal seats in silence. László stared at his plate. Miklós was tight-lipped and almost glaring.

Juliska appeared at that moment to clear away Andor's plate. László said, "What happened?"

"Andor wishes to eat in the Great Hall this evening."

"Yes. I saw him return there and seat himself. Why?"

Vilmos spoke up before she could. "I offended him. I am sorry. I will apologize to him after dinner."

László made no answer, and the look he gave Vilmos was unreadable.

The soup Juliska brought out then was Ambrus's famous

sheep soup, thick with meat, eggs, vegetables, and smoked bacon. Mariska was glad she had not seen it being dished out, for László had told her that Ambrus's secret was to leave the sheep's head in the soup pot while it cooked, and she didn't think the sight would have helped her eat. It was also spicier than she was yet used to, but she had made up her mind to acquire the taste for food as her new family liked it, rather than trying to use her influence to have it prepared more mildly. She promised herself, however, that she would have her father's chef send her recipes for *palacsinták*. No one made them like Hanna.

She looked up from her soup and found László looking at her, as if trying to read her face. She gave him a quick smile and, suddenly nervous, returned to her food.

László cleared his throat and said, "What have you been talking about?"

"The Palace, of course," said Mariska.

"Ah. Of course."

"I asked Vilmos to help with some of the work, but he said that he had already agreed—and begun, in fact."

"Yes," said László. "I should have told you."

"It's all right," she said. The artificiality of the conversation made her uncomfortable, and it was building. But it was not for nothing that she was the daughter of a Count—and a Countess. The best thing about being Queen, she had written to her father, was that she would no longer be called Countess. That title was her mother's, and would always be her mother's. Mariska could see her clearly, though she had been only a child when "the Goddess had called her."

Miklós interrupted her thoughts. "Tell me," he said, fixing those oddly compelling eyes on her, "when you first looked at the tree . . ."

"I remember," she said carefully. She shot a quick glance at László and saw that the muscles of his neck were tense as he watched Miklós. She had the sudden urge to rub them and smiled to herself.

"You said something to Brigitta," Miklós continued. "Something about the tree serving no purpose. What did you mean?"

Mariska took more soup to give herself time to think. Had she really said that? How foolish. She must have been distracted. She cursed to herself, but was careful not to let any of it show.

"Are you certain that is what I said?"

"Something like that."

No, the tree wasn't necessary. The changes she required around the Palace could have been brought about without it. But how could she explain that? They would see her as manipulative, or worse.

"I can't imagine what I might have been thinking about," she said. "The soup is excellent, isn't it?" This last was addressed to László, so she could see how he was reacting. Poor László. He was, for the most part, a fine King, but he could never keep what he was thinking about from jumping up off his face. None of these people could. It must be a family trait. Now, she could see that he was bothered by Miklós's question. Well, no doubt, being who he was, he would ask her about it later. She must have an answer ready by then.

Miklós was still looking at her, frowning, but he finally turned his attention to his soup. Another thing about this family; with the exception of Andor, they were all patient men. Miklós wouldn't forget either, nor would he be as easily satisfied as László.

The King said, "So, Mariska, you still think we can solve the problem of the tree by strengthening the walls around it, eh?"

She nodded. "Yes. And more, I think that is the *only* solution. I, like the rest of you, would like to learn what is causing this, but we can see that every other action is closed to us. It may be difficult—this is an old building, and to strengthen it will be a difficult choice, but there is nothing else we can do."

"Viktor doesn't agree with you, you know."

"I know Viktor," she said tightly. The force of her feelings about the captain accidentally slipped out in her tone of voice. László looked at her sharply.

"What do you mean?"

Over the mountain with it, then. "He considers you a fool, László. Have an eye on him. Not everything he thinks is mirrored in his face. He controls the Palace Guards. More, he is a closer friend with Henrik than you know."

László put his spoon down. "What are you saying?"

"I don't trust him," she said. Now that she had begun, there was no going back. "I have seen how he looks at you when you aren't watching, and Henrik controls the army."

László glared at her. "What does this have to do with anything?"

"It means that he may very well be plotting something against
you."

"'May very well' doesn't mean much. Have you any proof
of these charges?"

Mariska shook her head, frustration beginning to build
in her. "I am not making charges, László. I am warning
you—"

That was as far as she got. There came a deep, booming
rumble that seemed to come from below their feet. It lasted
for the space of half a dozen heartbeats, and seemed to be only
sound, yet Mariska noticed ripples in the wine in her glass.
She found herself gripping the edge of the table for no reason
that she could discern.

Far below them tiny stresses and gradual weakenings that had
been building up for years finally had an effect. A support
wedge, compressed and pulled by the weight of sandstone
blocks, moved slightly away from the wall against which it
stood. A sandstone block, worn away by nothing more than
the passing of gentle air currents, shifted. The shift changed a
balance that had held precariously for more than ten years, and
the entire wedge, one of six supporting that block, ripped and
fell. The block of sandstone tried to redistribute its weight onto
the remaining five. Two of these were nearly as weak as the
first had been; they lasted for no more than the drawing of a
breath.

It is unlikely that the three remaining wedges could have
held the block, but it doesn't matter. The distribution of weight
was now hopelessly wrong, and the block, almost sighing, gave
up, cracked, and fell. Floor tiles, supported by wedge and
block, caved in and collapsed. Hundreds of pounds of material
landed in the cellar, breaking a stairway and scattering more
sandstone. Wood and tiling and sandstone lay at the bottom,
choking in dust created by their own destruction.

On the other side of the cellar, more sandstone was supported
by more wedges. These tried to absorb the additional weight—
and succeeded. They didn't like it, and anyone listening would
have heard them complain loudly, but, for the moment, they
held.

*   *   *

When there was silence once more, Mariska found she had been holding her breath and exhaled. They all looked at each other and around the room.

László broke the silence first. "What was that?" he asked in a whisper. No one answered him.

"I'll go look," said Vilmos, starting to rise.

"I'll go with you," said Miklós.

László said, "No, wait. We will be told soon enough, and I want all of you near me. If we are under attack I don't want to have to send someone looking for you."

"But we need to find out what it is," said Miklós.

"Everyone knows where I am," said László. "Someone will—ah!"

This ejaculation was caused by Viktor's appearance at the doorway. The captain made a brief bow to the King.

"Out with it," snapped László.

"Your Majesty, there has been an accident."

"Accident?"

"A section of the floor, near the main doors, has collapsed."

László squeezed his eyes closed for a moment, then opened them. "Was anyone hurt?"

"No, Your Majesty. That is, no one was hurt seriously. Károly—the door guard—twisted his ankle getting away."

"Very well." He was silent for a moment. To Mariska, it seemed that he was aging before her eyes. "Have it cleaned up. And rig a plank or something so we can get in and out."

"Yes, Your Majesty."

When Viktor had left, László turned to Vilmos. "See about helping them."

Vilmos nodded. He started to rise, then froze, half in and half out of his chair. His eyes grew wide, and it seemed to Mariska that he grew pale. Then, with a speed that astounded her, he was through the doorway.

László said, "What was that about?"

Even as he spoke, it came to her. She glanced at Miklós, and saw that he, too, realized what had happened. She said, "The floor in front of the main door."

Miklós nodded. "The norska."

Mariska and Miklós rose as one and headed for the door.

"Miklós!"

They both turned. "Yes, László?" said the Prince.

"Stay with me. I'll want your advice."

He glanced at Mariska. She read his indecision, then saw him suddenly yield. He turned and nodded to László. Mariska continued up through the Great Hall. Andor was on his feet, looking around almost desperately.

"Mariska, wait a moment," he said.

She shook her head and kept walking. A moment later she heard his footsteps behind her. She ignored him, hurrying to the stairway and down to the main floor. She came near the entrance and saw a ring of guards and servants around it.

She repressed a desire to push them aside. Even now, she thought, I must maintain my role. Especially now. She gently cleared her throat and allowed a servant to see her, look startled, and cry, "Make way!"

By this time Andor had caught up and was at her elbow. A path was cleared for her, and she walked up to the edge of a hole in the floor, perhaps twenty feet by fifteen. She looked to the side, and saw that part of the hallway containing the stairway down to the cellar was gone, too, leaving two wooden beams hanging limply from the ceiling and swaying gently. The air was alive with dust motes, shimmering where the light came through the partially opened door to the courtyard. The stairway to the cellar had apparently collapsed too. The effect of it all made it seem to her like an open wound in the Palace, already festering around the edges with bits of broken floor tile. Yet perhaps the most dreadful part of it was how even and rectangular the hole appeared, despite the jagged edges.

Someone said, "Careful, my lady." She ignored him and looked down, but saw only a pile of broken sandstone. At that point, she heard a cry, and knew that it was Vilmos's voice.

She turned to the guard nearest her. "Help me down," she said.

"Mariska," said Andor, "I'm sure it is nothing but the norska. There is no need—"

She turned to him. "Keep still." He jumped as if stung, and opened his mouth to retort, but no words came out. She looked at the servant she had spoken to. He hadn't moved. She read the consternation on his face and interpreted it.

"It is not necessary," she said, "that you find a dignified manner to help me down. It is not a dignified request. Just do as I say. At once."

Someone muttered something about a rope ladder, and the servant rushed off. He returned a moment later with the ropes bundled under his arm. He and several others held on to one end as the other was lowered into the hole. She gingerly stepped onto this, wincing as her skin struck the edge of the pit. She used one hand to hold onto the rope, the other to keep her gown close around her legs. They slowly lowered her onto the pile of rubble.

The cellar was brighter than usual, due to the light from the torches on the main floor that appeared as a wide sunbeam. She stepped carefully off the rubble and raised her eyes. Vilmos was directly before her, a norska cradled in his arms. He was stroking its fur. The twin lines of tears running down his cheeks told a story for which no words were necessary.

She hesitantly approached him. "Who is it?"

"Bátya," he said softly. His voice choked, and he began crying with great, gasping sobs that tore her heart like a jagged knife. She looked around quickly for the others, and saw that Atya and Anya were still in their cages, staring intently at Vilmos, their noses quivering as if they smelt death and didn't understand what it was. The other cage had clearly been directly under something. One end was smashed, and there were jagged pieces of it sticking both inward and outward. There were no norska in the cage.

She turned back to Vilmos to ask him where the others were, but saw that Húga was at his feet, sometimes standing on her hind legs, her ears working quickly back and forth. A moment more of looking showed Csecsemő. She was lying on her side a few steps from Vilmos, looking around wildly and breathing very quickly. Her flank was covered with blood. She went over to her.

"Leave her alone," said Vilmos, without looking up.

She ignored him and knelt down next to the norska. Setting her fan next to her, she very carefully stroked the fur on the side of Csecsemő's neck, then ran her hand down her side. When she reached her flank, the norska jumped and reached around with her fangs. Mariska barely got her hand out of the way in time.

Mariska firmly placed one hand around the norska's ears to hold her head in place, then carefully lifted her hindquarters. This didn't seem to bother her. She set her down again. Still holding her ears, she parted the fur above the flank and saw a gash there, with a piece of bone showing through. She started to gag, but closed her eyes before actually doing so. She took three deep breaths, then opened her eyes again. She forced herself to examine Csecsemő completely, despite the norska's jumping in her hands and piteous cries.

She carefully set the norska down and searched the floor until she found a splinter of wood.

"What are you doing?" said Vilmos.

"Lend me your knife."

"Why?"

"Please."

He handed it over, but stepped between her and Csecsemő, watching her suspiciously. She cut off a small piece of the rope ladder that still hung from the ceiling, then broke it into several strands. She brought two of the strands and the splinter of wood over to Csecsemő, and knelt down next to her.

"What are you doing?" repeated Vilmos.

"Hold her," she said.

He set Bátya's body down, very carefully and, perhaps, reverently. His hands trembled. Húga came over, sniffed the other norska, and began chittering. Vilmos took Csecsemő's ears with one hand and put the other hand under the norska's stomach. Mariska took hold of the bottom of the injured foot and pulled. Csecsemő chittered in what was plainly an agonized scream as Mariska tried to align the bones. In a moment, the baby norska's screams were drowned out by Vilmos's sobs. In another moment, she was nearly blinded by her own tears.

It seemed to take hours.

When they were done, Vilmos sat in the rubble holding Csecsemő in his arm. With his other arm he held Mariska, who clutched him with both hands, her face buried in his shoulder.

Night had fallen by the time Vilmos helped her back out of the cellar, holding Bátya's body in one hand. They didn't speak. Vilmos left the Palace to bury the norska while Mariska remained within. A pair of boards had been stretched across the hole in the floor to the doors of the Palace.

She tried to decide if she needed companionship or solitude. The thought came to her that if she were in company with others, she must hold to her role as future Queen. She started. Hold to her role? She glanced down into the cellar. The idea seemed ludicrous.

She was still standing there when Miklós came in through the doors. His face was covered with sweat. As he walked across the boards, it seemed to Mariska that he was near tears.

"I've seen Vili," he said. "Thank you for helping him. I wish——" He stopped and shook his head.

She squeezed his shoulder. He continued around the corner of the hall toward the room he was sleeping in. Mariska pushed down a compulsion to follow him. He was handling his own grief. Perhaps it was only grief on Vilmos's behalf, perhaps there was more to it, but it wasn't her place to intrude. She leaned against the wall and allowed herself two deep breaths, then began the long walk back up to the Great Hall.

Rezső and Sándor were deep in discussion in one corner, Viktor napped in another. Mariska found a third. She carefully seated herself and nodded to a servant. "Brandy," she said.

When the liquor arrived, she forced herself to sip it, suddenly hating the mannerisms she had adopted over the years. She wished for nothing more than to toss the drink down her throat like Vilmos did, but it was less effort to do as she'd always done.

Rezső and Sándor came and sat next to her.

"Yes?"

Rezső said, "How is Vilmos?"

She studied him. Rezső always struck her as more careful than anything else. He knew a lot more then he ever let on. He was an observer, and, when he acted, it was through others. She said, "He'll live. It was quite a blow to him, of course. I did what I could."

Sándor nodded. "Then he'll be up to helping us tomorrow?"

Mariska stared at him. Had he no idea what this meant to Vilmos? No, he probably didn't. How could he? She turned away and didn't answer.

"Is something wrong, Countess?" asked the wizard.

She wanted to say, "Just go away," but she couldn't. Anything else would have been wrong, so she said nothing. She heard Rezső whisper something to him. The King's advisor said, "Perhaps later, Countess," and they walked away.

Goddess, what is wrong with these people? Andor entered the room from the other side. Mariska stood up quickly, knowing that, above all else, she did not want to speak to him just then.

She left the room quickly by the nearest exit, and only after walking through the doorway did she realize that this way led up to the King's Tower. She stopped, not wanting to go where she wasn't wanted, yet unwilling to expose herself to what Andor might—no, *would* do to her. After a moment, she continued up the stair. It was only lit with one lamp, and this did little to illuminate the stairway. But she could see that the walls were dirty and, like the rest of the walls in the Palace, cracked in some places and crumbling in others. She shuddered. The stairway was long, the steps high, and the walls were so close together that her shoulders brushed against both side as she climbed.

The stairs ended in an actual door, like the main entrance, with leather hinges. She knocked softly. The wood of the door felt thick and heavy; the dullness of the knock seemed not to penetrate. She knocked harder, but still had the feeling that the door defeated her efforts to be heard.

At last she lifted the latch and pushed it part way open. She called, "László? It is I, Mariska. Are you there?" She looked through, but couldn't see anything. There was a very faint luminescence coming from just out of sight. She stuck her head through the doorway.

László lay on the floor, naked, spread-eagled. Hanging in the air above him there seemed to be a gently glowing ball. As she looked closer, she thought she could almost see a face in it. She continued staring, and the features became clearer. She knew the stories that were told of the Kings of Fenario, and László spoke of these same stories as if they were everyday occurrences. The face could only be that of the Demon Goddess.

Then something inside of her stirred, and she suddenly knew that she must not look at that face. She tightly shut her eyes and closed the door. She found that she was trembling as she leaned against the wall.

She made her halting, stumbling way back down the stairway, grateful for the close walls which kept her from falling. She stopped just inside the door to the Great Hall and caught her breath. *I need a bath*, she thought, and almost laughed at herself for it.

She stepped out into the Hall and found Viktor staring at her. His eyes traveled past her to the doorway she had emerged from; then he raised an eyebrow. She turned away. In the center of the room, Andor was speaking to Sándor in hushed tones. The wizard seemed bored; Andor seemed excited. She tried to make it to the doorway that would lead to her rooms, but Viktor caught up to her.

"Countess," he said, "I see that you have been——"

"Have you seen Vilmos?" she cut him off.

"No. He isn't in the King's Tower, however. No one goes there except——"

"Very well. I'll look for him elsewhere."

"That is fine. I wish to know, however——"

"You know what happened to one of his norska, don't you?"

He brushed it off. "Yes, yes. You cannot blame the Palace for that. I still wish——"

"Blame the Palace?" She caught her breath. "What an interesting thought. It hadn't occurred to me to do so. Excuse me."

She turned on her heel and left him. As soon as she was past the doorway, she began walking faster, almost running. She nearly tripped on the stairway. In the hall, she saw Brigitta walking in a direction that could only lead toward Miklós's room. Mariska nodded and would have passed her by, but László's whore stopped and said, "Wait a moment."

Mariska halted, trembling, and said, "Yes?"

"Vilmos is in his room. Perhaps you should speak to him."

The Countess blinked. "Yes," she said at last. "Thank you."

Brigitta nodded and walked by her. Mariska found Vilmos's room and stopped outside of it.

"Vilmos?"

"Yes?" came the voice from the other side of the curtain.

"May I come in?"

"Yes."

She found him lying on his side, staring at the far wall. Vilmos's room was completely bare, save for one dresser and the bed. It seemed more a common laborer's room than that of a Prince of the Blood. He didn't look at her. At first, she thought that his face showed sorrow, but then she realized that he was glaring, as if he were afraid to move lest he flare up into a rage that would destroy everyone around him.

"What is it, Vilmos?"

He sat up suddenly. Usually, when Vilmos would change position, it seemed to be an effort to make his tremendous girth behave the orders of his will. This time, however, his motion was quick and fluid. The difference took Mariska's breath away, as if she were seeing a different person. She found that she was frightened; yet it was a different kind of fear than what she had felt in the King's tower.

Vilmos looked at her, not saying anything. "What is it?" she repeated. He shook his head. He was still glaring, and he was looking at her, but the anger seemed directed elsewhere.

"Has . . . anyone spoken to you?"

He nodded. "Sándor."

"What did he say?"

"He blamed it on the tree that is growing in Miklós's room."

"What? But that is impossible. It didn't happen anywhere near Miklós's room."

He nodded.

She sat down next to him. "You are angry, but you don't know who or what to be angry at. Is that it?"

He nodded.

She said, "I'm sorry. I know it doesn't help, but I'm sorry. I wish there were something I could do."

He didn't respond. After a moment, she stood and went to the doorway. She paused. "Must you blame someone?"

He nodded.

"I'm sorry," she said.

INTERLUDE

WHEN I WAS A LAD I took service with a peasant who lived in the north part of Bajföld County, near the village of Készpeńz. The first thing he told me to do was to find water for his fields. Well, I went walking north. I walked and walked until I came to the biggest lake I'd ever seen. I tasted the water and it tasted like salt, so I knew that would never do.

So I walked back until I came into the mountains. There was a dragon there, and a nasty-looking one at that. I sang the dragon to sleep so I wouldn't have to worry about it. Then I saw a big hole in the ground, with a willow standing over it. I kicked the willow until it woke up, and it kicked me back. It hurt so much I started crying. The tree was ashamed of itself, so it started crying, too.

Well, that tree cried so much, it filled up the hole with water. I tasted the water and there was no salt in it. Then I picked up the dragon (I was strong in those days) and used its head to plow a big gap in the side of the hole so the water could get out. I plowed and I plowed until I came to the fields of the peasant I worked for. But by then I couldn't stop. I just kept going until I came to the far mountains, and I plowed right through them.

Of course, the dragon was pretty angry by then, and I was starting to have some trouble with him. So I went over to the Demon Goddess's house and said, "Here, you can have this."

She thanked me, and I went back home. Well, the peasant

was happy with me all right, because now he had water for his fields, so he gave me all the grain I could carry, and he also gave me a pair of cows, so I could have milk with my grain.

And that is how the River first got started. It is the truth, too. Ask anyone.

chapter thirteen

The Goddess

MIKLÓS STARED AT the walls of his chamber—one of three
guest rooms in the Palace. It was larger than his old room, and
the paint, a neutral pale blue, was newer. Furthermore, it didn't
have a tree growing out of the middle of the floor.

The spot Miklós stared at (absently, not intently) was marked
by a vein of slightly thicker paint running diagonally, then
straight up. The vein, no doubt, covered a crack.

Brigitta had been with him until just after noon—a few
hours ago—when she had found herself, as she put it, unable
to cope with his moodiness at the same time as she tried to
cope with her own. She had left to visit Bölk. Miklós had not
objected to her leaving because he hadn't thought she was doing
anything to help his melancholy. Yet, now that she was gone,
it was worse.

Was it his last encounter with László that was upsetting him,
he wondered? No. It had been unpleasant, certainly, but he
could understand why Bölk's words had offended the King,
and László had understood why he, Miklós, had been so irate.
There was no real sign that their hard-earned and long-awaited
friendship was about to end. No, it had to be the norska.

But why had its death had such an effect on him? Was it
only sympathy with Vilmos?

A thought came to assail him: If you are so concerned about
Vilmos, why are you sitting here feeling sorry for yourself?

He stood and made his way into the corridor toward his brother's room.

"Vili?"

"What is it, Miki?"

"May I enter?"

There was a pause, then, "Yes."

He came in and stood uncomfortably. "You need a chair in here." His brother didn't answer. Miklós finally sat on the floor with his back to the wall. It came to him that, many years before, he had sat that way in this room, watching his brother build models of the Palace or boats of paper to sail in the River.

"How are you, Vili?" His brother nodded. Miklós bit down an impulse to ask about the other norska. There was no doubt that Vili was taking care of them as best he could, and the question would be presumptuous.

Miklós tried one more time. "Is there anything I can do?"

At this the giant looked up. He blinked. He looked down at the palms of his hands, then back at Miklós. "Yes," he said at last. "Tell me, who am I to blame for this? Is it my fault?"

"Huh? Of course not. Who could know the floor was weak there? It is no one's fault."

Vilmos nodded, and his head sank again. Miklós suddenly realized that his brother needed someone to blame. He should have pointed to someone. But what could he have done? It *wasn't* anyone's fault. Yet his sense of failure was real enough.

"It is nearly time for dinner, Vili. Shall we eat?"

Vilmos nodded, and was willing to be led to the dining room. Mariska looked at the giant with sympathy in her eyes, but they exchanged no words.

As the meal began, Miklós noticed that Vilmos was staring intently at László, who was taking small bites of his food, alternating with sips of wine. Vilmos suddenly put down his spoon, stood up, and left the room. By the time he reached the doorway he was running.

Miklós looked at the others, but they seemed as puzzled as he.

Brigitta came to him again that night.

It seemed that to make love with Brigitta was to allow her to absorb some of his pain and indecision. He spoke to her of it, asking if she felt that way as well and, if so, why did she wish to?

She laughed lightly. "I don't know," she said. "You find the oddest things to talk about."

"Do I?"

"Mmmm. Or perhaps the oddest times to talk about them."

He cast around for another subject. "What did you and Bölk find to talk about?"

She laughed again, louder this time. "Oh, Miki, Miki, Miki," she said. She kissed him on the lips and rested her head on his shoulder. "Let's go to sleep."

"I can't."

"Why not?"

"I don't know. Something's bothering me. Maybe it's that stupid norska. No, I don't mean t. I don't know what it is."

Brigitta propped herself on he. .lbow and studied him in the dim candlelight of the room. "Perhaps," she said, "you're just tired of being acted on. Perhaps it's time you became a mover, instead."

She settled onto her shoulder again.

Miklós stared at the ceiling, wondering if she was right. He was still wondering when he fell asleep.

When he awoke, he knew.

Brigitta was still sleeping. She stirred a little when he climbed out of bed, but didn't open her eyes. He dressed and went into the small dining room to take some bread. As he picked up a piece, he noticed a fine white powder on top of it. His first thought was that Ambrus was trying something new. Then he noticed that the same white powder covered part of the table as well.

He looked up. Some of the plaster from the ceiling was crumbling, as if someone had rubbed an abrasive over it. He put the bread down on the table, walked out, up, and down, and went out to the stables to visit Bölk.

There were no guards outside of the door this time. Good. He slipped inside.

"Good morning, master."

"Good morning, Bölk. I am ready."

"Ready?" The horse turned his head to the side. "For what?"

"I'm not certain yet. But something must be done, and I'm now ready to do it. I imagine you know what it is."

"No, I'm afraid I don't, master."

Miklós stared. "You don't?"

"No."

"But—" he laughed. "How ironic. I thought you had every-thing worked out and were just waiting for me to agree to act. Now I agree, and I can't do anything because we don't know what to do."

"You might start," said Bölk, "by telling me what problem it is that you propose to solve."

"Huh? Why," he waved his arms, "the Palace! It's falling apart around our ears! You heard about Vilmos's norska?"

"Yes. I am truly sorry for him."

"Well, how much longer is it going to be before it is one of us? It could just as easily have been, you know."

"Men are not so easily killed as norska."

Miklós felt suddenly disgusted. "You mean, none of this worries you?"

Bölk shook his head. "I am not unworried, master. I am merely confident."

"Confident? Why, when I don't know what to do, and you don't know what the problem is?"

"I am confident because you have agreed to take action. You are correct. That is all that was missing."

"But if we don't know—"

"We shall find out. Together."

Miklós sighed. "I don't understand."

"You will, master."

Miklós stared at him, half a dozen possible responses com-ing and going. Finally he said, "Very well," and seated himself against a post opposite the stall. "Let us begin."

Rather than laughing or making a condescending remark, as Miklós had more than half expected, Bölk nodded. "Our problem," he said, "is the condition of the Palace, is that cor-rect, master?"

Miklós nodded.

"Very well, then. Can the Palace be made safe?"

"I don't know."

"Let us assume it can. How?"

"Perhaps Sándor's spells, or strengthening the walls with wood or even iron."

"Was it a wall that collapsed?"

"All right, the floor then. Put in more supports."

"But master, I thought that it was the blocks themselves that were worn away, as well as the supports."

Miklós studied him. "How did you learn all of this?"

"Brigitta spent much time here yesterday. She has sharp eyes. They miss little."

"Oh. All right. Then we must support the floor and replace it."

"Yes. And replace the supports."

"Yes."

"And the walls, too."

"Hmmm. This is starting to sound like replacing the entire Palace."

"That is right, master."

Miklós blinked. Then the full import of what Bölk was saying struck him. "What? We can't replace the Palace!"

"It has been done before, has it not?"

"Well, yes, but—László will never agree."

"That is true. It isn't László who must replace it."

"Me? Bölk, where am I to get the resources for a new Palace?"

"What has been done before?"

"The King has ordered materials taken from the Riverbed, and sent in from east and west. And salvaged material from the building he was replacing."

"The King will not do so this time, master."

"That's what I'm saying."

"Another way must be found, then."

"*What* way?"

"What must a Palace be?"

"A shelter for the family. A place from which the King rules. A symbol of our land. A place that will withstand the attacks of our enemies."

"I think, master, that the symbol may be left to itself."

"Well, all right."

"How long has it been since the Palace was needed to defend against enemies?"

"Three hundred years," said Miklós. "That is when the cellars—"

"Yes, master. And the cellars and tunnels are still there, are they not?"

"Of course. Why?"

"And was not the wall strengthened around the Palace after that?"

"Well, yes."

"Then much of our defense against enemies of Fenario will
exist no matter what, isn't that so?"

Miklós hesitated, then, "All right."

"Now, if the King is of the family, then any place where
the family gathers is the place from which the King rules."

Miklós chewed on this but finally nodded.

"Then, master, what we are left with is a shelter."

"If you think that we can replace this Palace with some
hovel, I don't—"

"Do you wish for it to collapse on you, master?"

Miklós glowered, but at last he said, "No."

"Very well then, a shelter is required to replace the Palace."

Miklós opened his mouth and closed it a few times, unable
to fully grasp what Bölk was proposing.

Bölk ignored him. "Here," he said, "we reach the limits of
my knowledge. What makes something a shelter? You must
decide this."

Miklós shook his head. *All right, then. It's a game he is
playing. I'll play it, too, and see where it leads.*

He chewed on his thumb for a while. "What makes a shelter?
Well, I guess it depends what we are being sheltered from.
Mostly the weather, I guess. The wind, the rain—"

He stopped. A memory returned. A rainstorm, high winds.
Walking through the Wandering Forest, then running, desperately in need of—shelter. Pieces fell into place.

He said in a whisper, "The tree? In my room?"

"Brigitta says it is beautiful, master."

"I don't believe it."

"Do you not?"

"You've known all along."

"No. I cannot know more than you. I can only know it more
clearly and more certainly."

"I don't understand."

"You will."

"What should we do?" He laughed without humor. "Is my
task, then, to sneak around at night and water the tree, loosening
support beams in the meantime?"

"I suspect not, master. But certainly, the growth of the tree
must be encouraged."

"It's been doing well enough on its own."

"Has it? It has been growing quickly, true. Yet, if it had
grown quicker, perhaps it would have reached its full growth

before the floor fell on the norska."

Miklós shifted uncomfortably. "Are you saying it is my fault for not being here? What could I do? László would have killed me."

"Perhaps, if it was your fault, it is because you annoyed László unnecessarily. Yet, I think not. Could you not have hid yourself in the Palace?"

"Heh. I tried. Andor betrayed me."

"Why?"

"Because," said Miklós sarcastically, "the Goddess told him to."

"I hear scorn in your voice, master. Do you doubt that he spoke to the Goddess?"

Miklós was silent for a moment. Then he said, "No. Many in our family receive dreams from her. I have no reason to think that he is different."

"So you believe him?"

Miklós cursed. "Yes! I believe him. What is the point to this?"

"I think you have found your task, then."

"What do you—?" Then, "No."

"No, master? I thought you had agreed to act?"

"But—the Goddess? You can't be serious."

"Have I ever been anything else, dear master?"

"But *how?* How can I fight the Goddess?"

"It is what I am for."

"But you said you couldn't—"

"I cannot. You can. I shall be your weapon."

"But what will it gain us?"

"It will remove a powerful weapon from those who wish to destroy the tree. It is the Goddess who inspires them against it. Without her, much of their will to fight will be gone."

Once more, the memory returned of Andor revealing his hiding place to László. "You're right," he said. "But they'll kill me, you know."

"Perhaps they will, master. But I think they will be too stunned to do so until it is too late."

"Too late? What do you mean?"

"If the tree is a shelter, as you said, then surely it will protect you."

"I am to run and hide under a tree?" He heard his voice becoming hysterical, but could do nothing to stop it.

"I think that, too, will prove unnecessary."

Miklós closed his eyes until he felt himself growing calm enough to speak. Then he opened them and stared at his feet. "There must be another way."

"There is."

"Eh?" The prince looked up at him. "What?"

"Are you prepared to kill László?"

"He's my brother!"

"Yes."

"No!"

"Then there is no other way."

Miklós stood suddenly. He felt light-headed. He felt his pulse throbbing in his temples, and he felt feverish. "All right, then. We go fight the Goddess. Why not? Let's do that. Right now."

Bölk merely nodded. As if on its own, the door to the stable swung open. Bölk walked out.

Miklós stared at him, then swallowed. The horse stared back. "Well?" said Bölk.

"All right," said Miklós, hearing a tremor in his voice. "How do we go about it?"

"We must bring her to us."

"How?"

"I am not certain, master. Have you any thoughts?"

Miklós walked over to the doorway that led out into the courtyard. He looked for a while, then said, "Maybe. But what happens after we have summoned her?"

"You will destroy her."

"How?"

"I will be your weapon."

"I don't understand."

"You will."

They spent half an hour discussing how they would summon the Goddess, and then they emerged into the autumn sunlight. The courtyard was almost free of shadows and looked hot. The breeze, however, was pleasant on Miklós's face. He had left his cloak on the stable floor and loosened his blouse, so the air moved over his chest, cooling him.

When they were in the middle of the courtyard, he faced the wind, which was from the west, and let it play over his face. Bölk waited for him patiently.

"Tell me," said the Prince, "why are you being so mysterious about just what we do after the Goddess appears?"

"Am I being mysterious, master? Or are you merely unable to understand?"

"You are being mysterious. I can tell the difference. Why?"

The horse snorted. "Come. We have a task to perform."

Miklós chewed his lip. Bölk had been evasive all through the discussion on the summoning. There was certainly a reason. He sighed to himself. There was no real question, however. If he couldn't trust Bölk, there was no point in doing anything.

"Very well," he said.

The courtyard was all but deserted. A few of the guards on the walls looked at them idly. They came to the sculpture of the Demon Goddess that stared back at the Palace. Miklós studied it. It was twelve feet in height, plus three feet of pedestal. The Goddess stood with both hands stretched out before her. There was something peculiar about her hands, but Miklós couldn't quite see what. Odd that he'd never studied it before. And the smile! Was it warm, or was it malicious? It changed with the angle at which he studied it, or the amount of light, or even his mood. Perhaps that was why she was called the Demon Goddess. An odd name for a patron deity. Even odder that he'd never questioned it before. In Faerie, gods were thought of—but never mind that now.

He turned to Bölk. "Is it true that Fenarr himself brought that back with him from Faerie?"

"Perhaps it is, master. I do not remember."

Miklós nodded. He touched the base. Both it and the statue were in good shape for stone that been there for hundreds of years. The base was granite, and the surface had been left rough. The figure was done in marble, and had lost none of its smoothness. Miklós touched the leg. It was cool but seemed almost alive.

Yes, perhaps this would, indeed, work. He ran his hand briefly up and down the leg, and smiled to himself. Was this a desecration or perhaps the expression of a sick perversion?

He stepped back and looked once more at the entire figure. Yes, there was beauty here. More importantly, there was power. He glanced around the courtyard. Still, no one seemed to be paying any attention to them.

"Let us begin," he said.

Bölk spun and kicked. There was a surprisingly loud *thud*

as his hooves struck the figure's right leg, just at the knee.

"The knee is weak on a man," he remarked. "Why not on a statue? Or a Goddess?"

He kicked again. Miklós looked. Was there, perhaps, the slightest indication of a crack? In solid marble? But this was a *táltos* horse, after all.

Bölk kicked once more. Yes, there was a crack in the marble, at the knee.

Someone called, "Hey!" Miklós looked up and saw the two guards from the tower above the gate staring at him. "What are you doing?"

Miklós smiled and waved. Bölk kicked again, and a pyramid-shaped piece of marble fell from the knee. Bölk kicked again, and a larger piece fell.

Miklós looked around. Now they were beginning to receive attention. Servants and guards stared at them as if paralyzed, save for a few who were running toward the Palace, doubtless to tell someone.

Bölk kicked once more. "That will do for that leg," he said. He seemed to be blowing hard. Miklós realized with a shock that never before had Bölk shown any signs of exhaustion.

Bölk began kicking the other knee. Miklós watched the Palace door. It swung open, and László appeared. From where he stood, Miklós could see other forms behind him, standing on the planks that covered the hole in the Palace floor.

Bölk kicked again. László rushed toward them but stopped about twenty feet away, his eyes wide. Behind him came Andor, Sándor, Viktor, Mariska, and Brigitta.

None of them moved. Bölk kicked again. Miklós, turning his head, saw the figure begin to tilt. Andor gave a cry then and rushed forward, his expression one of mixed rage and anguish.

Miklós moved away from Bölk a little, to see which one he would attack. Andor's direction did not change—it was the horse. The fool! To attempt to battle a *táltos* horse, unarmed, was sheer idiocy. He was liable to get himself killed.

As he ran by, Miklós tripped him. Andor sprawled on his face. Bölk kicked the sculpture again. It tottered and seemed ready to go over.

He grabbed Andor's shoulders and pulled him. "Better get up, brother."

Andor rose to his knees and looked up at Miklós. "Why?" he whispered.

Bölk kicked again, then quickly walked away.

For an instant, the figure seemed to hang on by one knee. But it was leaning too far forward. There was a crumbling sound, and the Demon Goddess fell forward; landing first on her outstretched hands, then on her side next to where Andor had lain a few seconds before. To Miklós's surprise, the statue didn't shatter—or even crack, as far as he could tell.

Andor stared, stricken. Miklós looked at those around him, who stared at him wide-eyed.

"We should not have long to wait, master," said Bölk.

They didn't.

The dust had hardly settled over the fallen sculpture when it began. First, the wind picked up. It took a moment for Miklós to realize it, but the wind didn't seem to come from any one direction—it blew in everyone's face, whichever way he looked, and the dust on the ground was not disturbed. The sky seemed to darken, yet there were no more clouds than before. It was as if the sun were giving off less light. Less heat as well, it seemed, for Miklós was suddenly chilly.

Someone—Andor, perhaps—gasped. Miklós turned. Near the fallen idol, above the head, the air seemed to be shimmering. At first it looked like sunlight on the River; he couldn't quite look at the dancing, dazzling specks of light. Then it seemed to grow and weaken at the same time. Very gradually, it took a form slightly larger than human. Then, rather than turning into the Goddess, she seemed to appear from within it.

The winds died.

She must have been over nine feet tall. She wore shapeless gray robes, and her face was sharp and angular, her ears pointed, her eyes slightly slanted, her hair curled dark. She reminded Miklós of someone, but he couldn't remember who. He strained his neck looking up, but could read no expression on her face.

She pointed to the icon. Miklós noticed that each of her fingers had an extra joint. She said, "Who has done this?"

No one spoke. Miklós looked around and saw that he was the only one who had not fallen to his knees. It was strange that he had had no urge to do so, yet it had seemed involuntary with the others. It was even more strange how calm he felt.

He was prepared to find his voice and answer her, but there was no need. He was the only one not kneeling, and all of the others were looking at him. The Goddess turned to him fully. He could suddenly imagine that there was a shield around him, for her glance didn't seem to penetrate past the surface of his eyes. He could still read nothing in hers.

Then, as if from another world, a voice intruded. "I did it."

Miklós, startled, glanced in the direction of the voice. Brigitta had stood up. Her hands were on her hips, and the look on her face was stern, but Miklós could see that she was pale.

The Goddess looked at her and smiled. "You are very brave, little girl." Her voice was thin and airy, yet deep. It seemed to come from miles away. "But," she added, "I'm sorry to say that I don't believe you. Your effort speaks well of your— *lineage*." She laughed, then, but it was not an evil laugh; more a sad one.

She turned back to the Prince. "Your name is Miklós, is it not?"

He found his voice. "Yes, Goddess. I am Miklós."

"Why have you done this, Miklós?"

Of all she could have done or said, this was the most unexpected. How could he answer such a question. To kill you? Because my horse told me to? He finally managed, "To bring you here."

Someone, off to his left, gave a gasp. Probably Andor.

The Goddess looked around, and seemed to see Bölk for the first time. She said to Miklós, "The horse aided you."

Since it wasn't a question, Miklós didn't answer. It seemed none was needed. To the horse, she said, "You are Bölcseség, aren't you?"

"Yes, Goddess," said the horse. "I am surprised you remember me."

"You have changed."

"You have not."

"Is that why you think you can destroy me?"

"Yes."

"I must kill your new master, you know."

"I know."

"Then you."

"I know."

"I wish you had not forced this upon me."

"Perhaps it will work the other way, Goddess."

She laughed. "In that case, I will wish even more that you had not forced this upon me."

She's so human, thought Miklós.

Bölk didn't answer. She stirred then and said, "Well, let it be done as it must." She turned to László and said, "Oh, King, I am sorry that this must be, but it must. Perhaps you feel a need to intervene on your brother's behalf, yet feel loyalty to me. I do not wish to torment you so. Therefore, this!" Her hand moved slightly, and László jumped a bit, then stopped. Miklós had never seen anyone so still. He didn't even seem to be breathing.

"He is well," said the Goddess. "Merely unable to move. Now, let us be done. Are you prepared?"

Miklós faced her fully. *What now, Bölk? You haven't seemed surprised by anything. What is to happen? What will prevent her from destroying me?* It was unclear whether the terror that Miklós was holding at bay was stronger than his trust in Bölk but he had no choice so he couldn't find out. "I am ready," he said.

She pointed her right forefinger at him. There was a flicker of motion to his right. He saw that Brigitta was running toward him, and a cold fear paralyzed him for a moment, but she could never make it in time. Then there came a flash of blue from the Goddess's finger. At the same time, a dark shape flashed in front of him, so close that he fell backward.

There was a loud *crack* followed by the sound of a falling body. Miklós rolled over and came to his knees.

Bölk lay on his side not far away.

"NO!"

He ran to the horse and saw there was a great rent in his side, and all around it were burn marks, as if a hole had been cut and a poor attempt made to cauterize the wound. Miklós could see the horse's ribs and pale strips of muscle pulsating, and the ground around him was covered with blood. Miklós knelt next to his head. "Bölk."

"Master, listen to me."

"Bölk, don't die!"

"It was necessary, master. Now, here is what you must do."

"Bölk! You can't—"

"Quiet, master. I had to. Now listen closely, or all is wasted and you will die."

"I don't care!"

"Yes, you do. You must."

"This is why you wouldn't tell me what you were going to do! You knew I'd never let you do this."

"Bring your head closer. I must whisper, for my strength is waning."

He shot a quick glance at the Goddess, who was watching sadly. She caught Miklós's eye. "I am sorry," she said. "We were allies once."

Then Bölk spoke to her. "If you please, Goddess, a word with my master before I die."

She frowned but nodded. There were no other sounds in the courtyard. The wind had died.

Miklós turned away from her and put his ear next to Bölk's mouth. An instant later he pulled away. "I cannot!" he said in a fierce whisper. There was commotion around him now, but he ignored it. He leaned closer and listened more. He shook his head, feeling overwhelmed with horror and disgust. Bölk continued to speak for a moment, then his head fell back against the ground.

The commotion stopped. Miklós looked around and saw Brigitta stretched out a little way away. He turned. "What—"

"She only sleeps, my sad Prince. Had she done as she wished, I would have had to kill her; yet I did not wish to leave her awake but unable to intervene, to watch you die."

Miklós felt he should thank her, but the words wouldn't come out of his mouth. He felt tears well up in his eyes and wondered how he could do what he must—what Bölk required of him.

"Stand away," said the Goddess. "I have no wish to further harm his body."

He stood up and steeled himself. "A moment," he said. "A request from Bölk before he died." Without giving her time to answer, he moved so he could shield his actions from her view and drew his knife.

"What are you doing?" she asked.

"Only what he wished," said Miklós, without turning around. Once, in the service of a lord of Faerie, he had butchered a calf. One slit to open up the rib cage, then reach in with the knife and . . . He knew what to do, and, hating himself, he did it.

It was only seconds later that, dropping the knife, he turned around. The Goddess saw what he held in his hands, and her eyes narrowed in disgust. "What is this?"

"He wished me to offer it to you, Goddess."

She stared at him. "I don't wish to have it, Prince."

A sudden, terrible anger flared in him. "I don't wish you to have it either, Goddess! Demon Goddess! You who kill me and my friends, while showering us with kindness—you deserve no part of him. But he said to give it, so, by the River, I'm going to give it to you one way or the other!" He took two steps forward, until he was inches from her. Then, into her face, he flung Bölk's severed heart.

She reeled back a step, and, with a wave of her hand, the heart vanished. Only a few drops of blood remained on her face. Her eyes lit up with rage, then widened in surprise.

Then she screamed.

The walls and the Palace seemed to shake, and he desperately tried to cover his ears. He found himself on his back, then he was rolling away. He looked up and saw that László was moving, and a quick glance showed him that Brigitta was stirring; but he couldn't look because the sound hurt too much. He kept rolling.

The scream ended abruptly. He glanced over, and the Goddess was on her knees. Her lips were moving, but Miklós heard no sound. Was she praying, he wondered? To whom?

She fell onto her face next to her idol and clawed the ground. Then, shimmering as she had when appearing, she vanished.

Beside her, the icon cracked in many places. Then it fell to pieces. Then the pieces crumbled to dust.

Silence settled over the courtyard.

Brigitta came to Miklós and put her arm around him. Andor gave one great sob, then ran off into the Palace. Miklós followed him with his eyes, understanding something of what he felt. He, too, had lost a god this day.

INTERLUDE

By NOW, IT HAD filled the room completely. All four walls and the ceiling trapped its expansion. But the tremor that passed through the entire structure freed it from somnolence, and it began to push.

Gently, gently, so gently, but firmly, irresistibly, it began to push. The strengthened and reinforced walls felt it. They pushed back.

Who would win this match of strength? The chick, seeking to escape, or the egg, seeking to contain and smother it? The answer is unknowable, for things could not remain in this state; something else had to happen.

And something *did* happen: the scream of a dying Goddess pierced the air and the walls.

Even before the scream found its way into the room, that which grew there was having an effect on its enclosing structure. It couldn't break the walls, but it could bend them. And, when bent, perhaps they could break themselves. If anyone had happened to walk over that spot on the floor above, he would have noticed a bulge from where the ceiling in Miklós's room was being pushed up.

Then the scream came, at such volume and pitch that the very roots of the Palace vibrated for a moment in sympathy with the dying Goddess.

Now a few cracks appeared in the walls.

chapter fourteen

The Wake

SHE STROKED HIS HAIR.

They sat in the courtyard, and Brigitta watched as Andor
entered the Palace and Miklós followed him with his eyes.
What was he thinking?

When she had worked at the sign of the Two Rivers, she
had often carried the mugs of ale and glasses of wine without
thinking about it while she amused herself by studying the
people there, learning to read their faces and their gestures to
see what they were thinking or guess at their conversations
from across the room. She was good at it. Why couldn't she
read Miklós? He mystified her. She had even been able to read
Bölk.

That brought it back again.

Bölk and the Goddess and death.

The events had been going in and out of her head since she
had awakened after the sleep the Goddess had cast upon her.
Anger flared again, anger she knew was irrational. But to miss
Miklós's moment of glory! To have seen him—but put that
aside.

The King was looking at her. She felt herself flushing, and
tossed her head defiantly. What must he think of her now?
Casting herself at his brother now that he no longer wanted
her. And why hadn't he sent her away?

She had risen in the world, though. To have been the King's,
albeit for a while, would give her pleasant memories when she

was old and ugly and—no! Don't think of it. Never think of
it! But why was the King—?

Then she realized that he wasn't looking at her at all; he
was looking at Miklós. In his face she read only shock. He
had not yet accepted what had happened, perhaps couldn't
accept it. When he did—then what? Would he have Miklós
put to death? She must help him get away from here! She
looked at him then, and knew that he would never leave. This
was his home.

Why wasn't she afraid of him? He was a Prince, which
ought to count for something. And more, he had slain the
Goddess. She ought to be afraid to touch him. Strange.

She looked closely at Miklós, trying to see what he needed
now. Did he want to be left alone? Why couldn't she tell?
Perhaps that was what fascinated her so much about him. And
it was fascination—or had been at first. The mysterious vanished Prince, practically walking into her in the middle of the
night. But it was more than that, now. He was gentle, sometimes too gentle, she thought wryly. And the way he moved—
so graceful, as if he danced. And his shocking innocence never
failed to amaze and delight her.

He was staring now, at Bölk. That brought it back again.
Bölk—she couldn't think of him as a horse, *táltos* or not. He
was a friend. They had only spoken a few times, but he could
see down to the tiniest hidden corner of her soul and liked her
anyway. Everyone, it seemed, had the feeling that, "If he knew
me he would despise me," and most knew that it wasn't true.
But the certain knowledge that there was someone who knew
her and still liked her brought her a kind of peace she had never
felt before.

But Miklós was like that too, almost. He didn't know her,
but she knew, without trying it, that if she were to dredge up
her most shameful secrets, he would find ways to tell her that
it was all right, that none of those were horrible things. That
was how he was. She smiled to herself. *Yes, my Prince. I am
starting to know you. I still can't tell what you're thinking
about, but I'm starting to know you.*

She looked up suddenly and saw László standing over them,
looking at Miklós. He stared back.

"You have slain the Goddess," said the King, whispering.

"Yes," said Miklós.

László shook his head. His mouth moved between the shape

for "How" and "Why," but no sound came forth. Miklós only shook his head. At last László took a deep breath and said, "I must think, Miki. Do not leave here. I will speak with you and—do whatever I must."

He turned and walked back into the Palace.

Miklós stared at the ground. Brigitta squeezed his arm. He stirred, then stood up. "He doesn't want to kill me," he said, as if this surprised him.

She stood up also. He gave her his arm without thinking. They walked to Viktor, who still watched the empty pedestal. Viktor looked at Miklós, and Brigitta read hate—hate so strong it almost took her breath away. Viktor was hiding it well, so Miklós probably didn't see it, but it was clear to Brigitta. Miklós said, "Viktor, have someone dig a hole. Here, in the courtyard. I want the horse buried next to the pedestal. I'll find something to put over it later."

Viktor gave no answer except to stare inimically. "Well?" said Miklós, almost harshly.

Brigitta squeezed his arm as she saw the captain's lip trembling. Was he going to attack Miklós? Now? But he seemed to get himself under control. "I must ask the King about this."

"No, you must not," said Miklós. "It is nothing to bother him with. If you ask him, he'll be forced to refuse. If you don't, he won't care. I want it done at once. See to it."

Viktor's wooden face worked to let nothing past. Brigitta suppressed a shudder. The captain nodded, however.

Miklós returned to the Palace. As they entered, Vilmos was emerging from the cellar on a rope ladder.

"I heard something out here," he said. "What happened?"

Miklós stared at him. "You were inside the whole time?"

"Yes? What was it?"

Miklós shook his head and walked past. Brigitta said, "Miklós has slain the Demon Goddess," and left him gaping behind her.

They came to the guest room that Miklós was using and lay down together. She held him, and they didn't speak for some time. But she wondered. . . .

What had he seen, when he had taken the power into himself? That was certainly what he was doing; nothing else made one look or act that way, though it was funny how different it looked from the inside and the outside. But had he seen the same things she always saw when—

No. Don't think about it. It is behind you; part of another life. But the memories, the visions, returned anyway. Euphoria, streaming patterns and flowing, blending shades of texture. It was all there. And, just behind it, her father, assuming his natural shape to torment her mother, or bringing his "friends," to her. "Here, Brigitta. Here is what you will do. . . ." And the smile. The horrid, horrid smile. "Lineage," the Goddess had said. She had recognized her.

Finally the escape to—to the city, at the last. Best not to think of what had gone before, either. Leave the pleasure with the pain and accept contentment. But Miki. Dear, dear, Miki. He must not become one of *them,* as she was. He must not.

But how to tell him without telling him too much?

"He planned it all, you know," said Miklós suddenly, jolting Brigitta out of her reverie.

"I . . . excuse me." She struggled to recall what they'd been discussing, and it came back with a sudden ache that she had forgotten about Bölk. "I was not awake for much of it," she managed. "What happened?"

He briefly told her what she had slept through. He shuddered as he spoke. When he had finished, she fought to hold back tears. How could he have done it? She would never have had the strength to—

"Brigitta."

"Yes."

"Thank you. For trying to save me twice, and for everything you've done since. You—I could never have spoken to the Goddess that way, trying to make her attack you. I don't know how you did it. I hope, someday, I'll be able to—never mind."

Brigitta said nothing. How could she claim credit for those things? She had never really willed to do either of them, they had just happened. She held him closer.

Miklós whispered, "Bölk."

She felt rather than heard his sobs, and she did her best to comfort him.

After a while, Miklós stirred. He looked around the room, then settled onto his back.

"What are you thinking about?" asked Brigitta.

He shook his head.

"You don't want to tell me?"

"I don't think you'd want to know."

"You are probably right," she said. "But tell me anyway."

"Very well," he said. "I am going to gather wood and oil and spread them throughout the Palace. Then I am going to burn it to the ground."

Brigitta suppressed a gasp. "Why?" she said after a moment.

"Because I hate it. There has been too much death here. The norska. Bölk. Even the Goddess. Too much."

"But if you destroy the Palace—no, it doesn't matter to you."

"What?"

"The tree. You will destroy that, too, but it seems I'm the only one who sees anything of value in it."

He *didn't* answer for a moment, then he said, "There was also Bölk."

"Bölk? What did he say about it?"

"Didn't he tell you what it was?"

"No. What is it?"

"Then he told the truth. He really didn't know."

"What?"

"Later."

"Now."

Miklós sighed audibly. "You are right. Bölk would not have wanted the tree destroyed. He says—this is going to sound strange."

"Let it."

But still he said nothing. He stood up abruptly. "Come, then. Let us look at it."

She took his proffered hand and allowed herself to be led out of the room. On the way down to the main level they passed Mariska walking toward the Great Hall. She appeared not to see them, except to turn her body slightly to avoid collision. Brigitta glanced at Miklós. His lips were pressed tightly together.

They reached Miklós's room and stepped past the curtain into it. The tree had grown even more. On all sides it was pressed fully against the walls. She turned to Miklós. "Well?"

"Bölk says that the Palace must be replaced and that this tree is what will replace it."

She stared at him. "How can a tree—?"

"I don't know. But that is what Bölk said."

She shook her head. "Then how can you even consider doing anything that might harm it?"

He sighed and slumped against a wall. Thin leaves brushed

against his face, but he didn't seem to notice. "I don't know," he said.

She turned back to the tree. Once again its beauty struck her, almost physically. It wasn't merely the perfection, the symmetry of its form. Nor was it just the tiny perfection of every detail of every leaf. Had she passed it in the woods of home, before she came to the city, she would hardly have spared it a glance.

No, what was so shockingly beautiful about this tree was its newness, here, amid what was old and decrepit. The very thing, she reflected wryly, that prevented Miklós from admiring it. But on that score there was nothing to be—

"I see what you mean," said Miklós suddenly.

"About what?"

"It is—attractive, isn't it?"

For a moment, death and horror were swept from her mind and her heart was filled with clean joy, the like of which she hadn't known since she was young. She crossed the three steps to where he stood, feeling as if she were skipping and, laughing, embraced him.

He laughed too. "I didn't know it meant so much to you."

She leaned back and looked at him. "Didn't you?"

"Hmmm. Well, I suppose I did. But I've never seen it before. I suppose it's a matter of attitude. Beauty ought to be independent of such things, though."

"It is," said Brigitta.

"If you say so," said Miklós and squeezed her until she thought her ribs would crack. Then, smiling, he stepped away and began looking around the room.

"Come here," he said after a moment.

She went over to him and looked where he pointed. There was a noticeable depression in the wall where one whole side of the tree was pushing against it like a battering ram.

She went to look at another spot where tree met wall and found a similar depression. Looking up, she saw the same thing was taking place on the ceiling.

"Mariska will be disappointed," said Miklós.

"Why?"

"She is the one who thought that all that needed to be done was to strengthen the walls. Well, they tried, and it isn't working. Your tree, here, is winning the battle."

Brigitta laughed. "Good for it!"

Miklós nodded.

"I wonder what they'll do next?" said Brigitta.

"I don't know. We'll find out soon enough. Do you think anyone else knows?"

"If not, they will. I imagine they look in on the tree pretty often."

"Yes." Miklós sat down with his back to a wall. "Why is it that they can't cut through it, though?"

"Why does it matter?"

"I want to know its strengths. And its weaknesses and what it needs. If I am to aid it, I must know how."

Brigitta said slowly, "Then, you are committed to doing what Bölk wanted?"

Miklós nodded. "If I can," he said, as if he were speaking of the weather.

"And what of what you said earlier, about destroying the Palace?"

He shook his head. "Never mind. I still want to in some ways, but you're right. I have to do what Bölk wanted."

Brigitta nodded but didn't trust herself to speak. His attitudes were so changeable, who knew what he might decide if she said the wrong thing? She shook her head. No, no. She couldn't work like that. She had to *know* that she could count on him.

He seemed lost in thought. After enough time had passed she said, "You might want to share it with me."

"What? Oh. I've been trying to think of what we should do. They are certainly going to try to destroy the tree. How are we going to protect it? We can't stand up to them directly, so we have to find a way—"

"What about Vilmos?"

"Eh? What about him?"

"He could stand up to them."

"Do you think he will?"

"I'm not sure. We should speak to—"

At that moment, László and Viktor appeared at the doorway. The two pairs stared at each other. Then László stepped through, nodding his head. Viktor followed. The captain's eyes were on Miklós, and, once again, the hate that gleamed from them shocked Brigitta. She felt trapped, as she had never felt trapped since she had run away from her father. But they were between her and the door. Her breath came in gasps.

Miklós cleared his throat. "We have been looking at the damage, László."

The King grunted. "To the walls or to the tree?"

"To the walls."

The King muttered something under his breath. "Where?"

Miklós pointed out the damage. Viktor also looked.

"Well," said the King speaking to the captain, "Sándor and Mariska were wrong. It isn't going to work."

"No, it isn't," said Viktor. "It must be destroyed. And that, quickly."

Brigitta looked at Miklós. He seemed unhappy, but she could tell no more than that.

László faced Miklós fully. "What is your reaction to that, brother?"

Miklós held himself perfectly still, as if there were a knife at his throat. "Why do you ask?" His voice sounded slightly hoarse.

"Exactly what was it you did out there today? And, moreover, why?"

Miklós sighed. "I'm not altogether sure what I did. But I believe the Goddess will no longer be appearing to us."

Brigitta noticed that the King's hand seemed to jump for his sabre, but steadied itself. Viktor was not so restrained; his knuckles were white where he gripped the hilt of his own.

"Why?" said László.

"Because she tried to kill me! You saw that."

"Yes, I saw it. But there's more to it than that. Why did you summon her? It seemed you were deliberately trying to provoke her. You must have had a reason."

Miklós didn't answer.

"Very well then," said the King. "I will ask you this: When Viktor and I, and the others, attempt to remove this tree, will you aid us or not?"

"You have already asked me that, haven't you?"

"Yes. Days ago. Much has happened since then. I must hear your answer again."

Miklós chewed his lip. Why was he being so evasive? Brigitta could tell nothing from looking at him. Then she studied László's face, and from the pain there, she suddenly understood. Miklós could do whatever he had to do except for one thing—he couldn't turn his brother into an enemy once more.

Not for the first time, she was nearly overwhelmed by the pain he must be feeling. She leaned closer to him and squeezed his arm. László looked at her and barely scowled. Miklós, apparently seeing the scowl, stiffened.

"You're right," he snapped. "You should ask again. The answer is no. I will do nothing to help you destroy this tree. There. Now you know. Excuse me."

Miklós walked forward, bringing Brigitta along with him by the arm. Before the captain could respond, Miklós had brushed between him and the King, and they were walking down the hall.

Brigitta felt a relief that was almost palpable. Her legs felt weak for a moment, and Miklós had to pause to let her lean against him. They continued up to the Great Hall. On the way, they passed Sándor.

"Excuse me," said Miklós, stopping.

The wizard glared at him. "Yes?"

"I find that I must, with thanks, refuse your offer."

Sándor's eyes widened, then he laughed. "So I had already guessed, young Prince. So I had guessed."

As he went past, still laughing, Brigitta squeezed Miklós's arm. He pressed her hand.

In the Hall they found Vilmos speaking with Mariska. As they came near, she looked up; then, muttering something to Vilmos, walked away.

"I think she doesn't like us," said Brigitta.

"Huh? Who?"

"Never mind." She poked his arm affectionately, which earned her a puzzled glance. They sat down on either side of the giant.

"So," said Vilmos. "You have killed the Demon Goddess, have you?"

"Yes," said Miklós. "Poor Andor."

The giant chuckled. "I think he'll be all right. He was looking around for something else to do anyway."

"That's good."

"Yes. But *why*, Miki? Why kill her?"

"I had to, Vili. I—" He stopped and seemed to concentrate for a while. "All right. I need to ask a question of you. What is it you want, right now, more than anything?"

The giant's face fell for a moment, and Brigitta saw Miklós wince. The wrong question. But Vilmos shook his head, perhaps clearing it of wishes that could not be, and thought over the question.

"What I want? To keep my norska safe."

Miklós nodded, as if that were the answer he'd been expecting. "Good. The danger to the norska is the Palace, isn't it?" Vilmos nodded. "Then the way to save them is to make it so the Palace isn't a danger anymore."

"Ha!" said Vilmos. "Easily said. I have been working for the last two days to—"

"I know. But listen, Vili, remember the tree in my old room and how you couldn't make yourself destroy it? Perhaps there is a reason for that."

Vilmos watched him carefully, still not sure where he was going. Andor came into the room, saw them, and walked over. Brigitta motioned to him not to speak. He sat down next to Vilmos. Miklós nodded to him.

The giant said, "What reason?"

"Maybe you understood, without really being aware of it, that the tree was something you should be preserving." Vilmos still seemed skeptical.

"What if it is?" he asked.

"There are those who wish to destroy it. Chief among them was the Demon Goddess."

He thought for a moment. "Why would she wish to destroy the tree if it is good?"

"She, like László, wished to leave the Palace standing rather than replace it, even though it has become a danger to us all. You, of all of us, know that it is danger. If we leave it standing, it will collapse upon us."

Andor stirred. "Just what are you trying to do?"

Miklós glanced at him, then looked away. Brigitta found herself studying the intricately patterned tiling on the floor.

"No," said Andor, "don't answer. I know. You are trying to convince Vilmos to help you. Aren't you?"

Miklós didn't answer. Brigitta said, "That seems obvious, Prince Andor."

"You are manipulating him. Playing on his fears. You—"

"No," said Miklós. "I don't think so. I am trying to convince him, as you said. But manipulate? Look around you. Look at the cracks in the ceiling beams, the breaks in the walls. Look at the hole in the floor in front of the main doors. I think we are *all* being pushed into doing something; Vilmos no more than the rest of us."

Miklós looked at his brother through slitted eyes. "What about you, Andor? From as far back as I remember, you have been looking for something to make life meaningful for you. Time after time, you have failed. Why? Maybe it isn't something *you* have been doing wrong, as we've all been thinking it was. Maybe there just isn't any way to find out who you are, when everywhere you turn you are surrounded by either the collapse of your home or desperate efforts to hold back this destruction.

"But I have another alternative for you: embrace it. Embrace the collapse of all we've lived with and work to create something better in its place."

Andor fell silent. Brigitta stared at Miklós. Yes, he was growing. For the first time since she'd been in the Palace, someone had been able to speak to Andor as harshly as he deserved, yet respectfully. And, too, Miklós seemed to have more understanding than she had thought he had. What had he and Bölk said to each other, right before the end?

At last Andor spoke. His voice was harsh, yet Brigitta could see that he was shaken. "Better? How, better? You've been saying what is wrong with the Palace, but how do I know that what you want to replace it with is better?"

Miklós didn't answer. Brigitta, trying to continue what Miklós had begun, said, "I feel that it will be, Andor. Miklós feels that it will be. But how can you know? You have two choices there. One, undertake a long and hard study of the tree that is growing in Miklós's room. Try to see it clearly, without prejudice, so that you can judge. That would be difficult, I know, but I can see no other way for you to know, save to wait until it has reached its full growth—if it does—and see then. Of course, then it will not matter what you think."

Andor blinked. "You said I had two choices."

"Yes. The other is to consider this. Whether it is better or worse than what we have now matters not in the least."

Andor made a brushing-off motion, as if to clear the air of nonsense. Brigitta reacted. Without warning, blood began to pound in her ears, and she felt gripped by a great and terrible rage. She found herself standing, looming over the Prince. *"Are you mad?"* she cried. "This place is collapsing! It's going to kill us! How can you stand there like a flag with no device on it and ask if that is better than this, when, at any moment, the ceiling above your head might fall on you and break every bone in that thick, impenetrable skull of yours!"

She sat down, fuming. There was silence for a moment, while Brigitta cooled down. *I should probably apologize. He is a Prince, and I am nothing. But I can't, Goddess help me.* And, *No, the Goddess will help no one anymore, for good or for ill.* Miklós was looking at her, with a smile playing about his lips. He gave her the smallest nod. She closed her eyes and found herself trembling.

"Then why don't you just leave?" said Andor.

She glanced quickly at Miklós, then looked away.

"None of us can leave, Andor," said Miklós. "This is our home. We belong here. We have nowhere else to go. That is true for the family, and for those who have chosen to tie their fates to our own. We must stay."

Without another word, Andor stood and left. Brigitta's eyes snapped open and she looked at Vilmos. He sat leaning forward in his chair, his hands clasped together and his eyes cast down. As if he felt Brigitta looking at him, he raised his head and met her eyes.

"I . . . will consider—"

"Vilmos," said Brigitta.

"Yes?"

"The King knows now that Miklós is not going to aid him in his efforts to fell the tree. He may have guessed already that Miklós has decided that this Palace must not stand. If he has not, then he soon will. When that happens, he will try to kill Miklós. You are the only one with the strength to prevent that. Will you?"

Vilmos was silent for a long time. Miklós and Brigitta exchanged glances, but let him think in peace. At last he said, "It isn't fair to make me decide between my brothers."

"No," said Miklós quietly, "it is not. But László is only doing what he feels he must. That is all I am doing. That is what you must do."

After another pause, Vilmos said, "I will consider what you have said." Then he, too, stood and left the hall.

When he was gone Miklós said, "I will have my dinner sent to my room tonight."

Brigitta said, "Do you think he will defend you?"

"I don't know," said Miklós. "If he doesn't, I am a dead man."

INTERLUDE

ONCE THERE WAS A boy who was born with all of his teeth. He lived beyond the beyond, right at the very shore of the great sea. Every day he would go down to the beach and dive for fish for his poor mother, who otherwise would have starved to death, as she had no one else to care for her.

When he was seven his mother passed away and he buried her in the sand near the tiny hut in which they lived. Then he went out to the beach and wept for five days.

On the sixth day he looked up. Far out on the waves of the sea he saw a lady, and he thought she was his mother. She was riding on top of a great sea turtle.

He called to her, "Mother, mother! It is I, Jancsi!" For that was his name. But she didn't seem to hear him.

So, quick as the wind, he jumped into the sea after her. Oh, but you should have seen him swim! I didn't see it myself, but my Uncle Béla was there, and he said that Jancsi swam so fast he plowed a furrow in the ocean that is there to this day.

For ten days he chased the lady on the turtle. Finally he caught up to her, and he saw that it wasn't his mother after all but a beautiful lady. He looked back, but the shore was out of sight. "Please," he called, "My name is Jancsi, and I thought you were my mother, who only just died. Won't you help me?"

The lady laughed at him and shook her head. Then he was close enough to see that each finger on her hand had an extra joint, and he knew that she was the Demon Goddess, and the turtle must be one of her demons.

Quick as thought, Jancsi grabbed on to the tail, determined to follow the Goddess to wherever she went. But when he looked again, she was gone. He climbed onto the turtle's back.

Then night came. He looked up, and saw that the six stars that we now call Fenarr's Shield seemed to be falling from the sky. When they landed, they made a tunnel in the sea. The turtle dived into the tunnel, and soon Jancsi was riding beneath the waves.

For a hundred days he rode the turtle in the ocean and under the ground, until at last they came to a place where the water rushed out of the ground. The turtle didn't want to go up. It tried to turn around, but Jancsi wouldn't let it. They fought for a year and a day, and their battle made the water so hot that it remains blistering even now. But Jancsi had grown strong eating the eggs of the turtle, so at last he bested it and made it bear him up.

He emerged high in a mountain. The first thing he did was to kill the giant turtle and eat it. Then he found that the meat of the turtle allowed him to understand the speech of the birds and beasts.

He turned to a bull and said, "What land is this that I have come to?"

But the bull only said, "Find out for yourself, young Jancsi."

So Jancsi said, "Very well, I shall. But because you wouldn't help a man, man shall always be your master." And he put a ring in the bull's nose.

Then he turned to a bat and said, "What land is this that I have come to?"

But the bat said, "See for yourself, young Jancsi."

So Jancsi said, "Very well, I shall. But because you would not share your vision with me, you shall be struck blind." And he covered over the bat's eyes with a layer of its own skin.

Then he turned to a horse and said, "What land is this I have come to?"

The horse said, "This land is called Fenario, and you are to be its master and save it from those of Faerie who oppress it."

"Very well," said Jancsi. "Because you have aided me, you shall ever be the friend of man, who will care for you above all things, as you care for him. And as this land is called

Fenario, and as I am to be its savior, from this day I shall be known as Fenarr."

Then he went to the body of the turtle that he had ridden all that way. From the turtle's shell he made a shield, and from its tail he fashioned a sword with which to oppose those of Faerie.

Then he mounted the horse and rode off to the great battle of which our histories tell.

My uncle told me about all of this. It must be true, because I know my uncle, and he is as honest as me.

chapter fifteen

The Staff

MIKLÓS AVOIDED HIS brother for the rest of the day. He spent much of the night sleepless, wandering along the Riverbank or through the empty courtyard, stopping often by Bölk's grave, yet finding no words to say. He finally slipped into the stables, and in Bölk's stall he was able to sleep.

When he awoke in the morning, Brigitta was next to him. "How did you find me?"

She shook her head. "I didn't. I just came here because— well, I suppose for the same reason you did. I shouldn't have been surprised that you were here also."

For a moment, Miklós felt something like jealousy, but he quickly forced it down into the place where he kept all such things. He studied her face in the dim sunlight that sliced through slats in the stable walls. She was mostly in shadow, but the hollow of her cheeks and the arch of her throat were clear. He reached out and basked in the thrill it still gave him when she placed her hand in his.

But in the next moment of silence, the stall around them reminded him of Bölk and of his duty. He squeezed her hand and released it, then clasped his hands together as he tried to decide what his next step should be.

At length he said, "Vilmos has had enough time to think. We must get agreement from him."

"Are you not afraid that you will frighten him off if you push him too hard?"

"Last night we told him that we weren't pushing him—the very condition of the Palace was pushing him. Did you believe it then, or were you just saying it?"

Brigitta glared at him briefly, but then shook her head. "No, I meant it. But will he see it that way?"

"He has to."

"How will we show him?"

Miklós wrapped his arms around his knees. *Good question,* he thought. *But remember, Vilmos isn't stupid. He acts that way sometimes, but he isn't. Very well, Miklós my friend, how were you convinced?*

He stood up, brushing straw from his clothing. "Come," he said.

She took his hand again, and they made their way into the courtyard, past the pedestal and the fresh grave. They stopped there for a moment, heads bowed. *I am on my own now, my friend. I hope you would approve of what I'm doing.*

They entered the Palace, Brigitta going first over the plank. When Miklós was on it, he knelt and called down below, "Vili, are you there?"

The answer was muffled and confused with echoes.

Miklós said, "It is I, Miklós. I wish to speak to you."

There was another muffled response, then the giant's head appeared. "Yes, Miki?"

"Have you a moment? I'd like you to come with me."

Vilmos squinted up at him, then shrugged his massive shoulders. He ignored the rope ladder that still trailed into the cellar, and, standing on the pile of rubble, pulled himself up into the Palace proper.

He dusted himself off. Miklós and Brigitta led him around the main passageway to the diminutive corridor, with its pale, dim walls and oppressive dust-laden atmosphere, where the Princes' chambers were. They came to the room where the tree waited. *It took me a long time before I could see it for what it was,* thought Miklós. *Will Vilmos? But then, he must have felt something for it or he would have destroyed the roots.*

Miklós came to the curtain. Before he could open it, he heard voices from within. He held up his hand. Whoever was inside, they were speaking loudly. But then, he realized, they must be deeply involved in what they were saying or they would have noticed the trembling of the walls as Vilmos approached.

The first voice he heard he identified as Viktor's. "We must act at once, Your Majesty, before it gets any worse."

Mariska spoke next, saying, "And I still think—"

László cut her off. "I know what you think. You have explained it repeatedly. But it has gone beyond that. Very well. Viktor, send for the guards and have them bring oil and torches—and water. Lots of water. Line up buckets outside. We can at least try to keep it from spreading."

Miklós looked at Brigitta, who was looking back at him. *It is time,* she said with her eyes.

"Come," said Miklós softly, and motioned to Vilmos.

At that moment, Viktor appeared from within the room, saw the three of them, and stopped cold.

"You!" he said, and the hate in his voice was unmistakable. Miklós stared at him. *What have I done to him?* Then he almost laughed. The Goddess, of course; it was what he had done to everyone. He matched the captain's gaze, though it made him feel queasy. Anger, somehow, was easier to contend with than hate; anger could pass. What would Bölk have said? *Get used to it, master,* or something equally helpful. Miklós braced himself, then nodded to him and proceeded into the room. From the corner of his eye he saw Viktor walking away.

He stood in the doorway. Arrayed before the tree were László, Mariska, Andor, and Sándor. One by one, they turned to look at him.

"So," said László.

"Good morning, brother," said Miklós. He felt his heart begin to hammer within his chest, and it came to him that his body knew, somehow before his mind, that this was to be the decisive confrontation between them. He felt that his hands were shaking but forced himself not to look.

"Good morning," said the King. "It is time to destroy this thing before it destroys the Palace. I assume you are here to aid us?" His tone of voice told Miklós plainly that he assumed no such thing.

"No, László. I have discovered that it is the Palace that must be prevented from destroying the tree."

Now it was the King's hands that trembled, though Miklós could see that it was from rage. "What do you think to do about it?" said László.

"I must protect the tree, László."

"I see."

Miklós turned and saw Vilmos, whose eyes were wide and

fixed on the tree as if seeing it for the first time. Miklós turned back to László. "We defend. If you do not attack, there will be no cause for conflict between us."

László spat. "Don't play the hypocrite now, Miklós. The role doesn't suit you."

Miklós waited for rage to build in him, but it didn't. After a moment he said, "You're right. The conflict is inevitable. I just wish it didn't have to be."

László's shoulders relaxed, and he smiled slightly. "On that, brother, we can agree."

As they looked into each other's eyes, Miklós felt that now, of all times, they were actually close and could understand each other. The expression on his brother's face was not hate, nor even anger, but sorrow that mirrored what he, Miklós, felt. László had seemingly learned more than Miklós had thought. He had learned more than to cut and to thrust, or to attack or to retreat, or to plead or to threaten, or to tax or to export. He had learned duty. And, with painful empathy, Miklós knew that he, himself, would never understand it to the depth that his brother did.

Miklós heard sounds from behind him and the spell was broken. He turned and saw that the entire hallway was filled with guards, their bright red uniforms making them seem as if they were a vision from another place, planted in the pale, dim corridor by the hasty brush stroke of an apprentice painter; one who would never graduate from charcoal to oils, or from needle-point to portraiture. Instead of torches and oil, however, they carried naked swords. Miklós felt his pulse quicken even more and wished there were someone he could pray to.

Viktor called past Miklós, "We are ready, Your Majesty."

"Very well," said László. He looked at Miklós. "If you leave here and promise never to return, you may have your life." He gestured at Brigitta. "That one may accompany you."

Not trusting himself to speak, Miklós shook his head. He felt Brigitta touch his arm. "What?" he whispered.

"Whatever happens, let us be fully in the room when it does."

He nodded.

They took a step forward. László's eyes were burning, almost feverish. Sándor remained calm, but Andor's hands were twitching nervously, and he was blinking rapidly, his head making tiny motions. Mariska said, "A moment, László."

The King glanced at her impatiently. "Yes?"

Her eyes darted back and forth between László and Viktor. At length she said, "We should speak privately, Your Majesty. Before anything else is done here. It is important."

The King studied her and blinked twice. "Just say it, Countess."

"I think," she said slowly, "that that would be ill-advised."

Miklós stared at them, feeling as if he were a servant who happened to be present while the lord and lady of the manor discussed their private affairs.

"I insist," said the King.

She looked at him again, looked at Viktor, then back at the King. "Very well then," she said. "I do not believe you should enter into battle here under the impression that your Captain of the Guards is trustworthy."

Miklós glanced quickly at Viktor, who, notwithstanding that he turned pale, stiffened and could not keep his eyes from darting to (for some reason) Sándor, nevertheless put forth an amazing performance of being unconcerned. A few of the guards behind him gasped.

László's eyebrows arched. "How is that, you say?"

"I have reason to believe that he is conspiring against you for the throne. I have only just received proof. I know this is not the best time to say it, but this may be just the opportunity he wants to strike. I feel you must know, and you insisted it be spoken of publicly."

"Quite right, quite right," said László evenly. "Well, if that is all—"

"All!" cried Mariska.

He looked at her curiously. "Mariska, my dear, you must know that Viktor is, by birth, not excessively far from the throne."

"You knew that?" she said, saying in words what Viktor seemed to be saying most eloquently without the benefit of spoken language.

"It is Rezső's job," said the King, "to be certain that I know such things. And naturally, in a time of crisis such as this, Viktor's thoughts will stray to how much better he could do at managing it than I can. Don't you know the story of the Baron and the Runaway Coach? '"Well then," said the coachman, "You can have them!" And he vanished in a puff of smoke.' Is that what you think I'll do? Or am I to lose a fine soldier like Viktor merely because he takes his duties very seriously? No, no. I knew of this, and I've sent word to Henrik to make sure he gets no support of the army. This sort of thing always happens. My father tells me—"

"Your Majesty," said Sándor.

The King looked at him. "Yes?"

"Excuse me, but these fine people seem to be awaiting our pleasure. I think it unseemly to delay them further."

Viktor seemed to have something caught in his throat. "Your Majesty," he managed, "I—"

"Hush, Viktor. We have no time now to discuss it."

Miklós stared at his brother as if he were a stranger. *So this is what it means to be King.*

László nodded to Sándor. "Yes. You are right. Now, where were we, Miklós?"

Mariska threw her head back in a gesture that was both like and unlike Brigitta's. "I have no wish to see this. May I leave?"

The King waved her away as if he were brushing a bee from his face. She walked past Brigitta and Miklós without appearing to see them. Miklós watched her as she entered the hall. She looked over at Viktor and his guards, and shuddered. Then she turned to Vilmos. "I am leaving here. Will you come with me?"

He looked at her, appearing almost puzzled, but said nothing.

"Please?" she said. "Let us visit the norska. I'd like that. We have no part in . . . in what they are about to do."

Vilmos blinked twice, then shook his head. A sigh seemed to pass through Mariska's body. Her left hand clutched air, and, for the first time, Miklós noticed that she wasn't holding her fan. She turned away and, without looking back, went down the hall. Miklós could almost fancy he had seen tears glistening on her cheeks before she passed from sight.

László, standing perhaps six feet from Miklós, licked his lips. Then he drew his sabre. Állam caught a beam of sunlight from the window and glittered wickedly. László held it out, low, pointing up, yet not quite at Miklós. Andor backed away. Miklós felt himself pulled toward Brigitta and felt her sudden touch against his side.

László said, "Now, Viktor." He smiled slightly. "Prove yourself. Get him."

Miklós turned to face the door, while, by unspoken consent, Brigitta kept her eyes on László.

Miklós said, "Vilmos."

The giant stirred and looked at him. Viktor appeared in the doorway, stepped through and to the side. He turned back toward those he commanded and said, "Take Prince Miklós. Kill him if necessary."

Miklós said, "Vilmos."

The sound of footsteps. His heart sank and he was certain that, by now, his trembling was visible. He met the giant's eyes. The first of the guards appeared in the doorway, found Miklós, and raised his sabre to chest level, arm straight, wrist turned over, exactly as Viktor taught for fighting in close quarters.

"Vilmos."

The guard stepped fully into the room.

He got no farther. Vilmos reached out and took the guard under his armpits, lifted him over his head, and threw him down the hall. There was a curse and a cry as he landed. Vilmos looked startled. "He cut himself on someone's sword," he explained.

Vilmos moved forward, positioning himself in the doorway. Miklós felt a wave of relief rushing through him; it momentarily left him as weak-kneed as his fear had before. He stole a quick glance at László. The King stood as still as the idol of the Goddess had. He held his sabre pointing up. He stared at Vilmos, eyes wide. His self-confidence seemed to be wavering for the first time that Miklós could ever remember.

When Miklós's glance returned to the doorway, he could barely see past the giant's form that two guards stood facing him there. One struck at Vilmos. Miklós could not see what he did, but in an instant the guard was on the floor and the giant had the sword in his hands. He broke it in half as if it were flint and cast the pieces onto the ground before him.

As far as Miklós could see, the other guard got as far as raising his sword before one of Vilmos's mighty hands came down upon his head; he dropped like a lead weight.

Two more red uniforms took their place and were treated with equal courtesy. Miklós glanced at Viktor. The captain still held his sabre. He watched Vilmos carefully and licked his lips. He seemed unwilling to attack.

Miklós watched his brother deal with two more guards, take a step back into the room, then turn and give Miklós a quick, almost shy smile. Then he returned to the doorway.

At that moment, Miklós heard Brigitta's voice next to his ear. "Do nothing, wizard," she said.

Miklós spun. There was a look of concentration on Sándor's face, and he was staring at Vilmos. Thoughts of his own power came to Miklós's mind, but—*You must find a new weapon, master.* He looked around, as if hoping to see something lying on the floor. Behind him, he still heard the sounds of Vilmos scuffling with guards.

Sándor was still concentrating. As Miklós tried to decide what to do, Brigitta acted. She stepped forward with a speed Miklós could not have guessed at. She reached Sándor before the wizard was aware, and, placing both hands on his chest, pushed him into the tree.

He fell backward, startled, and slid to the floor. Brigitta rushed past him as he started to rise. She stood behind him and took into her hand a trailer covered with thin leaves. She wrapped this, tendril-like, around his neck and pulled tight, gripping both ends with her left hand.

Sándor seemed startled, but raised his hands in a gesture that reminded Miklós of the Demon Goddess. He wanted to yell to Brigitta that the power could be summoned from the source faster than she could strangle him, but there was no need. With a strength he hadn't realized she possessed, her closed right hand came crashing down directly onto the top of Sándor's head. The wizard sighed and fell back, senseless.

Miklós, cursing himself for doing nothing, stared at the tree. *There's your weapon, fool.*

How then? What did the tree conceal within its massive leaf covering?

László still hadn't moved. Brigitta's eyes widened suddenly, staring over Miklós's shoulder. As Miklós turned, there came a sudden motion from the side.

Brigitta had seen that as Vilmos was soundly drubbing the guards, Viktor had finally begun sneaking up on the giant from behind. But the flash of motion was Andor.

To the wonder and amazement of Miklós, if not everyone in the room, fat, slow Andor had jumped and fallen onto Viktor and was wrestling him to the ground. The captain would have had no trouble in a contest of strength with Andor, but the combination of sheer dead weight along with the arms wrapped tightly about his body took him some time to deal with.

"Vilmos," called the young Prince. "Look to your side!"

The giant did and saw what was occurring. He took a moment from his bashing of guards to drop his fist on Viktor's head, just as Brigitta had done to Sándor. Viktor lay still. Vilmos looked at Miklós, gave him another quick, shy grin, and returned to facing the guards. Andor looked at Miklós, started to smile, then dropped his eyes.

From what Miklós could see of the number of bodies piled in front of the door, he doubted that many guards were left by now.

Then Brigitta called, "Miklós, 'ware the King!"

The Prince spun and saw that László was moving forward steadily toward Vilmos's back, Állam leveled in front of him. *Now is your time, Miklós,* he told himself. And, even as he did, he wondered if he would have the courage to act. Yet, to his own surprise and eternal pride, he found that he was moving forward. His hands empty, he came behind László and tried to take the wrist that held the sabre.

But the King was quicker and stronger. Almost absent-mindedly, László struck the Prince in the forehead with the pommel of his sword.

For an instant, all he saw were the colors and patterns on the inside of his eyes. Then Miklós found that he was on his back, near the tree. Brigitta, next to him, met his eyes. Then she, too, charged the King. Miklós wanted to cry to her to stop, but there was no time. With a similar disdainful gesture, László struck her with the flat of the blade, and she fell back, dazed, next to Miklós.

Then it was Andor's turn. He knelt, then squatted, then sprang like an attacking norska. Állam flashed, and Miklós saw blood. Andor howled like a wounded animal, and Miklós saw that he held the stump of his right arm in his left hand, staring at it in horror. His right hand lay, palm up, on the floor next to László's feet.

His eyes met Miklós's for a moment, then he fell backward, sprawling. His upper body was still, but his legs kicked out, pitifully. Brigitta crept over to him on all fours and began tearing strips from her dress to bind his maimed arm. Miklós looked at László, whose eyes were wide with horror. Yet the King stared not at Andor but at Állam gleaming in his hand.

And, even as Miklós watched, the blade began to tremble, as
if László couldn't control it. The King looked up at him with
an expression of helplessness.

Vilmos, finished with the guards, stood and took another
step into the room. He faced László, his arms held out in front
of him. The King shook his head in denial; then it seemed that
his arm was nearly pulled from its socket by the sabre.

Állam struck at Vilmos like a snake. Miklós saw it connect
with his side, and blood spurted, mixing with the pool that had
formed when Andor's hand had been cut off. Vilmos looked
puzzled, and took another step toward László. "Miki," he said.

The expression on the King's face twisted, as if the rage
embodied in the weapon had worked its way into his soul. He
moved toward Vilmos and thrust for his heart, but the giant
twisted, so the sword only grazed across his chest. A rip appeared in his jerkin, and line of blood showed against his skin.

"Miki," he said.

*Now, what, princeling? Take another dive at László to at
least die fighting? For what?*

László stepped back before the giant's advance and cut down.
This time blood came in a smooth, even flow from Vilmos's
cheek. "Miki."

*Your weapon, idiot! Find your weapon! You don't know what
it is, but you damn well know where!*

László tried another cut for Vilmos's side. The giant stepped
back, but the blade caught him above the previous cut; he
stumbled, and there was more blood flowing from his body.

With a wrench that was almost painful, Miklós turned his
back on the battle and dived through the foliage. Behind him,
as if from a great distance, he heard once more, "Miki."

Inside, under the cover of the leaves and branches, there
was a pale light that seemed to come from all around. Miklós
cast his eyes to the trunk, now thick and solid, almost bursting
with life.

Growing from it, sticking straight out, was a single, large,
bare branch; thick and heavy in appearance, as if it were put
there for just this purpose. *Perhaps it was*, thought Miklós, as
he reached for it. It came away in his hand with a sharp crack.

He took it with both hands. It was nearly as big as he was.
It was as heavy as a stone, and Miklós found that he could
hardly lift it.

Yet, only a few feet away, Vilmos was dying.

Miklós cradled the branch in his arms. His back threatened to break, and his legs felt weak and watery. He forced his legs to carry him forward a step, but he nearly fell over and was forced to take two steps backward to avoid falling and being crushed beneath the weight.

He cursed silently, found his footing, and leaned forward slightly. He ran, rather than walked, back into the dim light of the chamber.

When he stepped back, Vilmos was only inches from him. There was another wound on his face now and a gash high on his right leg. His stomach had been cut open. Miklós could almost see the quivering of Vilmos's organs, but he allowed himself no time for nausea.

With all of his strength, he held the massive staff out with both of his arms.

"Take it, Vili," he said in a barely audible whisper.

The giant reached out his right hand and took it. Although he had never, as far as Miklós knew, used a club or a staff, he gripped it in both hands as if he knew what he was doing. Yet he seemed almost unaware of his actions; seemed to be concentrating wholly on László. He stumbled forward with the staff held out before him like a shield.

Miklós sank to the floor. László stepped back a few paces, until he was nearly in the far corner. He was uninjured, yet sweat beaded his forehead and his breathing was labored. He took a few tentative passes through the air with Állam, but Vilmos didn't seem to notice; he merely took another step forward. László's eyes narrowed as he studied the unadorned staff, and he shot a quick, speculative glance at the tree.

Állam seemed to jump in his hand, as if unwilling to refrain from battle. Vilmos took another halting step forward. László's mouth opened, and he broke forth with a yell that echoed throughout the room: the snarl of a cornered dzur or the battle cry of a charging dragon.

Almost faster than Miklós could see, the sabre swept down in a great arc toward Vilmos's head. The giant raised his staff. It was almost too late—almost, but not quite.

Steel met wood in a flash of white light that left Miklós with spots in front of his eyes, and with a clap like thunder that left a ringing in his ears. At the same time, he felt the tree behind him sway and tremble.

When Miklós could see again, Vilmos still stood, the staff

resting against the floor. László stood facing him, the hilt of Állam still in his hand. On the floor next to the King lay the blade of the sabre, now only a broken piece of burnt and twisted metal.

Vilmos tottered. But before he fell, he lifted the staff once more and thrust it into László's stomach. The King cried out and fell to the floor, where he lay moaning softly and moving his head from side to side. Vilmos collapsed to his knees. A faint smell of smoke filled the room.

For a moment no one moved. But then a breeze came from the open window, bringing the clean scent of the River, mixed with the fresh growing fragrance of the tree. Vilmos turned and there were tears in his eyes, but he said, "Thank you, Miki."

Brigitta stood and came over to the giant. She stroked his forehead, and, with his own garments, bound some of his lesser wounds. The blood still flowed freely from his side and his stomach, but there was little that could be done for those. László still moaned quietly on the floor.

Miklós saw that Andor's stump had been bound and was no longer bleeding. His severed hand still lay where it had fallen. Miklós turned his eyes from it. Viktor was still as death, yet Miklós could see the slow rise and fall of his back as he breathed.

There was a thud as Vilmos let the staff fall next to him. Brigitta looked at Miklós and caught his eye. She glanced down at the giant, then back at Miklós, and shook her head.

Miklós felt a lump rise in his throat, and for a moment he couldn't swallow. Then, with an almost desperate need to do something, he stepped between Vilmos and László, over to the branch he had taken from the tree. He looked at it, wondering whence it had come. It was plain and seemed almost to have been polished. There were no marks of twigs or leaves or other branches on it. The end where he had broken it from the tree was, impossibly, rounded and smooth.

Yet he was not then able to complete his inspection, for at that moment the Palace itself, from its very foundations, began to moan and rock back and forth, as if to match the actions of the King as he lay hurt and stunned before the tree and his brothers.

Miklós rose to his feet, but was knocked down again by the shaking of the Palace. Brigitta sprawled over Vilmos, who seemed not to feel her weight. Miklós looked up, and he saw that the ceiling was tilting, ready to come down upon all of them. Cracks appeared in the floor and walls, and Miklós longed for the strength to reach out to Brigitta, but his knees were weak and she was too far away. He caught her eye for an eternal moment of love and anguish, but another tremor pulled her attention away.

Yet even then, Miklós's eyes were drawn back to the staff. The one end was rounded, but the other had a peculiar shape to it. Miklós, despite the agonized tremblings of the chamber, looked closer. Yes, there was no doubt: it had been carved.

Carved into the shape of a horse's head.

Even the eyes seemed to be there—sparkling like jewels. And as he watched, they seemed to come alive and look at him and see him.

The chamber swayed, cracked, and fell apart.

The tree shook itself and seemed to reach out in all directions. The horse's head carved upon the staff opened its mouth then and said, "Fear nothing, master. You have done well."

INTERLUDE

THE PALACE SEEMED TO vanish around the tree.

Freedom! it cried. All of the energy contained within it burst at once, and it grew as if in all the time since it began it had been changeless. It grew as a mountain will from a volcanic pit, or as love will when two predestined souls find each other, it seems, at that one time when they both need to.

What is this? A falling ceiling? Its roots could now support far more weight than that and not feel it; it guided the ceiling safely to the side. A crumbling floor? It cradled those who stood on it as if they were babes and it a mother with a thousand arms. A dying man? This is no time for death—this is a time for growth and renewal. Another man has lost a limb? It grieves with him but rejoices that he yet lives.

It burst upon the world around it crying, Here! Here I am!

Parapets, golden and silver in the sunlight, sprang above the River and laughed with it. Streamers flew from towers that shone white and pure. Within, corridors exploded from nothing to join rooms that were yet to be, and the circular stairways it built were wide and comfortable, for the time for fear was past. It laughed at the world outside and dared it to join in its dance of creation.

Castles and palaces and hovels turned from it in fear and jealousy, but it only laughed, calling, join me, join me! You have life within you, too. They turned from it for now. But they could neither destroy it nor forget it.

A birth, and a death, as if they were one thing. For if they are not, they appear too often together to be far different.

Its story is barely beginning.

Yet the story of those within is not yet done.

chapter sixteen

The Tree

MIKLÓS LOOKED AROUND HIM, wondering at the sudden lack of motion. He recognized at once that he was inside of the area enclosed by the tree. He heard the sounds of crumbling and breaking but only as from a distance.

Andor knelt, clutching his arm, oblivious to his surroundings. Brigitta looked around, even as Miklós did. Vilmos stirred, and, unaccountably, his bleeding had slowed, even seemed to be stopping. Viktor shook his head and blinked. Sándor was sitting up, his eyes closed, seemingly lost in thought. László stopped moving. He stared up at the ceiling and breathed deeply.

Miklós found that he was still holding on to the staff. He stared at it, and Bölk looked back at him somberly.

"What is happening, Bölk?"

"A new beginning, master."

Miklós trembled. "How are you alive?"

"As ever. This my thirty-eighth incarnation. I am different, but then, it is always different."

"I am glad you're alive, Bölk. I can't tell you how glad."

"Thank you, master, I don't feel so myself, but that is as it must be."

Miklós blinked, and stared. "What do you mean *must* be?"

"How can I feel anything, master? You have removed my heart."

* * *

László's hand hurt. He looked down and found that he was squeezing the hilt of Állam. Next to his leg, he saw the broken, ruined blade.

He brought the hilt piece up before his eyes and saw there the ruination of the trust his fathers had had in him.

He didn't know how he was being protected or where he was, but somehow it didn't matter. The Palace was falling apart around him. He wondered if, in the tower high above, his parents were dying, being swept away with the tattered ruins of the building. He tried to grieve but couldn't. They had died years before, when he had taken the kingship. It was as well if they wouldn't live to see what he had done to it.

His eyes fell on Miklós, staring intently at that strange staff, his lips moving as if he were praying to it. What was it? It didn't matter. Brigitta was staring around her in wonder. Brigitta! Who would have thought it? A little tavern wench, to aid in his undoing. And now, of course, she would gloat over him along with Miklós. Or perhaps they wouldn't. That would be worse, in a way.

He pulled himself upright, then he stood. He thought to catch Sándor's eye, but the wizard's were closed. Was he preparing something? László looked at him closely. No; if he could do anything, he would have done so.

There was no sensation of movement, but he could still hear crumbling and falling from outside of this—what was it? Best not to know. He didn't ever want to know.

He cleared his throat to make sure his voice wouldn't crack when he spoke then said, "Miklós."

His brother looked up and seemed startled that he was on his feet. László tossed him the hilt of Állam. Miklós caught it, then set it down. László said, "This is yours now. Do as you will with it."

He stepped over to the green, wavering wall and was not surprised that he was able to step through it. He was not surprised to find that he was falling—in the open air, in daylight, in the real world of courtyard and crumbling walls.

He felt his ankle twist when he struck the ground and looked up in time to see some of the delicate tracings on the carved sandstone block that killed him.

Brigitta took a step over to Miklós. He took her hand. "I think he's dead," he said.

"László?"

"Yes. I felt it."

"I'm sorry."

Miklós held her hand to his cheek and pressed.

She said, "What are you going to do with that?"

He looked up and saw that she was looking at the hilt of Állam. "I don't know. Do you have any ideas? Bury it, maybe?"

She shook her head. "Use it. It is a useful symbol for now. Its power is broken, and I imagine it will rust away soon, but it isn't worthless yet."

"All right," said Miklós. He realized that he felt too numb to argue about anything. It was good that someone could make a decision for him. "Did you see Vilmos? He seems better somehow."

"Better?" She said, turning to look. When she turned back, there was puzzlement on her face. "You're right. I don't understand it; he was dying. I must go to him."

Miklós nodded. He sat down cross-legged on the floor and studied the jewels on the hilt. Some of the sapphires on it were missing; they'd probably never be found. Unimportant, yet sad.

He glanced around the room once more. Vilmos sat up, even as Brigitta knelt down next to him. Then Miklós saw Andor and his eyes narrowed. He stood up quickly.

Why is there no pain?

Andor studied the place he was in. *This is what I've been searching for,* said one part of him. But the other part stared at the bandages where his right hand used to be. *Why is there no pain?*

Maimed, by the Goddess! And now—a one-handed Prince? Doing what? He looked at those around him and felt a peculiar pride. He had done something, this time. Whatever else anyone could say about him, this time he had acted. There was that side to his wound, too. No one could ever look at him again without knowing that he had helped to save his brother's life.

It was a strange and oddly pleasing feeling. And there was no doubt in his mind that, if he'd been whole, he could have enjoyed it. He stretched both arms out in front of him. The bandages made them almost the same length. Why was there no pain? Never mind. Accept it; it probably wouldn't last.

Nothing of this moment would last, he realized.

He had taken his stand and done his part. From now on, he would be a useless fixture around the Palace. And with every passing year, his one useful deed would get smaller and smaller. Eventually he would return to being the parasite—now he could face it—that he had been up until now.

But now he could not go back to that.

He looked to where László had gone and suddenly understood his oldest brother. Andor's mind ran through all he had said and done since Miklós's return from Faerie, and his stomach actually churned with self-disgust.

But only two steps away from him was a wall of green. He knew that he could follow László through. He knew that death awaited him when he did. He had always wanted to be like László, he thought ironically.

For the one moment that resolve was strong in him, he stood, faced the wall, and stepped forward.

The transition from lethargic to energetic was almost enough to shock Miklós back to lethargy. But, the crisis upon him, he knew enough to act at once.

Andor had just begun his second step, the one that would take him into the wall, when Miklós reached him. He took both of his brother's shoulders in his hands, dropping Állam along the way, and wrenched him backward. *"No!"*

Andor fell back and stared at him, unmoving. His eyes were dead, and his expression one of puzzlement. "Why did you stop me, Miki?" he asked in the tones of a hurt child.

"Because we need you, Andor."

The other blinked. "For what?"

Miklós clutched him desperately, as if Andor might still tear free and throw himself outside. "Just to be. We love you. You're our brother. We have already lost one brother, we *can't* lose you, too. Please!"

Andor shook his head. "But what will I do?"

Miklós, somehow, understood the question. "I don't know, Andor. But it will be something useful, and it will make you happy. I promise you. I can't know what it is yet, but there will be something."

Andor didn't seem convinced, but after a moment he nodded and said, "All right. I'll try. Thank you, Miki. I love you."

Miklós buried his head in his brother's chest.

* * *

Vilmos took great gulps of air into his lungs and almost laughed for the sheer joy of it. He looked at Brigitta and matched her smile with his grin.

"I thought you were dying," she said.

"Ha!"

"How do you feel?"

"Weak," he admitted. "But good. There is no pain. I think I could lift—"

The sounds from around him. The place they were in. The tree. It was protecting them. It was protecting them from the Palace that was falling into pieces. All of it. Collapsing.

With a cry he sprang fully to his feet. He dimly heard Brigitta and Miklós calling to him, but he had no time for that. The wall before him was either solid or it was not, he couldn't tell, but there was no time to find out. He crashed through it, and wasn't really aware that it let him pass easily.

He landed in the courtyard and paid no attention to the maelstrom around him. He felt things brushing him, like leaves falling from a tree, and noted absently that they were boards, blocks, and beams from the Palace. He brushed them off.

He knew at once where the hole in the flooring was, but it was covered by rubble. That meant—no, he wouldn't think about it. The floor he stood on seemed to be bending from the weight of wood and stone falling on it, but he wouldn't think of that, either.

For a time his mind went blank. When he could think again, he stood by the hole down to the cellar, which was now cleared of blockage.

Then he was down it.

Anya and Atya chittered angrily at him and looked nervously above them as the bending planks from the ceiling slowly crushed the cage. There was no longer room for them to stand. Csecsemő and Húga crouched fearfully in the one end of their cage that hadn't been flattened.

Then Vilmos saw why they had not yet been crushed: the tree roots—the very roots that he had chosen not to remove— had stretched out and covered them, protected them.

Vilmos had no time to feel relief. The roots were giving way before the awesome weight pressing down on them. Even as he watched, the ceiling collapsed a little more. He crouched down until he was under it, then bent his head so the ceiling rested on his shoulders, neck, and head. Then he pushed up.

Never, in all his years, had anything been so heavy. Vilmos had never tested his strength, so he had no knowledge of its limits; the ceiling was heavier than he had ever imagined anything could be.

It fell another notch, and Vilmos saw rather than felt his knees bend. Csecsemő emitted a cry that was either terror or pain. Vilmos felt rage build up in him, and for the first time he understood how poor László must have felt those times when his eyes had become so fiery, and his mouth had twisted into a snarl.

The giant's fury was as red as his wounds that opened anew as he strained. A meaningless growl came from his throat as he demanded more of his body than he ever had before.

And, for just a moment, the ceiling lifted perhaps an inch.

He had left his arms free, and he faced the cages. He snatched them both with one hand to leave the other free to help him climb. He huddled down as the ceiling settled again. As he turned to run, he saw something white lying on the ground and, without thinking, picked it up and put it into his pocket.

He gave himself no chance to feel weakness, relief, or joy for his victory, however. He dashed to the hole in the floor. More rubble had fallen through it, so that now when he stood on it, his waist reached up to the bending, cracking floor. He leapt up onto it, almost lost his balance, and began running. He kept his body bent over the cages to shield them.

For the first time he looked up.

His eyes and his mind refused to grasp what he saw.

The air was filled with more collapsing stone and wood than Vilmos had thought the Palace could ever hold. And in the center was a whirlwind of green dust with lightning flashing from it. He could recognize no part of the Palace that he saw, except that, straight ahead of him, ran a circular stairway that had once led up to the Great Hall.

It seemed impossible that it still stood, almost as if someone or something were providing him a way of safety where otherwise there would be none. Yet was it true safety? It seemed so fragile. Even as he watched it shook and nearly fell.

And, to confound the impossibilities, the air was becoming even more filled with blocks of stone and with beams—as if the Palace had eaten these things over hundreds of years and was now disgorging them. They were becoming larger and heavier, too, and he knew that even he would not live if one of those fell on him.

There was no choice then.

But, just before he began to run, he saw Mariska, standing amid the falling ruins, staring at the heart of what had once been the Palace.

"Come, Countess," he said. "You'll be killed."

"No I won't," she said, as if she were saying, "I don't care." Then she saw that he held the norska, and for a moment almost smiled. "Bring them to safety, Vilmos. Hurry."

"But you—"

"I will be fine, my friend. Or I won't. Go."

"I—" As he stopped and turned to go once more, he realized what it was that he had picked up. Then, quickly, he set the cages down and dug into his pocket. "Here, lady," he said, handing it to her. "Here is your fan."

Then he sprinted to the stairway, hoping it would hold his weight, and started up.

For what seemed an eternity, Miklós stared at the spot in the wall where Vilmos had stepped through. Andor, next to him, rose to his feet and touched the wall. Then he turned away and walked back to the middle of the room. Brigitta touched Miklós's arm.

I will know it if he dies. I will feel it. I felt it with László, I will feel it with Vili. I know I will.

He held himself together in the same way one holds one's breath—with tension. He found that he had clenched his hands into fists.

His eye was drawn to another part of room, then, as Viktor stood up, still holding a sabre, and began walking toward him. Brigitta tensed at his side.

Viktor's hate was cold—almost passionless.

Something—he didn't know what—had happened to destroy all of his hopes, plans, and dreams. He could see no cause, but the feeling was unmistakable. Everything was different now. The notion of somehow removing László was now laughable; László himself was laughable. They were all laughable. It was fitting that he had chosen to kill himself and pleasingly ironic that Vilmos had joined him. This left no one to protect Miklós, who had been behind it all from the very beginning.

And Miklós would be so pitifully easy to kill.

His eyes went to the stump of Andor's arm. So, László had accomplished that much at least. On the floor between Andor and Miklós lay the hilt of Állam, and, seeing it, Viktor paused for a moment. What could have broken the sword? He almost went over to pick it up, but first things first.

He looked into Miklós's eyes, but the fear he had seen there earlier was gone, leaving only a tired resignation. Not what he would have wanted, but it would do.

He raised his sword. Brigitta stepped into the way. How sweet. He chuckled, then chuckled again as Miklós pushed her out of the way. Perhaps he should hold his stroke until they came to blows, and let them both die remembering that.

Something caught his eye, just past Miklós. He squinted, and realized that half of a small cage had pushed its way through the wall. A cage? And another one. And in them were norska.

Vilmos?

Vilmos.

The giant stumbled rather than walked into the room, tattered and bleeding, his eyes vacant. Cold sweat broke out on Viktor's forehead. He had almost had Miklós, too. But there was no way to defeat Vilmos; he could see that now.

The giant set the cages down, then bent over, not appearing to notice that his brother was about to lose his life, and held his knees, gasping.

Thank you, Goddess who is no more! A better chance there could never be!

He shifted his direction, and, with all the speed of which he was capable, struck down at the exposed neck.

Miklós cried, "Vilmos!" in a pleasingly agonized tone, but Viktor knew it was too late. The giant looked up and caught Viktor's eye just as the blade struck his neck.

A sensation passed through the captain's arm that was nearly identical to what he'd felt when striking at the root. His blade bounded back, and Vilmos straightened up. He looked at Viktor for a moment, then slowly reached out his hand.

It can't be! He knew he should move, throw himself through the wall and trust to luck, but he couldn't summon the will to move.

Vilmos's hand closed around his throat. He felt it constrict, then twist. He heard a cracking sound and wondered if, by a miracle, the giant's wrist had broken.

Miklós stepped over Viktor's body as if it were a lump in a carpet. There had been too much grief and joy intermixed for him to comprehend any of it anymore, and he felt that it still wasn't over. He could only act as the situation called for and try to understand it when it was over—if he were still alive then.

He helped Vilmos to lie down. The giant looked at Viktor sadly, then shook his head. He stretched out, then, mumbling incoherently, pointed at the cages. Miklós nodded and, finding the catches, opened the doors. All four norksa slipped out, the small one limping slightly. They clustered around Vilmos's face, nuzzling him, and a certain measure of joy for his brother penetrated the haze through which Miklós walked.

Brigitta knelt at the giant's head and began, once more, to treat his wounds.

Sándor continued watching through his almost-closed eyes—a trick he had learned early in the Palace. So. László was dead, Viktor was dead, Vilmos was invulnerable. That last was interesting; the legends of the heirs of Fenarr might have that much truth in them.

And what about the staff? Well, well, there was much to think of here. But first, he must find a place where he could feel secure. This wasn't it, certainly. There were too many conflicting patterns here; the destruction of the Palace, the battles among the brothers, and the staff all created too much confusion.

This would be a day to remember, all right. That in itself was pleasing. There had been fewer and fewer of those as the years wore on, and to think of being around for the destruction of the Palace itself! This would certainly make a fine story someday to amuse and delight the great-great grandson of this young Miklós, who had bungled his way to the cleanest usurpation of a throne Sándor could imagine.

He chuckled to himself. Enough of this, anyway; it was time to be leaving. He opened his eyes fully and stood up. Miklós, seeing the motion, turned to him.

"What now, wizard?"

Sándor shrugged. "I must be leaving. If you wish, I will be at your service after I've settled down a bit."

"No," said Miklós slowly, "I do not believe that will be necessary. I think this kingdom does not require the power of Faerie any more."

"As you wish." Young idiot! In a week he would be begging for help to handle the settling in of his rule. But Kings will be Kings, and young Kings will be young Kings. "I will be leaving you, then," he said.

He stepped through the wall at his back and called for the power. He looked down, and was instantly saddened to see the broken body of Rezső lying in the ruins next to the cursed river.

He realized that he was falling. Tch! Mustn't get overconfident now, Alfredo. He demanded the power to support his flight, and considered where to go.

He was still considering when he hit the water. The icy chill of the River struck him, and he felt water rush into his mouth and his lungs.

This is absurd, he thought, calling for power to propel himself to the surface.

Only then did he become aware of something big and powerful between him and the source. The next thing he realized was that his lungs were bursting. He felt his feet touch the ground at the bottom of the River, and he knew panic for the first time in more than a hundred years.

Panic was the last thing he knew.

Miklós watched the wizard vanish. He shrugged and turned away. Brigitta was tending Vilmos, and the giant, though his breathing was labored, seemed to be doing well enough. Or, at least, Brigitta did not seem to be worried. Andor was in a corner, staring at the staff.

Miklós went over to him. "What do you see, brother?"

Andor stared at him, wide-eyed. "Bölk. He says that Sándor is dead."

"Indeed?" said Miklós smiling. "Well, I'm not surprised. I—wait, you understood him?"

"Yes! I don't believe it!"

Miklós found himself smiling, though he would have had trouble explaining exactly why.

* * *

Mariska pulled on the reins of the horse she'd taken from the
Palace stables, turning it away from the smoke she could see
billowing up from the Palace.

So, László had had his way and burned down the tree and
the Palace with it. Who had lived and who had died? Would
Vilmos and the norska survive? Somehow she thought they
would. At least, they would share the same fate.

But, in any case, it was none of her affair anymore. She
was going home. Home! She was suddenly aching for the scent
of the spruce, the drone of the cicadas, and the song of the
mountain winds.

The title of "Countess" didn't sound so bad, after all. Her
mother would have understood.

She clutched her fan once more and was surprised to find
that, for the first time, it was a different face that appeared to
her.

Between them, Andor and Miklós rolled the staff over to where
Brigitta tended Vilmos.

"What is it?" she asked.

"How is he?"

She nodded. "He'll be fine."

Even as she spoke, his breathing seemed to be easier. To
Miklós's eyes he was pale, but his eyes looked about alertly.
"Good," he said. "There is something you should see."

He and Andor turned the staff so the carved end faced her.
Brigitta gasped. "Bölk!"

"As always," said the horse.

"No, different this time, I think," she said.

"Yes," said Bölk. "As always."

"Oh. All right."

Vilmos looked at Miklós. "What does he mean about being
different being the same?"

Brigitta said, "He means—"

"Pay no mind," said Miklós, wanting suddenly to laugh.
He looked into Brigitta's eyes, almost shouting with joy.

"What is it?" she asked.

"We both hear the same things now," he said.

Her eyes widened.

"Not all of us," said Andor.

"You will soon, I think," said Brigitta. Then, suddenly, she
turned to Miklós. "You are very, very happy," she said. "In

fact, you are finding it difficult not to laugh from sheer joy, although you aren't sure of the reason."

He nodded. "Yes. But why do you say it like that?"

She laughed. "Pay no mind."

Brigitta didn't know which brought her more happiness—the discovery that Bölk was alive or the pleasure of being able to see into Miklós's mind through his face.

She saw that he wished to hold her and wrapped her arms about his waist. Then she turned back to Bölk. He was staring at her somberly.

"What is it, Bölk? Is something wrong?"

"Wrong?" he said, "No. But there is something you should know. Something you *do* know, although you won't yet believe it."

"All right," she said. "Tell me what it is, then I shall know that I know."

"Do you wish me to say it aloud, to everyone?"

She hesitated, then, "I have no secrets," she lied.

"Then know, Brigitta, that you are with child. Miklós is the father. The child is, at this moment, healthy. Beyond that, I know nothing of it."

Brigitta stared at him. It took a moment for understanding to penetrate, bringing with it meanings and associations and repercussions. Then the world reeled around her, and she feared she would faint.

She turned to Miklós, and there was such joy on his face he seemed ready to burst.

She began to tremble.

To Miklós, this was all that was needed. The thoughts of his dead brother were driven from his mind. Before him was his first real love, and now they were bound together in a way that, in his naïveté, he had not foreseen as possible.

A child. *His* child. *Their* child. To bring life into the world and into a world that was now, he dared to hope, a better place than it had been. A son? Perhaps even that. Either way, a child.

In a sense, that is what they had done with the Palace; the old giving way to the new, a birth, with a death necessary to clear the way for it. Miklós chuckled. Was Rezső still alive? If so, he would be pleased that there was now at least one heir in the royal family.

He took Brigitta into his arms again, holding her head against his shoulder and rocking gently back and forth. He felt Andor's arm upon his shoulder and smiled at him. Vilmos said, "Uncle Vili. That doesn't sound bad, eh, Atya? What do you think? Do you like it?"

The norska chittered.

Miklós noticed that there seemed to be a wet spot on his shoulder. He pulled back to look into Brigitta's eyes. She was crying.

The old King and Queen had died quietly, unnoticed by themselves or the Palace as their tower gave way and fell to the ground, crushing them quickly beneath stone and rolling their bodies into the River.

László's body lay beneath a block of stone that had once been part of his tower. Perhaps he had found his Goddess again.

Andor had felt an urge to put a hand on his brother's shoulder, and had reached out before realizing that there was no hand there. Yet, Miklós had not seemed to notice. Miklós had turned and smiled at him, and never even seemed aware that there was the stump of an arm on his shoulder. Yet, in a way, it pleased him even more that *he*, Andor, hadn't noticed. Perhaps there was hope.

Vilmos closed his eyes and let Anya chitter into his ear as she tickled it with her vibrissae. Atya and Húga were sleeping, and Csecsemő was scouting around somewhere, perhaps looking for food. It was past their feeding time. Well, they could wait. He hadn't realized it before, but he had almost died, and several times at that. No wonder he felt such a need for sleep. and the wounds were enough to knock him out by themselves. He began to drift off. Uncle Vili! Nice sound.

Viktor's body lay on the floor for a while, but then, pushed by some invisible hand and unnoticed by anyone, it rolled past the wall and out, where it fell into the courtyard to lie at the feet of László's corpse.

And the wizard, dead, floated down the River he had always hated.

Mariska rode back toward her home, not looking back, afraid that if she did, she wouldn't have the strength to leave.

Brigitta buried her head in Miklós's neck and let the tears come as they would.

* * *

Miklós stroked her hair, speaking quietly. What could it be? How could news which filled him with such joy be such a sorrow for her? He wondered if it was a reaction to all they'd been through and somehow not really related, in any way, to the news itself. Yet, somehow, he thought that it was not so.

He brought her away with him into a corner and helped her sit. He let her cry for a while, then, when he felt it was the right thing to do, he said, "Would you like to talk about it?"

She looked up at him and shook her head. But, before she looked down again, he thought he saw in her eyes a vision of a Palace, new and strong and alive, glittering in the reflected light of the River.

INTERLUDE

FENARIO?

Fenario.

Where the Mountains overlook Faerie, but never go too close, nor stray too far. Where a rock still stands that Fenarr slept on, and turned over to find a sword.

Maybe.

Mountains, mountains, mountains. The River has cut a path through on the other side, called the Grimtail Fissure. See the geysers? Some say Fenarr came from there.

Why not?

Smell the pine trees, and the spruce, where the streams flow with silver, and the silver flows like water. The Forest? Big and dark, as a forest should be, and filled with all that forests should be filled with.

And demons, demons, demons.

They are everywhere, and doubtless have their own tales to tell. They gibber and they squeak; they chatter and they speak. They speak truth and tell lies, reward and chastise. They are part of life in Fenario, though not everyone knows this.

Pretty, pretty Margit, who lost her lover in the inn where the dzur stand. Will you never learn? Your daughter will learn, won't she? But only too late. Perhaps your daughter's daughter will fare better, and some say that will justify everything.

But in this land, which it is our pleasure to style Fenario, we don't ask to justify. We watch, and we wait, and we learn.

A mother cat carries a dead kitten by the neck, denying death as we thought only a man could, and we weep with her. A lad jumps backward into the River, splashing higher than anyone has ever splashed, and we cheer with him. Go elsewhere with your judgments; they aren't wanted here.

Get your feet wet on the shores of Lake Fenarr, and look around. You can see a long way, from there.

She sleeps amid the roses, or she lies on a bier, but she will awake in time to see pretty Margit wed the demon while Jancsi rides the turtle through the River, plowed with the head of a dragon by the biggest liar Fenario has ever known.

All we ask for is a miracle or two. Is that so much? All we need is to see ourselves as we are, so we can become what we wish, for Fenario is the place where that may be. But to do that we need to look, and to do that we need to stop.

If that isn't a miracle, what is? Stay here with us, with the Northman who built the River, rode the turtle, and fell in the inn where the pair of dzur guard the door. Or was it Jani?

Why Fenario? Why not. It is worth it for the glimpse of Margit, or so Miska tells us.

But why are we standing here?

There is a room that was green and existed in a tree that was not a tree. Now it is in a Palace, and it has many doors. In the room are those who, each in his own way, allowed the Palace—or is it a tree?—to achieve its destiny.

As is ever the case, each must choose his own door.

The horses are all *táltos* and the coachman waits.

chapter seventeen

The Palace

It took Miklós a moment to realize that the sudden change was the lack of breaking and rumbling sounds from outside. He looked about the room, nodding approvingly. The walls were solid now, and pleasing to look upon. He studied the room for a moment, until Andor touched his arm and indicated the staff that Miklós still held precariously balanced.

Miklós and Andor rolled the staff over to one wall and set it there so Bölk could look out at them. Andor looked around. "We'll have to find some way to secure it on the wall. Perhaps the throne could go over there." He stopped. "Do you think the throne survived?"

"It doesn't matter," said Miklós. "László rarely sat in it after his coronation. We don't need it."

"I suppose," said Andor.

Miklós looked at his brother with a new affection. His face was eager and alive, and he gave the impression that Miklós was now the older brother.

Andor went to speak to Vilmos. Miklós sat down in a corner next to Brigitta. He took her hand. She didn't resist, but there was no answering grip.

"Can you tell me about it?" he said.

She didn't look at him. "I don't know."

"Try. I need to understand."

After a moment, she said, "There is no place for me here."

He stared at her through eyes suddenly misted.

"Why?"

"I think because I was too involved in winning the battle; there is nothing left for me now that we have. Perhaps that is wrong. But I must leave, I know that."

Miklós fought to keep the trembling out of his voice because it wouldn't be fair to let her hear it. "You aren't telling me everything."

She inhaled sharply but didn't answer.

"Our child will have a place here," he said.

To his surprise, she nodded. "I know. I think that is why I cried. If it weren't for him, I could have slipped out, away from here, without pain—or at least without so much. You would hardly have noticed with all you will be doing, and—"

"That's not true!"

"Yes, it is. Only, now it isn't. I didn't want to have to tell you, but now I must, because of our child. I am sorry, Miklós, but I *must* leave."

He shook his head. *"Why?"*

She was silent for a long time. Then, sighing, she said, "Do you wonder how I found you and Bölk, the first time, by the oak?"

"You followed the river."

"And how it was that I could hold Sándor long enough to strike him?"

"You moved quickly. What are you saying?"

"And how—"

"Stop it, Brigitta. Tell me what you are talking about."

She looked at him fully. "When I was small, I used to walk through the woods—the Wandering Forest. Sometimes, even into the foothills. I continued to do this as I grew older. When I was fourteen, I—ran away from home. I went into the foothills—and beyond . . ."

He stared at her. "Faerie?"

She nodded. "I was there for more than a year. In that time, I learned much of the ways of the power. Not enough to challenge Sándor, but enough that it is now a part of me. Do you understand, Miki? There is no place for me here."

He shook his head. "I, too, learned of the power. I have put it behind me."

"I know. I cannot."

"Why?"

"There was a time when we spoke, in your old chamber. I knew what you had felt there, what you had experienced. I was afraid to say anything. But I have done that—I have allowed the power to flow through me until it became part of me, until to live without it would snap my mind. Don't you understand, Miki? *I'm not human. I'm not elf. My father was*—" She stopped and shook her head.

Miklós found that he needed to swallow several times before he could speak. He tried to clear his mind. Was she raving? Could there be truth in what she was saying? "Yet you understood Bölk."

"In my own way."

"The same as I did, at the end."

"It doesn't mean anything, Miklós. It was over, then. Don't you see?"

He shook his head. "I don't see how that can be."

"You needn't. I'm sorry, Miki, but you must accept it."

He bowed his head. Then, "What will you do?"

"I am going back there."

He stared. "To Faerie? Over the mountain? You can't! The path is gone; it is a sheer drop. I was hardly able to climb *down!*"

She shook her head. "There are other ways. The River turns south beyond the borders to the west. It runs a long, long way then, and it meets the sea. Mariska told me of it, how some of the peppers are sent that way. From the sea, there are ships that sail to Faerie and trade with them. I will take such a ship. The journey should not be beyond my powers."

He took both of her hands. He whispered, "Must you?"

"I am sorry, for I have loved you."

He released her hands and buried his face in her shoulder. "How soon must you leave?"

She stroked his hair. "It needn't be at once," she said.

A while later, Miklós felt a tap on his arm. He turned around. "What is it, Vili?"

The giant held out the two halves of Állam. "These are yours now, Miki. We must decide what we are to do."

He looked the jewel-encrusted hilt and the blackened blade. "Keep it Vili. I don't want it."

The other shook his head. "What am I to do with them?"

"You are older than I, brother."

"Yes," said Vilmos. "And Andor is older than I."

Andor, a few feet away, looked up. "Do not speak of me," he said. "I will have no part in it. I cannot hold even a broken sword with my right hand—or rather, stump. I will not waste the use of my left in learning to. You two decide."

"You see?" said Vilmos.

"Yes. There is nothing to decide. By the laws of the realm, you are King if Andor refuses. Further, we won only by your actions. You, of all of us, have the strength to wield the sword, broken or whole. The kingdom is yours."

"But it was your guidance—"

"It was Bölk's guidance, and you can understand him now as well as I."

"Not as well. And you have done more than that."

"Perhaps. But I am going nowhere. If I can help, I will be here to do so."

"But what about the Northmen? The southern invaders?"

"They are all quiet now. I am sure that you will find solutions to these problems if it becomes necessary. And, as I said, I will be here any time you wish to ask my advice."

"But I have no heir."

Miklós looked at Brigitta and fought back tears. "Nor have I. But wait, perhaps a year, perhaps less. Send for the Countess of Mordfal. She will come. She will be different, but she will come."

Vilmos said, "Are you certain, Miki?"

"I am certain."

He still seemed unconvinced. He turned to Andor. "What think you, brother?"

Andor drew himself up to his full height, then he bowed, low. "I think it is well, Your Majesty."

Vilmos blinked and a shy smile came over his face. "Then you will help me?"

"Whatever you command," said Andor. He paused, then smiled. "Or even ask for."

Vilmos sat on his haunches and addressed one of the norska that still ran about the room. "What about you, Atya? Will you be good for me?" The norska chittered. "Huh! No, Atya, I don't think I will send you out after dragons. You have enough to do, taking care of Anya and Húga and Csecsemő. So."

Miklós watched, smiling. When he turned back to Brigitta, she was gone. The door closed on its leather hinges. He started to follow her, then stopped. Why? One more tear-filled scene?

One more try at pleading with her? For what reason? Her will was as strong as his own, at least. She had granted him a few days; he would have to be content with that.

On impulse, he went over to the staff and knelt down. Bölk still remained there. "Is there anything I can do, Bölk?"

"Much, master. You can aid your brother in the ordering of his kingdom. It is most important that you be here now, for the first days are hardest. And you can write down what has happened so others will know of it when it is time for them to. You can—"

"I meant about Brigitta."

"I know. I am answering you."

"I don't understand."

"Yes, you do."

Miklós looked down at the floor, then back at the horse head. "Yes," he said. "I guess I do." Then, "Very well. What do you mean about when it is time for others to know?"

Bölk looked around the room. "Do you think, master, that this Palace, or any Palace, will last forever?"

Miklós shrugged. "It is too soon to think about that. It isn't even finished, as far as I can see. We will all be sleeping on floors tonight."

"That is true. You must help see to the finishing of it. But someday this Palace, too, will need to be replaced. It would be well if, when that happens, there are those who understand how it came to be built. Some will always insist on holding on to the old, no matter what. Those who do not will need to know how it was here and now, and that their fight, always new, is always old as well."

Miklós didn't answer. He turned away and found Vilmos. "I will begin inspecting the Palace," he said. "I am sure there is much to be done."

Vilmos nodded. "Yes. But take as much time as you need. If you wish to be alone—"

"Thank you, Vili. I am not sure what I need."

Andor, looking around him, said, "I will return in a moment, Vili. I must go out and see if I can salvage some food for these norska; they seem hungry."

Miklós looked at the horse once more.

"As you say, Bölcseség. As you say."

epilogue

THE AFTERNOON WAS BRIGHT and crisp on the balcony over-looking the River.

Miklós had hardly begun inspecting the new palace when he had found this place, and he knew at once that he would come here often. It would take a long time to learn all of the facets of the structure, but he was pleased that there was, at least, one place where beauty for its own sake could find a home.

He didn't doubt that there would be others, but learning them would be a long and difficult task. He—

He sensed, rather than heard, that someone was behind him. He turned, then looked down.

"Hello, Mister Miklós."

"You are . . . Devera! Yes, I remember. Hello."

"Hello. How are you?"

"How am I? I don't know. There is pain, and there is happiness. Those things exist in Faerie, too, I am sure. At least for those meant to live there."

"Yes."

"Have you seen what you came to see?"

"Yes, I have, Mister Miklós. Thank you."

"You will be going now? Returning to Faerie?"

"Yes."

"Could you—" He stopped. She looked at him quizzically,

her brown eyes huge in her face, her hair slightly unkempt. She seemed not to have aged at all. "You are fully of Faerie blood, are you not, Devera?"

"Yes."

"Then you will live a long time."

She giggled, then seemed to catch herself and turned somber once more. "Oh, yes, Mister Miklós. A very long time."

He nodded. "There is a thing I would ask of you. Do you know Brigitta?" She nodded. "She has left, to make her way to Faerie."

Devera nodded vigorously. "I know. She will—" she caught herself, then said, "She will arrive safely."

"You know that? Good. Then, will you, when you are older, watch out for her?"

Devera's eyes filled with tears. "I can't, Mister Miklós. She's going to . . . I mean, I can't."

He felt as if a dagger had been plunged into his heart. He gripped the rail.

"The child—"

"Your daughter will be fine, Mister Miklós. I promise."

He nodded. He tried to speak and failed. Then he said, "Daughter." Suddenly the child he would never see was as real as the woman he was losing. "Could you watch over *her,* then?"

The little girl ran to him and hugged his leg. "Don't worry, Mister Miklós." Then she looked up at him and smiled once more. "I won't have to watch *over* her; everyone else will have to watch *out* for her."

Miklós thought about asking what that meant but decided not to. It didn't matter. He would never see Brigitta again, but at least, it seemed, their daughter would live. It wasn't much, but it would have to be enough.

He turned back to Devera to thank her, but she was gone.

László was gone. Brigitta would be gone soon.

But Bölk and Andor remained, and Vilmos.

He turned and looked up at the Palace behind him, white and gleaming, with flags flying from the towers gracefully curving above him to pinnacles that challenged the skies.

He looked up the river once more, studying its flow. In the distance, he could almost imagine the Mountains of Faerie rising above it. In the other direction, the water was still clogged with logs and scraps of wood: the debris of the old Palace floating away.

Behind and above him, the new Palace rose strong and proud.

It would have to be enough.

...*és még ma is élnek
ha meg nem haltak.*

Stories

❖❖ of ❖❖

Swords and Sorcery

❖❖❖❖❖❖❖❖❖❖❖❖❖❖❖❖❖❖❖❖❖

Discover New Worlds with books of Fantasy by Berkley

COLLECTIONS OF FANTASY AND SCIENCE FICTION

BESTSELLING
Science Fiction
and
Fantasy